SHADOW

GURPREET KAUR SIDHU

SHADOW

Gurpreet Kaur Sidhu

Printed in the United States of America

Edited by Amanda Noon and Rebecca Bayuk.

Formatted, interior and cover art design by Vanessa Maynard

First edition published 2021

10 9 8 7 6 5 4 3 2 1

Sidhu., Gurpreet Kaur

SHADOW/ Gurpreet Kaur Sidhu

p. cm.

ISBN-13: 978-1-7322344-2-0

TABLE OF CONTENTS

To my dad, who always encouraged us to follow our dreams.

Acknowledgements

One of the things the global pandemic has taught me is to appreciate the people in my life, and to show my appreciation by making them feel seen, heard and loved. After I wrote my debut novel, *Storm: It's a Curse to Remember,* I made a promise to myself that when it came to the sequel, I would thank everyone who helped me along the way and supported me, whether by listening to my ideas, reading through rough drafts, or working on the editing and cover design of the book. You all have played a vital part in the success of The Storm Series.

I want to thank my dad and mom for supporting me through this journey in their own ways. I know that in the Punjabi community, being a writer isn't seen as a career. I'm thankful to my parents for allowing me to venture out and explore the depths of the talent I have been so lucky to be blessed with. I hope I have made you both proud, and as I continue my journey and expand into different industries, that I continue to make you proud.

I would like to thank my sister, Pavan, for allowing me to share every detail of this journey with her. Whether it was a horrible review from my debut novel, or my thoughts about the cover of the sequel *Shadow: Run, but You Can't Hide,* she listened with intent. Whenever I doubted myself, felt frustrated about an obstacle I was facing, or was simply feeling like I couldn't catch a break, she was the one I turned to. Sister, thank you for being the gem that you are and giving me unconditional love and taking this ride with me.

Harmin, my brother-in-law, is a straightforward and simple guy. So, I will keep this simple! Thank you for shining a light on me and sharing my book with everyone you have met as you started your own venture. I know you want everyone around you to succeed, and that has been clear from the support you've given me.

I had the pleasure to work with two editors, Amanda Noon and Rebecca Bayuk, on Shadow. Rebecca and I spent an ample amount of time working on the manuscript. She poured her heart and soul with each round of edit we went through. She treated my work as her own and consistently made sure everything was perfect. To see this story come to life has been such a thrill and I couldn't have made this book into what it is today without you.

I would also like to thank Kristen Hamilton for editing my first ever novel. I remember receiving the first draft of edits and feeling unsure if I even had a great story. However, with her guidance and her support in my vision, not only did Storm come to fruition, but I started work on a sequel. Kristen, *The Storm Series* exists because of you!

Deborah Brosseau is not only my PR manager; through the process of promoting Storm, she turned into a mentor and friend. As a new author, there were a lot of things I wasn't aware of and Deb always went above and beyond to make me feel comfortable with the process and has always been there to answer any questions I might have. She is someone who I know will always be in my corner, which I'm grateful for.

They say not to judge a book by its cover, but I think we've all found ourselves picking up certain books because the cover itself has looked interesting. Vanessa Maynard not only did such an amazing job with the cover for *Storm* but also for the sequel, *Shadow.* I never knew how much work and effort went into designing and formatting a book. It's been exciting seeing the initial drafts and designs and working with you on bringing the vision to life!

For the first time, I had book trailers created for both Storm and Shadow and as such I had the pleasure of working with Sarah Leeper on bringing the books to life. The visual representation of the story blew my mind. I've always wanted to adapt my series into a TV show or a movie; Storm started off as a TV drama series initially. Seeing the trailer has got me excited to begin writing the script and bringing the characters to the screen!

It's no secret that social media is the number one way people are made aware of the next new release in the literary world. One of the reasons *Storm* was a success because of the wonderful bookstagrammers and influencers I was able to connect with. They shared information about my debut release through their posts and stories and left reviews, which meant the world to me. A huge thank you to Lois Lim, Emily Ficeto, Helene Liakou, Karradyne Carter, Isabelle Henripin-Payette, Alexa Dudley, Karen Manabat, Tina Singh, Miranda Stardust, Olivia Danieli, Athina Skandami, Tejeshwar Singh, Maha Jahangir, Francesca Kishkill, Joao, and

Suri Singh.

My first radio show was with Sundeep Morrison, who has become a dear friend of mine. I often think back to that time in the studio where we connected and bonded as if we had known each other all our lives. Thank you for giving me time and a platform to discuss and promote my work.

The oldest and effective marketing tool to date has been word-of-mouth. I would like to specially thank Inderjit Kapoor, Mandeep Kapoor, Cindy Spencer, Arundeep Dhillion, Amanprit Randhawa, Balpreet Chhokar, Shaeli Gollaher, Avneet Kaur and Navpreet Atwal who read my debut work and shared it with their friends. Not only that, but for also being just as excited as I was when my novel was released. I appreciate you all so much!

From the bottom of my heart, thank you. I couldn't have come this far without you all!

FAMILY TREE

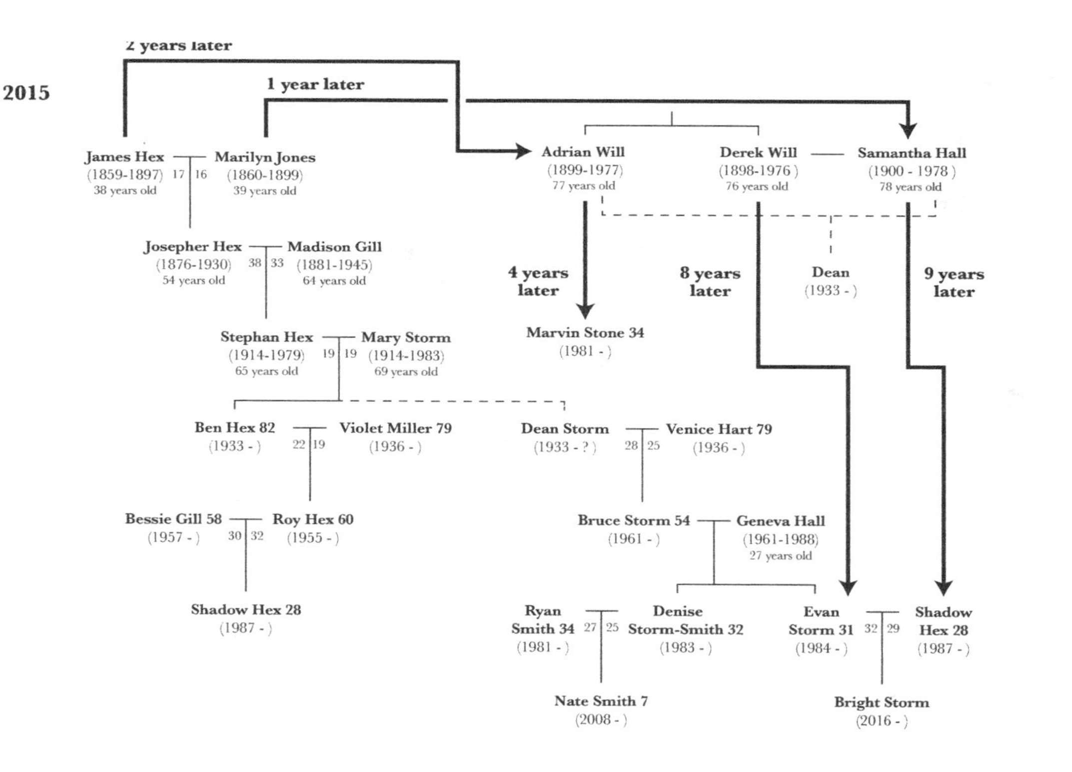
2015
2 years later
1 year later
James Hex
(1859-1897)
38 years old
17
16
Marilyn Jones
(1860-1899)
39 years old
Adrian Will
(1899-1977)
77 years old
Derek Will
(1898-1976)
76 years old
Samantha Hall
(1900 - 1978)
78 years old
Josepher Hex
(1876-1930)
54 years old
38
33
Madison Gill
(1881-1945)
64 years old
4 years later
8 years later
Dean
(1933 -)
9 years later
Stephan Hex
(1914-1979)
65 years old
19
19
Mary Storm
(1914-1983)
69 years old
Marvin Stone 34
(1981 -)
Ben Hex 82
(1933 -)
22
19
Violet Miller 79
(1936 -)
Dean Storm
(1933 - ?)
28
25
Venice Hart 79
(1936 -)
Bessie Gill 58
(1957 -)
30
32
Roy Hex 60
(1955 -)
Bruce Storm 54
(1961 -)
Geneva Hall
(1961-1988)
27 years old
Shadow Hex 28
(1987 -)
Ryan Smith 34
(1981 -)
27
25
Denise Storm-Smith 32
(1983 -)
Evan Storm 31
(1984 -)
32
29
Shadow Hex 28
(1987 -)
Nate Smith 7
(2008 -)
Bright Storm
(2016 -)

CHAPTER 1

1933

Stephan Hex and Mary Storm gazed into the worn bassinet at the slumbering newborn, so pure and delicate, as if they were looking at the rarest gem on earth.

"The midwife said the mother had not named this little one," Mary said.

"It is a pity, isn't it?" he said, thinking aloud. "For the mother to die after childbirth breaks my heart. I cannot imagine the pain her husband must be going through."

"It is very unfortunate," she replied, unable to peel her eyes from the newborn. "Very." She peered into the cradle with a smile. "I've had a name in mind."

"What is the name?"

"Dean," she said, smiling softly.

Stephan let the name sink in. He met her eyes, a grin

slowly creeping across his face. "My darling, that is a lovely name."

She looked at Dean and then back at Stephan.

"Stephan..."

"Yes, my darling."

"I want Dean to carry on my family name."

"You do?"

"Yes."

Stephan pondered her words a moment. He knew it was not traditional for children to take their mother's maiden name, but he loved Mary more than anything and wanted to see her happy. The last few months after the miscarriage had been hard. Mary hadn't been the same since they'd learned her chances of carrying a child to term were poor due to complications from the miscarriage. Mary wanted to be a mother more than anything, so now adoption was their next best bet.

Stephan already had a son, Ben, from a previous marriage, who was now nine months old. Mary loved being a mother to Ben. He had brought so much joy into her life, even though there were times that truly tested her patience. However, Mary had learned to gracefully walk through those challenging times with Ben, knowing they wouldn't last more than a few minutes. If she could weather the storm, a blessed calm would descend, and then there'd be hugs, and smiles, and Mary would feel the deep satisfaction of parenthood. Another baby for Mary meant double the work, but it also meant double the happiness, laughs, and smiles. And this time, she would get to experience the "firsts" with Dean that she had never experienced with Ben.

Stephan took Mary's hand and softly kissed it. "Of course, my darling."

She gazed at their new bundle of joy. "Our little Dean Storm," she whispered with delight.

***

Samantha sat slumped on her bed. The sun shone dimly through the drapes, which were still firmly closed despite the hour. Her world was spinning, round and round, leaving her disoriented and detached. No one knew the pain she was feeling. The moment she'd held her newborn baby in her arms for the first time replayed in her mind like a broken record, and she clutched the memory close to her heart, knowing she would never experience that feeling again. She'd shed every last tear there was. She forced herself to eat, but after taking one bite, she no longer had any appetite.

Derek hadn't asked how she was doing. They hadn't talked since the night Samantha had given birth. He would come home late, after he'd been to dinner with the men from the office, and retreat without a word to the living room, drink in hand. Most nights Derek spent alone, listening to the radio; on the weekends he'd play golf. He'd attend company events without Samantha. "She's under the weather," he would tell anyone who questioned her absence.

Adrian, on the other hand, would stop by whenever he

knew his brother wasn't going to be home. During these visits, he tried his best to comfort Samantha. Although neither of them said much to each other, it felt better to sulk together than alone. The loss of his baby with Samantha tore him apart. He had asked Samantha once what their son looked like. "He was a little piece of heaven," she said. As much as Adrian refrained from thinking about all the things he was going to miss as being a first-time father, he couldn't help but fantasize what it must have felt like to hold his son close to his chest. To peer into his innocent eyes. To watch him crawl, only to see him take his first steps months later. His son was somewhere in the world, and he was never going to get the chance to tell him how much he loved him.

Samantha looked down at her lap. A revolver sat cold and heavy in her trembling hands. For the past thirty minutes, she'd stared at the gun, weighing it in her palm, tracing her fingers over the metallic surface. She'd come to the realization that she could no longer endure any more pain. With one bullet, Derek would no longer be able to hurt or control her. With one bullet, she would be in control of her freedom. The answer was right there in her hands.

This was it...

She placed her finger on the trigger. Her heart pounded in her chest, louder and louder until it sounded like drums in her ears. She brought the hand holding the gun up to the side of her head as she looked at the drapes. If she squeezed the trigger, she'd finally be at peace. This torture would end and somewhere in the unknown, a new beginning was waiting for her.

She closed her eyes.

CHAPTER 2

Evan woke up, gasping for air. It was still dark.

It was the month of September, nine months after Marvin had set the kitchen on fire, leaving him to die. That night had changed everything for Evan, and life moving forward felt overwhelming. He feared for his life each day, knowing it wasn't over yet, not with Marvin still out there. He wondered whether he would find his attacker waiting for him in his bedroom after work, watching his every move and waiting to pounce, with Shadow nowhere to be found. At times, he felt the prickling of a panic attack rising while he drove to work. He'd endured months of sleepless nights studded with haunting nightmares, but he tried his best to keep his fears hidden from Shadow.

When Shadow spoke, her voice was soft yet distinct enough to break his reverie. "What did you do this time?"

Evan turned to look over at her. She was sitting up, her back resting against the headboard. She cracked a smile as she adjusted her position.

Evan rubbed his eyes and looked at her ever-growing stomach. As the due date neared, oddly, Shadow's body craved less sleep. Some nights, she would only get three to four hours and then spring out of bed, apparently feeling completely rested. Granted, she'd take a nap in the middle of the day or after work to wind down, but Evan didn't know how she managed to do it. Maybe it was anxiety, or excitement; maybe both. He wouldn't know because the doctors hadn't given them a particular reason for her wakefulness. If he was in her shoes, he could only imagine he'd sleep a good ten to twelve hours nightly on top of days spent taking it easy, but Shadow insisted on working until the last two weeks before her delivery, despite her lack of rest. Evan wasn't on board. He had to convince his sister, Denise, to put Shadow on maternity leave because she happened to side with Shadow on the matter. It didn't come much of a surprise to Evan, since Denise strongly believed women were capable of doing anything they wanted, pregnant or not. Denise and Shadow supported each other as if they'd been sisters from birth.

Overall, Shadow's pregnancy had gone smoothly, for which both of them were thankful.

"Was it the same dream? The one where I'm holding the gun?"

Evan nodded.

Shadow's words drifted away into thin air, letting silence take over.

The memories raised questions that neither of them

could answer. Who did these memories belong to? And why was Evan reliving them in the present? Evan woke up right before he was able to see what happened next, and that irritated him. And it made Shadow question herself. Were Evan's flashbacks hinting at the fact she, Shadow, was going to repeat the same cycle? Both Shadow and Evan would spend afternoons entertaining the answers to their questions, but neither of them found answers that made any sense. They'd forget about it for a couple of days until Evan woke up from yet another terrifying dream.

Evan placed his hand over her stomach and rubbed it in circular motions. "What's baby Bright doing?"

When Evan and Shadow found out they were having a boy, it took them a week to agree upon a name they both liked: Bright Storm.

She laid her hand on top of his. "He's being a good little boy. Sleeping like a little angel."

"I hope he takes after his mom, otherwise we're gonna be in big trouble."

Shadow giggled. "You know, I don't think everyone's going to be happy that we already named the baby without even asking for their input."

They had both agreed on the name 'Bright' for one reason: even though they had endured some of their darkest days, he was going to serve as a reminder there were far better days ahead.

"You're probably right." He leaned closer to her stomach and whispered, "Your mommy is sneaky. She's going to try and feed you mashed cauliflower and tell you that it's mashed potatoes."

She playfully shoved his face away from her stomach. "Oh, stop it."

"Let's be serious for a minute. They tasted nothing like mashed potatoes!"

She laughed as the image of Evan's face the night he tried her new dish came into her mind's eye. It was priceless.

"We need to be more health conscious. I don't want to feed our child processed foods. Have you seen the videos on YouTube?"

"No. I'd rather not know."

"It's disgusting what goes into the food we buy from the grocery store. Homemade is so much better because you know what's going in it."

Evan raised an eyebrow as he remembered the distinctly non-homemade foods Shadow had purchased only a few days before. He grinned.

"Don't be a hypocrite, Shadow."

She raised an eyebrow, unsure of what he was talking about.

"Yeah, that's right. Don't think I don't know what comes home in those grocery bags, Mrs. Storm," he teased.

"I'm pregnant!" she exclaimed as she grabbed his pillow from behind him and smacked him across the chest. "What am I supposed to do? Deny my cravings?!"

"And you've become so violent in the past few months, too," he giggled, taking the pillow from her hands.

She leaned closer and gave him the exaggerated glare that he never took seriously. "And again, I'm *pregnant*."

Evan stifled a laugh, placing the pillow behind his back. He gazed at her as she looked at him. "I love you so much." He kissed her on the forehead and wrapped his arm around her, pulling her in closer and leaving enough room for Shadow to switch positions whenever she felt the need to.

She laid her head on his chest, enjoying the peaceful time with her husband. "I love you too."

It was nights like these that made Evan feel like the luckiest man alive. Soon, he was going to become a father. His heart filled with joy knowing they were having a baby together, and that their child would be born into a family who would shower him with love and protection.

And then, just as suddenly, he was reminded of what Derek had done to Samantha, all those years ago. How he'd given her and Adrian's baby away. It pierced his heart thinking about what Samantha must have gone through the night Derek had instructed the midwife to hand their baby over to a family he deemed 'more deserving'. The truth was, Derek didn't want to be reminded of the lies and deceit that had resulted in a baby. Evan played the devil's advocate at times to make himself feel less like a horrible human being. Maybe giving the baby away in the long run was actually a good thing. *The baby would have a better life in a different home rather than with Derek*, he'd tell himself. Still, he couldn't justify what he'd done. The life he'd once lived as Derek Will was still unclear and disturbing to him.

He ran his fingers through Shadow's hair. "Are you

hungry? Are you craving anything?"

When Shadow didn't respond, he craned his neck sideways to find her fast asleep.

Evan replayed his memories of the family to whom Samantha's baby was given. The name Dean Storm circled in his mind throughout the day—his grandfather's name. Evan hadn't revealed this piece of information to anyone; his gut told him something had been hidden from the rest of the family. Perhaps, he thought, Grandma Venice knew about Grandpa Dean's past and the family who'd raised him. Knowing how secretive Venice could be at times—for legitimate reasons—he wasn't sure if she would be of any help.

From the new details emerging in his dreams, Evan knew that Shadow's great grandparents were the ones who raised Dean. What that meant for them all in the present day, he didn't know.

CHAPTER 3

September third was a perfect Saturday morning. The sky was clear and the sun already warm, making the weather perfect for an early swim or a walk around the neighborhood. Marvin, however, was doing neither of these things. Instead, he sat on a leather sofa in an empty office, looking over the assignment he'd been working on the past three months. He had a team of twenty agents working on this assignment, and it all boiled down to this week to execute the plan. There was no room for error.

He rose as the door behind him opened and then closed.

"How are you, sir?" Marvin asked as he watched Roy come around the desk.

Roy Hex took a seat behind the desk and proceeded to unbutton his jacket as he got comfortable. He ignored Marvin's attempts at small talk.

"What's the update on the home front?"

"Your daughter's due date is listed as the eighth. I have

my men in place, and they'll be making rounds this week at the hospital in case she delivers early, or late."

Roy nodded. "It's unfortunate for Shadow to be in this position. But the girl doesn't listen. She fails to understand what's best for her and what will be better in the long run."

"I agree, sir. She brought this upon herself."

"Although, if the baby is a girl, it changes everything. A girl won't be in line to take control of the agency even when she's of age. If you'd married Shadow as we'd originally planned, you would have a legitimate claim to the agency's reins. Without that tie by marriage, we need a male Hex heir. If Shadow's child is a boy, we can assume guardianship and prepare him for leadership as he grows, with you at the helm in the meantime. If it's a girl, we lose the Hex lineage, and I won't be able to appoint you to take over the agency after I step down, as we had discussed."

"Yes, I understand, sir." Marvin paused for a moment before pressing further. "In the event they do have a girl, who will take over the agency then?"

"I will have to appoint someone from the board of directors— the Hex dynasty will be done."

Marvin nodded, but he knew there was absolutely no way he was going to let anyone get in the way of him claiming power.

"Let's hope it doesn't come down to that."

"It's never happened in the agency's history. I'd like to keep the Hex's legacy running as long as I can."

"Legacy?"

Roy shifted in his chair, maintaining a steely eye contact with Marvin.

"The Hex family started this agency, and there are things that only the head of the agency has control over and can access. Without Shadow's baby, or in the event of a girl child, the public won't have access to what we've been working on for some generations."

"And what is that?"

"If you become the head of the agency, you'll find out. Now, if there isn't anything else you need to address, I have to do a board review."

Marvin rose from his seat and buttoned his blazer. "No, sir. This is it for now."

"Good. Please close the door behind you—and good luck."

"Thank you, sir."

***

Shadow and Evan sat on the porch swing in the backyard, enjoying their morning coffee together. Mr. Jingles, their cat, sat in the middle of the lawn, relishing the sunshine, his tail swaying back and forth. The center of the lawn had become his favorite spot in the past few months. Evan had mowed a couple of days prior, so the grass was dark green and short. Flowers bloomed in the beds around the lawn in beautiful hues of purple, pink, and yellow. The pathway through the grass was the same one Shadow had walked down in her wedding dress for their intimate wedding in July. Family and close friends had joined together to see Evan and Shadow exchange vows. However, only Shadow's mother was able to attend the wedding; Roy claimed to have other obligations back at the lab. To Shadow, it didn't matter at all even if her mother wasn't able to show up. The tension between Shadow and her parents hadn't lifted since she had moved to Lake View and seemed to grow even more after they found out their daughter was getting married to Evan, who her father referred to as an "average Joe." Even though her parents were outraged she wasn't marrying Marvin, the man she'd previously been engaged to for a year, Shadow was beyond ecstatic. She was marrying someone who made sure she was protected and loved, and that was all she needed.

Evan rubbed the back of Shadow's neck as he sipped on his coffee.

"Can you rub my shoulders, too? They're really sore for some reason," she said with a frown.

Evan shot her an "Are-you-really-being-serious-right-now?" look. "That's all you want? Me to rub your shoulders? Where's my pampering? What do I get in return for all this extra work?"

Shadow playfully nudged him as she lifted the mug close to her lips. "I'm giving you a baby, can't you see?"

Evan chuckled. "It's hard not to miss that big ol' tummy. Okay miss, I'll rub your shoulders if you rub mine."

Shadow scoffed as she carefully positioned herself so Evan could hit the right spots. "Anyway... making a pregnant woman do hard labor is not a very good look, mister."

"I'm only playing," he said before giving her a kiss.

He put down his mug on the concrete floor and began to massage Shadow. "Who do you think Bright is going to take after?"

"You already know that I want him to take after you. He's going to have a strong, amazing father, you know that, right? Probably won't be a good storyteller, but that's okay."

"You're out of your mind! I'm a great storyteller."

Shadow scoffed playfully. "Yeah, if you have nothing going on in your life and have weeks to spare, 'cause that's how long it takes for you to finish telling a story."

Evan let out a chortle. "You exaggerate *way* too much, my dear."

"I beg to differ. Denise will agree. Actually, Denise *and* Ryan."

Evan laughed, but he couldn't help but dwell on Shadow's answer to his earlier question. She clearly had total faith in his ability to parent their unborn child. When Evan thought about being a father to Bright, however, there was no such confidence. The only male figure he'd had in his life since the age of four was his neighbor, Mr. Brar. He was always there to listen whenever Evan had a situation he wasn't comfortable sharing with his grandmother, Venice, or Denise. Mr. Brar would set him straight whenever he felt Evan was off onto the wrong path. He'd encouraged him to embrace moving out of the house for college when Evan had fought hard to stay home. He showed him how a true man treated his wife. Even though Mr. Brar wasn't his biological father and didn't see Evan every single day as he got older, he still treated Evan like his own son. That kind of love was rare and unconditional. That was the kind of love Evan wanted to give Bright, but he couldn't help but worry that he wasn't going to be able to. What if he took after his biological father, who'd abandoned him and Denise as children, and not Mr. Brar? Not only that, but the Secret Eye Agency— SEA— still existed, and so did Marvin. He worried about the threat Marvin still posed to his family; the man was not the type to give up so quickly. Evan had pushed aside all unpleasant realities for some time now, but as Shadow's due date neared, Evan could no longer ignore the inevitable.

Shadow seemed to sense from Evan's silence the thoughts that were plaguing his mind. She smiled warmly and took his hand.

"You're going to be an amazing father, because you're already an amazing uncle to Nate. I see how you treat your family, the love and support you show them regardless of if you guys are on the same page or not. You show me love, care, and kindness even when I'm being difficult. Even though you weren't raised by your biological father, Venice and Mr. Brar raised you into the man I know your mother would have been proud of if she was here. You're not going to leave us when life gets tough. You've already demonstrated that. You had the chance to leave me when Marvin was a threat, but you didn't. You're going to show this baby boy so much love that you will cry at his kindergarten graduation. You're going to cry when he gets his first girlfriend, and cry when he gets his heart broken. You're going to cry when he goes off to college and then again when he graduates. You're going to be there, and loving harder each and every day, because that's who you are. So don't let yourself think you're going to be anything less than an amazing father to Bright. Okay?"

Evan craned his head sideways and looked at her in amazement. How did she know? He kissed her and let Shadow's words settle into his mind.

Shadow softly rubbed his cheek before he leaned back and continued to rub her shoulders.

"Did you check the grocery list to see if we have everything for dinner tonight?"

Evan took a brief pause from rubbing Shadow's shoulder.

"I thought you did..."

He leaned in and began to nibble on her ear.

"Oh, no, no, no mister," she said, adjusting herself to directly face Evan. "I'm not going to make a grocery run. Not today. I can pop any second now."

"I didn't say anything about you going to the grocery store!" Evan exclaimed. He leaned forward and kissed her belly. "Your mommy is crazy," he whispered.

Shadow giggled as she ran her fingers through his hair. "It's 'cause you drive me crazy."

"Yeah, yeah, I love you, too," he said sarcastically while rubbing her belly. He kissed her forehead and adjusted his position. "I should probably get started on that list."

"Yeah, sounds like a good idea."

Evan rose from the swing, grabbing his mug. "What are you gonna do all day?"

"Denise is coming over to help with the nursery, remember?"

Evan gave her a blank stare. "I thought you guys were doing that tomorrow?"

"Nooo. We said we would finish it up today since we were gonna have dinner at our place, anyway."

"Really? Where was I when this conversation took place?"

"You were sitting at the dinner table scarfing down chocolate cake. You need to start paying more attention."

Evan let out a chuckle. "You know I'm messing with you, right?"

Shadow shook her head and rolled her eyes but couldn't help hiding a smile.

"Get out of here!"

"I'm going, I'm going. Jeez. Do you need anything from the kitchen before I go? Water? Cookies? Meds for those moods?"

Shadow raised her eyebrows. "Moods? You're really trying me today, aren't you?"

"Sorry. What I meant to say was, do you need meds for the random… *heightened emotions*?"

"No, I think I'm good," she said as she laughed. "I'm gonna head inside in a bit, too. Denise is coming around eleven thirty-ish."

"You ladies have fun," he said, walking back

into the house.

"Thank you."

Shadow looked around the garden and felt blessed for the first time in her life. She was with a man who made her laugh and knew exactly how to cheer her up when she was upset. He let her be her own person, which was a breath of fresh air after previous relationships. And now, they were having a baby together.

Life couldn't be more perfect.

"You think he's crazy, too, don't you, Mr. Jingles?"

Mr. Jingles looked in her direction and meowed.

Her lips curved upward. "I thought so."

***

An hour later, Shadow headed upstairs and walked into the nursery. She stood in her grey leggings and white tank top and surveyed the room, with her hands on her hips. It was exactly what she had envisioned ever since she found out she was pregnant.

Starting from her left side, alternate walls were painted in Victorian Pewter, a dark shade of gray, with the other two in Distant Gray, which was an off-white color. Evan had put together the crib against the Victorian Pewter wall, and the hamper sat in between the crib and dresser. In the corner, there was a white rocking chair for whenever Bright woke up in the middle of the night and needed to be cradled back to sleep. Across from the crib and next to the closet was the changing table. All Shadow needed to do was organize the closet and figure out a place to hang up the photo frames that would display Bright's tiny foot and handprints. A photoshoot for Bright's one-month birthday had already been inked in the books, which Shadow was ecstatic about. She found inspiration through her favorite app, Pinterest, of photoshoots of newborns, some wrapped in pastel-colored blankets, curled up in a ball, placed in massive baskets to emphasize their tiny size. She wobbled her way over to where a portrait of their pregnancy photoshoot hung and took a moment to appreciate the photographer's hard work, which had resulted in a beautiful, intimate picture of the two of them.

Once Denise arrived, they went straight to work. They sat on the floor with clothes, toys, and other baby necessities dispersed around them.

Shadow was looking through the pile of clothes that she and Evan had bought for Bright and the ones they had received from her co-ed baby shower.

"I don't want to be rude, but I feel like my snobby Pool View side is kicking in. When they say all baby clothes are cute, they're lying."

Denise chuckled as she analyzed the stuffed elephants. "You don't like those outfits?"

Shadow shot Denise a look of pity. "No, not at all. I feel bad for saying it, because it sounds unappreciative, but I just don't like them."

She held up a brown sweater that had a tint of grey, coupled with corduroy pants. Then she held up another outfit: a white collared shirt with khaki pants.

"This is like something from the 1970s, and this one looks like my son is about to go to private school. He's not even born yet, and people are already preparing him for school, or to look like a grandpa!" Shadow shook her head as she tossed the two outfits to the side.

"Who were those from? Your aunt? The one whose husband came dressed in his golfing attire? I feel like they would've gotten you those khaki pants and collared shirt."

"No, not them. My mom mailed these in. I never got a chance to look at them properly. Actually, I didn't look at anything properly."

"You still haven't talked to her, I'm guessing."

"Nope. I was surprised she actually showed up to the wedding. She made all these excuses when I called to see if they had received the invitation. I didn't think she was gonna show. I know she only showed up so she could *say* she was here for me."

Shadow's baby shower had taken place not too long after the wedding. Evan had suggested combining the events, to kill two birds with one stone, but Denise spoke some sense into him, explaining how a woman's wedding should never be compromised. It was a day she was going to remember for the rest of her life, and it should remain separate from all of the other events in her life. Not to mention, it was a day that Shadow had been dreaming of ever since she was a teenager. Denise gave Evan an earful just for even suggesting the idea.

"Things with your mom sound tough," Denise said, before adding, gently, "that said, your happiness shouldn't be dependent on others. Just throwing that out there. You're important too. We often forget that."

"You're absolutely right. Evan reminds me of that a lot. Sometimes I just forget."

Denise smiled at her. "I'm super obsessed with these elephants," she said, wiggling them in her lap. "This is off tangent, but do you know who I think should get married?" She grinned impishly.

"Venice and Willow, right?"

"Yes!"

Shadow smiled as she thought of Evan's beloved grandmother and the gentleman she'd recently started seeing. "I was thinking about that a couple of days ago. They make such a cute couple. He loves and adores her so much, right?"

"Oh, he really, really does. When we had breakfast with them last week, you know what Willow said? I still feel a little weird calling him Willow— I'm so used to calling him Mr. Marx and thinking of him as the owner of that bakery we'd always go to as kids! Anyways, he said that Grandma was the girl all the guys wanted to date back in high school, and that he always had a crush on her but never had the courage to actually act on his feelings."

"Awww...that's so cute!" Shadow gushed. "I can see that. She had the looks back then— I've seen photos— and she still does. If he doesn't propose in the next couple of months, we're gonna have to get the ball rolling," she chuckled. "I can't believe she never dated after your grandfather passed away."

"Tell me about it! Look, I would miss Ryan, *immensely,* and I wouldn't be able to date for a while if something happened to him, but I would eventually, you know? I'd like to think I'd get remarried. I don't think I could stay single for the rest of my life. I know everyone's different, but with grandma... she just devoted all her free time to us. It was a huge sacrifice on her end."

"Hats off to her. I know I couldn't do it."

The women fell into a comfortable silence as Shadow began to color coordinate all the baby clothes while Denise started to fill the drawers with diapers, bibs, and some of the small toys that wouldn't be of use until Bright was a few months old.

Shadow looked over at Denise.

"While we're talking about couples...what do you think about Sky? Since she's dating your dad..."

Denise pondered the thought for a moment. "She's nice. I like her. She makes my dad happy, which is good." She kept her eyes fixed on the bib she was folding into a neat square.

"I sense a hint of hesitation." Shadow's eyebrows danced up and down. "You're still not comfortable with them, are you?" she added gently.

Denise flung down the bib.

"Not exactly," she blurted. "I don't *want* to be uncomfortable with their relationship... it's just that... I'm still trying to get used to the fact that my dad's been alive all this time, you know? I'm still digesting everything. Until recently, I thought he was dead. She's been a part of his life for the past five years. She literally knows more about my father's life than I do. I just feel, oh, I don't know—"

"Cheated, in a way?"

"Yeah, that's it. *Cheated*....I just feel like if he was able to pursue Sky and be in this relationship with *her*, well, why wasn't he pursuing a relationship with his own *children?* And did she not encourage him to get back in touch? It shouldn't have taken him this long to come back into our lives... I mean, on the one hand, I get it. He felt responsible for our mom's death. But on the other hand, it hurts." Denise sighed heavily. "Okay... I'm all over the place— sorry."

"It's okay, Denise," Shadow said. "Take your time."

Denise let out another long sigh. "To me it just seems like our mom's death was an excuse he used to not seek us out, but all the while he's been out there dating, which means he's been in a better mental state for *at least* five years. Right?"

Now Shadow sighed, understanding Denise's frustration. "I can see why you feel that way. Since they've been together for five years, you feel like he should've been here with you guys five years ago. I get that. But then... if you look at it from a different perspective— well— for some people, it takes *years* for them to heal from a broken heart. And given that your guys' mom took her own life... there are so many questions that are left unanswered. If your dad always felt responsible for what happened, maybe he couldn't face you guys. Maybe he thought you'd be better off without him? Coming back home would also be a reminder of what happened, and maybe that was something he just wasn't ready for..."

When it came to Evan and Denise's father, Bruce, Shadow always gently played the devil's advocate. She wanted to believe there were legitimate underlying reasons as to why it had taken him twenty-seven years to come forward with his truth, and that he simply didn't leave his children behind to start a new life because he no longer wanted to be a father, or because he didn't love them anymore. She couldn't judge Bruce for any of his decisions because she wasn't in his shoes. She also knew being an agent for the Secret Eye Agency most likely didn't help his circumstances either.

The SEA had been founded on the basis of helping people in circumstances in which the government had failed to provide the necessary protection and funds, but as time progressed, and as the successors changed, the values and morals of the agency had also changed. As a result, it produced agents who were power hungry and money driven.

Bruce had been recruited to join the SEA after the death of his wife, Geneva. The opportunity had come at a perfect time, given that he needed something to distract him. At the time, the agency's mission was, in simpler terms, to help those who couldn't help themselves. Bruce had felt his life had purpose again and it had helped with grieving the loss of his life partner. However, as time went on and as the ideals of the agency shifted— so much so that it no longer aligned with his beliefs— Bruce realized he didn't want to be a part of an organization which no longer possessed a moral compass. He worried he would lose his humanity if he continued being an agent.

Shadow had discussed Bruce with Evan on multiple occasions. The difference between Evan and Denise was that Evan had quickly adapted to the fact that Bruce was still alive. Surprisingly, he understood Bruce's delay in contacting his children. But Denise was the total opposite. Whenever Denise spoke about Bruce, it was as if she were that little five-year-old girl again, heartbroken after learning her father had died. He'd been a hero and her first love, and the pain of his death was surpassed only by the new pain of realizing he had chosen to abandon her. In some way, Shadow could relate to Denise. Shadow's bond with her father when she was younger was powerful. He had always been there and protected her. He was the one who consoled her when she was upset. She, too, felt a loss now that her father no longer played an important part in her life.

"Do you think they're planning on getting married? Or if they even want to?"

Denise shrugged. "She's still part of the agency. I'm not sure how that would work. Maybe after they shut it down? I guess we'll have to wait and see what happens."

"I can't wait until that's done and over with. It's going to be such a relief."

Denise finished organizing the first two drawers and then continued to do the last two.

"It's crazy how an agency like that has existed for such a long time without ever being exposed. You'd think the public would've heard about it at some point."

Shadow looked at Denise with serious eyes. "It's because they never let it get to that point."

The thought of people being brutally murdered and tortured to keep the agency's secrets sent shivers up Denise's spine. "It's like something out of a movie."

Shadow shook her head as she began to hang the first set of white clothes in the closet. "Tell me about it. When I was with Marvin, I couldn't even tell my parents about half of the things that went on, because it was just gonna make me sound like I was crazy and making stuff up. And in their eyes, Marvin could do no wrong. He was like the child they never had, in a way."

"How was it, being engaged to him?"

"At first, everything was great. He was amazing, and such a sweetheart. Always showered me with presents. Stuff like that. I didn't see any red flags until he told me what he *really* did for a living. So, he had lied to me, which was red flag number one. I don't like people who lie. It doesn't sit well with me. When he explained *why* he lied about his job, it took me a while to wrap my head around all of it and forgive him but then soon after, before things went back to normal between us, he started to become obsessive. Which was red flag number two."

"Oh wow! That's insane. What was he obsessive about?"

"About us getting married, starting a family. He would constantly push the idea, even after I had told him that I wasn't ready for it."

"That's strange."

"I asked him what the rush was—we were planning on staying together. There was plenty of time, in my mind anyway, for marriage and kids and all that, in the future. But he brought it up over and over, and he just wouldn't let it go. And that's when I started to see his obsessive side. We started to argue a lot and I started to feel unsafe around him. The idea of getting married to him, living the rest of my life with him, began to repulse me. I felt suffocated and my gut was screaming for me to run. So that's what I did... and I've been looking over my shoulder ever since."

"I can't imagine having to live like that."

"Let me tell you, it's not the type of excitement anyone needs in their life."

***

Later that evening, after Denise and Shadow were finished with the nursery, they sat at the kitchen table, teasing Ryan and Evan as they prepped dinner. Denise took a sip of her wine and giggled as she watched her husband attempt to mince garlic as finely as possible. "Looks like you're breaking a sweat there, hun."

Ryan looked up from the cutting board. "Babe, you can't get garlic this tiny without breaking a sweat. Trust me. You can't."

"His isn't...*chunky*, like yours," Evan chimed in, pointing jokingly at Denise. "Let the professionals handle this," he said, wearing a satisfying smug.

"Oh, here we go," Shadow giggled to Denise as she sipped on her water.

Shadow and Denise exchanged amused glances before Shadow picked on Ryan. "What are you guys making, anyway? Still spaghetti and meatballs? Or have you guys changed the menu again for the third time?"

"I'm going to keep my mouth shut," Ryan said. "I know better than to mess with a pregnant woman. I'm not gonna fall into your trap, Shadow."

Shadow and Denise chuckled at his response.

"As of right now, honey, it's still spaghetti and meatballs," Evan responded.

"Maybe we should just order in. What do you think?" Denise asked Shadow.

"With the way things are going right now, it seems like we might just have to. They should know better not to keep a pregnant woman starving," Shadow said, rubbing her belly.

"You two are horrible when you guys get together," Ryan said.

Nate sauntered into the kitchen with Ryan's phone in his hand and Mr. Jingles right behind him. He had been in the living room playing games on the phone, with Mr. Jingles resting in his lap.

"Dad, what's the password?" he asked, his eyes still glued to the screen. "I want to buy this app."

"Nate, you know you can't download anymore apps," Denise frowned. "You've already reached your limit."

Ryan and Denise quickly exchanged looks. Ever since Nate's birthday in July, he had become more demanding. His demands weren't followed by tantrums if they weren't met—it wasn't quite at that stage—but their formerly placid child would get irritated rather quickly. It was almost as if turning eight meant testing parents' patience on a regular basis.

"Mom's right. How many apps did you download this month?" Ryan asked, putting down the knife.

Nate glanced at Ryan before returning his attention back to the phone. "I don't know."

"What do you mean, you don't know? Count how many apps you downloaded. If it's more than four, you're going to have to wait until the next progress report comes home." Nate looked at Ryan and then at Denise with his eyebrows furrowed, extremely disappointed his parents were not allowing him to download another harmless app.

"Fine," he grunted.

Denise knew that Ryan was making every effort to ensure his relationship with Nate remained the same as it was before the accident a year ago. He scolded his son whenever he was being difficult to reason with. He began to coach Nate's soccer team; he still pulled pranks on Denise, just like old times. Despite all of it, he still couldn't remember life before the accident. Ryan had made peace with the fact that he wasn't going to get back the last seven years of Nate's life. It had taken him a while to come to terms with the cards he was dealt—and things had been tough with Denise, as well as Nate, for a while—but it was better to still be a part of his son's life rather than not being there at all.

When Nate left the room, Denise looked at Shadow. "Get ready, sista. They're cute and adorable when they can't talk. After that, you've got a tiny teenager on your hands."

"I wish they just stayed as little babies," Shadow chuckled.

"Alright ladies," Evan chimed in, "dinner is gonna be ready in fifteen minutes. Prepare to be blown away."

Once dinner was served, they all sat around the table, enjoying the last bit of the night. After the meal, the men loaded the plates and cutlery away in the dishwasher and set the timer to begin in the morning. Back at the table, Evan poured wine for everyone while Shadow enjoyed a glass of soda.

Nate had fallen asleep on the couch with Mr. Jingles keeping an eye on him. Over the past couple of months, Mr. Jingles and Nate had bonded. Whenever they were together, they had become inseparable. When Nate was around, Shadow and Evan were old news to Mr. Jingles; the new kid who had entered his life was much more fun and exciting.

"I think we need to address the elephant in the room," Ryan said, moving his attention from his wine to everyone else around the table. "What do you think about this whole taking down the agency plan?"

Shadow and Evan exchanged uncertain yet hopeful looks.

"It's a huge risk," Shadow began. "I don't know much about the agency, but I do know that there's a lot of corruption there. Marvin is a psychopath, and who's to say that there aren't far worse agents than him out there? One can only imagine. It gives me the chills when I think about it. But Bruce, Sky and Mr. Brar know exactly what they're dealing with," Shadow said as she changed position. "A part of me feels like because they've been around the agency for as long as they have, that they'll succeed in shutting it down, but then again, there's that fifty percent chance they won't. What happens then? It's all the uncertainty and just imagining the worst-case scenario that scares me the most."

Denise nodded her head in agreement. "When no one's done this before, there are just a lot of things that could go wrong. But then who's to say that others haven't tried before, either, you know? Which then comes down to... *if* people have tried, what happened to them?"

Evan nodded. "I talked to Mr. Brar about it a few days ago. He is nothing but optimistic about this whole thing. I still can't believe that he was an agent. It's mind blowing and makes you wonder: how many other agents live among us?"

After Evan was discharged from the hospital following Marvin's attack and met Bruce for the first time in twenty-seven years, he and along with everyone else in the family had learned Mr. Brar's true identity as a retired agent for the SEA. The wheelchair their neighbor had been tied to for as long as they all could remember was simply a ploy to keep off the SEA's radar. A disabled, retired agent was not someone they would keep tabs on.

"Dude... Mr. Brar had *everyone* fooled," Ryan inserted. "I don't blame him, though. It's pretty slick, keeping that appearance up as a handicapped agent so that no one would suspect him of anything. He's a smart cat."

"Just when you think you know someone, right?"

"So, what did Mr. Brar say?" Denise chimed in.

"He said dad doesn't want anyone close to this mission. Anyone meaning us. So, he wouldn't tell me the details, but he said with Sky working from the inside, it's giving them a huge advantage in shutting down the agency."

"Wait, is Mr. Brar a part of their team?" Denise asked, confused. "He's way too old for this, don't you guys think?"

"Oh, he is," Shadow responded, "but he's also the one who pulled Evan out of the fire, remember? That man wakes up every morning at four thirty and prays, has a light breakfast afterwards, and then works out for two hours. Even though he's in his old age, his body and mentality are still in their forties."

Evan nodded in agreement. "I was just gonna say that. He said he was only helping them strategize, but that's all I could get out of him."

Shadow shook her head and held her head in her hand.

"What's wrong?" Ryan asked Shadow.

She looked up at the three of them, knowing they had no idea exactly how truly difficult this task was going to be, based on what little information Marvin had shared with her when they were engaged.

"Thinking about your dad, Sky and Mr. Brar taking down a whole operation... it just stresses me out, to be honest. I just want it all to be over with. Have everyone back home safely and so we can just move forward with our lives."

Evan sighed. He knew Shadow wanted to have the SEA shut down and gone for good just as much as everyone else. But the one thing he knew which was shielded from everyone else was how much anxiety it gave Shadow whenever the SEA was mentioned. Marvin was linked to the agency, and anything that reminded Shadow of him made her feel uneasy.

"Same here. I just hope that they're able to shut it down successfully," Ryan said.

"Copy that," Denise said softly.

For a moment, they all sat in brief silence, each thinking about the potential outcomes of the mission.

"I think we should get going," Ryan said, breaking the silence. He looked at his watch. "Wow. It's almost eleven o'clock."

Denise covered her mouth as she felt herself letting out a big yawn. "Yeah, sounds like a good idea."

As Ryan and Denise slowly rose from the table and moved into the living room where Nate was, Evan sat up in his chair. He looked at Shadow and his face automatically broke into a smile. Over the past half an hour before the agency discussion, he had witnessed Shadow struggle to keep herself from falling asleep. He found it quite adorable. It was the little things about her that made him love her so.

Evan walked around the table to Shadow who was just beginning to get up from the chair. He held out his hand and waited for Shadow to take it.

Shadow looked up at him and smirked. "Are you going to help me like this when I'm old and frail?"

"Of course," he said, holding her hand tightly in his.

They walked into the living room where Denise and Ryan were putting on their shoes.

"Thank you, guys, for a lovely evening," Ryan said, tying his shoe.

"Yeah, of course," Shadow responded. "Thank you for cooking us dinner."

Ryan rose and walked over towards Shadow and Evan. "Anytime and anything for our ladies, isn't that right, Evan?" He slapped Evan on the back and then embraced him and Shadow before creeping around the couch and slowly picking up Nate, trying not to not wake him. He carried the sleeping boy carefully to the door. "I can't wait until your baby comes," he said softly.

"Me neither!" Denise said, hugging Shadow and then Evan.

"He's supposed to come Wednesday," Shadow responded as she looked down at her belly. "But honestly I'm ready for him to come today. I'm so tired of waddling around everywhere I go, and not being able to just jump off the couch when I need to go pee."

Evan chuckled and wrapped his arm around Shadow. "We're definitely ready."

Denise smiled at Evan. She'd never seen him so happy and was glad that her baby brother had finally settled down and was starting a family. Even though Evan and Denise's lives hadn't exactly gone smoothly, everything seemed to be falling into place at long last.

Denise and Ryan, too, were at a good place in their life. They had put all their hurt and suppressed feelings on the table, knowing the only way they would fully be able to move forward was to address the issues they had brushed under the rug before Ryan's car accident.

Although Evan and Shadow's relationship had likewise been tested, they too were in a great place and couldn't wait for the baby to come. However, life was never perfect. And just as Bright Storm was about to enter the world, everyone's lives were about to change in a way none of them were prepared for.

CHAPTER 4

Grandma Venice sat upright in her bed, wearing her reading glasses, with a book in her lap. She had made it a goal to read one book a week. She had picked up a couple copies of Stephen King's latest novels. It had been a while since she'd read a book that instantly engrossed her in the horrific and unknown. Willow, who disliked reading, would rather watch TV. And so, before bedtime, he would watch at least half an hour of *Late Night with Jimmy Fallon* while she settled down with her novel.

Willow and Venice were learning how to adjust to one another's likes and dislikes. Given that they were both in their early eighties, they were set in their ways and were content with what they were doing in life. Arguments between them were rare. If Venice wanted to go watch a movie, it didn't take a village to convince Willow to get on board. And if Willow wanted to go away for the weekend, Venice would agree, even though she was a little hesitant to leave Lake View, not knowing who would need her or what would happen.

Willow strolled into the bedroom, his hands in his pockets. He was wearing blue pajamas and a white V-neck shirt. His blue eyes sparkled as he let out a long yawn. Venice hadn't even looked up from her book, intrigued at the way Mr. King pulled the reader into a world that made them cringe in horror. She was hooked. Willow regarded her for a moment before he proceeded to get into bed. Once he got comfortable, he turned to Venice, waiting for her to look up from her novel, but her eyes remained fixed on the page.

"Venice, darling, we need to talk."

As Venice's eyes were still glued to her book, Willow's voice went through one ear and disappeared out the other.

"Venice," he repeated. "We need to talk."

When she still didn't respond, he gently nudged her elbow, hoping that would do the trick. After the first couple of attempts, Venice finally looked up from her book, peering through her glasses with her head tilted downward.

"What is it, dear?"

"There's something that's been on my mind."

Venice studied his eyes for a second and then slowly put the bookmark in its spot before closing the book. She removed her glasses, not having a clue what Willow wanted to talk about.

"What's going on?"

Willow held her hands in his and let out a deep breath.

He gazed at their hands and how they fit together so perfectly. Then he looked up at Venice, connecting with her soul by looking deeply into her eyes.

"I think it's time."

Venice nervously chuckled. "Time for what, hun?"

"It's time that I became a grandfather."

Venice was taken aback by what she had just heard.

Venice slowly put her book on the nightstand and gave Willow her undivided attention.

She looked at him with a little bit of concern. "A grandfather?"

"Yes."

Still confused, Venice looked at him, wondering if this was one of the jokes he would pull on her that she didn't get.

"I'm not following..."

Willow smirked and pulled out a little black box from his nightstand. He'd hid it underneath a few of his *Car and Driver* magazines. He opened the box, presenting Venice with the most stunning engagement ring she'd ever seen.

Venice was speechless. She covered her mouth out of excitement and looked at Willow with gleaming eyes. Happiness erupted in her heart.

It was a platinum topped 18k gold ring topped with a bezel set, old-cut oval diamond, surrounded by eight petal shaped emeralds outlined with a rounded border of smaller old-cut diamonds.

"What do you say? Make me the happiest eighty-two-year-old man on the face of this earth by giving me the gift of being your husband?"

Grandma Venice was at a loss for words. She ran her fingers through her soft white hair, feeling everything was moving rather quickly. She wanted to say yes, but in her gut, she knew the territory she came with.

"Willow..." she said.

"What is it? Is it the ring? You haven't tried it on yet."

Willow would ask questions and then answer them himself when he became nervous, or if the situation was looking like it was about to take a downwards turn.

"No. The ring is beautiful, Willow. I love it."

"Then why does it feel like you're hesitant? Should I have proposed in a different way? I should have. I'll re-propose then. I just thought—"

"Willow, it's not that. It has nothing to do with the proposal or the ring."

Willow sighed. "Then what is it?"

"My life is not stable. Just nine months ago, Bruce came back into our lives for good. Evan was almost killed. Denise and Ryan are—"

"What does any of that have to do with our relationship? I'm not trying to be rude, Venice. I'm wondering."

"They're my life, Willow. They constantly have things going on in their lives, and I have to be there for them. You know I would pick up and run to their aid in a heartbeat. You would always be trying to catch up because it's not the type of life you're used to."

"I'm in pretty good shape, Venice. I can run. Maybe not for long, but I can run."

She looped her arm into his. "What I'm trying to say is that I don't think they're at a point in their lives where they can enjoy peace. My life is hectic because their lives are hectic, and being married to me, you would...you would get fed up and frustrated. I'm too old for all of this, and I want to enjoy some peace, too, and not have to worry, but they're my family. I can't let them go and pick and choose when to be there and when not to."

"So, let me get this straight. You don't want to get married to me because you don't think I can handle the hectic life? Correct me if I'm wrong, but that's what you're saying."

"Yes."

Willow looked down at the ring for a moment before bringing his gaze back to Venice.

"Venice Storm," he started. "I said I wanted to be a grandfather and I meant it. So, I'm going to ask you again. Would you make me the happiest man on earth, happiest eighty-two-year-old man, by giving me the gift of becoming your husband? I would follow you over a cliff if you needed proof that I can handle being a part of your family."

Venice tried hard to keep the tears from streaming down her cheeks. She never once thought she was going to get remarried. Marriage was out of the question when she was raising Evan and Denise. This moment was something she didn't see coming and never expected, but she was happy. Willow made her feel like a twenty-year-old again, falling in love for the first time. She was overjoyed.

Willow wiped the corners of her eyes and smiled. "So, is that a yes?"

"It's a yes," she sniffled.

"I'm so happy, I could do a cartwheel right now."

"You'll break a hip if you do that."

Willow chuckled as he took the ring out of the box. "You're right."

Venice held out her hand and Willow slowly slid the ring onto her ring finger. Venice looked at it sparkle as she gradually moved her hand from side to side. She giggled like a schoolgirl as she analyzed the details of the ring.

"When did you get this? And what made you want to take the plunge?"

"I'm not going to stay young forever," he joked. "I wanted to make a commitment to the woman I had fallen in love with decades ago. And I know women like you don't like to wait around forever for a proposal. I did what I had to do."

Venice gave him a playful nudge before giving him a kiss. "You make me so happy, Willow," she said softly.

"Me too."

Willow held Venice in his arms as she digested the fact that she was an engaged woman and she had a wedding to plan. Even though she was able to predict the future, this was an event that she hadn't seen unfolding.

CHAPTER 5

Once Denise and Ryan arrived home from Evan and Shadow's, Ryan gently carried Nate upstairs, making sure not to wake him. Denise headed into the kitchen to quickly whip up some pancake batter for breakfast the next morning. She made a checklist as she shuffled around the refrigerator to ensure they still had some eggs, bacon, and sausages.

Sunday breakfasts were Denise's favorite. She would cook in the kitchen early in the morning before Nate woke up, and Ryan would come downstairs just in time to make himself a cup of coffee as breakfast was in the making. Then Nate would skip down the stairs in his pajamas and go straight into the living room to watch cartoons. They would all sit in the kitchen eating breakfast, talking about random things, creating memories they would cherish for years to come.

Denise set the list she had compiled on the table and switched off the lights on her way up to bed. Before she slipped into the bedroom, Denise slowly snuck into Nate's room and gave him a kiss as he was fast asleep.

Ryan was lying in bed, scrolling through his phone. Every night he would go through his inbox, reading, replying to, and deleting unnecessary emails. Then he would scroll through Pinterest and find several funny jokes to tell at the breakfast table for the following morning. He had his routine just like Denise, except that Denise's routine slightly differed from Ryan's. She spent time reading the Fortune 500 magazine to enlighten herself of what was happening in the business world and to learn tips on how to grow her own company, Storm Inc. All the long hours and jumping through hoops for tough-to-please clients had begun to pay off. Her company was doing well, maintaining steady sales increases and expanding by the day. Denise had hired ten more interior designers as the company was rapidly growing and was looking into moving into the corporate world.

She washed her face and brushed her teeth, following up with a thorough flossing. After changing into a tank top and pajamas, she slipped into bed. She tied her hair in a light bun as she sat crisscrossed in bed.

"Babe," she said, fumbling with her hair tie.

"Yes, my cookie bear?"

Every night, Ryan came up with a new nickname for Denise. It was something he'd always done after they had moved in together. Some of them were cute and to Denise's liking and others lacked creativity.

"Cookie bear, huh? I like that one," she said smiling. "I

think I'm ready to start trying again. I think this family is ready for another human being."

Without hesitation, Ryan put his phone down on the nightstand and pounced on Denise. Ryan had been waiting patiently for the green light for the past few months. They had talked about growing their family and both had come to an agreement that once Storm Inc. was on its way to expanding, their family would too.

"Sounds good to me," he said, kissing her neck.

Denise roared with laughter. "Not tonight. I'm super tired," she said playfully, pushing him off.

"Denise!" Ryan said as he rolled over.

She sensed the extreme disappointment in his voice. "Babe, I'm really tired. We will tomorrow though. Okay? I just wanted to let you know that I'm ready."

Ryan shut his eyes and moaned.

Denise leaned over as Ryan's eyes remained shut. "Give me a kiss." She ran her fingers through his short hair and tugged at it softly.

Ryan chuckled. "Woman, do you really think I'm gonna give you a kiss after pulling a stunt like that? You're a tease!" he began in a high-pitched tone. He opened his eyes and met hers. He couldn't help but smile. "Who am I kidding," he said before leaning in and giving her a good night kiss. "I love you."

"Love you, too. Goodnight, hun," she said as she made herself comfortable.

"Goodnight," he whispered as he pulled her closer to his body. Ryan picked up his phone and opened the home system app to turn off the lights. Although it was half past midnight, some of the homes on their street still had their lights on.

Meanwhile, in Brickwood, every house had dimmed their lights around nine o'clock. Only retired folks lived in Brickwood, away from the fast-paced world. Bruce, Sky, and Mr. Brar sat around the table in the kitchen, drinking hot tea. A map of the agency building was laid out in front of them.

Sky had her hair tied up in a bun and donned a black cotton V-neck shirt and black relaxed pants. Mr. Brar, like always, wore his black turban and a fitted tracksuit. Bruce wore a black shirt and jeans. They had been racking their brains to finalize the plan they had set in place to take down the agency.

Sky had recruited fifteen of the agency's top fourth-floor agents who had never been assigned with Marvin on any type of assignment or mission. They, too, were looking for an out from the agency but knew how difficult it would be to get rid of the SEA. Aside from that, their contracts hadn't come to an end yet, and some of them were still legally committed to the agency for another ten years. When Sky presented them with this once in a lifetime opportunity, to destroy the organization, which had taken over most of their humanity, all of the agents jumped on board without giving the offer a second thought. And of course, the pay grade for this mission was enough for each of them to retire after its completion.

"I think the plan is solid," she said, looking at Bruce,

then at Mr. Brar.

Bruce leaned back in his chair, looking at the map.

"This is going to work, Bruce," Mr. Brar chimed in. "Sky's got the best agents, and the plan is simple. No need to worry."

Bruce sighed. His mind thought back to when he first started with the SEA, and the man the agency had since turned him into. He had become stronger in a way and appreciated life more because of the SEA, even though the agency no longer was what it once used to be. However, that wasn't the story with every agent. What irked him about the entire plan of destroying the SEA was that it served as a reminder of how much he had missed in Denise and Evan's lives. It tugged on his heartstrings knowing he was never going to get that time back, which was his biggest regret.

"What's wrong, Bruce?" Sky asked, reaching over and softly squeezing his forearm.

Bruce shook off the feeling of disappointment and pursed his lips. "Nothing. It just feels surreal. I want to be overjoyed. I want to be happy that we're putting an end to this, but I also don't want to get ahead of myself. I won't be at peace until I see the agency blown up into pieces."

"Then let's get the ball rolling. We gotta inform the team about their duties and positions. Prepping them is going to take a few days."

Bruce ran his fingers through his greying hair. He refrained from making eye contact with either of them. His eyes began to well up slowly as they all sat in silence.

Sky and Mr. Brar exchanged confused and concerned looks.

Hesitant, Sky leaned in a little closer, not sure what was going through Bruce's mind at the moment.

"Honey, what's going on? If it's too overwhelming—"

"No, no," he said quickly. "It's not that."

Bruce pinched the corner of his eyes. His eyes, which were blue like the ocean, now looked as if they were swimming in a blood bath.

"I'm going to miss the birth of my second grandson. I don't want to miss his birth. I've missed so much already, but we can't put this off either. As long as the agency exists, no one is safe." He paused for a second, staring idly ahead before continuing. "I didn't think I was going to miss another big part of my son's life."

Sky got up from her chair and wrapped her arms around Bruce. She kissed him on the top of his forehead, hugging him tighter.

"Oh honey, you're not going to miss the birth of your grandson. Mr. Brar and I will prep the agents and get everything ready."

Bruce looked over at Mr. Brar. "He's going to want you to be there."

"I wouldn't miss it for the world." Mr. Brar took a moment to reflect on the plan, the birth of Evan's son, and the urgency of shutting down the agency. If he knew one thing, moments like this one only came once. "I say that we stick to the plan and roll it out once the baby is here. It would be a lot safer to execute once Shadow is back home with the baby."

Sky mulled over the suggestion. "I think that's a good idea."

"Okay. Then we meet here after he's born. Keep your burner phones on you. I'll give you a call when everyone is settled."

Mr. Brar nodded.

"Sounds good." Sky yawned. "I'm going to get going now."

Sky picked up her purse and rummaged through to find her keys.

"It's late. Why don't you stay the night and leave early in the morning?" Mr. Brar suggested.

"I really wish I could. But I've got a meeting in the morning, and I can't risk being seen out here..."

Bruce agreed. Even though Bruce was off the force, for the sake of the mission, Sky couldn't risk being seen with him. It would raise red flags and essentially guarantee that Sky would be placed under surveillance. He rose from his chair and gradually walked towards Sky.

They faced each other, knowing the next time they saw one another would be right here before taking down an entire agency. They knew the risks that accompanied this kind of plan. There was a chance they wouldn't make it out alive if they were captured in the process. However, it was a risk they were willing to take for everyone's safety. As long as the SEA existed, no matter where they might go, they wore invisible targets on their backs.

"Shoot me a text when you get home."

"I will," she said, wrapping her arms around him.

Bruce hugged Sky as tight as he could. He pressed his forehead against hers with his eyes closed. "I love you."

"I love you, too," she whispered.

She slowly slipped out of Bruce's arms. Her eyes flickered towards Mr. Brar, who was deep in thought.

"Good night, handsome," she said with a wink as she slipped her arm around him to give him a hug. "I'll see you soon."

Mr. Brar chuckled and patted the top of her hand. "I'll see you soon, dear. Take care of yourself."

On her way out, she looked at the oxygen tank and wheelchair that sat in the corner, then craned her head towards Bruce and Mr. Brar.

Her lips turned upward as she met Mr. Brar's eyes. "You've outsmarted us all."

Mr. Brar snickered. "I had to get creative to keep myself off their radar. No one suspects an old man in a wheelchair."

Sky flashed a grin and said goodbye. Moments later, she was out the front door and on her way back home.

Bruce proceeded to walk back to his chair, positioning himself across from Mr. Brar.

"Have you told them yet?" Mr. Brar asked.

Bruce broke eye contact for a moment.

"I'm guessing that's a no."

Bruce exhaled, knowing how strongly Mr. Brar felt about him telling his family what was going on. "They're just getting used to having their father around for the first time in over two decades. They don't need to hear that their father is dying of cancer now."

Two years ago, Bruce had been diagnosed with advanced prostate cancer, and it had since spread to his bones. Initially, he had completed androgen deprivation therapy, but his body was no longer responding to the therapy the way it had the first time. This pushed Bruce to face the reality of his case: his clock was ticking. Time was running out.

Mr. Brar sighed. He looked at Bruce and saw the young man he once was. He'd been happily married at one point and had helped raise two beautiful children for a short period of time. He was a good man, and this was how life was going to repay him? He pushed the thought far back into his mind, not wanting to deal with thoughts of Bruce's fate.

"Does Sky know?"

Bruce shook his head, and Mr. Brar let out a harsh breath.

"Flippin' heck, Bruce! You're not gaining anything by holding onto this."

"Yeah, I know."

Mr. Brar opened his mouth to press further, but, seeing the look on Bruce's face, thought better of it. Pushing this conversation wasn't going to lead to anything productive.

"Have you told Shadow and Evan who Shadow's father is?" he asked instead.

Bruce shook his head. "I told Evan. I don't know how to break it to her. Shadow's going to be devastated when she finds out that she went through all that shit with Marvin because of her father."

"It's going to be tough, but you can't hide this information from her," he said, hinting that Bruce couldn't keep his diagnosis a secret, either.

"I know," he said solemnly.

"Sooner than later, Bruce. Sooner than later."

Bruce rubbed his hand against his chin, very well knowing that Mr. Brar was right. He had to let Shadow know who Roy was and quite possibly ruin any kind of relationship she had left with him.

"This sucks," Bruce said as he picked up his tea and finished it off.

"Not as much as knowing that you're dying from cancer." As the words slipped out of Mr. Brar's mouth, his eyes began to well up.

Bruce's eyebrows drew together, and he broke eye contact with Mr. Brar. Bruce knew he was bringing more pain to the people he loved than any sort of happiness.

Bruce recalled the day he had received the call from his doctor asking him to come in and discuss some test results. It took him a couple of days before he was able to digest the news but even then, he found himself in disbelief. For weeks, Bruce felt as though he was living in some sort of surreal alternate universe where nothing made sense. It was tempting to pretend nothing had changed. Finally, he snapped back into reality and realized what the diagnosis meant. He'd taken a week off just to sit and think about his life—all the decisions he had made, his regrets, his journey at the agency, the birth of his two children. His life flashed through his mind's eye as if it were a movie. That was the week he decided he needed to be a part of Evan and Denise's lives, before it was too late.

It was cancer that had brought Bruce back into his children's lives, and it would be the same disease that took him away from them again.

CHAPTER 6

The following morning, Denise was up at 8 a.m., running to the grocery store to pick up the items on her list. One of the things she loved about grocery shopping early in the morning was that she beat rush hour. She didn't need to force her way through aisles heaving with other shoppers, and the checkout counter was a breeze. A trip that would usually take her thirty minutes only took her fifteen. Once she arrived home, she unpacked all the goods and began breakfast. In the kitchen, she flipped the pancakes and let them cook as she scrambled eggs. On another pan she had sausages cooking. The aromatic flavor of the sausages and eggs drifted through the air.

On cue, she heard Ryan strolling down the stairs. When he entered the kitchen, he was still wearing his pajamas, his hair uncombed.

He yawned and stretched out his arms, trying to wake himself up. "Good morning," he said, his voice a little croaky.

"Good morning," Denise replied in excitement. "You look like a hot mess."

"I know. I took a good hard look at myself before coming down, my queen. What's cookin', good lookin'?"

"Pancakes, sausages and scrambled eggs."

Ryan nodded as he lazily pulled out a chair from the table. He sat down and rubbed his eyes. He let out an exasperated yawn and then looked over at Denise, who had her back turned. His eyes flicked toward the coffee maker.

"Babe..."

Denise turned around with the spatula in her hand. "What's up?"

"We don't have any more coffee grounds, do we?"

She thought a moment before realizing it was the one thing she forgot to check last night as she was wrapping up her list.

She frowned. "I don't think we do, hun. I totally forgot to check last night."

"It's okay," he groaned. "I'm just gonna take a pre-workout for energy. I don't know why I'm so exhausted, Denise."

She turned around once again with the answer. "Did you forget that you worked sixteen hour shifts at the hospital every day this past week? And then, during your free time, you were off coaching Nate's soccer team, running errands, playing basketball... and you had that father and son trip last Saturday. Remember that?"

Ryan looked at her funny. "Jeez… I hadn't even thought of that. This whole week feels like a blur. I think it was the trip that did me in. When these boys get together, they're fuckin' wild, man."

"I know. Soon, we're gonna have another one running around."

"Are you already pregnant? Because from what I remember, last night we didn't actually get down to business. Or did we?" Ryan's eyebrows furrowed, now genuinely confused on how the night ended.

Denise giggled. "No, we didn't. But I think this busy schedule will help both of us prepare for another baby. It's been eight years since we had a baby screaming in the middle of the night, around the clock. Do you remember those sleepless nights and long days?"

Ryan calmly proceeded to put his head down on the table. "At dawn, we will rise and conquer."

Denise chuckled as she turned the sausages. "You're gonna be fine. It's only been a month since you've been back at work. Your body is still adjusting to everything."

For Ryan, it wasn't just the sixteen-hour shifts or the errands that had him exhausted to the core. It was the adjustment he was making mentally to be a better and more active husband, and the type of father he wanted to be for Nate. Once he had settled in after coming home from the hospital following his horrific accident, they were both forced to address the issues that had been bubbling underneath the surface of their marriage. Of course, no marriage was perfect. It was ridiculous to think there was such a thing. A great marriage meant work, which the two of them had stopped putting in. Ryan had learned a great deal of what Denise had been going through and realized he needed to be a better partner for Denise. He didn't want Denise to carry the whole family on her shoulders as she had silently done for quite a while, on top of running a start-up company all on her own. It was an adjustment in his mind that he was trying to get used to.

"I know. Do you need any help?"

"No, I'm good. Thank you."

Ryan rose sluggishly from the chair to retrieve his pre-workout powder. In half an hour, it was going to kick in, and he would be blasting with energy. Although he generally refrained from using such supplements, preferring natural resources, he was in dire need of energy.

He stood in the kitchen and poured a scoop into his protein shaker. After adding water, he screwed the top back on and shook the bottle as hard as he could. It was fruit punch flavor and, in his opinion, was actually pretty tasty. He gulped down half the bottle and then set it down on the kitchen table, eager for the shake to take action. Ryan walked over to Denise and kissed her neck and then craned his head sideways, getting a better view at her face.

"Whatcha thinkin' about?"

She drew in a long breath before she answered. She lowered the heat on the oven and put down the spatula.

"I'm just thinking about my dad," she said, facing him. She crossed her arms against her chest with a concerned look. "I know that working as an agent for the SEA isn't exactly the safest or easiest, but... why did it take my dad *twenty-seven* years to come forward with the truth? Why that long?"

Denise looked into Ryan's eyes, hoping he would have the answer. But, just like Denise, he couldn't come up with a reasonable explanation.

There was a moment of silence before Nate came thundering down the stairs. Oddly, this time, he didn't go straight into the living room to watch TV. He walked into the kitchen with a big grin on his face, his eyes bigger than a tarsier's. His hair was ruffled still, and his little hands remained innocently clasped behind his back.

Ryan and Denise's hearts melted every time Nate had a smile on his face. It radiated with sweetness and innocence.

"Good morning, bud," Ryan said cheerfully. He opened his arms for a hug. As always, Nate hugged hard and clung on.

Denise ran her hand through Nate's messy hair, trying to tame it as much as she could. "You're not going to watch TV?"

Nate looked up with his big brown eyes. "Yeah..." he said, elongating the word. "But..."

"But what?" Ryan asked.

Nate stepped away, far enough to get a view of both of his parents. Denise briefly turned her attention to the stove. She quickly removed the pancake from the skillet and poured another round of batter onto the pan. The heat for the eggs and sausages was turned down to low now that they were almost done cooking. When she turned her attention back to Nate, he wore a timid look on his face. She knew that look. Nate was about to ask a question to which he most likely knew the answer to.

Ryan chuckled looking at Nate. He knew something was on his little boy's mind but couldn't quite tell what it was. He was still picking up on Nate's social cues.

"What is it, buddy?"

"Can I... get a puppy?"

Ryan and Denise exchanged uncertain looks with one another.

"Well," Denise began, "you need to understand what a huge responsibility it is to have a puppy first. You've got to feed it every day. Take it for a walk. Pick up poop, give it baths, play with it... It's a lot of hard work, Nate. More than just having a fish."

Ryan studied Nate's facial expression.

"This makes so much sense now," Ryan said, subconsciously putting the pieces together. He looked at Denise with a grin, just then realizing how sneaky Nate was. "For the past two weeks, do you know which books we've been reading?"

"Which ones?"

"*My First Puppy*, *Puppies Puppy Book for Kids*, *Just Me and My Puppy*, *Bath time For Biscuit*. I thought he was getting bored with all the dinosaur books, but now it makes sense. I didn't pick up on those hints there."

He smirked at Nate, who was anxiously waiting for his parents' response to his question. Ryan looked at Denise and knew she was on board. He sighed. "Alright, you can get a puppy, *but* first, we need to know that you're ready."

"Okay!" Nate said with utmost excitement.

"You know what that means, right?" Ryan asked.

Nate remained silent.

"You're going to have to do your research on how to take care of a puppy. How to give it a bath. When to feed it, and how many times a day. How much exercise it will need," he said, crouching down to Nate's level. "Then we'll quiz you. If you get *all* the questions correct, we can get a puppy. Sound like a plan?"

Nate nodded his head eagerly.

After getting his answer, Nate rushed out of the kitchen and into the living room.

"Don't you think it's a little harsh? Quizzing him?" Denise asked as she flipped the pancake.

"If he really is passionate about getting a puppy, he's gonna do whatever it takes and ace that quiz. If he's not as passionate as he thinks he is, the excitement is gonna fade away halfway in. Did you forget what you were like as a kid?"

Denise planted her hands on her hips and gave him the arched eyebrow look.

"You know I'm right," he said, chuckling.

"I know kids jump from wanting one thing to another, but I just don't want to break his heart."

"We're not going to break his heart," he reassured her. Ryan scanned the pans and the stack of pancakes.

Denise handed him a plate and placed two pancakes, some scrambled eggs, and two sausages on it.

"You read my mind," he said, looking down at his plate. He retrieved maple syrup from the pantry and poured it over his pancakes before taking a seat at the table. "Thank you."

"No problem hun."

As Denise fixed Nate his plate, the doorbell rang. She put the plate down on the counter and strolled past Ryan—who already had stuffed his mouth with scrambled eggs—and down the hallway to the front door.

She reached for the handle, with a grin across her face.

"Hey!" she exclaimed, as she opened the door. "What a nice surprise."

"How are you doing, darlin'?" Venice asked, giving Denise a hug and a kiss on the cheek.

"I'm good."

"Hey, Denise," Willow said, closing the door behind him. He turned around and gave Denise a hug. "How are you?"

"I'm good. We were just having breakfast. Should I fix you guys a plate?"

"No, thank you, honey. We had an early breakfast," he responded. "We wanted to share some exciting news with you guys. Are Ryan and Nate up?

"Yeah, they're both up. Ryan's in the kitchen and Nate's.... in the living room," she said, walking down the hallway with Venice and Willow behind her. "Nate, Grammy is here."

From the living room she heard Nate yell, "Yay!"

When they entered the kitchen, Ryan was almost

halfway done with his breakfast. He looked up, surprised to see Venice and Willow.

"Hey, you guys," he said, rising from his chair. He wiped his hands before giving each of them a hug. "What brings you by?"

"There's something we wanted to share with you," Grandma Venice answered, feeling giddy.

"Grandma," Denise blurted, "what is it?"

Before Venice could continue, Nate came rushing in to greet Venice and Willow.

"Hiya Nate! What are you up to, kiddo?" Venice asked.

"I was reading a book on how to take care of a puppy."

"You're getting a puppy?" Willow asked curiously.

Nate nodded his head, and Ryan and Denise exchanged glances. They were under the impression that Nate had been watching TV the whole time. It seemed Nate was serious about this puppy business.

Ryan washed down his breakfast with orange juice before he answered. "We agreed that if he learned how to take care of a puppy and the responsibility that came with it, he would be allowed to get one. Isn't that right, Nate?"

Nate looked at his father. "Yeah, dad."

"What did you guys want to tell us?" Denise asked, feeling like her chest was going to explode if she had to wait another second.

Venice raised her left hand and flashed the beautiful ring Willow had surprised her with the previous night. "We're getting married!"

Denise gasped once she saw the rock on Venice's finger.

"Willow!" Denise proclaimed. "You proposed? Oh my gosh!"

Willow chuckled. "I did. We're not getting any younger, and I'm in love with her."

"Way to go, Willow," Ryan chimed.

Ryan and Denise closely examined Grandma Venice's ring as if they were experts in jewelry. Denise couldn't get over the fact that her grandmother was engaged and that there was now going to be another wedding in the family.

"You did good with the ring," Ryan stated. "It's beautiful and unique."

"Just like your grandmother," Willow responded, giving Venice a kiss.

"Have you guys set a date? Where do you guys think of having the wedding? I know—"

"Hold on there for a minute, darlin'. That's another thing I wanted to talk to you two about." She darted a glance at Nate and raised an eyebrow. Denise took the hint and ushered her son back into the living room, out of earshot.

Venice took a moment to gather her thoughts before she proceeded. "Your father is working on the mission, and with Evan and Shadow's baby coming, we wanted to wait until the dust settled. There's just too much going on. So, we're going to have to keep this news just between us."

"That's fair," Ryan said as he proceeded to the sink to clean off his plate.

"And there's something else I wanted to tell you..."

Ryan was in the midst of rinsing his dishes when he

heard the tone in Venice's voice. He turned back and looked at her face.

Denise felt the need to sit down suddenly.

"What is it?" Denise asked cautiously. Ryan left his dishes in the sink and sat beside her, feeling anxious.

Venice looked at Willow, unsure how to break the news.

"Grandma, what is it?" Denise felt a lump begin to form in the back of her throat. She had a feeling that this was going to be connected with her grandmother's second sight. It wasn't long before her suspicions were confirmed.

Venice sighed. "I always tell you guys that my predictions aren't going to be a hundred percent correct, all the time. So, keep that in mind."

Denise nodded her head.

"I had a vision... of Evan and Shadow's baby... being stillborn..."

"What?" Ryan gasped.

Denise slowly leaned back in her chair, feeling her heart go numb.

"But your grandmother is not always right, Denise," Willow stated, trying to calm her panic.

"Are you going to tell them?" Ryan asked.

Venice ran her hand through her hair. It was something she'd contemplated for the past two weeks.

"Me telling them really doesn't help anyone honestly, darlin'. There's nothing anyone can do but hope when the baby is born, he's healthy."

Venice got close to Denise and rubbed her shoulder. "Denise..."

Denise lifted Venice's hand from her shoulder and interlocked it with hers. She sighed and answered. "It's... it's just a lot to take in. I'm worried about everyone...It honestly feels like no one can catch a break in this family."

Ryan moved closer and wrapped his arms around her, kissing her on the cheek and pressing his face against hers. He looked up at Venice, not knowing how this was going to affect Denise from now until Shadow's due date.

"Let's not worry about something that hasn't happened yet. Like Venice said, not all her predictions are a hundred percent correct. So, we shouldn't jump the gun, right?"

Venice managed to break into a smile. She appreciated the positive outlook Ryan managed to have. Given what everyone had gone through in the past year, somehow Ryan managed to be the positive light in the family.

"Everything is going to be fine," he said softly to Denise.

CHAPTER 7

It was Sunday evening. As per usual, Shadow and Evan planned on eating dinner on the couch in the living room with the TV turned on to one of their favorite shows. Sundays were Shadow's days to make dinner for the two of them. In their household, equality and gender roles simply didn't exist, and all the household chores, including cooking, were shared. It was how they planned on raising their kids, too. However, the last trimester had made it difficult for Shadow to stand on her feet, even though she wouldn't admit it. Evan could see the discomfort in her face when she stood in the kitchen to prepare dinner, so he decided to take over more of the cooking until after Bright was born and Shadow had recovered.

Evan was pulling out the ingredients he needed to make his famous seven-layered burritos when he heard Shadow scream from their bedroom. Dropping a bottle of onion powder, he ran up the stairs, believing this was the moment both of their lives were going to change forever. He entered the bedroom and saw Shadow standing in the middle of the room with a horrified look painted across her face.

"Your water broke!" Evan exclaimed. He looked at her grey leggings and could see where the fluid had spread across the fabric.

"I know!"

For a brief moment, Shadow looked at him, perplexed.

"Why are you looking at me like that?" he asked, catching his breath without realizing he had been huffing and puffing out of excitement.

"To be honest, I thought you were going to freak out."

"What? Me? No. Why would I freak out?" And just like that, he felt his nerves work against him. He felt butterflies in his stomach, surprised he was still capable of feeling that way.

Shadow took a deep breath before she pointed out the obvious. "Maybe you weren't going to freak out before, but I think you're about to any second now."

On cue, Evan leaned forward, planting his hands on his thighs for support. "Okay… you're right. I'm freaking out. I'm gonna be a father… we're gonna be parents! You think we're ready for all of this, Shadow?"

Shadow walked over to Evan cautiously with her hand on top of her belly.

"Honey," she began, "You're just as ready as any father is when they have their first. Now, c'mon and let's have this baby. I'm ready for him to come out of me already."

Evan's mind darted from one scenario to another. How was he going to do in the delivery room? Would he pass out at the sight of Bright crowning? Would Shadow kick him out for not being the supportive husband she needed him to be at a time like this? He felt his brain was going to explode. Shadow's hand grazed down his back and then traveled back up to his hair. She massaged his scalp for a few minutes. She had such a way of soothing his anxiety.

Shadow looked at him as a smile crept across her face. "You're overreacting, you know?"

Evan looked at her, stunned by how calm she was. "Have you even had a contraction yet?"

"No, not yet. But we should get to the hospital."

Evan rested his hands on his hips, still trying to process the idea they were finally going to become parents. "That sounds like a plan."

As Evan gathered Shadow's things—the overnight bag containing a change of clothes and other necessities Shadow had squeezed in—Shadow emerged from the bathroom wearing a new pair of leggings and a tank top. She'd applied her favorite shade of red lipstick and brushed on some mascara, her hair now tied into a bun.

Evan was stunned. He stood in the middle of the room, holding the overnight bag in one hand, taken aback by Shadow's beauty. In that moment, he'd forgotten Bright was going to enter the world. Evan's mind went back in time, reminiscing about the first day he'd met Shadow. She was just as beautiful, if not even more, to this day.

The nervous feeling of having a baby and becoming

a father slowly faded away and was replaced with the excitement of meeting Bright and raising him alongside Shadow.

"You look beautiful."

Shadow grinned. "Thank you. I figured since everyone's probably going to be taking pictures, I should look decent."

"Oh shoot! I forgot about the camera." Evan looked over at the dresser and saw the camera sitting there, charged and ready to go. He quickly grabbed the Nikon and slipped it into the overnight bag. "You don't need makeup. You're always stunning."

Shadow proceeded to walk towards Evan with her hands on her hips. She smiled and gave his cheek a slight squeeze. "Thank you, husband. Okay, we should really get going now."

Once they had checked in at the hospital and Shadow was in her white hospital gown, the contractions began. Evan called Venice to let her know Shadow had gone into labor and asked to let Denise and Bruce know along with Mr. Brar. After that, he turned his phone to silent, not wanting to miss a second of this experience.

Shadow paced back and forth in the room, trying to fight off the pain. Just like Denise, she opted for natural childbirth. Even though Evan was supportive of her plan to give birth naturally, he knew deep down he would never be able to imagine how painful the time leading up to the birth was going to be without the drugs. It scared Evan. All he was going to be able to do was give Shadow support, which to him didn't seem much.

Evan held Shadow's hand when she asked him to, retrieved ice-chips for her to chew on, and did his best to keep her comfortable. Since such tasks were simple and short-lived pain relievers, they didn't prevent him from feeling helpless.

As she paced the room, Shadow suddenly stopped in her tracks, doubling over in pain as her body readied itself for labor. Her face scrunched in agony. Grabbing the side of the bed for support, she cried out. Almost physically feeling the anguish from his wife, Evan came around from behind her, armed with lavender oil to massage her swollen hips.

Shadow was beginning to sweat, and her cheeks flushed from the contractions, each one rolling through her body like angry waves, pain coursing from her stomach into her back.

Seven hours had passed. It was past midnight and Bright was still in Shadow's womb. Evan stood by Shadow's bedside offering her whatever she needed.

"Why doesn't he want to come out?" Shadow asked with agitation.

Evan reached for her hand and brought it up close to his lips. "Because you made a wonderful home for him in there." He kissed her hand. "You're a strong woman, you know?"

Shadow let out a wailing sigh. "I'm *soo* tired, Evan, and I can't fall asleep. I want to sleep. My feet hurt. I can't see my feet. I just want him to come out already!"

"I know. I know. The doctor said you're five centimeters along. You're halfway there."

Shadow let out short, continuous breaths before adjusting herself. "Is Venice still in the waiting room?"

"Yeah."

"How about Willow?"

"He's there, too."

"How about your father?"

"He's also out there."

"Mr. Brar?"

"Yup. So is Mr. Brar. Denise and Ryan went home. Denise said they'll come after the baby arrives."

Shadow nodded. "I can't believe they're all still here. Did you tell them that they could go home and come back in the morning? Hopefully, Bright's here by then. They really don't have to be here, not that I don't want them here, but they're probably bored out there."

"They're choosing to stay, Shadow. So, don't you worry."

Shadow cracked a smile. "Bright is going to be overwhelmed with so much love from your family."

It took a brief moment for Evan to understand what Shadow was implying.

"Hey," he said softly, "your mom showed up to the wedding. She may surprise you and come after all. Who knows, maybe your dad will drop by, too."

She looked up at him, giving a halfhearted smile. "This is going to be their first grandchild. If they can't be here for his birth, I don't want them anywhere near my family."

Before Evan could respond, Shadow was gripped with

another contraction. He held her hand as she grunted and cried out in agony, waiting for the contraction to pass.

For the next couple of hours, the contractions came and went. The doctor came in every hour to check on Shadow to see how many centimeters she'd dilated, and every time, it was just one more than the last. It wasn't until 4:10 a.m., when Shadow was finally ten centimeters along, that she was moved to the delivery room.

Evan stood by Shadow's bedside, holding her hand as her doctor prepared for the delivery.

Dr. Channing Copeland was a gray-haired gentleman who had three daughters of his own. He had been recommended by Denise as he had delivered Nate and had made the entire experience smooth and comfortable.

Dr. Copeland sat on his stool, looking at Shadow through his eyeglasses. "This is it, Shadow. Just a couple more pushes and you're going to be a mommy."

Shadow peered up at Evan, tightly gripping his hand. "It's happening," she said, and before he could say anything else, Shadow began to sob. "Evan, we're going to be parents!"

Evan chuckled. He looked into her eyes, still holding her hand. There was a thin sheen of sweat on her forehead, which he patted dry with a washcloth he'd been using for the past half hour. As he leaned in, his eyes still locked in with hers, his eyes began to well up with joy and happiness. He cleared his throat and said, "We're gonna be parents."

He kissed her right before Shadow was instructed to

push once again.

"Well, what do you know!" Dr. Copeland exclaimed. "His head's making way. Would you like to take a look, Evan?"

Evan froze for a second. He had known that he wanted to be a part of the whole experience. He wanted to see Bright's birth. But in the moment, he wasn't quite sure if he was entirely ready to see what it was going to look like down there. Granted, Shadow had informed Evan prior that her nether regions weren't going to appear normal or pretty during delivery and that it would be helpful for Evan if he watched a birthing video to get himself more prepared for the big day. Evan vividly remembered his response to Shadow's helpful suggestion: "I'm going to be fine. I'm sure I've seen more… horrific things in my lifetime."

Evan now regretted his decision to pass up sitting next to Shadow on the couch as she watched the birthing video. He was clueless as to what he was going to witness.

"Evan?" Dr. Copeland repeated. "You want to come and take a look before Shadow gives us another big push?"

Evan cleared his throat, subconsciously trying to stall.

"Evan!"

Evan's head jolted in Shadow's direction. "Please hurry up and decide," she said, panting.

He cautiously walked over to Dr. Copeland, unprepared. And there it was. Bright's head peeked out from the birth canal.

To Evan's surprise, he didn't faint or even feel as if he

was about to. Instead, he was memorized by childbirth.

Evan looked up at Shadow, who was tired as could be. "You're amazing."

Her eyebrows furrowed. "I know. Are you done yet? I want to get him out of me!"

"That she is," Dr. Copeland agreed. "Now, Shadow, give me another push. A real big one."

Evan quickly went back to Shadow and held her hand and watched closely. Shadow grunted and screamed as she pushed as hard as she could.

"Just one more push!"

Shadow's head fell back onto the pillow out of exhaustion. "I can't do it," she cried. "He's just gonna have to walk outta here when he's ready. I can't do it."

Evan couldn't help but chuckle. "Yes, you can babe. I know you can." He ran his hand through her damp hair and leaned closer to her face. "Shadow," he said softly, tightly interlocking his hand into hers. "You're stronger than anyone I know," he said as he kissed the top of her glistening forehead. "Just one more push. That's all."

"I don't think I can, Evan," Shadow cried. "I can't."

"Yes, you can," Evan assured her. "You've got it in you, babe."

"C'mon Shadow, one big push," Dr. Copeland encouraged. "I know you can do it."

Shadow let out a few short little breaths before pushing with all her might. Her forehead creased and face flushed bright pink as she pushed one last time.

Then, there it was. The cry.

The next hour, everything around Evan and Shadow seemed to be more fast paced and almost a blur. Evan cut the umbilical cord a few minutes after Shadow held Bright. The nurse wiped the amniotic fluid and then promptly completed a physical exam to make sure he was healthy. A knitted blue hat was placed on top of his head, and then their new baby was wrapped in a blanket before the nurse gently handed him to Shadow.

A little while afterwards, Bright and Shadow were both issued ID bands to wear around their wrists, and then Bright's footprints were taken soon after. Evan informed Denise through text that Shadow had given birth while everyone in the waiting room anxiously waited to meet the new addition.

When the bustling of medical staff ceased and the room emptied, quiet descended for the first time in hours. Now it was only Evan, Shadow, and Bright, who was fast asleep.

"Oh my god..." Shadow gasped, as she analyzed Bright's little fingers and tiny nose. "He's so cute!"

Evan's eyes brimmed with tears as he gazed at his son. "He is. He's got your nose."

Shadow looked up at Evan with a grin on her tired face. "I'm so happy, Evan."

"Happy cause he got your nose or..."

Shadow shook her head and giggled. "Happy that he's finally here."

"Me too," Evan chuckled and then leaned in to kiss Shadow.

They soaked up as much time with their newborn as

possible before Evan left the room to tell the rest of the family to come meet the newest addition. When everyone shuffled in, they all quietly congratulated Shadow and Evan, surrounding Shadow's bedside and gawking at Bright as he slept. When asked what they had named their son, both Evan and Shadow proudly introduced Bright Storm to the family.

"That's a beautiful name," Mr. Brar chimed in, wheeling closer to Shadow's bedside to get a proper look at the baby.

"Isn't he adorable?" Venice asked as she turned back to Willow and Mr. Brar. Both nodded their heads, unable to keep their eyes off the tiny, perfect human Shadow held in her arms.

"Can I hold him, Shadow?" Mr. Brar eagerly asked.

"Of course."

Shadow carefully handed Mr. Brar the baby.

"My goodness, he is so precious."

Evan watched as Mr. Brar held the newborn and gave him his blessings. Evan had always known Mr. Brar to be a religious man, someone who practiced the Sikh faith with devotion. For as long as Evan had known him, Mr. Brar had always worn a black turban, which was one of the Sikh's five articles of faith and sported an unshorn beard.

Mr. Brar's light brown eyes flickered towards Evan. He grinned from ear to ear, crow's feet crinkling around his eyes. His beard, now snow white, stood out against his olive skin. Despite a few wrinkles on his forehead, he looked considerably younger than he really was.

"I feel like my heart is going to explode from happiness," Mr. Brar giggled.

"Now I think of it, we should've named him after you," Evan said.

Mr. Brar brought his attention back to the baby. "You're making me blush. His name is fitting. He's going to bring so much joy to your lives. All our lives, actually."

After a few minutes, Mr. Brar handed Bright to Willow.

Bruce stood beside Evan, overcome with emotion.

Evan caught a glimpse of his father wiping the tears away from his cheeks. Evan subtly put his arm around Bruce's shoulders and pulled him closer.

"You have a son, Evan," Bruce chuckled through his sobs.

Evan nodded through his own tears. "I do. I can't believe I'm a dad now."

Bruce stepped aside from the bedside as everyone continued to express their joy at the new arrival. He ducked out of the room and into the hospital hallway. Evan followed after him, knowing no-one in the room would notice his absence for a moment amid their cooing. Bruce slipped his hands into his pockets and looked down at the tile floor. Evan approached Bruce, standing in front of him, not sure exactly what was going on in his father's mind.

"Is everything okay, dad?"

After a moment of silence, Bruce's gaze met Evan's, his eyes ever so slightly pink at the corners. He gave a halfhearted smile before he spoke. "Thank you for letting me be a part of your life again, Evan."

Evan felt his throat begin to constrict. He saw the pain in his father's eyes.

"Dad, I wouldn't want you to miss out on anything else that goes on in our lives. You know that, right?"

Bruce thought about the cancer that was spreading throughout his body. "I know," he said, clearing his throat. "I'm beyond grateful to you, and Shadow, and Denise, for… letting me be here, with you guys."

Evan replied with a smile. "I know. I'm glad you're a part of our lives too." A blurry memory of Samantha's face, etched with pain, flashed through his mind's eye. Pain caused by *his* actions in another life, another time. He took a deep breath, reminding himself he was nothing like Derek. "You need to stop beating yourself up for the past. We're not there anymore."

Bruce slipped his hands back in his pockets and nodded. "I know, but it's hard."

***

After a little while, when Shadow began to doze off, Bright was taken to the nursery. Everyone crept quietly from the room to let Shadow get some rest before Bright woke up for his next feeding. When they reached the waiting room, the group stood in a huddle, aware that now Bright had been safely delivered, there was something else they needed to talk about.

Bruce, with his arms crossed across his chest, pursed his lips as he gazed from Willow to Venice.

Mr. Brar sensed Bruce's hesitation and decided to

jump in. He met Venice's eyes and began. "I think we all know what the plans are," he said, hinting at their operation. "It's going to be an intense week, and we just want you guys to know that..." Mr. Brar halted for a moment before lowering his voice. "Once the operation is underway, if you need to get in contact with one of us, call me. It's safer that way since they don't suspect me of being capable of... well, really anything because of this thing," he said, looking at his wheelchair. "Once we've completed the mission, you guys will know. Worst case scenario.... you don't hear from any of us. Then, you will get a letter in the mail from the agency letting you know our whereabouts— or, if we don't make it, they'll send you guys our belongings. That would be the bare minimum. I don't have any reason to believe it will come to that, but that's just the worst-case scenario."

Venice nodded, understanding the underlying message Mr. Brar was delivering.

"We've got a good team, so there's nothing to worry about," Bruce chimed in. "Mom, can I talk to you for a sec?"

Glances were exchanged in the group as Bruce and Venice stepped off to the side.

"What is it, honey?" she asked, pushing her purse strap up from where it had slipped from her shoulder.

He looked at her with pleading eyes. "I need you to understand that whatever happens, any predictions you might have... you can't... you can't prevent what's meant to happen. You can't always play the hero."

A confused look trickled over her sweet face. "I know

that, Bruce." She took a moment to analyze him. "What are you not telling me?"

The thought of the cancer plunged into his mind. He didn't know how to tell her about his diagnosis, nor was it the right time; they were not yet in the clear with the agency. There was unfinished business that needed to be taken care of. So far, from the moment he had come back into their lives, he'd only delivered Venice bad news. How was he supposed to tell his mother, after everything that they'd been through, that he was now dying from cancer? He looked into her eyes, brimming with hope, and lied.

"Nothing. Look, I know I've been back for just a little while, but there are some things that you don't ever forget about a person."

Venice crossed her arms at her chest. "And what do you mean by that?"

"This gift that you have, being a psychic. It always made you worry— *always*. It's not like you can return the gift," he said with a chuckle, "but you need to enjoy life without worrying about what's going to happen next."

"You say it like it's so easy, Bruce."

And she was right: Bruce's eyes shifted to the waiting room where he spotted a young couple watching over two children playing in a playpen. Their tired faces and grim expressions said enough for Bruce to figure out the folks were looking down a road with no hope. There was pain everywhere he went. It was unavoidable, but his mother wasn't getting any younger, and he only wanted her to enjoy the rest of her life without living in constant fear about what was going to happen to Evan and Denise.

His eyes floated to Willow, who was all smiles with Mr. Brar and Evan.

"Mr. Marx seems like a good man, from what I've seen."

Venice was caught off guard by Bruce's sudden switch in topic. She responded with caution. "Yes, he is."

"And you're happy? With Mr. Marx?"

She took a second before responding, trying to figure out where Bruce was going with this.

She let out a nervous chuckle. "I am," she said looking over her shoulder at Willow, who was in the middle of telling a joke, from what she could tell. "Why do you ask?"

Bruce opened his arms wide as he inched forward and reeled her in. "Congratulations, mom."

Venice gasped once it registered in her mind. "I had no idea he told you." Her eyes slowly filled with tears. She hugged him tighter, not wanting to let him go. When she pulled away, she looked up at Bruce, experiencing a mixture of feelings, sadness being one of them.

"He asked for my permission." Bruce smirked.

Venice's eyebrows rose. "He did?"

"Yeah. After I found out you two were dating, I started to drop by his bakery. I wanted to see if he was good enough for you. I wanted to feel him out and... he's a good guy. He's over the moon about you."

Venice covered her eyes with her palms out of embarrassment. She hadn't dated after the death of her husband, Dean. She rarely had the time when Denise and Evan were growing up.

"So, you've known this whole time?"

Bruce grinned. "Of course."

"I guess Evan and Shadow are the only ones left to break the news to."

"Seems like it." He glanced over to the three of them who were deep in conversation and then down to his watch. "Denise and Ryan aren't probably going to come until a little later, huh?"

"I spoke to Denise earlier. She said they were going to come after Nate got out of school."

"I see," he replied, drifting into deep thought.

Bruce knew Denise still had emotions bottled up after their first conversation they'd had when he reached out to discuss his absence. She was more hesitant than Evan to forge a new relationship with him, which he understood. He'd been gone for twenty-seven years without any contact, so it was expected, but he wondered if she would ever truly forgive him for being absent. His clock was ticking, and Bruce wanted to try as many times as the universe would allow him to establish somewhat of a healthy relationship with his daughter. He just hoped he would have enough time.

Bruce was reeled in back to reality by Venice, who had tugged on his arm several times.

"You okay?"

"Huh?"

"You were gone there for a bit. Is everything okay?"

"Yeah, everything's fine," he said, reassuring her.

She studied him for a bit, feeling that he wasn't being

entirely truthful. "Okay," she said slowly. "Willow and I should get going. I want to take a little nap before my first client arrives, and Willow, well, he's got to make sure the kids aren't eating all the sweets, as he puts it."

Willow's bakery was staffed with high school and college students who would occasionally snack in between breaks. Not that he minded, but there were a couple of kids he needed to keep an eye on when it came to free dessert.

Bruce smiled and replied, "No worries."

"Please be safe, okay? I want to see you as soon as it's all over."

Bruce opened his arms again and wrapped them around Venice. "I will. I promise."

"I'm gonna hold you to it," she murmured.

CHAPTER 8

"Did you receive the identification number?" Hector asked.

"Yeah, I did. But I can't go in just yet," Dominic hissed.

"What do you mean you can't go in yet? You guys need to get the baby and get the fuck outta there."

"The nurse is still in there."

"You're wearing a disguise, you fuckin' moron." Hector sat in the chair in the hospital hallway, next to his pretend wife, Christy, as he casually watched Evan and Bruce having a conversation. "You gotta make the switch or this whole operation is a fail."

Joella chimed in. "We've been in position for the past seven hours, dipshit. You're not gonna cost me this assignment." She walked down the hallway with a coffee cup in her hand.

Hector expressed his frustration. "You have one job. We went over the whole damn plan—"

Dale, who was sitting outside in the black SUV, interrupted the conversation. "What's the holdup, guys? Y'all are running out of time..."

"The baby is waking up... I think. You guys need to hurry the hell up," Stacy urged.

All the agents were waiting on Dominic, a third-floor agent, who was on the brink of promotion to the fourth floor. His apparent inability to carry out this simple task suggested otherwise.

There was a moment of silence.

"I'm going in," Dominic hissed into his watch.

He walked by the front desk in his scrubs, matching all the nurses, and opened the door to the nursery. To his surprise, all the babies were asleep in their incubators.

"You found the baby?" Stacy asked.

He walked down the row, searching for the 10-digit number he was given by one of the agents to match against the numbers on the baby's bands.

"No, I'm still looking."

"You guys need to let me know when y'all are ready to leave the nursery," Gavin gently reminded. "The low frequency receiver will create an alert if you guys go anywhere near the exit without authorization."

Dominic dismissed Gavin's caution. "Yeah, yeah... we got it."

There was dead silence for a brief moment.

Dominic's heart began to race as he moved about the nursery, trying to find the baby. The clock was ticking. Every few seconds, he would look over at the door to make sure no one was about to interrupt his assignment. Then he would focus his eyes back on the incubators, trying to find the baby Marvin needed.

"Found him," he said as he looked down at the baby boy with the matching number. He was overcome with joy. Perhaps that promotion was still within reach, after all.

He could hear the other agents let out a deep sigh of relief when the words slipped out of his mouth.

"Stacy, you ready to make the switch?"

"Been ready."

Under the fluorescent lights, Stacy walked past the waiting room where Evan and Bruce were sitting. She carried a convertible car seat nonchalantly, the baby who would soon take Bright's place strapped inside. Dressed in comfy jeans, sneakers, and a loose shirt, she walked to the elevator and waited patiently as it arrived at her floor. When the doors slid apart, she stepped in and pressed the button for the fifth floor.

She walked across the front desk, then halted before she smiled at the receptionist. "I love the way you did your hair!"

The brunette receptionist with the messy bun smiled and replied, "Aww, thank you. Do you need help with anything?"

Stacy smiled and responded, "No, thank you." Without any further exchanges, she continued to walk in the direction of the nursery.

"What are you doing?" Dominic hissed in her earpiece. "We don't have time for small talk, woman!"

As she tucked a hair strand behind her ear, with the watch close to her mouth, she replied, "How to rule yourself out as a suspect. Read the book. Maybe you'll learn a thing or two," she said, breathing heavily, the carrier becoming a little hefty for her. "Okay, I'm turning the corner. Let's make this quick."

"We've got the security cameras disabled now," Gavin alerted Stacy.

In due time, the missing footage would be replaced by an older one, deceiving security when it came down to reviewing the videotape. However, a guard with a keen eye for detail might eventually notice the duplicate, if all energy was poured into finding when and how the babies were switched without an alarm being set off.

When Stacy approached the nursery, Dominic opened the door for her. She quickly entered the room and placed the baby carrier on the floor.

"Okay, which one are we taking?"

"He's the fifth one in the second row."

Stacy moved quickly along the second row to the incubator where their target slept. She carefully lifted him up and handed the baby to Dominic. As he held the baby, Stacy crouched down, picked up the decoy child, and quickly placed him into the empty incubator.

"We've got the target," she said into the watch. "We're on our way back."

"Copy that," the agent in the sedan responded.

Dominic handed the baby back to Stacy before removing his scrubs and shoving them down the trash can. Stacy carefully placed the sleeping baby in the carrier, making sure not to wake him before lifting the carrier up off the ground.

"Y'all ready to leave?" Gavin asked.

"Yeah," Stacy replied.

"Okay. Give me one second."

Dominic looked at her with a scornful face as they waited for Gavin to give them the all-clear.

"Why are you giving me that bitchy look?"

Stacy raised an eyebrow. "I don't understand how Marvin picked *you* of all people to join the assignment. It makes no sense."

"It makes perfect sense. I have the skills."

She shot him with a look of disbelief. "Oh yeah, sure," she said sarcastically.

"Why are you such a bitch? Is it because Tyler dumped you on your birthday?"

Gavin broke their bickering by announcing he had disabled the alert for the baby. "Alright. Y'all are clear to go."

Stacy scoffed and signaled to Dominic to open the door. "You're just sensitive. You always have been."

"That's bullshit," he said as he walked out behind her. "I'm not sensitive."

"What was it that dad used to say?" she asked, contemplating for a second before continuing. "Oh, yeah— 'Stacy, make sure Dominic doesn't get picked on at school today, because his feelings *will* get hurt. You on the other hand, I don't have to worry about.' Dad knew you were sensitive."

Dominic rolled his brown eyes as he closed the door behind his sister. "Whatever. Which way did you come from?"

Stacy nodded to her right. "But we're not going that way. There's an elevator to the left around the corner."

"I know that," he hissed. "That's why I asked so I knew which way *not* to go."

"Y'all need to stop bitchin'," said the agent from the sedan. "It's gettin' annoying."

"Maybe *you* should've been out in the field," Dominic hissed at his wrist.

Joella tossed her coffee cup in the trash can as she passed by the waiting room. She saw Evan walking away, leaving Bruce by himself.

"Bruce is still here. And Evan is heading back to the room, from what it looks like."

"We're on our way out," Stacy replied as they stepped onto the elevator. "Everyone exiting the premises?"

Receiving everyone's confirmations, one by one, the agents made their way out of the hospital like regular civilians, the target in their possession, completing their assignment.

CHAPTER 9

Evan quietly entered Shadow's room. He hadn't noticed the balloons and gift baskets in the room until now. The room was adorned with flowers, some already in vases and some still wrapped in cellophane, all carefully arranged around Shadow's bedside. The moment Shadow gave birth to Bright replayed in his mind. His life already felt different, and it hadn't been twenty-four hours since Bright had come into this world. As he walked closer to Shadow, he found himself admiring her through a different lens. Not only was she his wife and best friend, but now she was the mother of his child. He was in awe of her, and believed every new father saw their partners in the same way. At least he hoped they did. As soon as the initial elation of Bright's birth began to subside, however, the fear of their lives being interrupted and turned upside down kicked in. The SEA still existed, which meant Marvin was still out there. Even though Evan wanted to believe everything was slowly becoming better, the truth was, they weren't safe.

He recalled the moment when he was in the hospital the night after Marvin had set him and the kitchen on fire. Everything had seemed a blur, and yet certain details remained crystal clear at the same time.

It was there, lying in his hospital bed, that Adrian Will had appeared to Evan for the first time. The words Adrian had spoken that night never seemed to fade away.

It's not over yet, brother.

What did that mean? He had racked his brain trying to find the meaning behind the eerie words that had come from Adrian that night.

Having barely slept since the previous morning, with only a slight nap in between, Evan was exhausted. He stepped into the bathroom, then flipped the light switch. The lights lit up the white bathroom as bright as a summer day. He analyzed himself in the mirror as if he was seeing himself for the first time. There was a single white hair in his sideburn that he hadn't seen before. Evan leaned in closer to the mirror to get a better look at the silvery strand. To his relief, he could not see any other white hairs, but as he took a step back from the mirror, he noticed dark circles around his blue eyes. It hadn't occurred to him to worry about getting older; after all, aging was inevitable. But looking at his face now, he felt as if he had aged ten years in the span of the last twenty-four hours. Life seemed to be moving rather quickly all of a sudden. He'd gotten married less than a year after meeting Shadow, and now Bright was in the picture before they had even celebrated their first anniversary. It wasn't that he didn't want any of this; he loved where he was in his life. Things were just moving faster than he had expected. A part of him didn't know if it was a good or a bad thing.

But two things he was sure about: He loved Shadow, and he was excited about fatherhood.

He turned on the faucet and let it run for a minute before the hot water came rushing through. Turning the knobs to get the perfect temperature, Evan splashed his face with the warm water and then picked up a towel the nurses had left earlier to pat his face dry. He hung it on the hook behind the door before quietly stepping back into the room.

To his surprise, Shadow was sitting upright in her bed, looking strikingly beautiful. Her hair flowed down to her shoulders, her lips were naturally rosy, and, when she broke into a smile, her cheekbones flushed a healthy pink.

"Hey," she said, her voice soft. She shifted in her bed, making herself comfortable. "Where is everyone?"

"Grandma, Willow, and Mr. Brar left. Dad's still out in the waiting room. He wanted to talk to Denise. How are you doing?"

When he got closer, he kissed Shadow and slowly backed away, admiring her.

"Everything down there hurts," she said with a giggle, "but other than that, I'm just a little exhausted but good."

"As you should be." He looked at her with a hint of

excitement and tiredness. "You gave birth… I would be surprised if you *weren't* exhausted."

Shadow chuckled. "I wanna see Bright. Can you get the nurse to bring him back from the nursery?"

"Yeah, of course. And I'll make sure they send over breakfast, too."

"Breakfast?" She shot him a confused look as she shifted from one side to the other.

Evan pulled out his phone from his pocket and then quickly shoved it back. "It's almost seven o'clock. Bright's probably hungry, too."

Shadow pulled the hair-tie off her wrist and began to put her hair together in a ponytail. "I thought it was like the afternoon or something."

Evan shook his head as he began to make his way to the door. "No, honey. It's only been a few hours."

She sat analyzing Evan with her hands folded in her lap.

"Evan?"

He turned around just as he was about to reach for the door handle. "Yeah, babe?"

"You're not telling me something…"

A nervous laugh escaped from between his lips. "What are you talking about?"

"I can see it in your eyes," she said with a sympathetic smile. "What's wrong?"

He let out a sigh under his breath and proceeded to walk towards Shadow's bedside. He did his best to hide the worry in his eyes, his facial expression, and in his voice.

She looked at him with genuine concern as he

approached.

"Everything's fine," he lied. He kissed the top of her forehead and stalled for a second longer, wishing he could tell her the truth. "Just need a little bit of sleep. That's all."

She slowly reeled back, taking a good hard look into his eyes, trying to find the truth.

"You would tell me if something was wrong, right?"

Evan managed to let out a soft chuckle. He reached out to her and cradled her face in the palms of his hands.

"Yes," he lied again. "I would tell you if something was wrong. Now, I want you to do me a favor."

"What is it?"

"I don't want you to worry about me. Your only focus should be on Bright and you. Okay?"

Again, before responding, her eyes searched his, waiting to find the hidden truth. Shadow was able to tell precisely when Evan was not being honest with her. In the past, it always had been because he didn't want to worry her. She wasn't sure if she was reading too much into Evan's behavior; her hormones, after all, were bouncing off the walls and she was exhausted, but she couldn't help but feel there was something off about her husband. When she finally nodded, Evan kissed her again.

"Is there anything else you need? Ice pack? Tampons or pads? I don't know how many you need..."

Shadow cut him off before he could continue any further. "Honey, I'm good. We've got everything we need in our overnight bag. I just wanna hold my little baby, and ever since you mentioned breakfast, my stomach started to growl."

"Alright, I'll go talk to the nurse," he responded. As he navigated to the door, he heard her soft voice break the silence just as he reached for the door handle.

"I love you," she added.

He looked over his shoulder, and his eyes lit up as he responded. "I love you, too."

When Evan closed the door behind him, guilt trickled throughout his body. He didn't enjoy lying to Shadow, but he didn't want her to feel the way he was feeling right now, either. He wanted her to enjoy these first moments with Bright like any mother did, without fear lingering in the back of her mind or worrying about the what ifs. More than anything, he was terrified of what might happen to his little family. The words Adrian hissed lingered in his mind: *"It's not over yet, brother."*

As he walked down the hallway, he spotted Denise and Ryan talking to the receptionist, Nate at their side. Evan was excited to see them and sped up. As he got closer, his footsteps made the three of them look up.

"Hey, Papa!" Denise exclaimed.

They all enveloped Evan in a hug and congratulated him.

"What's up man? You're a dad now!" Ryan eagerly declared as he reeled him in for another hug.

"I know. It still feels a little surreal," Evan said, running his fingers through his hair. He looked down at Nate and pinched his cheek. "You ready to meet your new baby cousin?"

"He's not going to throw up on me, is he?" Nate looked

distinctly skeptical.

They all exchanged uncertain looks before breaking into laughter.

"We'll make sure he doesn't, okay?" Evan replied.

To that, Nate nodded.

"I thought you guys weren't going to come until after work?"

"When we found out Bright was already here, we couldn't wait, so we decided to stop by before work to meet him and check on Shadow," Denise replied, smiling.

"I see," Evan managed to say, "Shadow's gonna be happy to see you guys. I was gonna see if they could bring down Bright and get breakfast for her. Shadow wanted to spend time with him. She slept for about two hours, but she's wide awake right now."

"Only two hours?" Ryan cocked an eyebrow.

Evan nodded and rubbed his eyes in circular motion. "Tell me about it. I'm exhausted and just wanna fall asleep anywhere at this point, and she's in there awake. I don't know how she's doing it."

Denise chuckled. "It's a mother's instinct. I was like that, too, with Nate. You don't want to be away from them. We won't be staying for too long, though. Ryan's gotta drop off Nate at school. What room are you guys in?"

"We're in five twenty-six."

"We'll see you in a bit, dude," Ryan said to Evan as the three of them headed in the opposite direction.

"Oh wait," Evan said, turning around and smacking his forehead with his palm. He met Denise's eyes. "I almost forgot. Dad's in the waiting room. He said he wanted to talk to you before he left."

"Oh."

Denise and Ryan swapped looks with one another. Without a word, Ryan and Nate proceeded to make their way down the hallway, leaving Denise behind with Evan.

Evan watched as Ryan knocked gently on the door before entering Shadow's room. His mind jumped to a few years down the line, picturing himself with Bright right alongside of him visiting Shadow to meet another new addition. It was only the first day they had Bright in their lives, and as odd as it was, Evan already wanted to have baby number two.

When he met Denise's eyes, she looked back somewhat reluctantly.

When he spoke, his voice was soft and low. "Look," he started, stepping off to the side in the hallway to let some nurses pass. He knew how much Denise was struggling with their father's reappearance. "I know you and dad aren't on the same page and... I know you have every right to be mad at him. I can't force you to forgive him or get to a place in your life where you're ready to forgive him. But... he's going on this mission. Who knows what might happen? I don't want you to regret anything now that you've got the chance to talk to him about everything that happened."

Denise let out a frustrated sigh, partially because she knew her brother was right but also because she was still uncomfortable talking to her father. Deep down, she wanted to forgive him, but a little part of her wanted Bruce to suffer for the pain he'd caused her. She wanted to punish him until she was ready to move forward, but as a mother herself, she knew she would do whatever she needed to do to protect Nate—just like Bruce had done after Denise and Evan's mother committed suicide.

There was a pause. "Which way?" she finally asked, not entirely convinced the conversation with their father needed to happen right away.

"He's down the hall," Evan said, pointing past Denise, "to your right." He ran his fingers through his hair, turning again in the direction of the nursery. "Just hear him out when he talks," he added, gently. "He does feel horrible."

Denise managed to hold her tongue, even though she wanted to argue.

"Okay. I'll go talk to him," she said softly. She tugged at her purse string nervously before turning towards the waiting room.

As Denise walked away down the hallway, Evan stared blankly into space a moment, entirely forgetting why he'd left Shadow's room in the first place. It took a few seconds before he remembered he'd left to bring Bright back from the nursery and request some breakfast for his exhausted wife. Proceeding to the front desk, he was baffled by how disconnected he felt. He'd been a parent for less than a day and already he couldn't think straight! He marveled again at Shadow's stamina. He now saw women as warriors who could fight in a battle without any armor and still come out stronger than the enemy.

CHAPTER 10

Wordlessly, Denise sat down next to Bruce in the now-empty waiting room. She fiddled with her hands in her lap, sensing Bruce's eyes on her.

Bruce tugged at the inner lining of his blazer, crossing and then re-crossing one leg over the other. He cleared his throat. Denise looked up from the floor, assuming he was going to initiate the conversation. Bruce met her eyes for a brief second before looking away. What had once been an orderly list of things he'd wanted to say was now scattered. His mind went blank. He didn't know where to begin and was absolutely sure that whatever came out of his mouth wouldn't sound right.

All he wanted was to not mess things up further with Denise. This might be the last time he saw his daughter. There was no guarantee whether he would make it out alive from the mission.

Silence swelled between them.

An older gentleman with a cane shuffled in and sat in the far-left corner of the waiting room, in Denise and Bruce's eyeline. The old man picked up the newspaper off the seat of the chair next to him and began to skim through the pages until he found a section that intrigued him.

Bruce observed the man for a moment and realized again that he didn't have much time. He wasn't going to get a chance to grow old, like that old man. Even if he came out alive after shutting down the agency, cancer would eventually take his life, and sooner rather than later.

"Denise... I will never be able to apologize enough for what I did. I know I hurt you, the both of you. I know I caused you pain for reasons that made sense at the time, at least to me. I know I don't deserve to be sitting right here next to you. But I do want you to know this: I never stopped loving you or Evan. Never. I watched you two grow up from afar, which isn't nearly the same as being there, but I never wanted to miss out on seeing you two grow up." His eyes welled up as he continued to speak, but he held himself strong. He needed to get everything he wanted to say out there in the open while he had the chance. He brushed away a tear before he continued. "At the time, when I made the decision to go, I wanted to leave everything that was associated with your mother behind... and I convinced myself you and Evan would be better off without me. I know it's the most selfish thing anyone could do when they have two other lives depending on them; all I can say is that at the time I genuinely felt I was doing the best thing for you both. I wouldn't have been the father you two needed at the time. So I left. Had I known this was going to be the outcome... being gone for twenty-seven years, being a part of the agency, all the pain that I've caused... I wouldn't have left in the first place. I really wouldn't have. All I can do is ask you to let me be a part of your life now, on your terms. That's all that I'll ever ask and even that, I know I don't deserve. But you have been the love of my life since the day you came into the world, and I would regret it for the rest of my days if I didn't ask."

The room fell silent once more, but for the sound of the slow turning of the old man's newspaper pages.

Denise let the words digest in her mind. She sat still, her lips pursed. She let out a deep breath, unaware she'd been holding it in the entire time Bruce spoke. Without looking at her father, she cleared her throat and used the arm rests on the chair for support as she rose from her chair. Crossing her arms over her chest, she walked away, leaving Bruce alone with the old man.

Bruce's eyes welled up as he watched Denise walk away without looking back. He let the tears stream down his cheeks. His heart shattered into tiny little pieces. Though he'd known there were two ways this conversation could go, some desperate sense of optimism had kept him from dwelling on the possibility that Denise might not forgive him. The feeling of utter failure and heartbreak brought him right back to the day he'd found Geneva's limp body, unconscious, in their bed. The letter she had left behind had made him want to end things as well, to punish himself. He'd known his wife had been unhappy in their marriage, which had led her back to her old, self-destructive ways, but he hadn't wanted to admit it to himself. Bruce remembered touching her lifeless face, begging for her to wake up. Had it not been for Venice's pleading and convincing that he wasn't responsible, Bruce too would have been dead.

Bruce pulled out his handkerchief from his inner pocket, unfolded it, and patted his face dry of tears. He'd known nothing was going to be the same once he came back to Lake View, but he'd hoped that the journey to rekindle his relationship with his children would be possible.

Denise walked back into the room just as Bruce was putting his handkerchief back into his pocket. Her face was flushed, her eyes brimming with tears. All the pain Denise had suppressed had come to the surface.

Bruce looked up at his daughter. He choked up at the view before him. He'd caused her this pain, and all he could do was to be there to heal what he had hurt. Was she going to give him a chance to do that?

As Bruce rose from his chair, Denise came towards him. Her heavy sobs brought back the tears in Bruce's eyes. He felt his throat constrict and his face flush with heat.

"You *left* us!" she choked, "You *never* came back! I was only five... you were supposed to be there for us! You were supposed to be my dad!"

Bruce's voice cracked as he forced himself to speak. "I know." He clenched his jaw, as his heart tore itself into shreds.

"I missed you *so* much," Denise began to sob. "And I hate you for what you did."

Bruce's eyes began to water again. "That's okay, Denise. That's okay. I understand."

Bruce opened his arms, tears flowing down his cheeks. And when Denise stepped slowly into his arms, he held her tight. "I'm so sorry," he cried. "I love you, honey, and I'm really sorry. I really am."

"I hate you so much," Denise sobbed into his shoulder. Her body shook with tears.

Bruce kissed the top of her head. "It's okay, Denise."

"No, it's not. I shouldn't feel this way. You shouldn't have left us. We meant nothing to you?"

"You guys meant the world to me, honey," he replied, struggling to get the words out. "And I didn't want to mess that up."

"No. That's not fair," she cried. "You were supposed to be there for us. You were our dad…you were supposed to stay."

Not knowing what else to say, Bruce only hugged her tighter.

CHAPTER 11

Back at the agency, the agents appointed to Marvin's assignment sat in the conference room. The carrier in which the kidnapped baby was soundly asleep was placed right in the middle of the table, like a prize. They waited for Marvin to come back with the results from the lab to confirm that this baby was, in fact, Bright Storm.

The room was filled with nervous excitement. This had been a big assignment for all the agents. A good review for an agent working under Marvin ensured a pay raise, assignments to more high-profile cases, and other benefits which were addressed in the contract they all signed beforehand, such as an all-expenses paid weeklong vacation anywhere they desired, a personal driver and private security for their homes.

A bronzed-skin agent sporting an undercut fade was the first to break the room's silence. Gavin's voice was needle sharp when he spoke. "What do y'all think he wants with the baby?" he asked, scanning the room.

Dominic, who was sitting right across from him, responded with a grin. "I heard the guy..." he leaned closer and whispered, "is a little cuckoo."

"Why do you care what he wants the baby for, Gavin?" Stacy chimed in.

"'Cause," he said, looking around the table, "aren't y'all curious about the baby? And what he wants with it? I mean, is it his? Is that why he made us kidnap the kid?"

Hector, whose hazel eyes glowed against his dark skin, joined the conversation from the end of the table. "Look man, it don't matter why," his voice was soft and raspy. "We got the job done. That's it man. No questions."

When Stacy spoke, all the agents turned their attention towards her. "Hector's right. It's not our business as agents to know the 'why' unless it's specified in the document." She paused before stating the truth none of them liked to admit. "Anyway, if we knew why we had to kidnap the baby, most of us probably wouldn't have agreed to get on board." She was under no illusion that this mission was somehow serving a greater good: she was far too cynical these days.

"You say it like you *know* it's a bad thing," Christy chimed in.

Stacy scoffed. Wasn't it abundantly clear? "It's a baby," she pointed out. "What good ever comes out from kidnapping a baby?"

"You sound rattled," her brother asserted. "You've done an assignment like this before, right? And besides, didn't you just say it isn't our business to know?"

Stacy rolled her eyes and crossed her arms in front of her chest. She looked down the table and met her brother's eyes. "I'm just saying," she retorted, "that you don't exactly need to be a rocket scientist to work out that what we were assigned to do wasn't for any good reason."

"Damn, Stace, when did you grow a conscience? You don't need to yell."

Before Stacy could reply, the door burst open. Marvin stormed in, his face twisted with fury, waving a piece of paper. Most of the agents began to shift in their seats uneasily. It was apparent nothing good was going to come out of this meeting.

"Which one of you *imbeciles* was in charge of making the switch?" he shouted.

Usually, Marvin reviewed the pre-task report of how his team was going to carry out the assignment before approving, so he was aware of each agent's responsibility throughout the entire assignment. This time, however, Marvin was so desperate to get his hands on Bright that approval of the report was not a top priority, and he'd given it only a cursory glance, preferring the mission to go ahead as quickly as possible.

"Somebody answer the damn question!"

Dominic exchanged a terrified glance with his sister.

"I was in charge of making the switch, sir," Stacy finally blurted.

Marvin's eyes followed the direction of her voice.

"*You?* You were in charge of making the switch?"

She looked at him dead in the eyes. "Yes, sir."

"That baby," he spat, pointing at the carrier sitting in the center of the conference room table, "is *not* the baby I asked for! You took the *wrong* baby!"

Stacy's eyes flicked involuntarily over to Dominic, who had told her which incubator the target baby was in. She could see the fear in his eyes and tiny beads of sweat forming right at his hairline. In that instant, she knew her brother had messed up.

"I don't see how that's possible. We were given the ten-digit identification number for the target, and that number matched the wristband on this baby."

Marvin did not react well to being challenged in front of his whole team. His face reddened and his eyes glinted maliciously. A tense silence filled the room.

He tossed the paper towards her. "The results came back from the lab, and the DNA does not match the father, nor the mother." He slammed a hand down on the table, making several of the agents jump. "You brought me the wrong fucking baby! Do you understand what you've done?! You tanked the entire goddamn assignment!"

He waited for her response, but she merely continued to review the results he'd tossed at her. Marvin stared at her accusingly, his face almost crimson with rage.

Ignoring Marvin's rage, Stacy looked up from the papers. Her tone was measured when she eventually spoke. "Then the only explanation is that—"

"Stop talking!" he bellowed, the volume of his voice startling the agents assembled around the table, though mercifully not waking the slumbering baby. "You do not get to speak!" he hissed. "Not anymore."

Stacy knew what that meant. Though none of this team had worked with Marvin before, they had all heard tales about how neurotic and unreasonable Marvin could be. Abrupt firings were not uncommon. As keeping emotions in check was one of the first things agents had to master when they were recruited to the agency, none of them had much experience dealing with a commanding agent flying off the handle like this. But given the other agents' wide eyes, Stacy didn't think any of them would be jumping to her defense any time soon.

"You have *absolutely* no idea what you've done. I want you out of my sight!" When Stacy didn't budge, Marvin roared with fury. "For fuck's sake! Get out of my room! *Get out!*"

Stacy scooted her chair back slowly and rose from the table, her heart thumping in her chest.

"The board is going to want to hear from you before they decide whether to suspend or terminate you."

This was the final straw. Stacy's eyebrows furrowed and her eyes flashed with anger. Her former cool evaporated. "Are you fuckin' serious? You're reporting me to the *board* all because of one mistake? Isn't it enough that you're firing me from this team? I worked my ass off for this assignment and I'm not getting paid for it."

Her response took him by surprise and for a moment Marvin stood in stunned silence. Then his face darkened once more, and he smirked cruelly.

"Oh, you'd better believe I'm reporting you to the

board," he said archly. "This was an *important* assignment. Clearly, you have no regrets and show no remorse for what you did. It's quite concerning that you do not take your duty here at the agency as seriously as the rest of us."

Stacy couldn't believe the bullshit this man was spouting.

"You're *dismissed*," he added, with his signature malicious smile.

Stacy took a second to look around the room and everyone in it, not knowing if this was going to be the last time she would ever sit among other agents again.

***

Later, when the other agents had been dismissed—the baby sent off with them, to foster care, presumably—he didn't really know, or care—Marvin stood alone in the conference room. He paced back and forth, his arms folded at his chest. He practiced a few calming techniques he'd learned from some therapist his parents had sent him to when he was younger and out of control. Though he hated to admit it, the therapist's strategies did help him, for the most part, from making rash decisions, if not preventing the rages. He sat down at the table, still overwhelmed by this extra load of work he was forced to deal with now thanks to the incompetence of his agents. Marvin needed to get Shadow's baby to Roy, and quickly, but it was evident that if he wanted things done right, with no more screw-ups, he would have to do it himself. To his disappointment, however, each plan he came up with involved recruiting some sort of team. It would be so much easier, he mused, if he could simply carry out all steps of the operation himself. He slammed his fist on the table, frustrated by Stacy's negligence. If it hadn't been for her, Marvin would've handed the baby to Roy by now, locking in his seat as the next head of the agency. Within the next couple of days, the baby would be at home with Shadow, and it would be that much harder to carry out the plan.

Why did nothing ever work in Marvin's favor when he needed it to?

He let out a deep sigh and got back to work.

CHAPTER 12

1934

Adrian sat quietly in the corner of the Ritz Central Oyster bar, at a table draped in a heavy black and white checkered tablecloth, shiny utensils gleaming either side of the white plate in front of him. It was late autumn in Pool View; warm enough to wear shorts or a summer dress, but with slightly harsher afternoon winds and the onset of gloomier days. As usual, Adrian dressed in black slacks and a maroon, half-sleeve button down shirt and no jacket. A battered black fedora hat hung from the back of his chair.

It was midafternoon, and the restaurant was half-full. It wouldn't be busy until after five o'clock, when a heavy rush of customers would begin to appear after work.

A waiter dressed in black slacks and a white, full-sleeved button down under a black vest, with a fancy napkin hanging off his arm, approached and gestured towards Adrian's half-finished water.

"Sir, would you like me to refill your glass, or perhaps you'd care to take a look at the wine menu as you wait?"

Adrian held his gaze for a moment as he watched the door.

"My guest just arrived, actually," he said pointing in the direction of the entrance. "We'll be ready to order in a few minutes. Thank you."

"No problem, sir." The waiter nodded and left.

Adrian was beginning to feel nervous. He'd been anxious all morning about this lunch.

"Adrian Will?" the man approaching his table asked in a gravelly voice.

Adrian rose from his chair, almost forgetting his manners, and held out his hand. "Yes, that's me," he said, shaking the gentleman's hand.

Adrian watched the man as he took his seat. He had a full head of dark brown hair and looked awfully young. Adrian concluded he couldn't have been more than twenty-five years of age. His light, deep-set blue eyes almost seemed welcoming, though his swagger as he walked through the door screamed "mobster." He had a light beard that covered his slim jaw line and accentuated his thin, pink lips.

Stephan Hex. Better known as the "Handler" amongst his family and close friends.

"Sorry I took so long. There was an unexpected issue at the office. An emergency."

For a minute, Adrian remained silent. His stomach was

in knots. He brought his hands down to his lap and began to massage the back of his right palm, as he always did whenever he was tense and nervous—a habit he'd picked up when he was a little kid.

"I see reticence in your eyes, Adrian," Stephan observed. A tiny grin danced on his lips as he reached for his water. He took a sip, his eyes fixed on Adrian's. "You're the one who called me. I'm here because of you, Adrian. Let me remind you, I do not like any folks wasting my time."

Adrian nodded. He was aware of the overdue meeting *he'd* scheduled with Stephan.

Adrian brought his hands back up to the table. He drew a long breath before he met Stephan's eyes. "I need a favor."

The sound of Adrian's words was music to Stephan's ears. Again, the tiny grin crept up, and his eyes gleamed with delight.

Before Adrian could say another word, the waiter came back and kindly asked to take their orders. Adrian chose the shrimp and Stephan opted for grilled sirloin steak with vegetables. Stephan selected a 1929 Bordeaux for the table, one of Adrian's favorites.

Once the waiter left, Stephan continued. "You need a favor from me. Did I hear that correctly?"

"Yes."

Stephan shifted in his chair, amused. "What are the chances? A Will brother needs a favor," he said almost thinking out loud to himself. "This is interesting."

Stephan was known as the go-to man if a situation

needed to be *managed*. But from what Adrian knew, he had exacting criteria very few people were able to meet. Those who did were the only ones he'd decide he could help.

"Continue," he said, now that Adrian had his attention.

"From what I've heard, you run an agency that... helps people."

"That's correct," Stephan replied, proudly adding, "The Secret Eye Agency. Or, as we like to call it, the SEA."

"Well, I need your help." Adrian paused and took a deep breath. "It's my brother. I want to have him...killed." His stomach twisted as he spoke.

Stephan shook his head, not sure he had heard correctly. "What did you say?"

Glancing around the restaurant to ensure they were not overheard, Adrian leaned forward and lowered his voice. "I want ... my brother, Derek Will, killed."

There was a moment of silence as the two men stared at each other.

Finally, Stephan spoke. "Derek Will. You want *Derek Will* dead? The most powerful man in town? Besides my agents of course..."

Adrian nodded.

Stephan leaned back in his chair and scrutinized the man in front of him.

He shook his head. "You don't want your brother dead."

"Yes, I do."

"No, I don't believe you do." The words hung in the air. They were almost enough for Adrian to start doubting himself. But he *did* want his brother dead.

Vivid images came rushing back of the day when Samantha told him Derek had given their baby away. Derek had given *his* baby away. It had been a year now, and not a day went by in which Adrian didn't think about how he was going to make Derek suffer for the pain he had caused.

Torture. Then kill. That was Adrian's plan.

"I'm more than sure of what I want."

Stephan mulled the idea over in his mind as he looked out the window. Despite the emptiness inside the restaurant, the streets were occupied with shoppers and whooping gaggles of kids making their way to the ice cream parlor on the corner. One tiny girl, her face flushed with excitement as she raced past the window, brought Stephan's son Ben to mind. The thought of his bright smile filled Stephan's heart with joy and pride.

Stephan calmly turned his attention back to Adrian. "What did he do?"

Adrian pursed his lips. "It's something I'd rather not discuss."

"Your brother really did a number on you, it seems."

Adrian nodded. His mind jumped back to his son, who he'd never get to see.

"Killing is a last resort in our line of business. We like to settle our feuds in a… more *civilized* manner."

"Unfortunately, this is the only option left."

Before either one of them could continue, they were interrupted by the waiter with their food.

Once the waiter was safely out of earshot, Adrian spoke.

"Is this a service your agency offers?"

Stephan seemed in no rush to answer. He carefully cut a piece of his steak. Spearing it with his fork, he held it up to get a better view of the meat, then devoured it. He chewed thoughtfully, indicating with a dismissive wave of his fingers that he'd heard Adrian and would respond after he washed down his first bite with a swig of wine.

"It didn't used to, back when my father ran the agency, but now we've expanded our operation and are slowly building on that. However, we don't offer that particular service to just anyone. It's also quite costly. As I said before, we generally like to settle feuds without having to resort to any such— *irreversible* options."

Ignoring this, Adrian pressed, "What would the rate be for a job like this?"

As Stephan ran the numbers in his mind, Adrian chomped on his shrimp nervously.

"To kill? Seventy grand."

Stunned, Adrian almost choked on the piece of shrimp he was about to swallow.

"Seventy grand? I don't have that kind of money laying around."

Stephan cut off another juicy chunk of meat and stabbed it with his fork. "Another reason we'd suggest settling the feud in a civilized manner. If you are certain there is no other alternative, then that's what your favor is going to cost," he said, popping the steak into his mouth. He chewed and analyzed Adrian, who looked crestfallen as he stared at his almost untouched plate. "I might have a proposition for you, though, if you're interested."

Intrigued, Adrian asked, "What is it?"

"As I said earlier, we're expanding the agency. We're looking for more agents in the People's Department as I focus on the project my father left for me. You would work as a field agent first and then gradually move up the ladder to take on assignments from clients. You would run your own department and team at some point, if you were to be successful. Fifth-floor agents, as we call them, have that luxury. You would be required to take courses to learn about the human mind, the brain, trauma, and psychology, which we'll provide. You'll also need physical training, a lot of it, to become an authorized agent."

Adrian was confused. "So— you're offering me a job? How does that help me with the problem that I came to you with?"

A faint smirk danced on Stephan's lips. "If you become an agent, you can kill him yourself," he said, pausing to let the words hang briefly in the air. "As I see it, if you really wanted to kill your brother, you would have done it by now. Something's stopping you from pulling the trigger. That's why you came to me, Adrian. They don't call me the handler for no reason." He picked up his wine glass and took a sip. "If you join the agency, you'll have time to think about whether or not you really want blood on your hands. If you ultimately decide that you want your brother dead— big man about town that he is, even— well, then it won't cost you a penny. Of course, there is a process before you can execute a mission, but that's a conversation for another time. And if you decide to let him live, you'll have a wonderful career." Stephan looked at Adrian. "I have two sons myself. I would hate to know that one of them wanted the other dead. You might come to change your mind."

Adrian was left to make a decision. "What's in it for you, exactly?" he asked.

Stephan smiled a wolfish grin.

"Why, I get an agent, either way," he said. "Once you sign with us— well, let's say we take that commitment very seriously."

As Stephan explained further in detail about what exactly the agency did, Adrian wrestled with the decision before him. Joining this agency would certainly benefit him in one way, and that was in getting rid of his brother. That said, Adrian knew that realistically, it would take weeks before he would be able to take Derek out of the picture if he became an agent. And there was something in Stephan's grin that made Adrian uneasy.

What Stephan didn't mention was that if Adrian decided to join the SEA, he would no longer be afforded the rights of a private citizen. If Adrian had a sudden change of heart and decided he wanted to leave the agency before his contract came to an end, it would result in having a target on his back until his last breath. Ultimately, his life would no longer be his own, and attempting to rebel would incur the heaviest of penalties.

***

After lunch, Adrian met with Samantha at Shallow's Lake, a secluded area where they met each other at three o'clock on Mondays, Wednesdays and Fridays, their visits planned around Derek's schedule. Even though their secret was no longer so secret, for the sake of peace—whatever little they had left—they continued to meet.

They sat next to each other on the bench facing the lake. The sun danced on the ripples of the water and birds chirped in the trees, each trilling their own unique melody. Samantha appeared thinner since the last time Adrian had seen her. He peered over at her as she continued to stare out vacantly at the lake. She had barely greeted him when he arrived. Every time he looked at her face, his throat tightened, and tears sprang to his eyes. He'd let down the love of his life. He'd failed in protecting her and their baby. Adrian could no longer sit back and do nothing.

"I met with someone today," he blurted.

The urgency in his voice made Samantha's stomach somersault. "Who was it?"

"A man."

"That's very descriptive."

"A man who is going to help me... to help *us*."

"How?"

"He runs an undercover agency, and once I train and learn everything I need to know to become an agent, I'm going to have Derek killed. He'll never be able to hurt you again."

He let the words hang in the air.

The leaves rustled in a sudden breeze. The swells in the lake glistened under the pale sun. Two birds flew overhead, dancing and chasing each other through the air above the water.

When Samantha didn't respond, he reached for her hand and intertwined his fingers with hers.

"What are you thinking about, Sam?"

She gripped his hand a little tighter. "How did I end up here?"

"What do you mean?"

"I don't understand. Who did I hurt? I was taught to treat everyone with kindness, and this is the result?" She finally looked over at Adrian. She could see the pain in his eyes. "What did I do to deserve this, Adrian? What on Earth could I have done to live this miserable life? It's not the life I had imagined for myself." She turned her attention back to the lake once again.

After a moment, she asked, "I'm going to lose you, too, aren't I?"

"You're not going to lose me," he reassured. She felt his gaze fixed on her as she looked out across the lake.

Her head swiveled back towards him. "I don't want you to join the agency."

"Why not? Derek will be out of our lives—"

"Darling," she said, suddenly feeling her throat constrict. Her eyes welled up and she felt the pit in her stomach grow deeper. "You can kill him for revenge, but it's not going to undo what he has already done."

He glanced at her, surprised and taken aback by her

response. He knew she was right, but still, he wanted to live his life with her, and grieve the loss of their child together without having to schedule a time or be afraid that they would get caught. Moreover, he wanted justice. He wanted Derek to suffer as they had suffered.

"Sam," he said with a hint of frustration in his voice, "Derek out of the picture will do exactly that— at least, when it comes to us, to us being together. Right now, he *is* the problem, and this is the *only* way to resolve it."

Samantha gripped his hand even more tightly. A tear fell down her ashen cheek. "Adrian, do you know how much I love you?"

He gave her a blank stare. The sunlight highlighted the white strands that had begun to appear in his sideburns.

When he didn't answer, she pressed again. "Do you understand why I didn't pull the trigger that day?"

He took a sharp intake of breath at her words. His eyes brimmed with tears, recalling the day Samantha had confessed she'd considered taking her own life shortly after their baby had been taken away. He couldn't begin to imagine what the world would be like if she'd gone through with it. The thought alone made him nauseated.

"I thought of you," she said softly. "You know I couldn't bear to be without you, don't you?"

He responded quietly. "Yes."

"If you join this agency, then I'm going to lose you."

Adrian shook his head violently in disagreement. "That's not true."

Before he could argue, Samantha cut him off. "It sounds

as if you're going to war… becoming an agent. How many loved ones are lost in war? I will lose you, Adrian, if you join this agency. It's too dangerous."

"You don't know any of that for sure."

"I'm not willing to take that risk."

"I'm not willing to risk the love of my life, either. And Derek—he's killing you. He's killing *us*. I'm going to take this opportunity, Samantha."

Samantha's eyebrows furrowed and her eyes narrowed. Her voice shook as she spoke. "I've already lost a son. I'm not losing you, too. If you join… there's no more us. Do you understand?"

It was almost as if the words didn't register in his mind. Her ultimatum didn't scare him. Adrian loved Samantha deeply and believed that while she was opposed to his plan, there were certain things he knew Samantha wasn't capable of doing. He couldn't see her carrying out this threat. He'd made his decision; it was for her good, for *their* good. He hoped she would come around eventually. Given time.

As if she knew what he was thinking, Samantha spoke again.

"I am not bluffing, Adrian."

CHAPTER 13

Evan's eyes flickered open. His shirt was damp with sweat. Another memory. He lay there, trying to make sense out of what had come to him in his dreams.

This recollection seemed to have some correlation with the present time; Marvin, after all, was an agent for the SEA, and through his dreams Evan now knew Adrian, too, had made up his mind he was going to join the agency, all those years ago. It was intriguing, but like the other memories that came to him in the night, it was cut short. It left him with unanswered questions.

Evan propped himself up in bed. Sweat seeped through the fabric of his white t-shirt. He looked over to find Shadow sleeping peacefully. He smiled.

Evan staggered across the room and pulled out a fresh new shirt. He took off the old one and threw it in the hamper. After he visited the bathroom, he climbed down the stairs as quietly as possible. He passed by the living room, scanning his eyes around the dark room. It was something that Evan had never done until Marvin had tried to kill him. There was always a little part of Evan that feared seeing Marvin again. Evan liked to think he wasn't afraid of him, but the thought of Marvin standing in a dark corner in his home, waiting for the right moment to attack, sent shivers up his spine.

Once he flicked the switch in the kitchen, the room slowly came alive. His eyes slowly adjusted once he opened the refrigerator to search the shelves for something to nibble on. Nothing. Evan was still trying to get used to the new healthy lifestyle Shadow had implemented during her pregnancy—for the both of them. Even though he knew exactly where she kept some junk food stashed away, he knew Shadow kept a close eye on her treats to keep them out of his clutches.

He closed the fridge with a sigh. He debated risking the lecture he would undoubtedly get once Shadow realized he'd helped himself to some of her M&Ms and chocolate chip cookies. Then he looked down at his stomach. Where once was a deeply carved six-pack, now only a light outline of muscle definition remained—a physical reminder that if he snacked tonight, he was only adding to the decline of his once-athletic physique.

After some reluctant deliberation between his mind and stomach, he turned and poured himself a glass of water. In a few hours, he would have breakfast, anyway. To treat himself for not giving in to his urge, he would make one of his favorite breakfasts: chocolate chip pancakes, glazed with Nutella.

Evan stared out into the dark from the window and appreciated the backyard. Excitement rose as he imagined playing with Bright once he was old enough to walk. He planned on playing soccer, catch, tag and all sorts of other activities that would build a strong bond between the two of them. He wanted Bright to have the childhood that he wished he'd had, and he wanted a lot of pictures of their memories, too. Evan and Shadow were adamant about making sure there were stacks and stacks of photo albums for their children to look back to one day when they were older. Evan knew his children wouldn't appreciate all the photoshoots they would be expected to be a part of, but as someone with few images of his younger self with either of his parents, he knew that in due time, their children would come to see that their parents' annoying habit was a gift in disguise.

Evan gulped down the last sip of his water and placed the cup in the sink. His thoughts drifted away as he felt an odd presence take over the room. The hair on the back of his neck prickled. He slowly turned his body around to see a figure standing in the shadows between the dark hallway and the illuminated kitchen. Fear reeled through Evan. He pressed his body against the sink with both of his hands, trying to contain the emotions that were running through his mind. Was it Marvin, come to finish the job? The figure moved forwards into the light. Evan couldn't believe what he was seeing. Derek.

In his arms, Derek held Bright.

Evan felt paralyzed with fear. His mind darted from one thought to the next. Evan heard the sound of his heart pumping fast in his ears. Sweat trickled from his hairline down his forehead faster than he could blink. He scrunched his eyes closed, as if in doing so he could banish the scene before him.

He's not real. He repeated the line to himself over ten times.

Afraid to open his eyes, he walked himself through breathing exercises. *Breathe in. Breathe out. Breathe in. Breathe out.* He needed to get his mind back in the driver's seat and kick the fear out in order to take control of this panic attack he was having.

"This isn't real," he repeated, slowly, out loud. He opened his eyes, only to see everything in the room shift and distort, as if he were looking in a funhouse mirror.

"He's not real," he repeated. His heartbeat drummed in his ears. Derek still stood before him. Breathing rapidly, Evan squeezed his eyes closed once more, his legs trembling underneath him. It didn't work. When Evan's eyes flickered open again, Derek was even closer.

His voice, almost sounding soothing, settled in Evan's ears. "He'll be safer with me."

The words made Evan's heart drop down to the deep pit in his stomach. *No.*

"He needs to be with me. It's for a greater cause. One day you will understand."

No, no, no! Derek couldn't take Bright away from him. Evan pressed his palms against his face as hard as he could, willing the hallucination away. The harder he pressed, the more it felt as if his hands were slowly melting into his cheeks. He tried to slow his breathing, but it was no use.

Derek spoke again.

"Don't come looking for Bright. He will be in safe hands."

And just like that, Derek was gone.

As Evan's breaths began to slow down, his vision was slowly becoming clearer. Suddenly, his body dropped to the floor, and his cheek pressed against the cold hardwood floor. He let out sighs of relief and closed his eyes. It had all been in his mind. There was no Derek in his kitchen. Bright and Shadow were sleeping peacefully upstairs.

Bright was safe.

***

Later that morning, Evan woke up with a headache reminiscent of his college days after a night of binge drinking. The encounter with Derek earlier replayed in his mind as he lay there, not wanting to get up from bed. He forced himself to shift his gaze from the ceiling to his side but found only the imprint of Shadow's head on her vacant pillow and the sheets ruffled.

As Evan mustered the will to get out of bed, he couldn't stop thinking about his earlier encounter. Was there something he needed to worry about? After all, it was a delusion—wasn't it? He shouldn't worry about a man who didn't exist, but when Bright was brought into the equation it was less easy to dismiss. He was left uneasy and terrified, which he knew he'd have to mask in front of Shadow. He didn't want her to worry about anything other than spending quality time with Bright. Everyone always said how kids 'grow up so fast' and 'to enjoy every single moment' you were given with them.

Counting to three in his mind, Evan sat up straight and swung his legs out from underneath the sheets. The thought of having chocolate chip pancakes he'd fantasized about only hours before now made him want to puke.

What he needed right now was a run to clear his mind. At times, Evan drove himself crazy when he couldn't figure out the meaning behind a dream or hallucination. It was frustrating, to say the very least. If he knew anything, it was that these hallucinations and dreams had some connection to his present life, but he couldn't figure it out.

If life were simple, he would have all the answers in his hands by now. But life didn't work like that.

Evan rose from the bed, stretching to relieve the tension in his back. He walked to the window and turned the shades, squinting as the beaming sun flooded into the room.

"Hey, honey."

Shadow's voice made Evan jump.

"You're finally up," she said, softly patting Bright's tiny tush.

When he turned around, Shadow was standing in the doorway carrying Bright. She softly cradled his precious little body, rocking him back and forth, her eyes on Evan.

"You didn't get good sleep last night, huh? You kept tossing and turning when I woke up to feed Bright."

He rubbed his eyes before leaning in for a kiss. "Really?

I feel fine. I was gonna go for a run."

Shadow carefully handed Bright to Evan.

Evan was in awe when he laid his eyes on his son, almost as if he was seeing him for the first time. He marveled at the innocence of his child, and at the same time, feared for the impact the world would have on him.

Bright's big blue eyes gazed steadily up at him.

Evan kissed his forehead, feeling like the luckiest man alive. His eyes traveled back to Shadow, who couldn't help but smile at the view in front of her.

"I just can't get enough of him!" she squealed.

"Tell me about it… Aren't you a cute little boy? Yes, you are! You take after your momma, of course." With a smile, he looked at Shadow.

She leaned in and kissed Evan on the cheek, and then kissed Bright.

"What time did you feed him this morning?" he asked.

"I woke up at six on the dot to check on him and he was just wide awake, staring up at the ceiling."

"He didn't cry?"

Shadow shook her head. "He's not giving mommy a hard time. Isn't that right, baby?" She traced Bright's nose with the tip of her index finger.

They stood together, marveling over their little baby boy, taken aback by how in love they both were with their newborn.

Suddenly, Evan didn't feel the need for a run anymore.

***

That afternoon, Evan and Shadow took Bright out for a walk in the stroller to Cherry Park. After reading almost all the parenting books they could get their hands on, they took what they learned and applied it. They exposed Bright to the real world and to fresh air. Spending time outside, exploring different colors, shapes and noises, was okay as long as they made sure they didn't take him to a crowded area, keeping in mind that Bright's immune system wasn't as strong as it would be when he hit the two-month mark.

The sky was mostly clear, with only a few wispy clouds. The trees blazed orange and bronze, and the ground underfoot was littered with leaves. The park was relatively quiet; everyone was either at work or school, and they'd have the place to themselves until later in the evening.

Evan imagined bringing an older Bright to this park for soccer or basketball practice and then out for ice cream afterwards. He imagined all the things they would do together as father and son, the special bond they would share. It was something he deeply wanted, since he never had the chance to have that kind of bond with his own father.

He looked over at Shadow, who was staring intently into the distance. He craned his head to see what she was looking at but saw nothing in sight.

"Hey," he said, halting the stroller. "You okay?"

When she turned to meet his eyes, he saw that they were filled with fear. Despite his attempts to preserve a blissful baby bubble for Shadow, it was clear the reality of their situation was bothering her, too. After all, this was just the beginning of the storm they were about to endure.

Shadow pressed a palm against her forehead and took a deep shuddering breath. Her lips quivered as she spoke.

"I don't feel safe out here," she said. "I don't think I can do this. I thought I could, but I can't."

With one hand on the handle of the stroller, Evan reached over with his other hand towards his wife, inviting her closer.

Shadow ignored his outstretched hand. Her breathing remained ragged.

Evan felt his grip on the stroller handle tighten as he remembered Derek's promise to take Bright away.

Evan heard the fear in his voice as he spoke. "Babe, come here to me," he pleaded. He could practically see the wheels turning in her mind.

Shadow exhaled long breaths to keep from losing control. Her eyes darted around her, scanning the park for lurking figures. Evan's voice began to drown out under a rushing noise in her ears, but she could see his lips moving. She let her bun loose, her hair dropping down past her shoulders. It decreased some of the pressure about her temples slightly, but in the bigger picture, it made little difference to her mounting panic.

"Shadow," Evan repeated, trying to keep calm, "everything's going to be okay."

She shook her head. "I can't do this..."

"Yes, you can. Just come here. Hold my hand."

"I just want to run, Evan."

"To…?"

"Just away from here. Far, far away."

Shadow knew the truth no matter what Evan or anyone else said. Everything wasn't going to be fine. She'd been fooling herself throughout the pregnancy, refusing to acknowledge the danger. Now that Bright was here, she couldn't ignore it any longer. She shook her head in despair as she looked first at Evan and then into the stroller at their innocent son.

Bright lay in his stroller, wide-eyed, looking up at the sky.

Shadow rubbed her chest. She felt as if she were suffocating. Nothing was fine.

***

An hour later, having been coaxed back into the car and home by a worried Evan, Shadow sat shakily on the sofa with a glass of water. Evan walked in, holding a cold beer in one hand and the baby monitor in the other. Bright had fallen asleep as soon as they walked through the doors and now slept peacefully in his crib. Placing the monitor on the table, Evan sat next to Shadow.

"What are you thinking about?" For a moment, there was silence. When she jerked her head towards him, Evan knew what was about to come next wasn't going to be pretty.

"What do you think?" she snapped, her voice low, keeping in mind that Bright was a light sleeper.

Evan regarded her for a moment. He ran a hand through his hair, trying to keep himself calm.

"We're not safe here," Shadow continued. "I'm scared, Evan, and I don't think—"

"Look. I'm scared, too," he said, cutting her off.

Shadow opened her mouth to say something but then closed it. Evan could see the change in her demeanor. She looked almost defeated.

"You think I don't worry about us? About Bright? About our reality? I don't know what to do. I want to live a normal life, with no fear, not having to worry about Marvin or the stupid agency," he said. "It's all I do. I really didn't want you to worry about any of this."

"It all just came rushing in," she began. "It was like an alarm went off, reminding me that we're not okay. Anywhere we go, we're not safe…" Her eyes brimmed with tears.

Evan leaned in and wrapped his arm around her.

"As long as he's still out there, we're not safe, Evan. We will never be. Now that Bright's here, it just seems..."

Evan rubbed her shoulder softly, resting his chin on top of her head. "I know," he whispered.

In the quiet, both of them thought of alternative options that would allow them to live a life where they wouldn't have to look over their shoulder; a life where they could raise their children in peace. Evan's mind jumped to the encounter with Derek he'd had earlier this morning. He still hadn't told Shadow about it and felt it was unnecessary information to burden her with. Unexpectedly, the sound of the doorbell startled them both.

Evan and Shadow parted, exchanging a confused look.

They weren't expecting anyone, especially during the middle of day. Evan jumped from the couch, locked eyes with Shadow, and held his finger up to his lips. He walked slowly and quietly towards the door, making sure not to make a sound. For all he knew, Marvin could be standing on the other side.

Shadow watched carefully as Evan made his way to the front door.

When Evan managed to peek through the peephole, he let out a deep sigh.

He opened the door to Venice.

"Hey Grandma," he said, hearing the relief in his own voice.

"Hi, darlin'," she said quietly. Something in the look she gave him before she walked into the house left Evan with the feeling that something wasn't right.

Her eyes found Shadow, who was just getting up from the couch.

"Hi, sweetie," Venice said, opening her arms for a hug. "How are you doing?"

Evan closed the front door and joined them in the living room.

"I'm doing okay," Shadow replied. "Bright's upstairs sleeping. How are you?"

"Sleep, poop, and eat. That's what they do," she chuckled.

Venice hesitated for a moment, feeling the uneasiness settle in her chest.

She looked at Shadow and then Evan before proceeding. "There's something I need to talk to you guys about."

Evan and Shadow exchanged concerned looks.

"What is it, Grandma?"

Venice sighed as her eyes flicked over to Shadow.

Evan felt a knot forming in his throat. His cheeks flushed with anger. He sensed whatever Venice came to tell them had Marvin written all over it.

"I'm just waiting—"

She was interrupted by the doorbell. Both Evan and Shadow felt their panic increase.

"I'll get that," Venice ventured.

When Venice came back to the living room, she was accompanied by Bruce, dressed in dark jeans and a black, short-sleeved shirt.

Evan's eyebrows furrowed at the sight of his father. He wasn't supposed to be here. "Dad, what are you doing here? I thought—"

Venice spoke quietly. "I think you should tell them," she said to Bruce.

Bruce nodded.

"You guys," Evan began, feeling the panic in his own voice, "what's going on?"

Shadow slowly sat down on the couch, rubbing her knees in circular motion. The tension in her shoulders had come again, and she felt as if invisible hands were grasping her around the throat. She looked up at the three of them, feeling nothing but fear overtake her mind. Everything *wasn't* okay.

Bruce scratched the back of his head. He never had the right words when it came to delivering bad news.

"Umm..." he started. His eyes naturally flicked in Shadow's direction.

He wondered how long she had lived in fear. He knew very little about her, from the few conversations they'd had with one another. From what he could gather about Shadow, he had concluded she was one of the sweetest human beings he'd met. She reminded him of Geneva in a way. She had a pure heart and was full of life, but there was a darkness cast over Shadow, which was dimming that part of her. Since Bruce couldn't save Geneva from her own battles, he was determined to help Shadow where he'd been unable to help his wife.

"The plan is still in motion. That's not why we're here though."

Bruce and Venice exchanged long glances.

"Dad!" Evan cut in, feeling his anxiety rise to a tipping point. "What's going on?"

Venice spoke up quickly. "I had a disturbing vision before Bright was born," she said. "I didn't tell you because I didn't want to upset you, and, when Bright arrived healthy and safe, I thought I'd got it wrong. But I think— I think it was a *warning*."

Evan was frustrated. "A warning for what?"

Bruce sighed. "Your Grandma had another vision. One of Bright being taken from here. Now, I know not all of her visions come true. But with everything that's going on, I think it's best that you guys hide out until we're done with what we need to do. Just as a precaution."

Shadow's eyes brimmed with tears, her worst fears

seemingly confirmed. She picked up the baby monitor from the coffee table and carefully looked at the screen, which showed Bright calmly sleeping in his crib.

She held the monitor close to her chest. Her eyes darted from Evan to Venice. Her lips quivered as her mouth parted. "I'm *so* tired of living this way!" she wailed.

Without any hesitation, Bruce pushed forward and sat down beside Shadow. He put his arm around her, his chest heavy with sadness. "I know," he whispered. "We're going to end this. No one will ever bother you again, you hear?"

Shadow nodded as she sobbed.

Evan clasped his hands behind his head. His eyes welled up, feeling helpless.

If only this was a nightmare I could just wake up from, he thought.

Venice spoke, her voice unsteady. "I know my visions haven't been accurate these days, but with two so close together—"

"It's the safest thing to do," Evan responded softly. "I get it."

Pushing aside his fear, Evan slowly lowered himself down and sat on the edge of the coffee table. He looked over at Bruce, whose arm remained wrapped around Shadow.

When Shadow met Evan's gaze, she managed to crack a watery smile.

"You kids need to pack a suitcase and leave tonight," Bruce said. He rose from the couch. "We don't have a lot of time."

"How's this gonna work?" Evan asked his dad. "Should we book a hotel in a different city, or—"

"I've got everything taken care of."

Bruce had made sure he had a game plan in place if he needed Evan and Shadow to move into a safehouse. Bruce had driven a rental car to Evan's house, so Evan and Shadow could then drive the car to a house Bruce owned in Brickwood. No one would look for them there; Bruce's name wasn't on the deeds of the property. Everything remained in the name of the previous owner, thanks to a favor he owed Bruce. The address wouldn't show up on anyone's radar.

It didn't take long for Evan and Shadow to pack for a week-long stay. However, packing for Bright was anything but a walk in the park. Shadow made a list of everything they would need for their stay and checked off each item as they both scattered to gather everything.

After three hours of packing, checking, and rechecking their lists, they were ready to leave. Evan and Bruce drove the rental car with Bright buckled securely in his car seat in the back, while Shadow drove her car with Mr. Jingles in his cat carrier and Venice as her passenger. Taking extra caution, Bruce had instructed Shadow to take route one, which consisted of back roads leading straight to the downtown area. Meanwhile, Bruce took the highway, frequently checking his rear-view mirror to make sure they weren't being followed.

When they arrived at the West Villa Mall, Bruce drove through the parking lot, taking odd turns every chance he could get, finally pulling into a parking garage. Right on time, Shadow drove in from the opposite direction. They had only a few minutes to make the switch.

When they were ready to depart, all that was left was to say their goodbyes.

Evan faced his father and looked at him briefly before his eyes welled up. "Thanks, dad," he said, wrapping his arms around Bruce's neck.

Bruce hugged him back, not wanting to let go. He shut his eyes, doing his best to stay strong. There was no guarantee whether they would see each other again. When they parted, Bruce held Evan's face in the palm of his hands, remembering the face of the little boy Evan once was. Memories of Evan as a child charged through his mind. He would run to the front door as soon as he heard Bruce come home from work. He would insist on playing "ride the horsy" on Bruce's back and before bedtime, Evan would refuse to go to sleep unless Bruce read him his favorite book, *Franklin Goes to School.*

"There are two burner phones at the house," Bruce said, his voice low, "so if you need to get in touch with any one of us, you'll be able to, without having to worry about being traced."

Evan nodded.

"And… there's something you need to tell her."

Evan looked confused. "Tell her what?"

After Bruce mustered up the courage, he responded, "That her father runs the operation." Bruce looked deep into his son's eyes, knowing the questions and anger that would soon follow. "He might be one of our casualties. There's no guarantee."

Evan's eyes grew wide. "You said you were gonna tell her! Why do I have to tell her?"

Evan turned back and glanced at Shadow, who was in the middle of a conversation with Venice. He turned his attention back to his father, with fury in his eyes.

"*You* said you were gonna tell her. What changed?"

"Look, we can go back and forth but—"

"Tell me how is this fair, dad?" Evan was frustrated. "Why do I have to break her heart?"

Bruce placed his hands on his hips. "She loves you, that's why. It'll be a little easier for her to hear the news come from you."

Evan furrowed his eyebrows. "I'm pissed at you."

"That's fair. I know I should have told her, like I said I was going to. I'm sorry."

"So, to be clear, you're telling me that on top of everything else that's going on, I'm gonna to have to tell my wife her father is the one who runs the fuckin' organization? And she may not have a father after this is all done with? I'm guessing I'm gonna have to tell her about Marvin working with her dad too."

Without hesitation he responded, "Yeah. That's exactly it. Now, as much as I'd love to be with you guys, you *have* to go." He wrapped his arms around Evan one more time. "I love you, Evan."

After Evan let what Bruce had said register, he responded. "I love you too, dad."

Once Bruce peeled away from a seemingly upset Evan, he nodded at Venice, signaling it was time to go.

Venice and Shadow hugged. "Be safe, okay? I love you, sweetie."

Shadow nodded. "I love you, too, Venice."

"Evan?" Venice said as she slowly unwrapped herself from Shadow.

"Yeah?"

She walked over, fear dancing in her eyes. "I love you, darlin'."

"I love you, too, Grandma. I'll see you soon."

"Yes. We will see each other soon," she said adamantly. "And we'll throw a party to celebrate all the good in our lives."

A corner of his mouth lifted. "Sounds like a good idea."

Bruce and Venice watched as Evan peeled out of the garage.

"I'm tired of lying to them," Venice admitted.

Bruce let out a deep breath. "It's not necessarily lying."

"You and I both know I didn't have that second vision."

Bruce peered into her exhausted eyes and replied, "I know, but it's for their own good. They wouldn't have gone to the safe house otherwise."

***

The two-hour drive to Brickwood was quiet and boring; there wasn't much to look at on the way. Evan glanced over at Shadow a few times and could see how tense her face looked. Not saying anything and leaving her alone with her thoughts was a smart idea for now. Although, then again, leaving Shadow with her thoughts for too long wasn't a good idea either.

Bright had been asleep, and Mr. Jingles sat next to Bright's car seat, curious where the road trip was going to take him. Shadow would crane her neck every once in a while to check on them. And every so often, Evan would check his rear-view mirror to make sure they weren't being followed.

"The GPS says we're only two minutes away," Evan said. He'd been careful to turn off his phone so they couldn't be tracked.

Shadow remained quiet.

Evan pulled in front of a two-story house on a suburban street. It was a large neighborhood. Evan suddenly felt nervous. What if they weren't safe here, either? What if they were in fact followed, even after taking the necessary safety measures? What if Marvin was waiting for them inside? He gripped the steering wheel a little tighter and exhaled a sharp breath.

"You have the keys?" he asked Shadow.

"Yeah."

He took note of her weary response.

"I'll take the suitcases and Mr. Jingles, if you can get Bright inside."

Without acknowledging what he'd said, Shadow opened the car door and went back to unbuckle Bright's car seat. Mr. Jingles watched her through the netting of his carrier as she proceeded to lift the seat out of the car, closing the door behind her. Evan took their suitcases, the carrier and headed inside.

The house inside had clearly been recently refurbished. The floors were polished. The décor on the walls, the area rugs, and the sofas all appeared new. When he walked into the kitchen, that, too, was brand new. The tiles and marble countertop were a sparkling white to match the white cabinets. The appliances were all chrome and gave the impression they hadn't been used. It looked like a show home.

Evan set down their suitcases and let Mr. Jingles roam around their temporary home. He placed his hands on his hips, taking in everything around him. He had so many questions about this place and the many mysteries of his father's life.

Upstairs, Shadow quietly stepped out of one of the bedrooms, closing the door softly behind her. In her hand, she carried the baby monitor.

Evan peered over at his wife as she came down the stairs and towards him. He bit his lower lip, turning his body towards her. "Just say it..."

She looked up at him, her mouth agape. For a moment, she stared at Evan as her thoughts spun out of control in her mind. She spoke, breaking eye contact. "This was never a good idea. You know it too."

"What? Coming here to Brickwood?"

"No," she exclaimed. "*Us*!"

"Shadow—"

"Look at us, Evan," she began, her voice shaking. "Because of us, everyone is in danger. *Everyone*."

"Everything's going to be alright," he responded,

trying to sound as confident as he possibly could. "We're safe here. By the end of the week, our lives will be back to normal."

"Do you seriously believe that, Evan?" she snapped. "Huh? Do you really think we'll ever live normal lives?"

"After they shut down the agency, I believe so."

"What if their mission fails? Then what? What's our life going to look like?"

He looked at her with a blank stare. He didn't know what to think. More importantly, Shadow was bringing his own fears back to life. He didn't want to believe anything she was saying.

"You can't put that kind of energy out into the universe and expect a different result. You can't be negative and focus on everything that could go wrong."

She scoffed and pulled at the roots of her hair. "I'm not being negative. I'm being realistic. I believed we would live a normal life yesterday and we wouldn't have to worry about Marvin or anyone else but look where we are. We're in a safe house, Evan. We have no protection—"

He gradually moved towards Shadow. "This *is* our protection, Shadow. No one knows we're here."

"Evan… as long as we're together, everyone's in danger." Her eyes filled with tears. "He wants me, and since he couldn't have *me*, they're coming for our baby." She drew a long breath before continuing. "If we hadn't met, none of this would have happened. Do you ever think about that? All of this is happening because we chose to be together."

He stood before and watched as her tears streamed down her cheeks. "I think about a lot of things." He grazed her cheek with the back of his hand. "I think about the day Marvin set the kitchen on fire to kill me, and how my dad was by my bedside when I woke up. I hadn't seen him in twenty-seven years. That day brought my dad back into my life. I think about us. I fell in love with one of the sweetest souls I've ever known— a sweet soul with a sarcastic edge." He smiled. "If it wasn't for us, Bright wouldn't be here. I believe everything happens for a reason. I know we're not in the best situation. But I'm not going to let people control how I live or who I spend my life with. We fell in love. How was that in our control? I'm happy with you by my side. Despite how our life looks right now, I'm still happy about the decisions I made. I'm not living in la-la land, Shadow. I see what's happening and it hurts me too but… I'm happy."

"The bad outweighs the good here, though."

"I know," he replied, wrapping his arms around her waist. He pulled her in closer. "Even so, I'm still happy and I wouldn't change any of it. We're going to get through this, no matter how crazy it gets. That's what partners do."

She rested her head against his chest. "You sound so sure," she whispered.

"Like they say, everything's going to be okay in the end. If it's not okay, it's not the end." He kissed the top of her head. "Let's get some rest. I was thinking we should finally check out Zack's Ice Cream parlor. We can go tomorrow.

Remember when we were supposed to go last year?"

"Yeah," she responded softly. "We were also supposed to go to the beach. You had planned a nice romantic day for us, but *someone* got food poisoning the night before." She smiled weakly.

Evan let out a soft chuckle. "That was not a good weekend."

CHAPTER 14

Marvin stood in front of the mantel, looking over the framed pictures there. Some were pictures of smiling, chubby babies, others were of a wedding day. There were family portraits and Christmas cards. None of the pictures were recent, which took Marvin by surprise. After all, there'd been much to celebrate over the past nine months.

He walked around the two-bedroom bungalow. He skimmed through some magazines sitting on the coffee table. Once he was done, he placed them back exactly how he'd found them. The room was elegantly decorated with white and glass furniture with teal accents. *She has good taste*, he thought. He walked over to the window and looked outside. It was a sunny day, and the skies were clear. He heard the birds chirping from where he stood. On his way into the house, they'd been silent.

Marvin was in the bedroom when he heard the front door open and close. Footsteps traveled to the kitchen, and he heard what he believed to be the sound of grocery bags being put down on the table. Marvin strolled his way out of the bedroom towards the kitchen.

The woman had her back turned as she put the milk carton in the fridge.

"You're home," he said calmly. "I've been waiting for you, Venice."

The unfamiliar voice startled her. She froze. With her hand on the door handle, she slowly rotated her head around and eyed Marvin, who stood by the kitchen table. Her heart began to race, and her eyes widened with disbelief.

"Sorry to frighten you like this," he said, unbuttoning his blazer. "You probably don't know who I am."

She talked through gritted teeth. "I think I have a good idea."

"Why don't you have a seat then?" He motioned her to take a seat in the chair in front of him.

He scooted another chair back and sat down, as relaxed, Venice noted, as if he were in his own home. A menacing smile danced over his lips. He folded his arms neatly across his lap.

Venice closed the refrigerator door and cautiously approached the table.

"How did you get in here?"

"I assure you that's the least of your worries," he said with composure. "Please, sit." He motioned her to the chair across from him.

Venice's heart raced and her throat began to close. She

felt her chest burn. She knew what this man was capable of, and she became nauseous thinking about the reasons why he might be here in her home. She pulled out the chair and sat down.

"You look like you've seen a ghost, Venice," he chuckled.

She kept her voice steady when she spoke. "Why are you here?"

"How is Evan doing these days?"

"What do you want?" she hissed.

"I'm going to be honest with you. I need to talk to Shadow. I went to pay them a visit, but they weren't home. Would you happen to know where they are by any chance?"

"What do you want with them?"

"That's none of your concern, now, is it?"

"When my family's in danger, I make damn sure it's my concern," she responded, raising her voice.

Marvin chuckled. "You want to watch how you talk to me, old woman," he warned. "Now, look, what I'm asking is very simple and reasonable."

"I can only imagine what you'd do to them if they were anywhere near you."

His eyebrows furrowed and an exaggerated frown appeared across his face. "Oh, come on now. I'm not that horrible, am I?"

"You set Evan on fire! You stay away from my family."

He studied her for a moment. He was going to get Bright one way or another, and he was going to make each member of the Storm family feel pain they had never experienced before.

"It seems you want to do this the hard way. That's fine by me," he said, rising from his chair. "Let me make one thing clear here. You had the chance to do what was right. All I wanted to know was where your precious Evan and Shadow are hiding. You refused to provide me with that information. Now, if anything happens to the people you so dearly love, know that the blood will be on your hands. This was your warning, Venice."

Venice stared into this devil's eyes. She knew better than to give in to a bully. What she feared now was Marvin's next move.

"I'll let myself out."

Venice watched the door close behind him. Panic roared inside her. Even though Bruce assured her that no one knew of the house in Brickwood, she couldn't stop herself from wondering if Evan, Shadow, and Bright were really safe. Her eyes welled up, and a wailing cry filled the room. Her heart ached knowing that they were going to have to face one hurdle after another until the agency was destroyed, preventing them all from living a normal life. Venice wanted, urgently, to call Bruce and tell him Marvin had threatened her, but she knew if she ever so much as mentioned his name to Bruce, it would act as a distraction, and she couldn't risk any mishaps with the mission.

All Venice could do was hope that Bruce successfully executed his mission, leaving Marvin useless and powerless.

Outside, Marvin slid into the back seat of the sedan

that had been waiting for him. He raised his phone to his ear. A moment later, a man answered.

"Yeah."

The malicious smile once again appeared on Marvin's face as he spoke. "Today's your lucky day."

CHAPTER 15

Evan took Shadow and Bright to Zackery's Ice Cream Parlor. It was only fifteen minutes away from the safe house. Aside from Bright's initial cries, the drive was peaceful and quiet. There weren't many cars out on the road during the day, unlike in Lake View. Granted, Brickwood was a city retirees migrated to. Most of the folks there either stayed indoors or walked to the nearest park, depending on the weather.

After they had parked and retrieved their belongings from their car, they made their way to the entrance. When they walked into the ice cream parlor, the interior caught their eyes, despite the heavy traffic of teens and kids with their parents. The entrance was decorated with red and white stripes, with all the colors in the rainbow dripping from the corners. Sections of the ice cream parlor had different themes. One section was painted with various superheroes. The table and chairs were bold and bright in color. Other sections were a mix between hip and elegant.

The scoopers wore white attire and white WinCo chefs' hats. As a whole, Zackery's Ice Cream Parlor catered to all types of personalities and was aesthetically pleasing to those who were in dire need of social media content, if the number of patrons taking selfies or photos of their ice-cream was any indication.

Shadow had Bright in a baby carrier close to her chest. When she peered down, she found him fast asleep. She was in love with his long eyelashes and tiny, irresistible nose. Luckily, his sleeping schedule consisted of long naps. She wondered how some parents were able to function if their baby wasn't a good sleeper. Shadow knew she would have struggled, having to wake up every two hours to change, feed and then soothe Bright back to sleep, but one thing she had heard from other moms was that it all became basic instinct.

They stood in line patiently as the customers in the front sampled flavors and debated on what they wanted. They both took a quick scan of the area, to make sure they hadn't been followed. The habit had become mechanical. Everything and everyone appeared to be normal. It was a relief for Shadow to feel, for even a brief moment, as if everything were right with the world and they were simply a normal family enjoying an outing with their new baby.

"It's *so* unique. I've never been to an ice cream shop with so much character," Shadow said in awe as she gazed at the walls.

"Wait until you see how you can design your ice cream."

"Design?"

"Yeah. You can have your ice cream rolled up in cotton candy and they cut it in half like a burrito. Or you can get it rolled and add your favorite toppings to it. You can get it in a donut, freshly baked cookies or in a cone if you wanna go simple. They have crazy sundaes, which are ridiculous in size. This is *the* place for ice cream."

"No wonder the line is super long. I wouldn't know what I'd want with all the options they have here. I'm surprised they don't have one back home."

"I'm actually surprised, too," he said, taking another look around. "All the old folks live out here. Well, a majority of them... but if you look around, they're all young people here."

Shadow chuckled. "But if you think about it, it's cheaper out here for them to open up a shop. The rent is probably way cheaper compared to Lake View, and it's clearly gaining a significant amount of attraction because it's not surrounded by competition."

She could see the wheels in his brain turning.

He raised an eyebrow. "You know what, honey? That makes a lot of sense."

Shadow leaned on one foot and then on the other. A grin appeared when she responded. "I'm more than just good looks, honey."

His eyes crinkled at the corners. "I know," he replied. He leaned in and kissed her softly.

To kill time as they waited for their turn, they entertained fantasy business ideas perfect for the secluded yet accessible suburb of Brickwood. It was easier than thinking about the reasons they found themselves in this neighborhood in the first place.

***

Stacy slouched in her chair at her desk, looking at the box that contained all her belongings. She was due to leave the agency in another hour. A part of her didn't want to leave the place that had become a home to her. Her history with the agency up until today was clean, and she had made memories she'd never forget. The other part of her felt disgusted for even agreeing to take on an assignment involving the kidnap of an innocent baby.

A knock on her door prompted Stacy to sit up straight, unsure as to who would be seeking her out at a time like this.

"Come in."

Sky slipped into the room, closing the door behind her. She peeked into the box of Stacy's belongings, pursing her lips.

"You got a lot of stuff in there."

"Yup."

"How are you holding up?"

"I'm fine. I didn't think I'd get fired. The most I expected was to get suspended, you know? But it's all good. I'm moving on to better things."

The truth was that Stacy had no clue what she was going to do next.

Sky beamed with satisfaction. "You're absolutely right."

Stacy scowled. She didn't have time for inane conversation with a member of the board that had just voted to fire her. "Is there anything I can do for you?" she said curtly.

Sky smiled again. "That's why I came here to talk to you."

Stacy leaned forward, now curious.

"If you don't want to leave the agency just yet, you don't have to."

Stacy raised an eyebrow, confused. "What? I don't have a choice..."

"You do now."

"This doesn't make any sense. The board, *yourself included,* all voted to fire me."

"I'll explain that later. I'm here because I wanted to talk to you about a special project that I'm working on and it's highly classified. We've got a team in place to run the mission, and given your track record, I believe this mission is probably something you're going to want to do."

"How are you so sure about what I'd want?"

Sky grinned and pulled the chair out in front of her. She sat down, a look of pure contentment on her face.

"Here's something I know about every single person working here," she began. "Not everyone executes their missions or assignments the same way, and the way they execute them tells me a lot about their character. Now, the agency isn't... let's say... as *clean* as it used to be. But there are still some pure-hearted souls that walk amongst us. Agents who are in it for the right reasons. I believe you to be one of those agents."

Stacy studied the other woman. The two of them had never had a conversation prior to the board meeting, but Sky was speaking as if she knew all about Stacy. She was intrigued.

"Well, that makes sense given that you have access to all our files and personal information. I don't know anything about the people I've never worked with, so there isn't much that I can say about everyone else here." Stacy leaned back in her chair and crossed her legs. "But I don't trust anyone here. Not even you. So yeah..."

"I'll give you that. After what happened with the assignment you were working on, I would have my guard up as well."

"Then I guess this concludes our conversation."

Sky nodded her head, understanding Stacy's pique. "Okay. Let me ask you this then. "Would you agree that this agency has taken a toll on your life and changed you as a person?"Stacy nodded without any hesitation.

Sky looked steadily at her.

"So, what would it take for you to seek revenge on someone—or something—that had taken such a toll on your life?"

Stacy thought about her question carefully. She shifted in her seat and looked at the box full of her belongings. "I don't know. I haven't had the time to really think. I'm not sure there is anything I can do."

"You could be a part of this mission," Sky offered.

It didn't take long for Stacy to answer. "Yeah, about that...I'm not too sure if I want to be a part of any mission. I'm still trying to wrap my head around the last mission I was a part of..."

Sky rose from her chair and pulled out a white business card with an address written on it in red ink.

"For the safety of this mission, I can't say much about the details. All I *can* say is that you will be compensated well if you decide to get on board." Sky handed her the business card. "When I see you at this location, understand that you've already agreed to be a part of this once in a lifetime mission and there will be no turning back."

Stacy flipped the business card of a restaurant to find the time and day of the meeting. She looked up at Sky, not entirely convinced she wanted to be a part of this mission.

"I know *you* won't regret joining us, Stacy," Sky said. She paused for a moment as she turned around to make her way to the door. "Hopefully we'll be seeing each other soon."

"Wait," Stacy called out. "What's the comp?"

Sky reached for the door handle and looked over her shoulder. "One point five million."

Stacy's eyes widened in disbelief. The hair on her neck rose.

The door behind Sky closed, leaving Stacy alone.

She leaned back in her chair, her eyes lingering over her empty desk and the box of her belongings. She held on tight to the business card. She had a big decision to make in the next few hours.

CHAPTER 16

Bruce peered over the table, reviewing the blueprint of the SEA. Their team was on standby and ready to execute the plan on his say-so. He picked up his glass of Coke, finishing the last of the remaining liquid.

From the kitchen, Bruce could see Mr. Brar outside in the backyard, pacing back and forth on the porch, reciting a prayer. They were in Highland View, at a safehouse Mr. Brar had bought with his wife, which they had rented out over the years. When Ekam passed away, Mr. Brar had decided not to rent out the property again. Since then, the house had been sitting idle, accumulating dust. The thought of selling the home they had bought together didn't sit well with him.

Mr. Brar turned around and faced the house. He knew Bruce had been watching him for the past few minutes. He signaled for him to come and join him on the porch.

"Finished?" Bruce asked as he closed the screen door behind him.

He slid his hands into his pockets. "Yes." His eyes glistened with tears. "I remember when you moved in next door to us. We bumped into each other on a run. That was the first day we met. You remember that?"

Bruce nodded.

"Your energy was contagious. You were a chatterbox, and I couldn't help but wonder if you always had that much energy or if you were on drugs. It was hard to tell," he chuckled. "You had done a five-mile run, too, I believe." He paused for a moment as he gathered his thoughts. "You reminded me of myself when I was that age. Full of life, a little carefree, no tension. And then you guys had Denise and then Evan..." Tears began to roll down his cheeks, but he smiled through the pain. "I remember seeing the change after you lost Geneva. I know it wasn't easy, Bruce. I know," he whispered. "I waited for your phone call telling me you were going to come back home. Twenty-seven years is a long time not to see someone you love with every fiber in your body. It tore me up inside, Bruce. It really did."

The sadness in his voice made Bruce's eyes well up too.

"You have no idea how much it breaks my heart to know that you have cancer," Mr. Brar continued, his cheeks visibly pink. His eyes flickered towards the garden. "I ask God why, out of all people, he chose to put you through so much pain." He wiped away the tears with the back of hand. "He hasn't answered yet, if you were wondering."

Bruce drew in a long breath. He looked up at the sky and closed his eyes. "I don't know, Mr. Brar. I ask myself the same question. But you of all people have made me into a stronger man. You know that, right?"

Mr. Brar craned his neck sideways and peered into his eyes. "You deserved better, Bruce."

"I think we all do," he said as he wrapped his arm around Mr. Brar. "You just have to make the best of what you have, right?"

"Do me a favor, will you?"

"Anything."

"Don't go before me," Mr. Brar pleaded, his voice cracking. "I won't be able to handle it. I know death is a part of life and it's just another journey we all take, but the attachment I have to you, to your family..."

"I'll try my best," Bruce chuckled.

"It's been a privilege to be a part of your lives, Bruce. I count myself as one of the lucky few in this world who can call his friends, family."

Bruce laughed quietly. "It's been *our* privilege to have you in our lives. You have gone above and beyond with everything. I honestly don't know what we would've done without you."

All Mr. Brar could do was smile through teary eyes. He couldn't believe Bruce's life was going to be shorter than his.

***

A little while later, Sky dropped by the safehouse to review the plan. The three of them sat at the kitchen table once more, the blueprint in front of them.

"How did it go with Stacy?" Bruce asked.

"I'll find out later tonight, if she shows up to our meeting. We're supposed to meet at Mean Burgers, seven o'clock sharp."

"You really want to bring her on?" Bruce asked.

Sky nodded. "We owe her this."

"You think we have enough time to bring her up to speed?" Mr. Brar asked.

"This wouldn't be her first time joining a mission at the last minute. Looking through her files and reviews, I don't know why she hadn't been promoted to the fifth floor. I hope she shows up tonight."

"Has everyone got their updated packet?" Mr. Brar asked Sky.

"Yup. I gave them a number to call— a burner phone, of course— if they had any questions, but so far, I haven't gotten a single call."

"Sounds good," Bruce replied. "I still can't believe Marvin went as far as trying to kidnap Bright."

"Well, we know a few things," Sky began. "Roy and Marvin are working together, so Bright is an asset to the both of them. He's the missing piece of whatever plan they're working on, and he and Shadow will always be targets until the agency is gone."

Mr. Brar shook his head. "I thought I had lived long enough... to see everything. But this world continues to surprise me."

"I was going to ask Stacy about the mission, but every assignment description Marvin has ever issued is deliberately vague. And because Roy signs off on most of them, he's not exactly going to offer up that information, either. My feeling is that there's definitely something bigger that they're working on and, for some reason, Bright fits into it. I'm not sure if we'll ever find out unless we lure Roy in somewhere and torture the information out of him."

For a moment, the room fell into silence.

"The execution of the plan will still take place at night, correct?" Mr. Brar asked.

Sky nodded her head. "It's the only way we'll have the least amount of casualties. From our research, the agents who are still around working in the evening, are mainly fifth floor agents, or trainees. As for Roy and Marvin... their schedules have been unpredictable. They've only stayed past seven pm ten times in the past six months. There's no guarantee we'll be able to get rid of them at the time we blow everything up."

"It would make everyone's lives easier if we did."

Sky and Bruce both agreed with Mr. Brar.

"Where are you placing Stacy if she agrees to the mission?" Bruce asked, taking a glance over the blueprint before meeting Sky's eyes.

"If she agrees, she's going to take second lead for the finance operation. Right now, we have Prem as our main lead."

"How is our inventory looking?" Mr. Brar asked. "Do we have all the gadgets signed off?"

Sky mulled over the question for a moment. "We're

waiting for two suits to come back from inspection. Everything else, we have booked. Once the suits come back, we can solidify the date and go over the mission as a team before execution. Answer any last minute questions."

Mr. Brar rose from the table and retrieved a glass from the cupboard. "Anyone want anything to drink?"

"No, I'm good," Sky answered.

"I'm fine, thanks," Bruce replied.

Mr. Brar set the glass on the counter and made his way to the refrigerator. "You two need to get your affairs in order."

Bruce and Sky exchanged brief sidelong glances. It was the one thing they both were leaving to the last minute. Even with the level of confidence they each had about the success of their mission, it was important that all necessary documentation, such as wills and deeds, were up to date. This was every agent's least favorite task because it served as a reminder that this could very well be the mission that they didn't return from.

Mr. Brar pulled out a carton of milk and closed the refrigerator door behind him. The silence told Mr. Brar everything he needed to know. He shook his head in a disapproving manner. "You two need to have everything sorted out by tonight. Alright?"

They both nodded in agreement.

"I'm going to check in tomorrow morning," he said as he poured a cold glass of milk. "I shouldn't have to remind you. I'm going to need you guys to bring me your papers so I can make sure everything is good to go. We've all worked too hard and sacrificed a lot to let these things slip through the cracks. Especially you, Bruce."

***

Evening had arrived, and unlike the other September days, the sky had quickly become gloomy, and the trees whistled as the wind picked up. Ryan, Nate, and Skylar, Nate's friend, had spent their afternoon playing soccer in the backyard while Denise prepped for dinner.

Denise could hear the kids screaming while Ryan yelled out words of encouragement. At times she would stand by the window to watch them play. Sometimes she would randomly remember Ryan's accident or the initial interaction he'd had with Nate when he first came home, and a rush of anxiety would fill her chest. Somehow, despite the severity of that accident, everything had eventually gone back to normal. Somewhat.

Ryan fell in love with Nate, and it almost seemed as if Ryan had never really lost his memory. He managed to have conversations about things he didn't remember with Nate. When he didn't remember a story Nate would ask him about, he would simply let Nate know he was getting old but would do a better job to remember for the future.

It took some time for Denise to realize that the accident, in hindsight, both tested their love for one another and bonded them as a family. When she looked back how far they'd come, she realized that their marriage had been in dire need of saving. This realization wouldn't have come to light if it hadn't been for Ryan's accident. In a way, it was a blessing in disguise. Not so long afterwards, Denise began to practice gratitude by journaling and tried her best to make each day better. As her priorities shifted, one of her main goals was to make sure each day was filled with nothing but positivity and happiness. Granted, some days were harder than others, but it was the effort and progress that mattered.

Work had become a second priority. Storm Inc. was reaching new heights, enabling Denise to take a step back and spend more time with family.

As she diced the avocado, she could hear Ryan's voice nearing the house. She looked up and saw Ryan waving at her as he approached the porch.

He removed his shoes before stepping inside the house. "I think I'm done playing soccer for the day," he said, almost out of breath.

"It looks like it," Denise chuckled.

She threw the avocado into a bowl with lettuce and tomatoes. She poured the dressing and tossed the salad before beginning the vegan tacos.

Ryan raised his eyebrow, like he always did when it was clear Denise was trying to instigate a debate. "What are you implying?"

She grinned and turned around to grab the tortillas. "You don't think cardio is important and haven't been to the gym in over a month. I didn't wanna have to say this, but it looks like your abs have been… a little shy these days." She pursed her lips and turned around again to retrieve the cauliflower from the refrigerator.

Ryan pulled up his shirt and looked down at his stomach. He met her eyes. "Really, Denise? You know how insecure I am about my looks, and it's literally the only thing in my life that gives me purpose. My looks. I mean, we got a good deal on this house *because* of my stunning good looks, and you're gonna just take a shit all over it?"

Denise bit her lower lip to refrain from laughing. She had always secretly enjoyed his sarcasm. "I'm sorry to burst your bubble, honey," she responded in all seriousness. "I thought it was more about personality than looks."

Her eyes flickered towards the sink, and she tried her hardest to maintain a cool and calm demeanor as she washed the cauliflower.

"I'm disappointed about this, Denise. All of it. I just lost my appetite. You are a mean woman!"

Her mouth was agape. "Honey, I'm kidding!"

He chuckled as he made his way around the counter. He stood next to her as she started to cut the cauliflower into bite-sized pieces. "Oh, you sure about that?" He poked her in the middle of her waist, tickling her. Denise giggled and jumped up.

"Stop." She tried to sound serious but couldn't help but smile.

He crossed his arms at his chest and leaned against the counter. "What are you making?"

"Vegan cauliflower tacos and avocado salad."

His eyes flicked towards the salad bowl and then back at her. "Wait. The tacos...don't they already have lettuce and avocado in them?"

"Yeah..."

"The salad has the same thing. Lettuce and avocado. You just added the tomatoes to it."

She stopped cutting the cauliflower and met his eyes. "You always have something to say. You're worse than those two out there," she said pointing the knife towards the backyard.

Nate and Skylar had abandoned the game of soccer to play a round of pick-up sticks on the cement. In the age of electronics, Denise and Ryan made a conscious effort to limit screen time as much as they could. Granted, at times, it was all they had at their disposal to keep Nate occupied.

"Yeah, I know," he grinned. "Hey, tomorrow I've got an early shift, so I'll pick up Nate from school, and we'll go get some ice cream, then come home."

"What time are you starting tomorrow? Cause I have to go in for a meeting at eight."

"Seven in the morning, babe. You got new clients?"

"Yeah," she sighed. "Everyone I deal with now is like a top executive or a CEO."

"That's great! More money, more honey!" he said gleefully. "Are you still working with the founder of that dating site? The bachelor pad dude?"

"No, I finished that project like a week ago." She lined a baking tray with foil, sprayed it with canola oil and preheated the oven. "It was actually a lot of fun working with him. But not all my clients are as interesting as him, or as patient."

Ryan pulled up his sleeves to wash his hands. "I'm so glad my job isn't client focused. I don't have to interact and deal with patients one-on-one like you."

She smirked. "You definitely wouldn't last a day in my shoes. I can totally see you losing your shit if a client kept going back and forth with what they wanted."

Ryan chuckled at her response. "Yeah, I don't have patience for that kinda stuff." Especially not with adults. How do you go through life and still not know how to make decisions? Honestly, I have a hard enough time as it is with Dr. Jackson. You have no idea how many times I've had to bite my tongue when he comes around with his latest ridiculous demands."

Denise nodded.

Dr. Jackson, the Chief of Surgery at Ryan's hospital, was known for the unreasonable expectations he had for his staffers. She knew Ryan sometimes found it difficult to keep from giving Jackson a piece of his mind.

"You should seriously come work for me for a week," she giggled, thinking of some of her own more demanding clients. "You can be an intern. It'll help you practice diplomacy!"

"No, thank you. I think I'm good," he chuckled, knowing all too well he wouldn't survive an hour.

After drying his hands, he started to help coat the cauliflowers.

"Since you're working at seven and I've got to leave the house by seven-fifteen, I'm gonna ask Grandma if she can drop off Nate."

"Yeah, okay. Sounds like a plan," he answered. He lowered his tone as he continued. "How are you doing with everything that's going on? I know we try not to talk about it here, but…to be honest, it scares me, and I feel terrible for Shadow and Evan. I can't imagine having to run away and go into hiding."

Denise and Ryan had made a pact to not discuss the agency at home. Life was challenging as it was, and their lives didn't have room for more worry. Their home was their sanctuary, and they held each other responsible for maintaining the positive energy inside of it.

Denise let out a deep sigh.

She looked at him with concern. "I'm always worried, Ryan. That's my baby brother, you know? It's depressing if I think too long about it. And the thing is, we can't get away from this agency, either. What if we're the next target? I think about that too sometimes, even though we have nothing to offer that they might want to take… but it just seems like you've gotta be on your toes with these people."

Ryan sighed, feeling his mood dampen. "I just want life to be normal again, whatever normal means these days. We know too much about things we should know nothing about."

***

Twenty minutes later, Zack Moore dropped by to pick up his son, Skylar.

"Dad!" Skylar exclaimed, as he stood in front of his father

with a pleading look. "Just ten more minutes. Pleeease?"

"Another time. Your mom is getting dinner—pizza. Your favorite."

Skylar crossed his hands over his chest and frowned. He stared at his father for a few seconds before turning to Nate. "I guess I'll see you at school tomorrow."

"Okay. We can play Captain during recess."

They gave each other a high five, establishing a deal.

"Thank you, guys, for having Skylar over. He always has a blast playing with Nate. It's all he talks about on the way home and at the dinner table," Zack said.

"We love having him over," Denise responded. "I wish you guys were staying for dinner. We were gonna have spicy cauliflower tacos tonight."

"Ah, that's okay. We've got pizza coming. Maybe another time." He smiled. "I'll see you guys later."

"It was nice seeing you, Zack," Ryan chimed in. "You and I should go for a round of golf. It's been too long."

"My department is organizing a charity golf tournament. Once the details are finalized, I'll send over an evite."

"Sounds good."

"Good night, you guys," Denise said.

"Good night."

They watched Zack walk down the pathway, Skylar right beside him, before closing the door.

CHAPTER 17

1934

It had been three months since the day Adrian had seen Samantha at Shallow's Lake. It hadn't been easy on either of them. They knew deep down the loss of their baby was tearing them apart. Adrian sought revenge on Derek, while Samantha was wise enough to know the answer didn't lie in Derek's death. As much as she wanted to kill him herself, she knew violence wouldn't solve anything. In the end, it wouldn't make her any better than Derek. And she supposed a part of her still loved the man.

It was a sunny Monday afternoon, and Derek had gone to work earlier than usual. Samantha had taken the opportunity to prepare dinner in advance, so she wouldn't have to rush back before Derek, who expected dinner to be waiting on the table when he arrived home.

Now, she surveyed her surroundings— Charles' Restaurant, a fine American and Greek foods bistro—wondering what the man she was meeting with looked like. She wore a white fedora hat and a white floral dress, accented with red lipstick. Her hair was tied back tightly, which was giving her quite the headache.

The waiter arrived with menus and filled two glasses with cold water. Samantha was beginning to feel antsy waiting. The longer she waited, the more she began to think maybe he wasn't going to show up. It had already been thirty minutes. She wondered if it was the universe's way of giving her a sign to leave and never look back at this day, which could possibly change the future for her.

After another two minutes of agony, Samantha grabbed her purse and rose from her booth. As she walked past a table full of businessmen, chattering loudly and drinking cold beers, a man in a long black coat over a three-piece grey suit made his way towards Samantha. He slowly lifted his hat from his head, revealing thick black hair combed back. He held his hat close to his chest as soon as he locked eyes with her. Her beauty struck him in a way no other woman's had.

She froze. Her heartbeat quickened. Samantha smoothed the front of her dress, maintaining tense eye contact with the man in front of her.

He had a moustache and piercing hazel eyes. He struck her as someone she should fear, though she didn't know why.

When he got closer, he smiled. "Shall we?"

Samantha turned around and went back to the booth she'd just left and sat down right across from Neil Harper, one of the SEA's Board of Directors.

He sat across from Samantha and set the hat to his side. He studied her eyes before anything else. He could see pain etched there.

"I apologize for having you wait. I had a meeting that ran a little longer than it should have."

She nodded.

"What can I do for you, Mrs. Will?"

Without any hesitation, Samantha got straight to the point. "I want us to work together."

He leaned forward and folded his hands together. His eyes flickered towards the tablecloth. He scoffed. "What business do women have working with the agency?"

Samantha held his gaze for a moment, slightly appalled but unsurprised. "Men are under the assumption that women are weak and hold no power, which is false. A woman who has had everything taken away from her yet has found the will to live is very powerful. You will very well have signed your own death warrant if you were to cross her," she said, taking a moment to keep her courage intact. "Women will rise and rule the world one day, Mr. Harper. I assure you of that. That day will come soon, and you may want to get on the right side of history before it's too late."

Neil used his index finger to trace an imaginary circle on the tablecloth, choosing his words carefully before he spoke. It was evident that before him sat a potent woman.

He cleared his throat when he responded. "Why would we want to work with you, Mrs. Will?"

He waited for her to respond.

"Have you ever heard of WIP?"

"Yes, I have. I believe it stands for Women in Power."

"Yes, that is correct," she said, pausing for a moment. "I'm the founder of that organization."

"You?" he asked, shocked.

Samantha nodded. "Yes."

She could see the wheels turning in his mind.

"Well," he said, still in disbelief. "What do you want in return, Mrs. Will?"

"I want my freedom. I want protection. In exchange for our organizations working together, those are my requirements I want guaranteed, in writing."

"Who are you seeking protection from?"

"From my husband. I'm sure you have heard of him—Derek Will."

"That name rings a bell. Is that all?"

"There is one more thing."

"What is it?"

"I want to enforce the WIP code of conduct as a law. With the power the SEA holds, and its connections, I'm sure it will be easy for this law to be passed and be in full effect by the end of the year."

Neil reviewed the proposal in his head.

Women of the WIP organization were demanding the following: equal pay; for big businesses to address misconduct that took place in the workplace against women; an increase in maternity leave to a year with pay; and the elimination of taxes on feminine products. But, most importantly, they were advocating for the implementation of the WIP code of conduct: *Any female, regardless of color, creed, religious background, or sexual orientation, owns the right to her body, mind and soul. Just as males have rights to their bodies, females too shall receive the same acknowledgement and rights. No male or female is in any position to make a decision for a sole individual on what the individual can and cannot do with their body. Any act that places a female in harm's way, in a vulnerable position, will be considered a violation of human rights. If a female is unconscious or does not have the ability to say 'yes' or 'no' and is taken advantage of without her consent, will be considered a violation of human rights. Any human rights violation will result in the perpetrator serving a minimum of ten years in jail, without bail. Good behavior will not result in a lighter sentence. The severity of the violation will determine whether the sentence of ten years will be increased by the court of law. Any and all legal fees the female may face will be covered by the defendant.*

It sounded like a hefty demand but considering how men had been treated from the beginning of time in comparison to women, Samantha knew they weren't asking for much.

"I'm curious. As the founder of this organization... I would assume you would have the power to set yourself free."

"It's easy to say, Mr. Harper. But you wouldn't understand."

"You will have to try."

Samantha took a deep breath and told her story, leaving nothing out. She saw the emotions change across Neil's face when she explained in detail the beatings she received from Derek that would leave her unconscious at times. But most importantly, for the first time, she told her story without struggling to keep herself from breaking down in tears. She was always going to grieve the loss of her baby. Deep down, however, she knew that one day, hopefully, her grief would be easier to bear.

Neil nodded. "I can imagine it wasn't easy to relive all those moments just now. Here is what I can do. The SEA can offer you protection and the freedom that is rightfully yours. However, I cannot guarantee that we can put the WIP code of conduct into place."

Without any hesitation, Samantha asked, "Mr. Harper, are you married?"

"Yes."

"Do you have children?"

"Yes."

"Boys or girls?"

"A son and a daughter."

"We have no idea what tomorrow holds, isn't that correct, Mr. Harper?"

"Yes," he replied.

"This law will protect your wife and your children even in the instance you cannot. You must have seen or at least heard of things that some women and children are subjected to— things that should never happen to a woman or to a child. If you help make the WIP code of conduct a law, you will be a part of making history. You will have contributed to legislation generations to come will talk about; you will be deserving of the praise that will inevitably follow. You will be leaving a legacy behind for your children. Either you take it upon yourself to see this through, or someone else will down the road."

Neil slowly clasped his hands together and studied Samantha. The truth was always in the eyes. He had met eyes with thousands and thousands of people throughout his career at the SEA and could always determine whether a person was telling him the truth by their gaze.

After some contemplation, he responded. "Okay, Mrs. Will. I think we can make this happen. It will take some time, please keep that in mind."

"Yes, of course."

Samantha gathered herself and tried not to act too excited about the support she was now going to receive.

"I will do everything in my power to implement this into law," he said, extending his hand across the table. "Congratulations, Mrs. Will. Once we have the official documents signed about our agreement, we can move forward with the next steps."

"The WIP organization will be excited to hear about our new relationship," Samantha replied with a smile.

"I'm sure they will."

***

That evening, when Derek arrived home from work,

he was in an entirely different mood compared to that morning. He kissed Samantha on the cheek as she was putting dinner on the table and was liberal with his compliments. To her further surprise, he'd even bought her a gift. When she opened the black suede box, she laid her eyes on a diamond bracelet. Far from being delighted, all she could think was that Derek knew about WIP and her secret meeting with Neil earlier, and this was a way to lure her into confessing. This could be merely a beautiful, sparkling trap. Even if he was simply in a good mood, she knew from experience it would eventually pass. Either way, there was trouble to come.

She sat at the dinner table, admiring the shiny bracelet. "This is an expensive bracelet. What is it for?"

He forked a roasted potato into his mouth and looked at her with confusion. "What do you mean?"

She locked eyes with him. "I mean, it's lovely, but I don't know what I did to deserve this. What's the occasion?" She forced a smile.

"It's a celebration gift. I will be opening my own firm in the coming months."

Samantha wasn't at all surprised by the news. He continually and purposely kept her in the dark about anything that was related to work or money. She had given up on the idea that one day he would open up to her. Trying to sound enthusiastic, she responded, "Well, that's wonderful."

"Thank you."

Samantha took a sip of her wine and entertained the

thought of what her life would be like without Derek. She glimpsed at Derek and the past came rushing back—the good and the bad. Despite the years of abuse, part of her still loved her husband, or at least imagined she did. Moments like this, when he was kind or even loving, were confusing, even after so long. It had taken her time to grasp the idea that what Derek professed to feel for her wasn't really love. But by the time she'd come to this realization, she had stayed far too long in a relationship that had slowly deadened her soul. Though she fantasized about life without Derek, in truth, Samantha hadn't known how she'd even begin to leave. Lately though, something was shifting.

Could it finally be time to let go?

CHAPTER 18

It was happy hour, which drew in an unusually large crowd for a weekday. A line had formed outside of the entrance, and the patio was buzzing with laughter and the excitement of first dates. Luckily for Sky, she knew the owner, which allowed her to pass up the line. She pushed her way through the throng, her blazer resting over one arm, her purse in the other hand. The music was loud, but not enough to drown out all the noise made by the exuberant males cheering at the television screens that hung above the bar at Mean Burgers. Spotting an empty seat at the bar, Sky took a seat, placing her purse and blazer next to her.

Enrique turned around after closing the register. He was handsomely tall, with short black hair streaked with a hint of white through his sideburns. His thick black eyebrows drew attention to his seductive brown eyes. His nose was long and sharp and perched above slightly uneven, pouty lips, the likes of which many women were spending hundreds of dollars to duplicate.

"Well, well, well," he said, chuckling, "if it isn't Sky in the flesh! I'd give you a hug, but a guy threw a glass of beer at one of my bartenders, missed and got me. Then, get this. He wanted to fight me! He tried to jump over the counter but because of his weight, couldn't swing his short pudgy legs over. Ended up cursing his way outta here."

Sky chuckled.

"It's fine."

"What are you drinking?"

Sky pondered over what her taste buds were craving and after a long deliberation, settled for a glass of Cabernet Sauvignon.

Enrique, who she had known since high school, always had something interesting to share. Whether it was a story from a family trip that he'd taken with his siblings during the summer to Puerto Rico or Ecuador, or whether it was simply a regular day that took a sudden unexpected turn, Enrique knew how to tell a story. He knew how to keep his friends engaged, receiving *oohs* and *ahhs* from his audiences, their expressions changing from concern to outright chortles, making him one of the popular boys in school. He hadn't gone to college, like most of his friends, but had done well for himself after launching his first Mean Burgers restaurant, leading to multiple openings in major cities.

"What have you been up to?" He asked as he brought her the glass of wine.

"Just the usual. Working. Keeping myself busy. I see

you're still putting in the hours here."

Enrique peered around the bar, a satisfied smirk on his face, seeing another successful night. He shrugged his shoulders. His eyes swung back and met hers.

Sky took a sip and placed the glass in front of her.

"I get bored if I'm not here. I've got another location we're opening in a few months. It'll be a change of scenery for a while, which will be nice."

"Oh yeah? Where?"

"Brentwood. You'll be there for the grand opening, right?"

"Have I missed any of the other grand openings?"

"Nope," he chuckled. "Do you want me to get something going on the grill for ya?"

Sky turned her wrist inward, getting a view of the time. "Yeah, in a bit. I'm just waiting for someone… I may be looking at a no show."

"If he's a no show, then he's a borderline braindead idiot. That's for sure."

Sky grinned and took another sip of her wine. After taking a glance at the doors, she brought her gaze back to Enrique.

"It's not a guy. I have a meeting with someone. She was supposed to be here at seven, right on the dot."

The knowing stare which accompanied her words established the purpose of her visit.

"I'm going to need to borrow your warehouse."

"Of course," he nodded. Enrique understood perfectly. "People do run late from time to time, you know?"

he offered.

"It's called time management," Sky sighed. "If you look at your day and allocate how much time you will need for everything you're doing, you'll be on time for all your appointments and never be late. It's really that simple."

"Never be late? Oh c'mon. That's unrealistic. Life is unpredictable, Sky. You know that."

"What are cell phones for? If you're running late, call. Or at least shoot a text. Besides, I suspect that may not be the issue here. I'm not sure I have this one entirely convinced. Not yet, anyway."

Enrique chuckled. "Now I think about it, for as long as I've known you, being tardy is something that you've *never* been flexible about. Remember when we decided to grab dinner—"

"And you never showed up and I only heard from you the *next morning* with a lame excuse? Yeah, I remember that." Sky raised her eyebrows.

He let out a loud chuckle. "I cracked my phone an hour before and then one of my bartenders called in sick. I couldn't get my phone to work so I could call you—"

"I guess the landlines stopped working too, huh?"

"Who has people's numbers memorized these days?" he protested, weakly.

Sky grinned and shook her head, not believing his reasoning. "How's your mom doing?"

"She's good. She's traveling the world as much as she can. It reminds her of my dad. Keeping his legacy alive, in a way, I guess."

"It sounds like she's really enjoying herself though," she replied before taking another sip of wine.

Enrique's eyes flickered to the entrance, spotting someone he'd never seen before. He watched as the woman scanned the crowd, looking for someone in particular. "Wow. She's beautiful. That's not her, is it?"

"Umm…" Sky's eyes followed his and found Stacy. "Oh, yeah, that's her." Sky waved Stacy over.

Wearing a black bomber jacket, ripped jeans and booties, which made her look ten years younger than she did in her usual agency garb, Stacy quickly made her way through the crowd towards Sky.

"I'm so sorry," Stacy began as she pulled off her jacket, revealing a black halter top underneath. "I missed my exit and then when I got here, I couldn't find any parking. The parking lot was jam packed. I circled around for a good ten minutes hoping someone would leave. Eventually, I just gave up and ended up parking down the street."

"Even if that's the truth, she won't believe you." Enrique smiled and winked at Sky.

Stacy chuckled in confusion. "But… it *is* the truth."

Sky shook her head. "Don't listen to him. Once we get a table, we'll discuss the project." Sky cast her eyes back at Enrique, who couldn't help but stare at Stacy. "I'm going to need a booth. I would really appreciate it."

"Yeah. Let me talk to the hostess."

"Thanks."

"Anytime." He turned to Stacy with a twinkle in his eyes. "What's your name?"

"Stacy. You're Enrique, right?"

A little taken aback, he responded. "How'd you know?"

"I looked up the restaurant before I left the house. Your picture was in the *about us* section."

Sky studied Enrique. She couldn't recall the last time she had seen him blush. She had always known him as rather a womanizer. She was stunned.

With a giggle, he answered. "Yeah. I was advised to make my website as personable as possible. Building the brand and all that other business-y stuff. I guess it paid off," he said as he surveyed the room full of people.

"Alright," Sky inserted, noticing the conversation taking a different turn. "I'm really gonna need you to get us a booth, Enrique. We've got some *business-y* stuff to discuss as well."

Enrique tapped the counter. "Alright, alright. Let me go talk to the hostess. I'll be right back."

It didn't take long before a booth opened and was wiped down, allowing for the next set of customers to take a seat. Once the women had been seated, their orders were taken. Each ordered a burger with a side of shoestring fries. While Stacy opted for a soft drink, Sky ordered another glass of wine.

Stacy studied Sky for a moment, with a question in mind that had been simmering ever since Sky had dropped by her office.

"Why did you choose me for this assignment?" she asked.

"Already asking questions. I like it."

"Yeah. I mean, why would anyone in their right mind

hire an agent who was just fired over all the other agents that have a better track record? It doesn't make any sense to me. So, why me?"

"Because you are standing on the right side of history. And I know it wasn't you who tanked Marvin's mission. It was Dominic who screwed up. Not you. You saved his ass. At the agency, that kind of loyalty is rare to see, even if you are related to one another. You clearly have integrity. That's why I went back to the board and had them reverse their decision to terminate you."

Stacy allowed the words to sit in the air and thought back to the day when she'd sat in front of the board, in an attempt to save herself from being terminated. She had never felt more alone or scared in her entire life. If she were fired, what was her life going to look like? When the board had come back with their decision to let her go, it had felt as though someone had stabbed her in the heart. The agency had given her a sense of purpose, a sense of drive. Now, that was all gone, and it upset her that covering for her brother had led her to losing her position with the SEA. She wasn't convinced he would have done the same for her had the situation been reversed.

"Look, I appreciate you did that for me but—"

"I've already requested your transfer to the fifth floor," Sky interjected.

Stacy raised her eyebrows. "You're joking, right? I mean, how can you even do that? Agents are only promoted at the end of the year. It's not even December yet. And they did opt to fire me. That's hardly a vote of confidence in my abilities." Stacy couldn't help but feel bitter towards the agency who'd fired her despite years of dedication.

"I've been on the board long enough to make decisions on my own. Once you were reinstated, I made a convincing argument that it was time for you to move up the ladder. Your record is clean; you have a ninety eight percent success rate on all your assignments and missions. Now, I may be the only woman on that board, but they sure as hell know I would drag them through dirt if they overlooked the facts and denied your approval. So, you'll have your new office and position by next week, if everything goes well with this mission."

Stacy nodded her head, still trying to grasp the bundle of good news she was hearing. "What's the mission that I'll be on?"

"Taking down the agency. It's—"

"Wait, hold on," she interrupted. Her eyes narrowed, and her eyebrows furrowed with confusion. "I don't understand. *Taking down the agency?* Why? Are you insane? And why would you go through all the hassle of having the board reinstate me if you're planning on shutting it down anyways?"

"Stacy, you're a smart woman. And you've demonstrated you have integrity. If you're honest with yourself, do you think the agency still acts in accordance with its founding principles?" Sky looked meaningfully across the table at Stacy.

Stacy thought of the mission to kidnap the baby, how cloaked in secrecy it was, and felt a twist in her stomach.

Had that mission really been to benefit the wider community, or had it been solely to further the shadowy aims of Marvin and his superiors? She frowned and looked down at her soda.

Sky continued. "Stacy, it needs to be done. More than anything, the agency has ruined lives. The agency isn't what it used to be. Its interests no longer serve the people; instead, it exists to serve a selective group of people who have no intention of being transparent about their motives. Let's be honest, how many good agents are left?"

Stacy let the words sit with her.

"We have a team in place and a plan. I wanted to bring you on board because you're one of the few agents left with her humanity intact. *If* this mission fails— because we're talking about taking down an entire agency, remember, and that's no small feat— we don't want any of the agents who took part in this mission to have a target on their back. If you aren't discovered, then you have the option to continue working for the SEA. Obviously if you're captured, then you know your entire life will be under their radar. Are you following me?"

Stacy nodded. "I guess the huge paycheck is a way to make things a little easier if things go sideways."

"We value life. I'm not saying the compensation you're receiving reflects how much we think your life is worth, but it's enough so you don't have to stress about food or shelter and will be able to live comfortably if this mission doesn't pan out the way we hope."

When their orders arrived, they both took a juicy bite

from their burgers and munched on the fries.

Stacy wiped the corners of her mouth and took a sip of her Dr. Pepper. "How, exactly, are we going to take down the agency?"

"From the inside. We will destroy every single file, the servers, equipment, you name it. Let's face it, without the agency, agents are useless. And with funding avenues cut off, the agency will shrivel and die. While some of our agents will be out in the field, other agents will be working on the inside, freezing all the accounts. Once the donors get spooked, they'll be out of there, and they'll take their money with them. They're not going to want to risk their association coming out into the open once the agency's corruption is revealed publicly. We're going to make sure we cut these financial and society ties, so Roy can't begin another agency right after. If he does, it'll take some time. Unless, of course, he dies in the process, then we won't be really having that problem."

Stacy nodded. "Is he a target? How many casualties are we predicting?"

Sky chewed on her burger, letting her eyes wander. She took a sip of her wine to wash down the last bit of the burger before answering. "Here's the thing. We aren't planning on killing anyone. We just want to shut down the agency. But the building will be blown up to bits. There should be no trace of the SEA left when we're done. We're going to carry out the mission when there's less traffic inside. We'll have agents make rounds and get everyone inside the agency to leave the premises. Whoever refuses will be... collateral damage."

"How long have you and the rest of the team been working on this mission?" Stacy asked, taking a bite out of her burger.

"Six months."

She raised her eyebrows in shock. "Why are you *just* adding me to your team?"

"If you hadn't taken the fall for your brother, we wouldn't be here right now. I didn't want *that* to be your last mission. You worked extremely hard and gave every mission and assignment your best. You deserved better. That's why it was last minute."

Stacy's eyes welled up. "Wow. Thank you," she said, taking a moment to digest the information. "I really appreciate it."

"Of course."

Sky raised her glass of wine, leading Stacy to mimic the gesture. "To the end, and hopefully, to a new beginning."

Their glasses clunked, establishing their new relationship.

CHAPTER 19

Evan's eyes flickered open. His heart was racing, and his face was dripping with sweat. For a moment, he lay still in bed. A memory replayed in his mind. Evan tried his best to recall every moment before they disappeared out of reach.

He reached over to his nightstand and picked up his cell phone: three thirty-three in the morning, as always. He opened his notes app on his phone and typed everything he could remember about his dream. After he finished, he slowly rose from the bed.

What did this memory mean?

For a moment, he wondered about what happened to WIP, an organization that was making a positive difference. He craned his neck to the side and found Shadow sound asleep. Even though they were now living a different life, a part of him was proud of Shadow for what she had done in a previous life as Samantha, creating an initiative to make a positive difference in the world.

Before heading into the kitchen, he checked on Bright, who was fast asleep in his crib. Downstairs, he made his way to the refrigerator and pulled out a bottle of water. He quietly pulled a chair from the table and sat down. As he turned the cap, he broke the ring, and then took a sip.

His mind replayed the memories of Samantha sitting on the bed with a revolver in her hand and then, later, sitting in the park with Adrian. Now, he had another memory to add to his storyboard. As he tried to come up with a theory of what all the memories were leading him to, the conversation he'd had with Shadow the night they arrived pushed its way through.

He couldn't help but wonder if she was right. What if they weren't meant to be together? Sure, his life would have been easier. His life would have been somewhat normal aside from the memories; he suspected they would have been there anyway. But love was tricky. Life without it was dull, and he couldn't imagine spending the rest of his days without Shadow by his side, no matter what life had in store for them. And surely, there was a reason they had met again, in this life. There was a reason for everything, right?

"Hey," a voice said softly. Shadow walked towards the table. Her eyes were tired and full of concern. "I didn't hear you get up." She came around and wrapped her arms around his chest, her face pressing against his hair. She felt the dampness of his shirt as she gently rubbed his chest. "Another dream?"

"It wasn't a bad one… I don't think."

"You're drenched in sweat, babe," she said, unwrapping herself from him. She took a seat beside him. She looked into his eyes and gave a sympathetic smile. "I know you're hiding things from me."

"Babe, I—"

"Evan," she interrupted. "I know *you* more than you think. You're not telling me everything, and maybe it's because you don't want to burden me, or because you're scared. I don't know what it is, but I know you're not telling me everything. And you need to. I can handle it. Whatever it is. I need to know. We can't expect to have a healthy relationship if we can't share our difficulties with one another."

He sighed, knowing she was right. "Okay, fine. But I just want you to know that I only didn't tell you because I feel guilty for what happened in… in our other lives."

Shadow smiled wearily. "You shouldn't feel that way. I've told you so many times. You can't change what happened. We both caused each other pain. I just wish I remembered my life as clearly as you do, you know? It could've probably helped us and given us some answers."

Evan nodded. "Today, I had a memory of the agency, and this man, Neil."

"You mean, the SEA? It existed back then?" Shadow's eyes widened. "And you— *we*— were connected to it, in those lives?"

He nodded. "You—*other you*—were the founder of this organization called WIP—Women in Power."

Her eyes lit up. "That's kinda cool," she said.

"That part is. But there is some other stuff, too..."

"Like what?"

Evan's eyes flickered towards his water bottle. He wasn't sure how she was going to react to what he was about to tell her. His eyes traced their way back to hers. "The man who ran the agency back then was Stephan Hex... I don't know if—"

"That's my great grandfather!" she cried in disbelief.

Evan could see her pupils dilate.

"When I discovered that in the dream, it sort of made sense," Evan began. Shadow looked confused. He took a deep breath and continued. "Okay.... look..."

"Evan, just tell me," she begged.

"I'm trying to... it's just...alright, there's no way to say it so it sounds any better. Here's the thing. It made sense that your great-grandfather was involved in the SEA once, because, well, your dad... he runs the agency now."

He watched Shadow anxiously. Her mouth parted but no words came out. He reached for her hand and held it tight. Evan hoped the truth might set her free, might answer some of the lingering questions she'd had for the past year; still, he'd feared seeing her reaction to the news. "Marvin and your dad have been working together. He set up Marvin to... seduce you, I guess, and then eventually marry you. Marvin wants to run the agency when your dad steps down later down the line, but he'd only be able to run the agency if you were married to him, if he became a part of the family."

It was apparent Shadow was slowly beginning to register

the gravity of what Evan had just told her. She looked away, feeling as if her whole world was crashing down on her in slow motion.

The next fifteen minutes were filled with a thick, tense silence. Evan's hand remained with hers as he waited for her to wrap her mind around the truth. Evan wanted to hug her and tell her everything was going to be okay—anything to make it easier for Shadow to accept the truth that had been hidden from her—but he knew the best thing right now was for him to simply sit there and wait until she was ready to talk.

When she cleared her throat as if to speak, Evan took a deep breath, preparing himself for the heavy conversation that was about to follow. But Shadow remained quiet. Her hand slipped away from his and her head lowered to her chest.

He could hear her breathing heavily, which began to concern him. He wasn't sure if she was about to have another panic attack. He stayed quiet and watched her carefully. The last thing anybody in a state of shock needed was more noise in their ears. The thoughts racing through Shadow's mind were enough for her to deal with. He just had to be patient.

"C-c-can you… get me a glass of… water, please?" she whispered, her voice breaking as she spoke.

"Yeah. Of course." Evan jolted from his chair, glad to be useful at last. He retrieved a glass of water and held it out in front of her. "Here you go, hun."

When Shadow raised her head, he saw the redness in

her eyes. Her hand trembled as she reached for the glass. "Thank you."

Evan sat back down, fear slowly creeping back into his chest.

Shadow took big gulps of water, finishing the glass halfway before setting it down on the table. She looked at him, her eyes brimming with tears.

"My dad? *My dad?!*"

Evan nodded.

"Holy mother..." she said under her breath. "My dad… and Marvin? Marvin… and my dad… My dad… My own dad?!"

The lump in Evan's throat caught him off guard. It broke his heart to see Shadow in complete shock about her life. It reminded him of the day he had met his father for the first time in over two decades, when he was taken to the hospital after Marvin had set his kitchen on fire, leaving him to burn to death. Even though he was beyond excited to have his father, for the first few months, Evan was in complete shock about the lies and deceit from Venice and Bruce. He imagined it was similar to how Shadow felt now, hearing the truth about her father.

Her nose wrinkled and eyebrows furrowed as the news slowly set in. She pursed her lips as they quivered. "But I'm his daughter…" She looked away the moment her tears began to stream down her cheeks. "He was working with Marvin… and *our relationship* was part of the plan?"

He could hear the dismay in her voice. Evan scooted his chair closer to her and slipped his hand into hers as she quietly sobbed.

She wiped the tears away and met his gaze, her vision still blurry. "He *pimped me out* for a stupid agency," she spat. "He put me through hell. Because of *him*, we're away from home, hiding. Because of *him,* you almost died? I can't believe he was behind all of this."

"I know, I know," Evan said softly, his eyes beginning to well up. "No one deserves to go through this. I'm really sorry you had to find out this way."

For a while, they sat in stillness.

Shadow looked down at her lap and focused on how their hands were intertwined. "I don't know what I did to deserve this," she whispered, wiping her eyes. "I adored my dad," she sniffed. "Yeah, as I got older, things changed, but my love for him never did. He was the *one* person I knew I could always count on... Marvin— I mean, I found out he was a jerk. But my own father? *Using me for his own personal gain?*"

"No matter how old you get, if you're ever wronged by a parent, it's going to hurt. Whether you're sixteen or thirty. The depth of that pain is never going to change," Evan said, pinching the corners of his eyes.

"Thanks to my Dad, not only are we in hiding, but your father, Sky, and Mr. Brar are risking their lives to get rid of the agency. You see how many people this is affecting? It's *never going to end.*"

"It will, babe. This isn't going to be our reality forever."

"I don't even know what to feel, or *how* to feel. I really just wanna scream and pull my hair out, but... I'm too tired to do that. Too damn tired. The lack of sleep and being constantly stressed is going to make me go insane. How are we supposed to raise a happy and healthy baby like this?"

"We'll figure it out. I promise. For now, how about we get some sleep, huh? We can talk about this tomorrow… or whenever you want to."

"I don't ever want to see him again. *Ever.*"

"You don't have to. It's justified. But he deserves to know how you feel, because I know it's going to eat you up if you don't get it off your chest."

Shadow remained quiet.

"It's just a suggestion. I'm not saying to do it tomorrow. Just when you're ready. Or not at all. For right now, I think we need to get some sleep."

Shadow looked up and nodded. She opened her arms and naturally, Evan leaned in and wrapped his arms around her.

"I love you," she said. "Thank you for being there."

"I love you too, hun. Let's go to bed."

They rose from their chairs and began to make their way to the bedroom.

CHAPTER 20

Ryan sat in the lunchroom, eating an apple, a handful of magazines sprawled messily in front of him. To his surprise, the room was empty when he entered. He'd been up since five thirty in the morning, and, in a rush, had forgotten to retrieve his lunch from the refrigerator at home. Not wanting to go to the cafeteria or to the nearest fast-food restaurant, he opted for a healthier option that was readily available. Granted, it wasn't going to fill his starving stomach, but it was going to hold up until the end of his shift. Today, all that was helping Ryan get through the day was his ice cream date with Nate after school.

Twice a month, Ryan and Nate would go get ice cream sundaes. It was a new tradition Ryan had started, to help build and strengthen their bond as father and son. After his accident and consequent memory loss, Ryan knew if he wanted to be the dad that Nate deserved, he needed to spend as much time as he could with Nate, just the two of them. Right after school, they would go to Rachel's Cream Bar, one of the popular places in town, known for its homemade creamy ice cream and treats. The ice cream parlor was constantly occupied with teenagers who had been released from school and would hang around until their parents picked them up.

Ryan rubbed his eyes, feeling rather tired even though he had gotten his eight hours of sleep. He looked down at his watch and noticed it was almost two o'clock. Nate was off at two fifteen. Calculating that he'd have to leave right about now to make it in time to pick up Nate, he quickly finished the last couple of bites that were left of the apple before tossing the core into the garbage. On his way out, he quickly stacked the magazines into a neat pile.

As he navigated down the hallway, he noticed the Chief of Surgery, Dr. Jackson—a man he wasn't fond of—taking long strides towards him. Dr. Jackson was a tall, white haired black man, who had risen through the ranks in the hospital. He was prone to putting work above anything else, and Ryan had a hunch that it was because Dr. Jackson was divorced and never had kids of his own. Everything that Dr. Jackson talked about or did, it seemed, was work related.

Ryan's eyes flickered towards the manila folders in the older man's hand, which only meant one thing: reviewing cases and patients before they went in for surgery. His role as an anesthesiologist extended beyond the operating room. Ryan was responsible for assessing the type of surgery the patient would need and the best anesthesia plan he or she needed based on their current health.

"Smith," he yelled.

Once Ryan neared, already dreading the conversation, he answered, "Dr. Jackson. What can I help you with?"

Dr. Jackson handed over the folders with determination in his eyes. "I need you to review these and have them back on my desk first thing in the morning."

Ryan looked over the folders and realized it was going to take him at least three hours to review the files and give Dr. Jackson a report on each case.

"I don't want to sound like I'm not a team player, but I won't be able to get you the information you're looking for by tomorrow morning."

Dr. Jackson studied him for a minute, bringing his index finger to his lips.

"Why not?"

"I'm supposed to pick up my son from school," he said as he looked down at his watch.

"Figure it out," Dr. Jackson said, crossing his arms at his chest. "If you want to succeed here, you're going to have to make sacrifices. We all do. Some of us have to stay longer than our hours to get what needs to be done. *Our* patients are counting on us to make sure we provide the proper assessment, care, and treatment they come here to get. So, I want the reports tomorrow by eight a.m. Good?"

Ryan looked him dead in the eyes, knowing that the lecture was unnecessary. Without saying another word, Dr. Jackson walked back in the direction he came. Ryan sighed and looked at the stack of files. As much as he loved his job and understood there were going to be times where he would have to stay later than usual, which he'd done in the past, he wasn't going to keep Nate waiting—especially not today. He decided to work on the files after putting Nate to bed tonight, and to get into work earlier the following morning so Dr. Jackson would have them in time.

***

When he arrived at Nate's school, there were still some kids outside by the parking lot, waiting to be picked up. A teacher, with black sunglasses perched atop her sharp nose, monitored the children as she snacked on some popcorn. Ryan parked his car by the sidewalk, with the engine still running, keeping a lookout for Nate. He looked at the dashboard and saw it was two-thirty. Nate should have been outside by now. He screened the playground and adjoining areas and then scanned them again. Nate was nowhere in sight. Ryan ventured a guess that Nate was probably still in the classroom, for reasons he couldn't figure out. He decided to check in the office in case Nate had decided to hang out there until he arrived.

He put the car in park and turned off the ignition, holding the key in his hand. He unbuckled his seatbelt and stepped out of his car, locking it as he strolled towards the office.

When he entered, there were two secretaries sitting at their desks, scrolling through their computer screens.

He approached one with whom he was familiar, Daniella Hayes.

"Hi," he said uncertainly. All of a sudden, he began to feel nervous, noticing Nate wasn't waiting inside the office.

"Hey, Ryan! How's it going? Coming to pick up Nate?"

"Good, good. Yeah, he wasn't outside. I was running a little late, and I waited for a few minutes... do you mind calling his teacher to see if he's still in class?"

"Yeah, of course. It's... Mrs. King, right?"

"Yeah, that's it."

Daniella looked up the extension number to Mrs. King's room and picked up the receiver before she began to punch in the numbers. She smiled at Ryan as she waited.

"Did you ask Mrs. Thompson? She's outside with the kids right now."

"Ah, no, I didn't."

She pointed to the phone, signaling Mrs. King had answered the call. "Hi, Shonda. I have Nate's dad here in the office and he was wondering if Nate was still in the classroom? He wasn't outside waiting to be picked up."

Daniella went silent. She nodded her head and thanked Mrs. King before putting the receiver down.

She looked up at Ryan and shook her head. "She said Nate was dismissed with the rest of the class. Did he know you were going to pick him up today?"

A sickening knot formed at the bottom of Ryan's stomach. His heart began to beat faster, and his throat immediately felt dry. Denise knew Ryan was going to pick up Nate and go for ice cream afterwards, and Venice wouldn't have picked him up without telling Ryan or Denise.

"Yeah."

"Just check in with your wife, in case she picked him up, and ask the sub, Mrs. Thompson, if she saw him outside."

Ryan only managed to say, "Okay," before he hurried out of the office and jogged all the way back to the sidewalk. Beads of sweat rolled down his forehead.

"Mrs.—er, Thompson, is it? We haven't met. I'm Nate's Dad."

The teacher looked blankly at him. He pulled out his phone and showed Mrs. Thompson the picture of him, Denise, and Nate.

"Have you seen him by any chance? Nate? He was supposed to wait for me to pick him up."

She leaned forward and removed her sunglasses to get a better look of the picture he was showing her.

"Ah, yeah. Someone picked him up like about... ten minutes ago..."

"And you didn't think to check the identity of this 'someone'?" Ryan spluttered.

The hapless teacher merely opened her mouth helplessly.

Without saying another word, he called Denise and jogged back to his car. He turned on the ignition and put on his seat belt. As the phone rang, all he wanted to hear on the other end of the line was Denise letting him know that she had picked up Nate because she had gotten off work early. He wanted to hear that Nate was going to be waiting for him at home and they would go for ice cream. Anything. The chain of events he wanted to believe played like a movie in his mind, but he knew, somehow, in his gut, that it wasn't likely.

Denise picked up, sounding chipper. "Hey, babe."

He let out a deep breath, wanting to hear a 'yes' to his question. "Is Nate with you? Is he with you?"

"No. Why would he be with me? Honey, we discussed this yesterday, remember? You said you were going to pick him up... wait, is he not at school?"

Ryan let out several long breaths. His fingers began to lose feeling and he felt a numbness from behind his eyes travel around his mouth.

"Ryan... Ryan?"

He heard the panic in Denise's voice.

"Ryan!"

Suddenly all the noise began to fade away. He couldn't hear the cars passing through the street, or the horns of late parents getting their child's attention now they'd finally arrived. Everything was dead silent. He wanted to grip his hand around the steering wheel and move the gear into drive, but it required strength he didn't have.

"Ryan!"

Something was wrong and he couldn't make sense of it. Mrs. Thompson's voice echoed in his ears. *Someone picked him up. I'm not sure who it was, though.* Nate would never step foot in another car unless it was family, or he was instructed by Ryan or Denise. He wouldn't have gone with a stranger. If Nate had gone with a stranger and that was a big *if*, he knew Nate would have struggled to get into the car, and someone would have noticed Nate struggling. Right? Why didn't anyone notice a screaming kid? Did he scream? Did he yell for help?

"Someone picked him up," he murmured into the phone.

"What?!"

"Someone... someone picked... him up," he said, swallowing the pain he wasn't ready to deal with. "Get to the house," he choked. "Maybe he's there. If he's not, we'll call the police. And call Venice. Just get to the house, Denise."

Once he was back on the road, Ryan pushed past the speed limit. It was going to take him ten minutes to get back home, counting all the stoplights and stop signs. All he could do was hope that his little boy was waiting outside the house. He racked his brains trying to think of a harmless explanation for Nate's absence at the school gates: could it have been a neighbor who'd offered him a ride home? Skylar's mom or dad, thinking they were doing him and Denise a favor by picking Nate up, too? He couldn't help but feel this wasn't the case, however hard he tried to convince himself. If someone had taken Nate... perhaps all he could hope was for whoever had taken him had a change of heart and decided to let Nate go. Ryan repeated to himself that Nate was going to be safe and sound, and he would hug Nate as hard as he could and wouldn't let go. Ryan would go on to tell him how much he loved him and kiss him until Nate playfully pushed him away.

His eyes welled up thinking about the alternative.

As Ryan pulled into Kentwood Drive, he pressed on

the gas pedal a little harder. When he pulled into their driveway, Nate wasn't there as he'd hoped. Putting the car in park, he quickly jumped out and slammed the door behind him. The house seemed unusually eerie. He stopped in his tracks, not wanting to go through the front door. What if Nate wasn't inside? Taking the next step was terrifying.

He pushed away the negative thoughts and moved toward the front door. Without any hesitation, he quickly pulled out his keys and unlocked the door. He subconsciously held his breath and stepped inside the house. Everything was quiet.

"Nate?" he yelled.

He scanned the living room as he marched by. "Nate!"

When he walked into the kitchen, a wave of relief washed over him. Nate's backpack sat on the kitchen table by a bowl of ice cream, melting away. So, he *had* been dropped off at home, at least—but where was he now? Nate was nowhere in sight. As he approached the table, Ryan's heart dropped into his stomach and any relief he'd felt evaporated as he spotted Nate laying on the floor, unconscious. Ryan jolted forward, his knees landing heavily on the hardwood floor.

"Nate!" He felt his face. It was still warm. He leaned in, his head hovering over Nate's face, to listen for breathing. A little relief washed over him as he heard the tell-tale sound of air hissing in and out of his son's mouth. "You're going to be okay, buddy. Daddy's here," he whimpered. "Everything's going to be okay."

He wiped away the drool around Nate's mouth with his hand and kissed his soft warm cheek. Ryan pulled out his cell phone and dialed 9-1-1. He answered the dispatcher's questions, his eyes still on Nate. He wiped away the tears and choked on his words as he responded.

"Okay… I'll stay on the line," he replied.

The police and ambulance were expected to arrive in a few minutes. While he waited, he stroked Nate's hair. Every minute, the grueling thought of losing Nate began to register in his heart. He couldn't stop from sobbing as he gazed over his son. He traced his nose and his lips, wondering when he'd get to hear Nate's voice again. Memories of them playing hide-and-seek and practicing soccer in the backyard replayed in his mind. Nate's laughter rang in his ears.

He kissed him on the cheek and held his hand.

"Everything's going to be okay, Nate. Mommy's gonna be here any minute. The ambulance is coming. We're going to take you to the hospital, okay? You're going to be fine…you're going to be fine," he sobbed.

The thought of never seeing Nate again pinched his heart. He wasn't ready. He resolved he wasn't going to lose Nate. Not today.

He heard the sound of Denise's heels hurrying to the front door, which Ryan had left open.

"Ryan!" Denise screamed as she stepped inside the house.

Ryan's face scrunched up with pain. He wanted to yell out to her, but he couldn't get the words out.

"Nate!" she hollered.

"Here," he said, his voice soft and weak. "We're in here, Denise."

"Ryan! Where are you?"

"The kitchen!" Ryan hollered.

Denise rushed to the kitchen and met Ryan's eyes, which were overflowing with tears. Her eyebrows furrowed and lips began to quiver as she slowly neared her husband and son. Her eyes peered over and saw Nate. They widened as she got closer, feeling as if the world was crumbling down around her. Her legs became weaker with every step. She reached for the table for balance, her heartbeat racing, unable to comprehend what she was seeing right before her eyes.

The corners of her lips quivered as she spoke. "No, no, no, no, no..." She met Ryan's eyes, feeling a lump form in her throat. "Ryan," she began but then couldn't manage to finish the question she feared to ask.

"I called the ambulance," he explained, wiping his face with the back of his palm. "He's not responding, Denise," he said, looking at her helplessly. "He's breathing, but he's not responding...Denise, he's not responding."

It was then when it registered in Denise's mind what this meant.

Her loud sobs filled the room. They were soon drowned out by the sirens nearing their house. She leaned over and slipped her hand into Nate's.

"Please wake up for Mommy," she whimpered. "Please..."

CHAPTER 21

1934

Stephan Hex finished the last of his drink. His usual: Scotch on the rocks. He was a lucky man, which he had been aware of: married to a wonderful woman, father to two adorable boys. But despite this good fortune, increasingly, he felt as if he had the weight of the world on his shoulders. Shortly before his father, Joseph, had passed away, the SEA had been handed over to him. Stephan had little choice in the matter. The agency had started with the Hex lineage and would remain under the control of only Hex men. Of course, rules over the century would come to change—such as women joining the force in the twenty-first century—and the fundamental tenets of the agency were tweaked with each new leader's tenure, which blurred the lines between ethical and unethical conduct. But the main focus of the agency remained the same: to help people who had few other options.

He flipped through the thick file in front of him. Derek Will had come onto the SEA's radar a few years ago, when it was discovered that the criminal nicknamed "The Lord" they had been tracking was, in fact, Derek Will. He was running a successful drug operation in broad daylight. A man had contacted Neil about a bag of flour his wife had purchased, which turned out to be a bag of cocaine. From there, the SEA had brought in their forces, set up surveillance, and created profiles on all the employees who worked in the store where the cocaine had been delivered.

If taking down "The Lord" wasn't a major task in itself, given how long it had taken the SEA to uncover his true identity, Stephan also had other pressing matters to deal with. For a start, benefactors were withdrawing their support for the agency. It didn't sit right with them that they would never be given clear answers regarding what their donated money was going to be used for, despite Stephan's reminders that secrecy was a core part of the agency's work.

Stephan also had a project that was on the top of his priority list now. Nothing else mattered as much, other than receiving more funding for the SEA to keep the organization alive. His father had left him with a considerable amount of unfinished business and, given how important this operation was, Stephan's days were long and stressful. It didn't help that he had to execute this task without the board knowing what the project really entailed. It was a secret project that had been in the works, dating back to when his great grandfather was the head of the agency.

Project X.

For Project X to succeed, a large sum of money was needed to fund the project. As part of the project, a proposal for a new hospital at Lake View needed to be approved in order for construction to begin. The only way that was going to happen was if there was enough money for running the agency *and* building Lake View Hospital. A dry spell would mean an end to the agency and could very well mean Project X would never see the light of day. Stephan knew how important Project X would be for the coming generations, especially for the Hex clan. It had to go ahead.

He looked up when he heard the knock on his door. "Come in."

His secretary, Jackie Murphy, a veteran of the SEA, slipped inside for a moment. "Mr. Harper is here to see you, sir."

"I hope he comes bearing good news, Jackie."

"One can only hope, sir," she smiled. "I'll send him in."

A moment later, Neil stood in front of his desk with a black folder in his hand. Being one of the board of directors, he shouldered the difficult burden of making decisions that could never make everyone happy, but which would be for the greater good for the agency and the people it served. Should Neil's decisions result in a financial loss or taint the reputation of the agency, the result would be Neil losing his position on the board.

Stephan could tell by the look on Neil's face that there had been a change of plans.

He sighed. "Am I going to like this?"

Neil looked at him with an eyebrow raised. His attention turned to the ground as he paced to the other side of the room.

"Not all of it, sir," he said. He took a seat in one of the chairs facing the desk. "We know the SEA can only last for a few more years before we lose our cash flow. That's the harsh reality we are looking at. The donors are stepping out, and I know how vital this operation is to you, from what you've expressed to the board."

Stephan brought a finger to his chin as he leaned back in his chair. "Go on..."

"If we seek funding from those who have a... certain—*reputation*—and who might be, therefore, looking to improve their standing in the public eye—we will not have to give them any information about where this money is going. They won't ask questions if it means they might get some public credibility via association with the SEA." Neil paused. "With that in mind, bringing Derek Will on board will be a huge asset to this organization. If we bring Derek on board, then it would solve our problem. He would supply us with the money we would need to keep the agency running."

Stephan leaned back, not quite sure how he was feeling about Neil's proposition. "You want to use his dirty money?"

Neil locked eyes with Stephan, unsure of which way

the conversation was going to head. "Yes," he finally answered. "Sir, if this agency has any chance of survival, we need him. This is the only way we will be able to fund this organization without losing any more donors. And believe me, we have the dog on a leash, sir. He could be a blessing in disguise."

Stephan leaned forward, his head lowered. The agency had never been involved in exploitation. To destroy corruption was the sole reason why the agency had been formed in the first place. Now, Stephan was torn between doing the right thing, which would ultimately end the agency's existence if the donors continued dropping like flies or working with the most notorious man he'd ever encountered to carry out Project X successfully and save the SEA.

"And what do you suppose we do with Adrian? We're at a crossroads here. I offered him a position with the agency. We certainly can't work with Derek *and* have Adrian as an agent. Adrian wants him dead," he replied. "We can't go back on our word, Neil. You know that. That's not who we are."

"I understand, sir. However, Derek is our asset. And it's stated in the Articles of Accordance that '*in order for the Secret Eye Agency to survive and be a means for the public to rely on when the government has failed to do so, it must deem what is necessary to survive.*' Section five, paragraph two."

Neil had a point.

Stephan closed his eyes for a moment. His decision was not only going to decide the fate of the SEA but how they conducted business moving forward. Stephan opened Derek's file again, scanning it over. Derek had made over a million dollars in drug money in the past year alone. Stephan concluded that the number would only increase over the years.

"We will have to offer Adrian something in exchange for his previous offer."

"I understand that, sir, and I will get to that in a moment," Neil said, excitement in his eyes. "The founder of WIP requested to meet earlier. We will be working collectively with the WIP organization as a separate division under the SEA. It will be another legal—and respectable—source of income for the SEA. The agreement is in here," he said, handing over the folder.

Stephan took the folder and reviewed the first page.

He raised an eyebrow in concern. "Samantha Will? Now we have three members of the Will family tied to the SEA in some way or another? Neil, you very well know this cannot work," he responded in frustration.

"I understand, sir. If you take a look at the proposal, you will see how this will come together."

An intense expression came over Stephan's face. Neil couldn't help but wonder what was running through Stephan's mind right now. The document contained all the background information Neil had obtained on Derek, Samantha, and Adrian, plus the proposal and the agreement that would allow the WIP to begin its professional relationship with the SEA.

Once Stephan had finished reviewing the documents

that Neil had put together, he closed the folder with a look of bewilderment and let out a sigh of relief.

"This is a clever plan. Good job."

"Thank you, sir."

Stephan nodded. "Let Derek know he is no longer in power. I don't know how you will find the baby—I'm sure he will not give up that information so easily."

"I will do what is necessary to find the boy."

Stephan pursed his lips and handed Neil back the folder, along with Derek's. He was relieved it was off his desk.

"You have quite the mission on your hands, Neil."

"It's been quite a while since I've had a challenging mission. I will have the draft for the mission execution for your review this week."

"No later than Friday, Neil. It's time we begin moving forward."

"Absolutely, sir."

***

It was a lovely afternoon at Shallow's Lake. The sun blazed, making the ripples in the water sparkle. Samantha sat on the bench, pondering what was going to happen, and how her life was going to change. Although she was happy about the direction in which things were going, she didn't feel the joy she thought she would experience from knowing Derek could no longer hurt her. Even though love didn't exist between them—at least for Samantha it didn't—deep down, she still cared for the man. She cared for who he once was, at least. Somewhere in her heart, she felt guilty for wanting Derek to suffer, though she didn't know why, after all he'd put her through.

Startled, she looked to her side to find Adrian sitting next to her. "How long have you been here?"

"I saw you arrive fifteen minutes ago. I wanted you to have some time to yourself. I know you like to ponder over your thoughts."

"What brings you here?"

"Are you still upset with me?"

Samantha studied the water. She was intrigued by how calm, yet powerful it was. Water that cleaned dirty hands and provided hydration during the summer was also capable of flooding cities and wiping away homes to thousands and thousands of people with one tsunami. Interestingly, water had both a positive and negative effect on its surroundings. She found herself to be like the water. She provided benefit to those around her, never asking anything in return. However, now that she had become tired of being taken advantage of, she was going to turn the tables and bring the tsunami.

"No, I'm not mad at you."

"I'm doing what needed to be done a long time ago. I'm doing this for us."

She looked at him with sadness in her eyes. "There's no more us, Adrian."

Confused, he pressed further. "Then you *are* upset with me. Otherwise, you wouldn't have said that."

She rose to face him. "I'm mad at myself for allowing a man to make me feel worthless. I'm mad for allowing myself to depend on a man to love me, only to get hurt. I'm mad for putting everyone above me. I'm mad for not loving myself enough," she whimpered. "You chose to become an agent over me, Adrian. I am tired of being pushed down to being second. It's time that I put myself first."

"This is absurd, Sam. I'm only doing this because I don't want you to have to worry about him again. We both know how powerful he is—"

"You were ready that night at the charity event to kill him. You were going to do it all on your own. He was as powerful then as he is now. The only person who has changed is *you.* You're running away from me, and you don't even realize it."

Adrian's lips parted but said nothing. His eyes flickered out to the glistening water. Samantha *was* right about one thing, but it wasn't that he was running away from her. Or from anything else, for that matter.

As she began to walk away, he ventured, "I put you first every single time and you chose to stay with him rather than leave. How many times did I ask you to come with me? How many times did I *beg* you to leave him because I worried he would end up killing you? Every single time, you said to me, 'Adrian, I can't. Not right now.' I worried that… the love of my life was going to take her last breath at the hands of this despicable, pathetic excuse for a human being. But you always put him first. *Always.* I'm running towards the problem, Sam, not away from it. It does not mean I love you any less."

When she turned around, he was standing, tears in his eyes. Samantha felt her heart break and was momentarily stunned to discover she was still capable of feeling yet more pain after so long of feeling things couldn't get worse. She brought a hand over her trembling lips.

"I'm scared of losing you," she said, her voice soft.

"You're not going to lose me."

Adrian opened his arms as he stepped towards Samantha and pulled her in.

She wrapped her arms around him, gripping tight, and let out a loud wail.

"You've always been first, and you always will be," he said, choking on his words. "I can't lose you, Samantha."

CHAPTER 22

It had been two weeks since Nate was injected with steroids strong enough to give him brain seizures that resulted in him going into a vegetative state. Ryan and Denise took time off from work to try to cope with the situation, but it was a universal truth that coping with something as devastating as this could very well take a whole lifetime. Some losses would hurt for a little while before the heart began to mend itself, while others would leave a person shattered until their last breath.

The police and detectives had worked together to piece together the puzzle of that day's events, but they'd been left stumped. The house had been clean of fingerprints. There was no footage from the school showing any indication of how Nate was lured into a stranger's car. Surveillance cameras in the surrounding areas picked up a black sedan heading in the direction of their home. But then there was nothing.

It was clear that the abduction was well thought out,

and whoever planned it had known exactly where the security cameras were, which homeowners had installed them, and how to deactivate the systems in perfect synchronization to pull off the perfect crime.

The mastermind behind such events always had been the SEA.

***

Bruce had his team in position, ready to roll out their plan, when he received the message from Mr. Brar that forced him to call off the mission temporarily. The guilt that this was all his fault was eating at him. He had lost his appetite and could hardly sleep. He'd forced himself to shower and go for a walk, only to repeat the same scenario in his mind over and over again. *What if I hadn't come back? None of this would've happened if I hadn't provoked Marvin.* The question that irked him the most was *who attacked Nate?* Marvin wasn't a viable option in Bruce's mind, nor was Roy, because Nate wouldn't have gone with a stranger. So, who was able to lure Nate? It had to be someone they knew.

Like Bruce, Shadow also blamed herself. Marvin wanted her, and he had successfully proved no one was going to get in his way. What had happened to Nate seemed like an obvious warning to Shadow: it didn't matter whose life he was putting in danger or taking; Marvin was going to do anything in his power to get her back, or at least punish her. If she hadn't gotten involved with Evan, or hadn't allowed herself to continue their relationship, Nate would have been at home, safe with his family. She felt responsible for Marvin's actions and the pain he inflicted on everyone around her.

Ryan replayed that day over and over in his mind. If he had left the breakroom ten minutes earlier, he wouldn't have run into Dr. Jackson. He would have arrived at the school on time to pick up Nate, and the abductor would've missed their chance. His mind ran different scenarios, and every one of them led to more questions. *How did the person know I was going to be late that day? The ice cream… they knew about our plans.* The abductor had known about their routine, which meant they had been keeping a close eye on them the entire time. He shuddered thinking about someone watching them without their knowledge.

Venice blamed herself for not alerting Bruce when Marvin had paid her a visit. She hadn't had any visions prior to his visit, or afterwards, that would've pushed her to keep her family safe, and that frustrated her. Why didn't she see this coming? She didn't think Nate was going to be Marvin's target when he came looking for Evan and Shadow, who were at Bruce's safehouse. She had assumed he was after Shadow, or Bright. Marvin's visit replayed in her mind's eye. He had warned her, and she failed to take all the precautions she could to ensure her family stayed safe. Had she called Bruce, Nate would still be here.

She wept through the nights as Willow held her, trying to calm her down as she drowned in grief.

Nothing was going to be the same again.

Their lives were forever changed.

***

It was a bright Sunday afternoon. The harmonious chirps of the birds filled the air. The clear blue sky practically called for a day out in the park or the beach. The chugging motor of a lawnmower from a neighbor's lawn and the laughter and screams of the children at a birthday party next door was a stark reminder that life was continuing as normal, no matter what was going on in Denise and Ryan's world.

Denise sat at the kitchen table, next to the chair where Nate used to sit. Every morning, when she passed by his room, she desperately wanted to find him fast asleep in his bed. It still hadn't registered in her mind that her son was in a hospital bed, fighting to wake up.

She nursed her morning coffee in her pajamas, hair uncombed. She'd skipped makeup altogether, revealing a face puffy and chapped from sleepless nights filled with tears, agony, anger, and sadness. She was startled when the refrigerator door closed. Her eyes flickered over to Ryan, who was making his way to the table, a mug in his hand. He took a seat opposite her, resting the mug on the table.

"Your dad called," he said.

Denise looked up from her mug, sadness filling her eyes. The redness around his eyes hinted that Ryan had cried while he was on the phone with Bruce.

"What did he say?"

"They still don't know who took Nate... there's no footage, nothing they can work with. But it's someone we know."

Denise's eyes glistened with tears. "That could be anyone."

"He said that whoever took Nate doesn't work for the agency but is somehow linked to it. And he says... he says we may never know who did it."

Denise nodded.

It was a while before either one of them said anything else. They sipped on their drinks, trying to make sense of their tragedy. Ryan wanted to hunt down the person who had taken Nate away from them and put an end to their life. Revenge felt fair. But deep down, the logical part of him knew seeking revenge wouldn't reverse history. It would only make matters worse for him and Denise.

The sound of partygoers singing *Happy Birthday* drifted through the open window from next door. It made Denise and Ryan's hearts ache in their chests. Would they ever get to sing happy birthday to Nate again?

Even though Ryan had only just begun to make new memories with Nate, the pain he felt was as if someone had ripped into his chest and slowly dragged a knife through his heart. He knew the pain that Denise was feeling was worse. She remembered everything—holding Nate for the first time; giving him his first bath, watching him take his first steps, celebrating his first birthday. Ryan remembered none of that.

He felt her gaze on him, prompting him to look up from his mug of milk.

With tears streaming down her cheeks, she sobbed, "I'm so afraid, Ryan. My mind... I just... what if... what if he never wakes up?"

He rose from his chair, holding back his tears as he pulled out the chair next to hers and took a seat. Wrapping his arms around her, he replied, "I know, honey. I know." He half choked on the words. "We have to try our best to be optimistic. It's the only thing we have to rely on right now. Miracles happen every day, right?"

Denise buried her face in his neck, feeling scared and lost. Nothing made sense. To her, life had lost all meaning. In a span of just one year, she'd had to deal with the near loss of her husband, and now her son's life hung in the balance, too.

***

Bruce had insisted on Evan and Shadow staying in Brickwood for their own safety, but they both felt there was little point continuing to hide after what had happened to Nate and had returned to their house in Lake View. Marvin had shown he was going to hunt them and their loved ones down and would do anything to show he was in control.

Evan peered over in the portable bassinet next to him to find Bright still fast asleep. Luckily, Bright was an easy baby. He slept for a solid four hours before he was up, and then the routine began. First, they would change his diaper, then feed him, which would be followed by a routine burp check. Then, check his diaper once again before communicating with him in a baby voice before he fell back asleep.

Mr. Jingles walked around the flower beds, sniffing and searching for anything that was out of the ordinary. For him, Bright was still a little mystery. Loud cries in the middle of the night prompted him to come to Bright's rescue. And when he was fast asleep, Mr. Jingles remained by his side most of the time.

For Evan, the past two weeks seemed as if they had all merged into one day. Sure, he knew it was the lack of sleep because of the newborn in the house, but at the same time, everything had happened so suddenly. From Bright being born, to having to relocate as a safety precaution, to Nate fighting for his life, it was hard for Evan to wrap his mind around everything. He loved his nephew as if he were his own, and his anxiety over Nate just intensified the worry he had over his son. He'd wake up some days thinking it had all been a dream, but soon after, it would hit him like a tornado. He held Roy and Marvin accountable for what they had done to Nate, even though Evan knew it was someone else behind the actual assault.

Looking down at his lap, he picked up a letter that had been delivered to their house while they'd been away. He looked over at Bright again, knowing he'd do anything to protect him. In the letter, the SEA demanded Evan and Shadow hand over Bright into their custody, as if he was a missing package. Of course, Evan wasn't going to allow the SEA to get their hands on Bright, let alone come anywhere near him. However, keeping Bright safe would only be possible if the SEA was destroyed. With the SEA no longer operating, agents were powerless to cause harm even if they wanted to.

What Evan had a hard time wrapping his mind around was how inhumane the world seemed to have become. Or had it always been like this, and he was only just beginning to see? He couldn't grasp the idea that there were people lurking in the shadows who would take innocent lives just for power. Yes, the world wasn't a fair place. People had unfair things happen to them every day. But now that his own family was the target of something bigger than them, it had profoundly changed the way he viewed the world.

He wanted revenge. He wanted to end Marvin's life and that of the person who had harmed Nate.

Shadow stepped outside from the kitchen, with sweat dripping down her face and her hair drenched. She took a sip from her water bottle and turned towards Evan. She'd gone for a run the third time in a week, in an attempt to cool off the anger that had been raging inside of her after processing who her father was and what he did for a living. With fear of the SEA ever-present, she struggled to step outside of the house without feeling a rush of anxiety, ready to swallow her whole. However, repeating positive affirmations to herself and negating the thoughts that brought anxiety helped Shadow immensely to a point where she was in a better head space to be out in the world. Granted, some days were harder than others and it was a constant reminder that she wouldn't be able to jump back into a regular routine as quickly as she hoped. Evan advised her to stay indoors for her safety, but Shadow knew if there was any chance of normalcy she could experience, it would have to start with small steps. A short run was a start.

The guilt of what the SEA did to Nate ate at her every single day. She woke up every morning thinking about what the day would hold for her and her family. What was the SEA's next move? She'd apologized to Denise and Ryan, even though they didn't blame her. She couldn't believe they didn't. And while all of that was going on, she was supposed to enjoy her newborn, which seemed unfair given the awful circumstances. How was she supposed to relish the miracle of life when she didn't feel deserving of it, when chaos reigned all around?

"Hey," Shadow uttered as she took a seat beside him. "Is that the letter?"

"Yeah..." He looked at her with his sorrow-filled eyes. "You know I don't blame you for any of this, right?"

She looked away, wanting to believe him. Evan would remind her every day that what the SEA chose to do was not her fault. "I want to believe you, Evan," she started. "I really do, but..."

He wrapped his arm around her. "No one blames you for what happened. I don't. Denise doesn't. Ryan doesn't. Grandma doesn't—"

"What if that was Bright? If Ryan's ex put our son in a vegetative state just to send a message, wouldn't you blame them for it?"

Without hesitation, he answered, "No, I wouldn't. Ryan and Denise can't control what someone else is going to do."

She sighed and wiped away her tears. "Ever since I

came here, there has been nothing but chaos and pain."

"I understand how you're seeing it, but I don't see it that way. I never have and never will, and neither does the rest of the family. If the SEA didn't exist, none of this would've happened. That's how *I* look at it, and that's what needs to be eliminated from the picture."

Shadow nodded. "I wish I was handling it as well as you are."

Evan held out hope that Nate was going to wake up from his coma and everything was going to go back to normal. Hope. That's what kept Evan going and believing that the future was going to be better than what they were facing right now. It wasn't until everyone fell asleep at night that he lay awake thinking of all the worst-case scenarios which could still come true.

"We can't change what happened, but we can do something about it now," he said, looking down at the letter.

"This only ends one way."

Evan let out a deep sigh, following her train of thought. "I know."

They sat in silence for a moment before Evan rose from his seat, folding the letter and slipping it into his pocket. "I'm gonna go for a quick drive. I'll be back soon. Bright won't be up for another hour, hour and a half."

Shadow promptly rose from her seat and grabbed his wrist. "Evan...."

"I'm only going for a drive. I won't be gone for long."

She eyed the pocket where Evan had put the letter and

knew the thoughts that were whirling through his mind. "Evan," she commanded. "Whatever you're thinking of doing... please... don't do it."

He sighed.

"I'm just going for a drive, babe."

Shadow's bottom lip began to quiver. She wasn't convinced. Her chest slowly began to feel heavy and her throat tightened slightly. "Evan..." she sniffled. "I can't lose you. Please don't do anything—"

"Shadow, I promise. I just need to clear my head, and I really don't feel like going for a jog. And I'm tired of watching TV. I really don't want to read. I just want to put some music on and roam the streets for a bit."

She peered into his eyes, searching for the truth. As much as she wanted to believe him, she knew he was lying. Shadow knew Evan wouldn't do anything purposefully to jeopardize their family; at the same time, he always needed to create peace for everyone else around him. In protecting them, she feared he might sacrifice himself.

"If you're not back in twenty minutes—"

"I'm *not* going to do anything stupid. I promise. I'll be back, maybe not in twenty minutes, but I'll be back. I promise I won't end up in jail," he said, chuckling.

"That's not funny."

Evan leaned in and gave her a tight hug. "I know. I know."

She let out a deep sigh of anxiety. She didn't want Evan to leave her sight, out of fear for what might happen to him. A forced smile appeared on her face when she leaned back.

"Okay, but if you do make a pit stop anywhere, just make sure you're aware of your surroundings. Text me."

"I will. I love you."

"I love you, too."

Evan peered into the bassinet for a moment, in awe of how beautiful Bright was. His face was scrunched as if he was dreaming of something frightening. He kissed him on the forehead and whispered, "I'll be back, little guy."

Shadow watched Evan slip from the yard back into the house. When he was out of sight, she sat back down, a series of nightmarish scenarios about what might happen running through her mind.

CHAPTER 23

Sky sat at the table, reviewing the mission she had organized and put into motion in the last two weeks. It had been years since she'd planned and executed a mission on her own. The last assignment she had worked on before becoming the first female to take a seat with the board of directors was with Bruce. Their relationship at the time was strictly professional, but when it came time to assign her open assignments to agents, she realized even though Bruce was one of the best agents she'd had the pleasure of working with, she didn't want to be the reason why he never came back to work. Instead, she handed all her open assignments to another agent, which had caught Bruce off-guard. She had fallen in love with him. It wasn't planned, nor had she thought she'd ever find love again after losing her husband in a motorcycle accident.

"Hey," Bruce said as he walked into the kitchen. He was sweating through his shirt and his hair was damp with moisture.

He and Sky had retreated to Bruce's safehouse in Brickwood after Nate was taken to the hospital, and had been there since then.

"Hey. How was your run?"

"It was alright. I ran about four miles, and then right before I was about to hit my fifth, my heart almost gave up."

A subtle smile danced over her lips.

His eyebrows furrowed, sensing something was off. "What's wrong?"

"How come we're not married? I know it's not the best time to bring up this topic, but the outcome of tomorrow isn't guaranteed, and well, with everything that's happened, it's got me thinking..." she said with a smile that only he knew disguised sadness. "Do you not want to or…?"

It was the question he had been dreading even though he'd known it was coming.

"I want to, Sky, and I see myself spending the rest of my life with you," he began, the realization dawning on him that the perfect time he had been waiting for to break the news to Sky was never going to come.

"But…? I know when there's something else goin' on, Bruce. Don't underestimate a woman's intuition."

He couldn't make the same mistake again by dragging out the truth. That would only make things worse. He pulled up a chair and let out a sigh, feeling at unease of the conversation that was about to take place. "The thing is… I've been diagnosed with… cancer."

It took Sky a few minutes for the news to register, and then the reality of what Bruce said finally hit her like a lightning bolt.

"I have advanced prostate cancer," he sighed. He reached for her hand as he delivered the rest of the news. "I was diagnosed with it about two years ago. They did androgen deprivation therapy but my body isn't responding to the treatment anymore. Nothing's working and it's… it's spreading fast, honey… it's just a matter of time."

Sky's eyes filled with tears, and she held her hand over her mouth. Her face slowly scrunched in pain, knowing she was going to watch the love of her life slip away right in front of her eyes.

"There's nothing they can do?" she asked. It took all the energy she had to ask the question. She couldn't believe what she was hearing.

Bruce's eyes welled up, knowing the truth. He reached for her hand and gripped it tightly. "I'm going to fight this until I take my last breath. I'm not giving up."

"But…" she sobbed. Her eyes swam with tears until Bruce's face was just a blur. "We were supposed to spend the rest of our lives together. After we retired, we were supposed to travel around the world…" Her voice rose as she tried to hold in her cries. "We were supposed to grow old together. That's what we talked about."

Bruce felt his throat constrict. There was nothing he could say to make this easier to digest. "Hey," Bruce began, "you wanna travel around the world? We can still do that. I'm not on the force anymore. You have a ton of vacation days. We can still do that."

Sky jolted from her chair. "I need to get some fresh air," she said, walking out of the kitchen, her voice filled with pain. "I'll be out front."

Bruce watched as she rushed out of the house, the door slamming shut behind her. He slouched in his chair, wondering how on earth one person could bring such tremendous amounts of pain to the people around him.

***

When Evan reached his father's house, he sat in his car for a moment before getting out and heading to the front door. Bruce had given them keys to his place, just in case they ever needed anything or, if under unfortunate circumstances, they had to pack up his belongings because he wasn't around to do it.

Evan approached the front door, key in hand. He paused, contemplating exactly why he was there. *What am I doing?* He thought. What was he hoping for? What was he going to find there that would end the madness that had consumed their lives? Would he even find anything that could do that? The whole drive over to his father's house, his thoughts scattered this way and that, like dead leaves in the wind. Perhaps he would find a map or some notes, papers, that would give him hints about where Marvin lived, or where the SEA was located. Anything that led him to Marvin would be helpful. Although, if he was being at all honest with himself, he knew that rummaging through his father's house was likely a mistake; really, he had no idea what he was doing. Somehow, he knew he wasn't going to find what he was looking for, whatever that was. Instead of turning around and heading back to his car, however, Evan turned the doorknob and entered.

He closed the door behind him and took in the view. Bruce's home was nothing like he had imagined it, but it's not as if he really knew what his father's taste was like. The man had been gone for twenty-seven years; there was so much he still didn't know about his father. They were still in the process of rekindling their relationship.

As he cautiously walked past the living room towards the kitchen, the floor creaked beneath his feet. To his right was a hallway, and he walked into the first bedroom, which he assumed was Bruce's. He looked around but found nothing. The dresser was filled with neatly folded clothes only; there was nothing hidden beneath the socks and shirts. The nightstand was stacked with books on psychology and philosophy, but otherwise turned out to be empty. He picked up the books one by one and skimmed through the pages. Nothing stashed in between the pages. Before he left the bedroom, he looked at the mirror that hung on the wall. He carefully lifted the bottom away from the wall and peeked behind it. Still nothing.

Evan made his way to the next bedroom, a guest room, but found nothing there either. Then, he moved onto the last bedroom, which was used as an office. It was evident this was the place his father spent most of his time. The executive desk, accompanied by a laptop, faced a large TV mounted on the opposite wall. There was a large synthetic plant in the corner by the window and a painting of the ocean on the wall. Bruce seemed to have put more work into creating his office space than the rest of the house, which led Evan to think that if he was going to find anything, it would be here. He rummaged through each drawer in the desk but found to his dismay that the first drawers he opened were empty. What was the point of having an enormous desk if it was going to be kept empty? It wasn't until he reached the last drawer that he found a single piece of lined paper, dated March 24, 2000. It read:

Bruce—

A little reminder for when you're doubting yourself:

You did this for them. No matter how guilty you make yourself feel for leaving, this was the right decision at the time. You'll see them again soon. But right now, you need to remind yourself that what you did was right, and it was in their best interest. Right now, you're not the father they need. It's better this way. Had you stayed, they would have remembered you as a deadbeat father. In the long run, being away from them is best for everyone. You can't go back just yet, not that you have a choice, anyway. They won't understand, but hopefully one day they will and maybe then, you'll get a second chance and start over again. Until then, just hang in there. This isn't permanent. You will be reunited with your family soon enough.

Evan reread the message until he had tears in his eyes. He couldn't imagine the pain his father had endured, but as a new father himself, he couldn't wrap his mind around spending even just one day away from his son. Evan hadn't realized until he became a parent himself how hard it must have been for Bruce to make the decision to leave his family behind, only to begin his life someplace else, with no love nor family, and watch his kids grow up from afar, without a mother and a father.

Evan wondered how many times Bruce had reached down into the drawer and read the letter to himself. He held the letter in his hands, feeling closer to his father, before slipping the paper back into the drawer. He looked around the room, realizing any important information wasn't going to be kept here.

Deciding it was time to head back home, Evan stepped out of the room and walked down the hallway. Before he approached the living room, he could see a black sedan parked in front of the house out the window. Evan's heart began to race, knowing very well someone was paying him a visit. He prepared himself to face Marvin, feeling the little hairs on his neck lift in fear. The last time he had come face to face with the man, Evan had been left for dead. When he entered the living room, his heart dropped. A man in a black suit sat on the couch, one leg slung casually over the other, apparently waiting for him. Evan recognized him from a picture he'd seen. This was Shadow's father, Roy Hex. They locked eyes for a moment, as if waiting to see who would be the first to speak.

Roy scratched his chin and looked out the window as Evan stood stock still, paralyzed with fear.

"Whatever you're looking for, you're not going to find it here," he began, at last. "Look, I'm not going to waste your time, Evan. We're both busy men. You're a new father and I'm, well... I'm busy making sure no one has to die..." He let the words linger in the air. "I understand you don't want to give up Bright. He's your first born and, well, he's your son. But he's really *ours*, you see, either way. Whether you hand him over voluntarily or we force him out of your hands, he belongs to us."

It baffled Evan how offhand Roy was and how smoothly the words slipped out of his mouth, as if he was asking Evan for a simple favor and not his child.

Evan could barely muster the energy and strength to respond. He didn't know where to begin. "How can you do this to a family? How can you do this to your *own daughter*?"

Roy rose from the couch and buttoned his blazer. He walked towards Evan without breaking eye contact, until he stood less than a foot away from his son-in-law.

Evan clenched his fists so tightly his fingers numbed. He wanted to prepare himself if he needed to knock Roy to the ground. Deep down in his gut, however, he knew that should it come to that, Roy was far bigger than he was, and he would likely destroy Evan in seconds.

"There are things you don't know... things you can't comprehend," Roy declared. "We need Bright, and it'll benefit not only you and Shadow, but your father, as well, in the long-term. I suggest you give him up— for the *greater good*."

"But why do you need Bright? He's just a baby..."

Roy turned away and began to walk towards the door, leaving Evan without any answers. As he turned the doorknob, he turned around, making eye contact once again.

"It's going to get worse, you know. Your hallucinations... they're going to get worse. You know that, right? You're going to become delusional and you'll lose everything. Shadow's hallucinations are going to come back. I care about my daughter, regardless of what you might think. I don't want her to lose herself—which she will—and you can't save her, Evan," he concluded. "You need to give us Bright. It's the only solution."

"How do you know?"

Roy let his hand slip away from the doorknob and turned to face Evan. His hands slipped into his pockets. Furrowing his eyebrows, he peered at Evan. "Look, I'm not going to go into great detail, but understanding who you are... it's part of the job. You've been on our radar ever since Shadow moved in next door to you. There isn't anything we don't know about you, Evan."

"How do you know they're going to get worse?"

"My agents are highly trained experts in human behavioral psychology. You're not exactly a hard case to crack, Evan. You take a run every time you're anxious. You run your hand through your hair whenever you're overwhelmed. You have a big, sweet tooth, based on what we've found in your garbage. You're great with animals but never had one your entire life, until Shadow came along with Mr. .... *Jingles*, isn't it?" Evan's eyes widened. "Your ex-girlfriend, Harmony—the one before Shadow—you were planning on proposing, were you not? And your relationship specifically ended because of your hallucinations and nightmares. Isn't that right, Evan?"

"How long have you guys *really* been watching me?"

Roy gave him a pained look. "Give us Bright, Evan. That's all I'm asking."

Roy pulled his hands out of his pockets and turned around. Again, he reached for the doorknob.

"She knows what you do," Evan blurted, almost as if this was going to turn the tables and make Roy reconsider his demands. To his dismay, Roy remained unfazed.

"The truth always comes out, Evan. You can't run or hide from it." He shrugged.

"Then why didn't you just tell her from the very beginning instead of putting her through that... *hell* with Marvin. Why not be straightforward...with your own *daughter*?"

Roy chuckled and looked over his shoulder. "Oh, Marvin's not so bad, you know. Under all the hunger for power and pain, he's just another man who wants to be loved."

Evan was taken aback by Roy's response. Roy was adept at selectively answering questions. Evan was left no wiser than before their encounter.

Before Evan could say anything, Roy disappeared

behind the door.

Evan approached the window and watched through the blinds as the black sedan drove off down the street. When the car was no longer in sight, he slowly made his way to the couch where Roy had been sitting moments before and took a seat. Evan thought repeatedly about how Roy knew so much about him, right down to the dreams he couldn't even explain himself. Why was Bright so important to the agency, and why wouldn't Roy tell him? In Evan's experience, vagueness was only ever an indication of someone trying to keep something hidden, to stop it coming out into the light. But whatever the reason, how could Roy demand Evan and Shadow give up their son? It was impossible.

Only one thing seemed guaranteed: no one was safe. No one. He rose from the couch swiftly and left the house, locking the door behind him. He needed to talk to Shadow.

CHAPTER 24

Shadow's heart thumped in fear, and her hands trembled. A half hour after Evan had left, she was convinced she'd heard the front door softly open and close, without Evan's customary greeting. She cautiously checked the first floor, afraid Marvin would be waiting for her in the living room, but no one was there. When she reached the kitchen, she heard the stairs creak. Afraid, Shadow rushed to the counter and pulled out a knife from the knife stand and scurried to the hallway, equipped to take on her attacker. She stood shaking with fear. As the moments passed, there was nothing but dead silence.

Could she be hearing noises now? Her world was closing in on her. She'd been convinced there was someone else in the house, but now, there was nothing but the sound of her rapid breathing. Had her mind taken over? She no longer knew what was real and what was a figment of her imagination. She called Evan, knowing he would reassure her, but, after a few rings, his phone went to voicemail.

"Why aren't you picking up?" she whimpered to herself. Something still felt wrong.

She needed to get Bright and herself out of the house and someplace safe.

Shadow carefully picked up Bright from his bassinet and put him in his car seat. As she fumbled around to find her keys, it dawned on her that she had left them upstairs when she had used the restroom after her jog. And her wallet was upstairs, too. She felt her heart quicken again in her chest. Shadow paced back and forth in front of the car seat, in which Bright was still sound asleep. She needed to keep him safe, and to do that, she had to overcome her fear of going upstairs. All she needed was to grab her keys off the dresser, and get out of the house, as fast as possible. That was it.

But she couldn't bring herself to move. She began to sob silently, feeling helpless. Her body quivered. She started to shake away the numbness that had traveled to her hands. She tried to regulate her breathing. *Okay, okay. Everything's okay. There's no one upstairs. No one's here. Just run upstairs, get the keys and wallet, then come back down. That's all you have to do. It's that simple. No one's going to hurt you. No one's there. No one's there.* Beads of sweat formed on her palms. Nothing seemed to be working: anxiety raged through her like a torrent. Tears streamed down her face. She crouched down and kissed Bright on the forehead and pushed through her fear as she headed for the hallway. The staircase seemed suddenly daunting, even though she'd gone up and down it hundreds of times. *Run up, grab your stuff and go. That's it.* She inhaled a deep shuddering breath and sprinted up the stairs. When she got to the top of the staircase, she looked down the hallway and, to her relief, no one had magically appeared. Her mind had convinced her that as soon as she reached the top of the staircase, either Marvin or someone else was going to be standing there at the bottom, waiting for her to come back down. She took another deep breath for courage and dashed into the bedroom, unable to shake off the feeling someone might still be watching. She spotted her keys on the dresser, right where she had left them. But her wallet wasn't there. She distinctly remembered she had left her wallet next to her keys, and now it was gone. She groaned softly in despair.

Where was her wallet? She needed it. Her cash, credit cards, driver's license—it was all there. She could leave the house without it, but was it smart? Not really. What if she needed to fill up with gas? Or had to make a pit stop at the grocery store for Bright? Or what if she were pulled over by a police officer? She *needed* her wallet, and it wasn't where she had left it. Someone *had* been here. And they'd taken it. She felt a tingling sensation in her legs. Her heart thumped louder by the second. She wasn't delusional. *Someone. Was. Here.*

Bright's cry pierced the silence.

Her eyes widened with terror. *Oh my god.* She whipped around. Why was Bright crying? He had been fed and wasn't supposed to be up for another hour. Was there someone downstairs? She hadn't heard anything— but then, she questioned in horror, could she have been so terrified of what she'd find upstairs that she'd missed the sound of the door opening in the front hall?

She squeezed her eyes shut for a moment, clenched her fists, and dashed out of their bedroom. She started down the stairs and, in a panic, tripped over her feet, gripping onto the hand railing just in time to stop her from plummeting the rest of the way down. Bright's cries continued. Staggering down the stairs, Shadow saw the car seat, just the way she had left it. She found Bright, wide mouthed and shrieking. She quickly undid his straps, picked him up, and put him against her shoulder. Softly patting his back, Shadow peered around the doorframe into the kitchen. No one was there. The latch was still intact on the back door. She cautiously moved towards the office. The door was slightly ajar. Shadow couldn't recall whether or not it had been like that all morning.

With a rush of courage, she stood at a distance from the doorway and pushed the door back.

Her soul jumped out of her body as Mr. Jingles ran out of the room.

"Fuck! Mr. Jingles!" she hissed.

He looked up at her, his tail swaying from side to side, a bemused expression on his face, and then sauntered his way over to the glass back door, meowing.

"You scared the shit out of me!"

Mr. Jingles peered at her, not sharing her concern. All he wanted was to be out in the garden with the flowers, which he appreciated more than anyone else.

Shaking, she opened the back door, letting Mr. Jingles free. She watched as he trotted towards the flowers.

The beginnings of something like relief started to come over Shadow. Bright's cries were fading. Shadow made her way back to the hallway and the car seat. She carefully put Bright back into the seat and buckled him up. She wasn't going to take any chances. As quickly as she could, she walked out the front door, closed and locked it behind her. Only once she was safely behind the wheel with Bright in the back seat did a sense of peace begin to return. She peeled out of the driveway, away from the house, from the danger she feared it contained.

CHAPTER 25

Bruce and Sky sat on the back porch. She rested her head on his shoulder, knowing that she had very little time left with the man who had captured her heart some time ago. She hadn't made peace with the fact that she was going to lose Bruce to a disease that should have had an effective cure by now, but she had shed all the tears she had in her for the day.

"We should execute the plan… as soon as possible. Then we can spend as much time as we can with one another."

"Yeah," he answered. His voice was rather hoarse. It was slowly hitting him after seeing how emotional Sky had become that he was going to die. It wasn't that he hadn't thought about death or what his last days might look and feel like, but he hadn't thought much about the emotional toll it was going to take on everyone else who'd be affected by the news. He'd been so wrapped up in coming home and seeing his family, cancer had taken a backseat.

She shifted away from him and looked into his eyes. "You have to tell your family after we complete this mission. You can't keep this from them. It's not fair."

Bruce nodded. She sounded a lot like Mr. Brar. He didn't like to hear it, but he knew it was irrational to think he could go on without telling them. And he couldn't risk leaving them in the dark a second time.

"You're right," he said, clearing his throat. "We should get back and go over the game plan one more time and begin prep."

"Yeah."

They headed back to the blueprint for the rundown.

After a long moment of silence, Sky looked at Bruce with concern. "What if this doesn't work?"

He was taken aback with the sudden lack of confidence, a rare occurrence with Sky. She was by far one of the most confident and secure women he'd met on the force. Bruce let out a nervous laugh.

"Of course it will. Why do you think it wouldn't?"

She looked at the blueprint that she had designed. Given that she had spent countless hours working on plans and contingency plans, every angle considered, exact routes mapped, agents assigned, there was only the tiniest chance that Sky had missed something that would lead to the whole plan collapsing. There was still doubt. Doubt that swelled in the chance—however small—that something might go wrong. It was enough for her to question the whole operation.

"Nate's in a coma," she reminded him. "No-one saw

that coming. They are *always* one step ahead of us, Bruce. What if this doesn't work? Or if we get caught? What if they get to you before we're able to roll out the mission? You're a target now, too, you know?"

Sky pulled her hair back and let out a long breath.

Bruce pursed his lips. "Yeah, I know," he replied.

He traced his finger on the edge of the kitchen table, his eyes focused on the pattern of the dark-stained wood. He'd built the table with Sky one summer. It was one of their projects that they'd done together after being inspired by a channel on the Home Improvement Network. There were similar projects all over the house: he thought of the bookcase in the upstairs bedroom they'd built one winter. The upstairs bathroom was another project they had worked on. Even though it took them a month to complete, they had thoroughly enjoyed annoying one another and creating a space that melted their stress away. They had built more than just a home together. Memories lingered in every room. One day, Bruce knew these moments with him in the kitchen, poring over the plans, would be but memories for Sky, too.

"There's always the possibility of something not working. All we can do is give it our all, right? Isn't that what life's about? Taking the leap with the ones you love and hoping it works out for the best? But in the end, you know… you know you've got each other, no matter how bad it gets." His eyes glistened with sadness. He knew where her heart was and where the doubt was coming from. She was afraid to lose him, and he wasn't ready to let her go, either. He cleared his throat and continued. "We've got a solid team behind us. They're trained and have been through every extreme mission we can think of."

She looked at him glumly. She placed her hand over his and whispered, "Aren't you scared?"

He placed his other hand on top of hers and rubbed it softly. His voice cracked when he answered. "I don't want to be."

Sky's lips quivered and her eyes filled with tears.

"Why does it have to be like this?"

"I don't know, honey. I ask myself that same question and all I can think of is what Mr. Brar said to me before I joined the agency."

"What did he say?"

"There are things that happen in our life that we will never be able to make sense of. It comes down to what we did in a previous life, how we lived before. Karmic debt. I think that's the only explanation that kind of helps me navigate through it."

"But... that's so unfair. You have been the sweetest, kindest person in *this* life!"

"I've tried my best, Sky. But the universe has its own plan. All I can do is continue to do my best and give it my all."

***

On the way back home, Evan had zoned in and out while he was driving, dwelling on the short, vague conversation he'd had with Roy. Either Roy was an extremely well-trained liar making threats, which was plausible, or he was, in fact, telling the truth, and the agency was prepared to take Bright by force. If it was the latter, it meant they were never going to be safe, and the idea of a peaceful life was out the window. Was there a scenario in which the three of them could live their lives without interference from the agency? Was there hope? Evan doubted it. Being realistic was the only way out of the predicament they were in. Their safety seemed dependent on them giving in and agreeing to what the SEA wanted, but Evan wasn't ready to surrender.

He'd reached the stop light, a long line of cars ahead of him. When the light switched from red to green, the cars remained at a halt. Evan couldn't see far enough to find the reason for the traffic. Five minutes had passed, and he'd only moved forward an inch. He pulled out his phone, figuring he'd be in line for a while given how slow the traffic was moving, and saw two missed calls from Shadow, but no text messages. He pressed the button on the screen and heard the ring. He waited, only to be directed to her voice mail. He tried again but this time it was no different. A text message later, he'd moved forward by a foot and could begin to see the cause of the traffic congestion. Flashing red and blue lights were visible up ahead.

Police cars surrounded the intersection, and a fire truck was parked off to the side. He looked back at his phone but there was no response yet. He presumed Shadow and Bright were sound asleep and put his phone back in the cup holder. Slowly, each car inched forward to be ushered towards a diagonal detour.

As he got closer, the accident site came into view. There was only one car involved. A black car. He stared at the scene, an uneasy feeling starting to wash over him. He checked his phone again. No response. His car crept forward, enabling him to get a better view of who was in the car. He saw the figure of a woman in the driver's seat, slumped over the steering wheel. As he inched forward, Evan could see the license plate on the Mercedes Benz but couldn't make out the numbers and letters. Evan inhaled a deep breath and exhaled, then picked up his phone to see if Shadow had texted him back. Still, no response.

He watched a firefighter trek from the truck in his black suit with neon stripes, hard hat on, carrying a hydraulic ram to the driver's side. Evan couldn't see that side of the car. It quickly registered in his mind that the car must have collided with another vehicle in order for the firefighters to forcibly remove the door. *Right?* Had there been another vehicle? Or, heaven forbid, a pedestrian?

The traffic was beginning to move more quickly than before. He leaned close to the steering wheel and watched like a hawk. As moments passed, his anxiety levels rose. It seemed to Evan the firefighter was taking his time opening the car door, and the suspense was killing him.

There was a detective on the scene. He was writing in his notepad, looking into the car, and talking to the officers, which struck Evan as odd. In most cases, there was no need for a detective. Usually, the regular beat cops would handle collisions. *Unless... there was a criminal case to investigate.* The more Evan analyzed the scene, the more he realized it was beyond a car accident. Something was off. He could feel it in his gut.

The person in the car next to him was watching the scene just as intently as he was. The line of traffic remained at a standstill. As the firefighter was still working on getting the driver out, the detective was writing down information and turning the pages in his notebook faster than the traffic was moving. Evan's eyes lingered over the firefighter still using the tool to break open the car door. He saw him motion his teammate over, and they exchanged a few words before the car door was finally cracked open.

Moments later, the EMTs pulled out a stretcher and prepared for the driver to be pulled out of the driver's seat. The detective approached the vehicle, looking in the backseat. He opened the back door with no trouble and leaned in. As the man continued to inspect the car, Evan grew worried. *What is he looking in the backseat for?*

The traffic began to move again. When Evan neared the intersection, he felt his chest tighten. His hands began to shake. Surely this had to be some sort of horrid mistake. The license plate of the mangled car, now clearly visible, was the number registered to Shadow's vehicle.

His mind began to shut down. Shadow was the driver, and she wasn't moving. *Where was Bright?* He released the seatbelt, turned on his emergency blinkers, and got out of his car. When his feet hit the asphalt, his body didn't want to move. Evan urged every fiber in his body to propel him forwards. His heart dropped with every step he took towards Shadow's car. He begged the universe to let it be someone else behind the wheel. He hoped someone had stolen the car out of the driveway and that Shadow was still at home with Bright. Anybody but Shadow. *Anybody.*

The police officer noticed Evan from a distance approaching the car and held up his hand.

"Sir, I'm going to have to ask you to stop right there."

Evan saw the officer's mouth move, but his mind didn't comprehend the words, or even the language. When he continued in the direction of the car, the police officer put his hand on his gun and this time shouted, "Sir, freeze!"

In that instant, Evan came to a halt. Wide-eyed and heart pounding, he stood still. A part of him wanted to puke, knowing that it was Shadow behind the wheel. The other part of his mind tried to convince him the woman was someone other than Shadow.

Deep down, Evan knew the truth.

"I'm sorry, sir," he stuttered. "B-b-but... I think... that's my wife."

The officer's hand lifted off the gun, and his face softened with concern. He approached Evan, this time his voice calm and soothing.

"What's your name, son?"

Evan looked around him.

People were watching him with curiosity. The world seemed to slow down a little bit, to the point where he was able to catch his breath and hear onlookers' voices that stood from afar on the sidewalk. The pace of the traffic around the intersection had begun to pick up.

"My name?" he asked, confused.

Evan noticed the officer's yellow mustache and the beads of sweat forming on his forehead. It was evident he had been outside for quite some time, and an unsettling feeling overcame Evan once again. Something about this accident didn't appear normal.

"My name's… Evan."

"Evan," he began, "I'm Sergeant Richard Crown with the ninth precinct. What's your wife's name?"

Evan's eyebrows furrowed at the question. "Shadow," he answered slowly. "I just wanna see if that's her. Can I just go see, please?"

The officer nodded his head. "That's your car over there?" he asked, pointing in the direction of where Evan's car sat idle with the emergency blinkers flashing.

Evan peered over his shoulder in the direction. He craned his neck back and nodded at Sergeant Crown. "Yeah… that's my car. Can I just—"

"Why don't you pull up off to the side here and we can run over a few things?"

Sergeant Crown wore a sympathetic but firm look which only left Evan with more concern. All he wanted to do was check whether the woman behind the wheel was in fact Shadow. He hesitated for a moment, but before he could open his mouth and speak, Sergeant Crown nodded at him to proceed towards his car.

Dazed, Evan stumbled to his car, disregarding the

grumpy stares from drivers finally able to put a face to the person responsible for further blocking traffic, with all their angry honks and furious hand gestures. Starting his engine, he slowly merged with the rest of the traffic in the direction they were going, before pulling up to one side, where Sergeant Crown had suggested.

When he got out of the car, he saw one of the firefighters lever the car door off to the side of the road. Sergeant Crown was standing in position with the detective by his side. Evan unsteadily made his way over to Sergeant Crown, his heart drumming in his ears. He couldn't see what was going on from where he was, but it was apparent they were getting ready to pull the woman out of the car and onto the stretcher. Questions raced through his mind. When they finally pulled out the woman and carefully placed her on the stretcher, he saw who it was. She wore familiar jogging gear. Her eyes were closed. A brace had been placed around her neck. A deep gash on her hairline spilled blood down her face. Although she wasn't recognizable as her usual self right now, Evan knew it was Shadow.

Her nose—he remembered tracing that Roman nose in the middle of the night. Her lips—he remembered those full lips he kissed every morning. The jawline that he kissed along so softly, making her giggle, was indisputably hers.

"That's my wife." The words traveled out of his mouth, leaving his body in shock. "That's my wife," he said in a panic as he rushed over. "*That's my wife!*"

The male EMT looked at Evan in the eyes and said

sternly, "Sir, please step back. We've gotta take her to the hospital."

Evan opened his mouth, but the words had lodged in his throat. His eyes brimmed with tears.

Sergeant Crown walked over and put his hand on Evan's shoulder. "Evan, Detective Lucas has a couple of questions he wants to ask you."

Evan cocked his head to the side and met his eyes. "Huh?"

Detective Lucas, wearing a pantsuit and glasses with black rims, stood beside Sergeant Crown, with his small notebook flipped open. He smiled briefly at Evan before looking back at the scene.

"Detective Lucas wants to speak to you," Crown repeated. "Maybe you can help point us—"

"Wait. Wait...Wait! Where's my son? Where's Bright? My son. Where is he?"

Sergeant Crown let out a sigh. His eyebrows furrowed and he hesitated slightly before speaking again.

"Detective Lucas has some questions he needs you to answer for the investigation."

"Wh—why is there an investigation?"

"Let's come here to the side," Sergeant Crown offered as he led Evan to the curb, away from the scene. "Your wife needs you by her side. The quicker you answer Detective Lucas's questions, the quicker you can go be with her."

Evan ran his fingers through his hair. He wanted to scream but couldn't. His body was slowly shutting down. He began to feel weak. His brain could no longer comprehend exactly what was going on, but deep down, he knew it was something so terrible his mind couldn't accept it.

"Okay."

Sergeant Crown stepped back to the scene, leaving Detective Lucas and Evan alone. The detective skimmed through his notes before meeting Evan's eyes.

"Your wife's name is Shadow Hex, correct?"

Evan nodded. "Yeah."

"They were unable to find her license or any kind of identification other than the registration for the car. That's the only way we were able to identify her. Does she normally drive without her wallet or purse?"

"No. She's not negligent. I… I don't know why she drove without her license."

Detective Lucas put his pen to the paper and noted his answer.

"Did you notice anything out of the ordinary today, or even in the past few days?"

Evan's eyes flickered over to Shadow's car as he scrambled to comprehend the detective's question. Glass was scattered everywhere. He watched the firefighters step over the shards as they began to prepare for their departure.

He didn't understand why Shadow had left the house. His mind jumped from Shadow to Marvin to Roy. The conversation he had earlier with Roy came forward in his mind, playing like a broken record. They had been watching them and waiting.

Slowly a lump formed in the middle of his throat. His

mind was spinning, and it all boiled down to this: if he hadn't gone over to his father's house, none of this would have happened.

Detective Lucas's voice dragged him back to reality. "Was there anything out of the ordinary you can think of that might help with this case?"

Evan wiped away a tear from the corner of his eye. "No. Not that I can think of."

"Whoever did this wanted your son for a reason I simply can't think of. Can you think of anyone who could be responsible for kidnapping your son? Any friends or families who have shown interest beyond what we would consider normal?"

Evan's face went pale. "Bright's *gone*?"

A flash of irritation passed over the detective's face. "Nobody informed you?" He sighed heavily. "I'm sorry to have to tell you this, but yes. From what we've gathered, it appears that your son is currently missing. We've got a search team in place that is equipped to handle these types of situations."

Nothing Detective Lucas said was registering in Evan's mind. He couldn't fathom that his newborn son had been taken. His mind revisited his encounter with Shadow's father earlier that day. This incident had Roy written all over it.

"Is there anyone who has threatened you or your family? Is there a reason why someone would want to kidnap your son?"

"No," he forced himself to say, knowing all too well who

wanted Bright, if not why.

"Mmm. Can you give me details about your son? His name is Bright? How old is he? Color of his hair and eyes?"

He cleared his throat and responded. "Yeah... Bright Storm. Brown hair, blue eyes, light skinned... under a month old."

Detective Lucas looked up from his notepad, shocked. "Oh jeez… I'm really sorry. I had no idea he was only a newborn. We're going to find whoever did this."

Evan nodded, knowing they were never going to find him. He was gone. Roy had what he wanted.

"Were there any eyewitnesses?" Evan asked, not knowing why or whether it mattered at this point.

"We had one witness who claims she saw your wife's car swerve as if to avoid hitting something, although there didn't appear to be anything in the way. Then she hit that pole." He gestured towards a street sign now listing at an angle. "There was a woman in the parking lot over there who said she heard a loud screech as she was putting her groceries in her car, and another woman was at the traffic lights when she saw two black SUVs pull up after the accident but before she could see anything else, it was her turn to go." His voice trailed off as he began to flip back to the beginning of his notes. "And that's it— that's all we've got in terms of eyewitnesses," he said, pausing and contemplating what to say next. "Once we get the security footage from around the area, we'll have a better sense of what happened. Right now, it's still a puzzle. The only piece we have is that it appears as if your wife was potentially being followed—which may or may not have led to the accident—and that your son is missing." He frowned. "Is there a chance you could also have been followed, Evan?"

"Ah, I'm not sure… it's a lot for me to take in. I'm still trying to… wrap my head around all of this."

"I understand," he said, slipping the notebook into his jacket pocket. "Right now, it would be best to be with your wife. She was taken to the Lake View Hospital. Meanwhile, we'll be working on this case and keep you posted if we find any leads."

Evan nodded and stood still for a moment before heading off to his car. His eyes welled up as he looked straight into the road and wondered, *what if Shadow was right?* If he had kept away from her the day she warned him about Marvin and the agency, they wouldn't be in this situation right now. None of this would have happened.

But there was no human in existence who could control fate. He was in love with her, and he knew nothing could ever change the way he felt about Shadow. But their love was only bringing pain. Was it worth continuing their marriage if their loved ones were going to suffer as a result?

The drive to Lake View Hospital consisted of more questions and theories, and a call to Venice; no solutions were found. After he pulled up into a parking spot, he sat and stared blankly through the windshield. How did they get here? Bright was missing. Shadow was in the hospital. Nate was in a vegetative state, with no guarantee he'd wake up. All Evan could do was obsess about the things they could have done differently, things that could have prevented this moment in time. From the minute Bright took his first breath, there was nothing but chaos surrounding them, no matter where they went. He couldn't help despair that no matter what they did, they were never going to live a normal life.

This day itself had been too much for him. All he wanted to do was break down and cry. He was exhausted and on the verge of collapse. But he knew if he gave in to that impulse right now, there was no telling how long it would be before he managed to pull himself back together.

Right now, Shadow needed him by her side.

Forcing himself to get out of the car, Evan hesitated by the trunk. If he was being honest with himself, he didn't want to know what had happened to Shadow. He wanted to numb the feeling, to run away from it, but that made him feel like a coward. He didn't want to walk into the hospital, afraid of yet more bad news. What he really wanted to do was get back into his car and drive away, but he knew running away wasn't the answer. But—what was he going to find when he went into that hospital room? Was Shadow still going to be covered in blood? Would she need surgery? Evan knew the only thing to do was to go in and find out, but he wasn't ready to face the reality. His chest began to pound rapidly, enough for him to realize that if he didn't take a step forward, he was going to unleash the huge anxiety attack that had been building inside of him since he saw the accident.

He took one stride towards the door from the parking

lot to the hospital, and then a second, following each with deep breaths. Moments later, he reached the automatic doors, where he paused, bracing himself for what waited for him on the other side.

Evan approached the help desk and found that Shadow was on the third floor; Venice had already signed in to see her. He walked under the fluorescent lights to the elevator. His heart drummed louder. When he reached the third floor, he searched for room twenty-six. He could hear the distant murmur of voices. Taking a deep breath, Evan walked into the room and noticed Venice sitting in the corner. Her eyes were fixed on a nurse, who was sitting on a chair next to Shadow. A medical assistant stood nearby, lending a helping hand. As Evan moved forward, he saw that the nurse was suturing the gash in Shadow's forehead. Relief washed over him as he realized Shadow was conscious.

Shadow peered at him with pain in her eyes. Her eyes glistened with tears, but she remained calm and silent.

Before Evan could formulate a sentence, he was intercepted by the doctor who stood by Shadow's bed, examining a medical chart.

"You must be Evan," the doctor said.

"Yeah," he responded softly.

He held out his hand and introduced himself. "I'm Dr. Davis. Your grandmother let us know you were on your way."

Evan nodded.

"Can we step outside just for a moment? I'd like to talk

to you about a few things."

"Uh, yeah. I just want to quickly see my wife first."

With a slight hesitation, the doctor answered. "Yes, of course."

Evan approached Shadow's bedside, across from the nurse and assistant who were focused on stitching the open wound.

"Hey, babe," he said softly, feeling his throat constrict with guilt and sadness. He looked into her eyes, not knowing where to begin. The short conversation he'd had with her before he left home came rushing back. She was here because of him. Bright had been kidnapped because of him. Reaching for her hand, he softly rubbed the back of her palm. "There's something—"

"Evan, I appreciate you want time with your wife," Mr. Davis interrupted, "But can I please speak to you for a moment?"

He peered over at Dr. Davis, reluctant to leave Shadow's side. However, sensing the urgency in Dr. Davis' tone, Evan slipped away from Shadow's bedside and followed Dr. Davis into the hallway. His stomach churned, suspecting that a conversation which required stepping outside was not going to be one that delivered any good news.

"Your wife is going to be fine. I just wanted to say that first before anything else. She's going to need plenty of rest and we're going to keep her here overnight so she's not up and about at home. Patients tend to do that. She doesn't have a concussion, so that's... incredible in my book. She said her wrist, head, and nose were hurting, so we're going to get her in for an x-ray once the nurse is done stitching her up, just to make sure she doesn't have any broken bones. She suffered a blow to her forehead, so she lost a lot of blood, but she's going to recover."

Evan's initial relief faded as he saw the slight shift in the doctor's body language. Here it was, the bad news the doctor hadn't wanted to start with.

"The reason why I pulled you out here is because—and I already told your grandmother this—your wife doesn't know about your son. That he's missing. She wanted to know where he was. To calm her down, we had to tell her that he was getting examined. She thinks he's getting evaluated right now..."

"Oh," Evan let out the breath he was holding.

"I just wanted you to be on the same page as everyone else. I know that the police are working on finding where your son is. It would be best to break the news once she's had her x-rays. She's most likely still reeling from the fact that she was in an accident."

"Yeah... I'll tell her once she gets back from getting her x-rays."

"I'm really sorry about this. I really am. It's awful. I've got two kids of my own. I can't imagine..."

Evan nodded. He knew at this point sympathy was all people could offer. They couldn't and wouldn't be able to do anything to fix the situation.

Dr. Davis placed a hand on Evan's shoulder. "Please let me know if there's anything you need. Our staff is here for you and ready to answer any questions you may have. We'll have x-rays done as soon as they're finished in there."

"Thank you," Evan muttered, forcing a smile.

And just like that, Dr. Davis whisked off in the opposite direction to attend to another patient. Like everyone else, Shadow was just another patient to him, Evan thought. She only held value for Dr. Davis up until she was discharged. Evan understood that it was the nature of the doctor's job, but he desperately wanted to have someone else shoulder a little bit of the weight he was carrying around. He wanted someone to understand, but no one could—except possibly for Denise. She might understand. She *would* understand. But like him, she, too, needed help with the enormous burden she was struggling with. He couldn't lean on her.

Evan let out a deep sigh before stepping back into the room. There was a vacant chair next to Venice, which he made himself comfortable in. He craned his neck towards her, hoping she would look him in the eyes and say something, but she didn't. She continued to watch the nurse suture Shadow's forehead.

"You're quiet," Evan managed to murmur under his breath. He couldn't tell what was going on in her mind. For the first time in his life, he couldn't read Venice.

"I saw it happen," she responded, her voice low but crisp.

"You saw the accident?"

She nodded. "In my vision. I asked the doctor when the accident took place. He gave me the estimated time of when Shadow was hit." Then, she finally met his eyes. "I had the vision of Shadow's accident ten minutes before it actually happened. Glass everywhere. Police at the scene. She looked… lifeless. I thought she was dead."

Evan could see tears forming in her eyes, but she was resilient.

She continued, "I wanted to call her. I wanted to tell her not to leave the house. But I couldn't. I wasn't able to, Evan." Her voice began to tremble. "By the time I managed to get up, I got your call." Her eyes flickered towards Shadow, who remained quietly cooperative. "They took him. But I don't know where," she said, pausing. "Why did you let her leave the house?"

Evan contemplated telling her the complete truth, but he knew this wasn't the right time for an interrogation. "I know. I should've been there."

Venice raised an eyebrow. "Yeah, you *should* have. Where did you go?"

"Grandma," he responded in annoyance, ignoring her inquiry. "Not right now. We can talk about that later."

Venice persisted.

"Where was she going, Evan? Why weren't you home? You should have been at home, knowing that with everything going on, you were both at risk. What were you doing?"

"This isn't the time or place for questions." Evan motioned to her to keep her voice down.

She stared stonily at him before whispering, "You went looking for trouble, didn't you?"

Before Evan could answer, the nurse made her way over

to them, peeling off her medical gloves. "She's all done," she said with a smile. "We're gonna take her for x-rays in a moment. It'll take about half an hour or so. You're free to come along if you'd like."

Evan nodded. "Thank you."

He got up and went to Shadow, whose eyes followed his every movement. Venice remained seated.

Evan reached for his wife's hand. "How... how are you feeling? Are you in any pain? Is there anything I can get you... water? A snack?"

"I feel sore. I'm not in a lot of pain, if that helps. They gave me plenty of meds."

He chuckled. "The doctor said you're getting an x-ray for your wrist and nose. Which wrist is it?"

"Yeah... it's my left wrist." Shadow looked at Venice, who had an odd expression on her face, with concern. "Venice... what are you thinking?"

"Nothing, honey," Venice responded, smiling weakly and rising from her chair. She held her purse in her hand as she strolled over to Shadow's bedside. "I'm in awe of your strength."

Evan managed to smile and added, "She's definitely one tough cookie."

Shadow let out a deep sigh. "As much as I want to cry and scream and seek revenge, it's not going to change anything that's already happened. There's no point." She glanced at them both before looking back at the end of her bed. "Listen. I know they took Bright. That's the only reason they'd come after me. I pretended that I didn't know he was kidnapped, because who was gonna believe me if I told them it was the SEA? Marvin took Bright. I recognized his voice before I blacked out at the accident site. Or at least I think it was his voice. There was more than one of them."

Venice and Evan exchanged glances.

"Did they say where they were taking him?" Evan asked, his heart pumping twice as fast.

Shadow sighed. "I only heard snatches of the conversation... I was fading fast after the car crashed. But I think I heard them mention my father. I heard the name *Roy*. It'll be someplace no one knows about. Bright's safe, though. I know they won't hurt him."

The room fell silent. Evan and Venice shot worried looks at one another, wondering how Shadow was so sure that the SEA wouldn't harm Bright.

"Why does your father need Bright?" Venice asked.

"I have no idea," Shadow replied. "But whatever it is, there's a bigger picture. They must *need* him for something. And because they need him, there's no way they're gonna hurt him."

Venice pursed her lips and met Evan's eyes. "This needs to end."

"Grandma, where are you going?"

"I need to call Willow," she said with tears in her eyes. "And then your father."

Without exchanging another word, Venice left the room, with her head held high, tears streaming down her cheeks.

"I feel so horrible," Shadow began. The room slowly

began to fill with the sound of her sobs.

"Babe..."

She looked at him, her eyes wet, her forehead knitted together. "I feel *relieved* that they took him. I shouldn't feel this way. But I do. And I hate it. What's wrong with me? I know I love my baby, but at the same time, I feel like I don't... because if I did, I wouldn't be feeling like this," she wept. "Why do I feel this way?"

Evan reflected for a moment about what it must be like to be standing in Shadow's shoes. He went down a mental list of things to find justification. She was sleep deprived. She'd just been in a car accident. He factored in postpartum depression, which their doctor had warned them of even before Bright was born. They were hiding from a malevolent agency that would do them harm. And now, as if all that weren't enough, their son was kidnapped. He ran his fingers gently through her hair, letting her express her emotions.

"Honey, listen to me for a second," Evan said, reaching for her hand. "Under the very best of circumstances, when a new mom gives birth, she goes through a lot of different physical and emotional changes. On top of that, we're dealing with all these awful things happening, all out of our control. It's not normal for parents to have to go away and hide someplace else, out of fear, because they're a target. It's not normal. *Nothing* about our situation is normal. You're feeling relieved only because you don't have to keep feeling scared or anxious about what's going to happen next. The worst has already happened. They took Bright. Not for good—we're going to get him back, I promise you—but the worst has already happened. Now you're not gonna be playing out a hundred different scenarios about how the SEA is gonna get to us. Just because you feel this way doesn't mean you don't love Bright more than anything."

Shadow gazed at him, her eyebrows furrowed. "I don't know what I did to deserve such a loving and compassionate husband."

Evan chuckled wearily as he leaned and softly kissed her forehead. "We both know that I'm the lucky one."

They gazed at each other as if this was the first time either of them had laid their eyes on one another. Their love for one another ran far deeper than they even knew. Their souls had connected a lifetime ago, and regardless of the tragedy that unfolded in front of them, or what storm they were heading into, or whether they knew *how* to love one another, they were always going to find their way back to each other.

"We're gonna get him back," Evan reassured her. "It doesn't end here."

Shadow nodded, feeling the tiniest amount of tension drain from her aching body.

Just then, the nurse reappeared, ready to take Shadow for her x-rays. Evan followed and sat in the waiting room as the technician moved ahead and began setting up the equipment.

Evan thought about what he and Shadow hadn't said out loud. Their lives were only going to become more complicated here on out. There were no guarantees, as much as they both wanted to stay hopeful. Evan felt afraid, and he knew Shadow felt it, too. Only time would reveal what was going to happen to their little family.

Was love going to be enough this time around?

CHAPTER 26

After learning that Shadow had fractured her wrist and was going to need to wear a sling, Evan stayed with her for a few hours until she fell asleep. Denise stopped by for a couple of minutes on her way to see Nate. They spoke briefly about Shadow's accident before Evan inquired about Nate. His health hadn't improved. He was still in a coma, but Denise remained hopeful about his recovery. "I've been through this once before, and we'll get through it again," she said confidently. It inspired Evan how strong and determined Denise was. Granted, it took every ounce of her energy to keep herself optimistic and to not let what the SEA had done to Nate define her, but like Evan, she refused to accept this was Nate's fate.

On his way home, Evan grabbed dinner at Mean Burgers and sat at a table by himself. The tables and booths around him were filled with a number of people. It struck him that he hadn't eaten alone since his own hospital stay last year.

As he munched on his burger, the earlier argument with Shadow replayed in his mind. For her safety, Evan had insisted on staying with her until Shadow was going to be discharged from the hospital. Shadow wanted Evan to get a good night's rest and had reassured him that nothing was going to happen to her: the worst *had* happened. The SEA had kidnapped Bright. Evan and Shadow were of little interest or use to them now. Even though Shadow had made a valid point, Evan felt uncomfortable leaving her all alone. In the end, anything was possible; he wouldn't put it past those responsible for Bright's kidnapping to come back for Shadow—a point he had made over and over— but as sweet as Shadow was, she was also stubborn.

While he ate his burger and fries, Evan scanned the room. There was nothing out of the ordinary that he could see. But he did notice couples, laughing and enjoying the night. He wished every person in the room would cherish the moments they had with their partners or spouses because, in the blink of an eye, everything could change. He wished they knew how lucky they were to have their loved ones with them tonight. Sure, they probably had plenty of issues, but how many of them had problems that included spouses laying in a hospital bed and the abduction of their newborn child? He bet himself there wasn't one single person going through what he was going through. Just as his thoughts began to derail, heading towards pity town, he shook away the miserable ruminations and finished his dinner before heading home.

Just as Evan approached the house, he spotted Mr. Brar sitting in his wheelchair on the front porch, with his oxygen tank close by. It brought back so many memories of a younger Evan finding Mr. Brar out late at night, pondering life's biggest mysteries. There had never been a time when Evan didn't take the chance to take a seat next to him on the porch for a little chat before going inside.

Mr. Brar broke into a smile followed by a light chuckle as Evan approached the porch. "Your face always brightens up my day," he said, opening his arms for a hug.

Evan grinned, pushing his pain deep down into the pit of his stomach. He hugged him tight, feeling a sense of ease flow through his body. "It's always good to see you."

Mr. Brar gazed at Evan with a hint of sadness in his eyes. He reached over and stroked Evan's head, remembering the little boy he once was.

"I want you to know," he began with his voice cracking, "you have a place in my heart no one can replace." He brushed away the tears before continuing. "When Ekam passed away... there was no one who was capable of putting a smile on my face like you were able to. Your love for me all these years made me feel like a father. And it breaks my heart to see what you're going through."

Evan's eyes welled up. His throat tightened. In all the time he'd known Mr. Brar, there hadn't been sweeter words exchanged between the two of them than in that moment. A part of Evan was beginning to feel the loss he'd been trying so hard to avoid all day.

"I love you, too," Evan sniffled.

They sat in silence for a bit in the still night. The street remained quiet. In the indigo sky above them, the stars glistened, as if a reminder that even in the darkest of times, there was still a glimmer of light to be found in the distance, however faint. It was only a matter of how long that journey was going to take before the light broke into the darkness.

At length Mr. Brar spoke. "We had to put that project we were working on, on hold."

Evan nodded, knowing they couldn't openly talk about what Bruce had been working on. After Venice had spoken to Bruce, updating him about Bright's kidnapping, he had phoned Evan, assuring his son that first and foremost, they would bring Bright back home.

Evan pursed his lips. "What are the chances of… this new project not working out in our favor?"

Mr. Brar let out a short sigh. His eyes flickered out onto the street. "Do you want my honest answer?"

"Yeah."

"They're high. I can't begin to imagine what else is out there that we don't know about. I mean, there are things out there that people have no idea about, stuff that I can't talk about. Knowing that they'll never give away all the information, it's hard not to think that there isn't another organization somewhere, and that the two of them are working together. Or that there are locations that aren't on the map, that they've turned into smaller agencies or incubators for God knows what. The possibilities are endless, if you ask me… but your father won't rest until he makes things right."

Evan mulled over his answer. His pupils dilated at the thought of never being able to see his son again. "Then he's gone... no one's gonna find him. If he can't find him, there's no chance of getting him back."

"I will fight until my last breath to bring him back home, Evan. That's a promise. There's always hope, and we have to hold on to that."

"Thank you," Evan offered.

"When do you go back to work?" Mr. Brar asked, changing the subject.

"I go back in the beginning of November."

"Oh, that's right. You've been off since August, right?"

"Yeah," he replied. "I have a question for ya if you don't mind me asking."

"After all these years, you're asking if it's okay to ask me a question?" Mr. Brar teased. "You know I welcome all dialogue. What's your question, son?"

"How come you guys never had kids?"

Mr. Brar smiled and looked out into the street again. "We tried so many times, Evan. So many. Miscarriage after miscarriage. Ekam...well, she felt defeated. I didn't blame her. We tried everything we could, but... the way I had to look at it, after some point, was that we just weren't meant to have kids. It was *hukam*."

Evan's eyebrows furrowed, hearing the novel word for the first time in his life. "What's hukam? What does that mean?"

"It means it was the will of God. I never used to be

a religious person, believe it or not. I didn't have this beautiful beard or wear a turban when I was younger. I used to drink and eat meat, things a practicing Sikh is prohibited from consuming. But after years of us trying to get pregnant, we finally came to terms that it was hukam, and that's when I started to build my faith and learn what it meant to truly be a Sikh. God had other plans for us. We ended up moving out here and then your parents moved in next door a few years later. When we had finally gotten to a place of acceptance, guess who came along?"

"Who?"

With a grin he responded, "Denise. Then, a year later, you. You two may have not been ours to raise, but my goodness, you two brought us so much joy. *So* much joy. Ekam and I both never wanted to be away from you two. Our hearts were so full. I believe it was around your fifth birthday, when it hit me, the role me and Ekam were supposed to play in your guys' lives. Venice was raising you two on her own, and we knew we wanted to help in any way we could."

Evan chuckled. "I wouldn't have thought of it like that."

"Ekam and I wanted to experience life in different cities. Explore the world. I'm not sure if we ever told you that. After we realized we weren't going to have kids, we decided there was no need to be stuck in one city for the rest of our lives. Nothing was holding us down at that point."

Evan was surprised. "But you've lived here forever."

Mr. Brar raised his eyebrows. "I know. Our plans

changed— *hukam*. We didn't want to leave after becoming so attached to you kids. It just didn't make sense. We were so happy. Leaving would've been a mistake and we both knew it."

Evan was taken by surprise. "I never knew that."

"You'd become such a huge part of our lives and we couldn't see ourselves living without you guys next door. So, we stayed put. It was one of the easiest decisions we had ever made."

"Not a lot of people would do that. Stick around for people who aren't even family."

Mr. Brar nodded. "When you truly love someone, you'll do anything for them."

Evan contemplated the words for some time as they lapsed back into silence. It was true, what Mr. Brar said. When you truly loved someone, you would do even the things you never imagined yourself doing. Love was both amazing and terrifying. It could make the most rational person irrational, the sane insane. Evan wondered how far he would go in the name of love.

"Did you know that my dad was going to leave?"

Mr. Brar nodded. "I used to sit here on the porch in the middle of the night when I couldn't sleep," he started, as the memory came flooding back and began playing in his mind's eye. "One night, I spotted your father standing on the sidewalk, his back turned towards the house. It was well past midnight. I waited a couple of minutes, wondering if he would turn around, but he didn't. So I went to him, thinking he would say something or at least look at me. But he just stood there, almost frozen. He had a blank expression on his face," he recalled. The porch fell back in silence. A flush of sadness filled his eyes. "I asked him if everything was alright. And he said... 'I can't find the will to live anymore.' I had never seen your father so... devastated. So, I had him recruited."

Evan raised his eyebrows. "Wait, he joined the agency because of you?"

Mr. Brar nodded.

"How come this is the first time I'm hearing about it?"

Mr. Brar sighed. "I know how it all sounds, and looks, but when someone is going through depression, nothing makes sense anymore. The only reason I wanted your father recruited was because I felt like it was something I could do to help him feel like he had a purpose again." He looked at Evan. "The SEA puts first floor agents through rigorous tests and molds them into... I want to say soldiers, but it's not the word I'm looking for. To put it simply, you don't come out as the same person as you went in. Agents develop a high tolerance to pain, to suffering. If you can hold on to your humanity, not become too detached—it can help, having that purpose. I thought your father needed that. A way through his grief," he explained. "Your father needed the SEA so he could overcome his battle, but I never thought he would be gone for twenty-seven years. I just wanted him to *live*. I wanted him to be here for you guys."

Evan remained quiet and let himself process the information.

"I have so many questions."

"I may have the answers you're looking for."

"So...why did *you* join the SEA?"

Mr. Brar peered over at him and smiled. "We're going to have to save that conversation for another time, son."

Evan grinned, despite everything. "Okay. I'm gonna hold you to it."

"I'll tell you this though."

"What is it?"

"Almost everyone who joins or is recruited has a past they need saving from. I'm who I am because of the SEA. Don't get me wrong. They've done some pretty messed up things, and things are only getting worse now, but back when I started, there was still some good left. I'm living proof of that goodness. Or at least I'd like to think so."

CHAPTER 27

1934

Derek stood in the middle of a newly furnished office overlooking the city. His law firm, Will & Associates, was going to officially open for business in the coming month. His top five clients had already moved their business strictly to Derek's firm. It was a plan Derek had been working on for the past three years. Having his own firm was not only going to attract more attention, but it would put the word out that he had just become more powerful than any other man in Pool View. After the ad had come out in the paper for positions available at Will & Associates, over two hundred applicants had responded. This dream of his had once included Adrian, when it seemed that the Will brothers were going to be unstoppable. But from where Derek stood now, it was apparent that Adrian's priorities had changed.

Derek's secretary, Beatrice Walker, quietly stepped

inside the room. "Mr. Will, there's someone by the name of Neil Harper here to see you. And there are five other men with him..."

Derek's eyebrows furrowed. He had no appointment with a man named Neil Harper. "Send him in. Only him," he stated clearly.

"Will do, sir," she responded, stepping outside the room.

A moment later Neil strolled into the room, alone. He observed the space around him, absorbing how Derek had set up his office and how expensive each piece of furniture was. When it came to Derek Will, money was no issue.

"How can I help you, Mr. Harper?"

Neil chuckled. "I'm here to help you, Derek. And please, call me Neil."

The light in Derek's eyes dimmed. In that moment, he knew he wasn't going to like what was coming. "Who are you, then, *Neil*?"

"That's not as important as what I'm about to offer you."

"I couldn't possibly imagine what you could give me that I don't already have," Derek said coolly.

Neil took a sudden step towards Derek. "As of this moment, you have nothing," he said.

Derek appeared unfazed. "I would be very careful of what I say," he said, taking a step forward and holding Neil's gaze. "Are you aware of who you're dealing with?"

"Here is the deal, Derek," Neil said, "I work for the SEA. Quite frankly, I have the authority to end your life right now, if I wanted to, which was the original plan. However, I don't want to do that. I would have to assign more of my agents to this assignment, which means more time would be allocated towards something we could have avoided. Ultimately, time and money will be wasted on a pathetic scumbag such as yourself. I'm here to save your life. All you need to do is to become a SEA donor. *Benefactor*, if you prefer."

Derek scoffed.

"And why would I do that?" he said. "Your threats to have me killed don't scare me, Mr. Harper. I'm a powerful man. You don't think I have security?"

"You're going to give us access to all of the sources of your income," Neil said, calmly. "We've been keeping an eye on you, Derek. Or should I call you '*The Lord*,' instead? That's the name, after all, some of your more nefarious '*business associates*' know you as, right?" Neil stated with a coy smile. "There is a lot you don't want going public. We are also going to need you to tell us who has Samantha's baby."

Derek scoffed a second time, but it seemed to Neil that he was rattled. "Your list of demands is not my concern."

"Is that so? It may be of interest to you that as of today, we have moved your wife out of the house."

For a moment, the room fell into silence.

"You can't do that," Derek hissed.

"The SEA can do whatever it pleases, especially when people are in danger. You have no idea the pain you have caused your wife. Or shall I say, your *soon to be ex*-wife. She's a powerful woman, and it seems you underestimated her," he said, smiling.

"She belongs with me, you fucking cunt! I will slit your throat in front of your entire fucking family!"

Neil chuckled at Derek's outburst. "You are not as powerful as you think. Not anymore, at least."

Derek's breathing quickened. The vein in his forehead had become visible at this point. "She's still *my fucking wife*," he hissed. "Tell me where she is, and you can have access to whatever it is that your agency wants."

Neil shook his head. "You're in no position to negotiate. You've had a good run, Derek. Now, it's time for us to take over."

Derek pursed his lips, and looked away, out of the window with its impressive view of the city. He was silent for a moment, his hands clenched in fists by his side. "You promised her you would find the baby?"

"Samantha's relationship with the agency will remain confidential. I will give you some time to think everything over, of course. I hope this Friday will mark the beginning of our relationship," Neil said, feeling satisfied.

Once Neil had left the premises, Derek weighed up their conversation. He paced back and forth in his office, his hands on his hips. Derek couldn't stand to be dictated to. He had to have the upper hand. His anger rose the more he thought about Samantha and her betrayal. He dropped to his knees, finally coming to terms with the possibility that the end of his life had come. He would lose everything he had worked for. His face turned bright pink as he let out a loud scream. With a fist, Derek slammed the floor, over and over, as tears rolled down his cheeks.

"No!" he repeated.

Beatrice rushed into the room, only to be taken aback by Derek's state. "Mr. Will, is everything alright?"

"Get out! Get out! *Get out*!"

Without another word, Beatrice hurried out of the room, terrified.

The life he once knew, the power he once had, was being challenged. But Derek Will never gave up without a fight.

***

Derek spent the rest of the week trying to come up with a viable plan that would remove him from the shackles the SEA had put him in. A lack of sleep and alcohol only clouded his judgement and sent him in a downward spiral every night since Neil paid him a visit. Alone, he sat at the dining table with a bottle of whiskey, taking a sip after every thought that crossed his mind. His eyes welled up when his heart reminded him of the good woman he had lost. He never imagined his life without Samantha, but deep down, he knew he didn't deserve her. Now, it was his biggest regret. It hadn't occurred to Derek that Samantha was capable of involving the SEA in their personal matters, let alone getting in touch with a very powerful agency. Derek couldn't force her back home, and he very well knew he wasn't going to find her easily. Now that the SEA had stepped in, reaching Samantha was going to be impossible.

But then it dawned on him. There was one card left that would keep him in the game.

If Derek was going to die, he was going to die as a powerful man with his dignity intact. He was not going to allow anyone to take the very last thing that took him years to accumulate: his reputation.

***

When Friday arrived, Derek had closed an account in the morning, which was a success for the firm. Meetings with prospects led to new clients. In his office, he sat resplendent behind his desk, feeling proud of himself. More than anything, he was looking forward to his meeting with Neil.

Beatrice popped her head in the doorway at around half noon, holding a notepad against her chest. "Mr. Will, Mr. Harper has just arrived."

Derek nodded. "Send him in."

Neil stepped into the office with a folder of his own. He could already taste his victory.

"Derek."

"Neil," he started, "Please, take a seat."

Derek watched as Neil settled himself in the chair facing his desk.

Neil began. "Let me be very clear. There will be no negotiations."

"Certainly," Derek said, chuckling under his breath. "I do not need to negotiate. I simply want to talk."

Neil hesitated for a moment. He studied Derek's demeanor and observed the surroundings for any visible threat.

"Do tell."

"They call me The Lord for a reason. I am sure you and your men have figured that out by now. I could tear this city apart if I wanted to, Neil. You may belong to the SEA, claiming to do all good in the name of the people. A '*transparent organization*,' you call yourselves," he scoffed, "but you are bullies. Like me. You may not see it, but years from now, that is what your organization will be. One big bully. But there is a difference between your organization and me," he said, leaning forward. "I don't lie about who I am. Now, I know why you have come to collect my money. Your donors do not want to be associated with an organization that won't reveal how the money is being handled. Am I correct?"

Neil kept his composure, though Derek's confidence was unnerving. Underneath his calmness, a fire was burning. Derek's words crawled underneath his skin.

Derek spoke again. "I am curious to find out what would happen if I accidentally let it slip to the press what the SEA has really been up to? Now, how would that look for you? Huh?"

"You are forgetting you are powerless. You have nothing."

Derek clicked his tongue and leaned back in his chair. A malicious smile crept over his face. "I would respectfully have to disagree. I have some *very* powerful friends, Neil. And, as long as I am alive, I have all that I need. Let me remind you— have me killed, and you will find yourself scrounging on the streets for pieces of bread. You would not want that for yourself or your family, now would you, Neil?"

At the mention of his family, Neil had to stop himself from lunging across the desk and choking Derek until he turned blue and his eyes rolled back in his head.

Derek pushed forward the folder he had for Neil. "The SEA is vulnerable. I know I am an asset to you. A massive one. So, here are my terms."

"I said no negotiations," Neil muttered through gritted teeth.

"It is not a negotiation. It's a deal. Take it or leave it."

Neil picked up the folder and began reading the document. The further he read, the more he realized, with horror, that Derek was way ahead of the SEA, despite how he might have appeared to react in their first meeting. Derek was proving himself to be one of the most intelligent men Neil had come across, and it irked him to realize he was torn between wanting to kill Derek and applaud him for his sheer cunning. Derek had his operation set up in a way that his suppliers would never be recognized for their product, and the dealings were complex enough to ensure the safety of everyone in his operation. All the roads led to Derek for one simple reason: to make it clear that he always held the power, no matter who was standing in front of him.

Derek had led the SEA right where he wanted them.

When Neil finished, he was almost speechless.

"Impressive," he finally said.

"I know as much about the agency as you know about me," Derek said with a grin. "You are not the only ones who have surveillance teams. Take the document and have Stephan take a look at it. Take this as well," he said, sliding another folder towards Neil. "Revenue and expense reports for my operation. Have the agreement signed and on my secretary's desk on Monday, and I will know we have a deal."

***

Stephan paced back and forth in his office.

"For fuck's sake, Neil! He put us in a fuckin' corner! A seat on the board?!" Stephan's cheeks flushed pink and red in complete rage.

It had been ten minutes since Stephan began roaring about the mess Neil had created.

"How did you let this happen?" he hissed.

It had been years since the last time Neil found himself in hot water. Even then, the situation was nowhere near as bad as the one they were dealing with now.

"Sir, we underestimated him."

"Underestimated? No, no. That is not what happened here. Our men failed, Neil. They *failed*! Two years. Two fuckin' years and this is what we get in return? He's got us by the balls. How did he get all this information about our activities? Where has it come from?"

Stephan stopped in his tracks for a second. He put his hand on his hip and ran his fingers through his hair before he started to pace once again. "There is a traitor in the organization. There's no other explanation."

"Sir, it was our top agents that were assigned to this

mission. They have been with the agency far too long to risk their title or payroll."

Stephan scoffed. He headed in the direction of the bar cart that was stationed in the corner of his office. He poured himself a scotch, straight. He took a sip and pondered in silence. Something about this was not making sense. There was a chance one of his top tier agents was the traitor, and the thought of being betrayed by one of his own sickened him. However, his gut was pulling him in a different direction. Slowly his eyes met with Neil's.

"The donors," he blurted.

"What about the donors, sir?"

"Six out of the ten withdrew their donation the same day."

Neil tried to follow Stephan's train of thought, but given the state he was in, his mind wasn't currently as sharp as it normally would be. He had thrown up in the bathroom prior to the meeting, dreading the conversation with Stephan. He was hardly himself and found it difficult to concentrate while all he could think about was how he was going to support his family if he lost his job at the SEA.

"You think Derek got them to walk away... but how?" he ventured.

Stephan seemed frustrated by Neil's confusion.

"How convenient is it that our donors step away around the same time Derek opens his new firm? He *paid them*, Neil. He has given them stakes in his company, which is by far more beneficial to them. They know they will be getting a return. Guaranteed. Moreover, he knew if the donors pulled out, we'd need funding, and we'd need it fast, and that we'd try to get it from him. He was planning this. If word gets out that Derek Will managed to bring the SEA to its knees, we are done."

"What do you want me to do, sir?" he asked nervously.

Stephan looked Neil dead in the eyes and responded. "There's nothing we can do at this point. He has us on a leash. Without Will's money, this organization is done."

Neil stood in position. The guilt trickled through his body, and he feared what all of this meant for his career.

"Sir, I'm sure there is—"

"There is nothing we can do now. He has been ahead of us this entire time. He is intelligent. It worries me what will happen when he is sworn in."

"Sir! You can't be serious. Bringing him in as a board member will only damage the agency. In that case, we are better off without him."

Stephan moseyed his way back to the desk and set his glass down. "I know," he replied with sadness. He hadn't foreseen any of the events unfolding that all led to this moment. He was forced to give up the upper hand, and it made his heart sink. Derek, the devious creature Stephan knew he was, would infect the agency with his corrupt morals, and the agency that was founded on good ethics would slowly slip away. Stephan knew eventually the SEA wouldn't be recognized as the agency his family had started. "But we can't afford to continue without funding, and we can't afford for our activities to be made public right now. It would jeopardize the safety of every client we've ever had." Stephan thought too of Project X, yet to be birthed, but didn't mention it to Neil.

"Give me the agreement."

Neil stared at Stephan in disbelief. "Sir—"

"Neil! Hand me the damn paper!"

He handed Stephan the document and watched as he signed their power away.

CHAPTER 28

Evan lay in bed, recalling the memory. His heart was still racing. There wasn't a day when he didn't wake up with more questions, and so far, he still had no answers. Now he wondered about the SEA and what they were hiding. The conversation he had with Roy at Bruce's house replayed in his mind. *Your delusions... they're going to get worse. You'll lose everything. Shadow's delusions are going to come back. I care about my daughter. I don't want her to lose herself, which she will, and you won't be able to save her, Evan.*

What was Project X? How was giving up Bright going to benefit not only him, but Shadow and Bruce, as well? The SEA was clearly prepared to do whatever they had to in order to get Bright into their possession, even if it meant almost killing Shadow, Roy's only child.

He looked over at the other half of the bed, empty. Everything came flashing back, reminding him of the nightmarish reality he was living in. He'd gotten used to having Shadow next to him when he would wake up in the middle of the night. Sometimes she was awake before his eyes fluttered open after having a dream, and sometimes she was sound asleep. His stomach turned itself upside down. He didn't want to lose her. He *couldn't.*

He sat up in bed and then headed for the bathroom. He peered at himself in the mirror, as he did almost every night, and wondered what the bigger picture was. *There must be a bigger picture.* But he was still missing pieces of the puzzle.

The faucet ran for a moment until the water warmed, and then Evan rinsed his face of sweat and patted it dry. He stood in his room for a minute before going downstairs for a glass of water. As he neared to the bottom of the stairs, he felt a presence in the darkness. He couldn't reach for the light switch from where he stood, and the heaviness in his chest pulled him back from taking another step forward. Like a child, he wanted to run up the stairs; the thought of someone grabbing him by the foot or his arm made the hair on the back of his neck rise. Beads of sweat began to form at the edge of his hairline.

His chest rose rapidly as he thought about what might lurk in the darkness. His hands trembled and as much as he tried to control his breathing, he couldn't seem to regulate it. His mind was spinning out of control each passing second. What if Marvin was standing in the dark, waiting to attack? He had done this once before. As he tried to calm himself, he knew he had only two options: either push past the fear and flip the switch or go back upstairs and wait for the sun to come up before heading back downstairs. Shaking, he took another step, now a little closer to the light switch. Sliding his hand across the wall, he tried to reach for it. He felt the base of the switch plate and knew he was close. As soon as he flipped the switch, the room came to life.

His eyes scanned the living room. No one. He let out a sigh of relief and trotted down the last few steps and navigated his way into the kitchen. Again, before taking another step in the dark, he switched on the light, illuminating the kitchen.

Mr. Jingles emerged from underneath the table, a spot he'd retreated to after they had returned home from Brickwood. The sudden movement took Evan by surprise and sent his heart racing once again. "You need to stop doing that, Mr. Jingles," he exclaimed. Before he proceeded towards the refrigerator, he bent down and scratched the side of the cat's jaw, resulting in soft purrs. Afterwards, he retrieved the water pitcher and grabbed a glass from the cabinet. In the silent room, all he heard was the sound of the water glugging into the bottom of the glass as he filled it. He felt a desperate thirst, his mouth dry from fear. He chugged the water gratefully. After taking a few more sips, Evan felt the presence again. He turned around slowly, but no one was there.

Gooseflesh covered his arms. Slowly he went towards the sink and placed the glass right next to the garbage disposal. As much as he didn't want to turn around and face whoever—whatever—might be standing there, he forced himself.

As before, no one was there. He convinced himself that it was just a figment of his imagination. And yet, the hair on his arm and neck continued to stand erect. Leaving the kitchen light on, he walked back towards the staircase cautiously. It was then he heard a whisper.

Evan.

He halted midway and waited. He wasn't sure if his mind was playing tricks on him or if he was indeed hearing his own name. When there was dead silence once again, he took a few more steps, hearing a creak as his foot pressed down on the wooden surface. He stood, paralyzed, afraid to move further. Then, once again, he heard the voice.

Evan.

All common sense and reason went out the window.

Evan... Come here.

The voice was coming from upstairs.

Almost under a spell, Evan found himself slowly climbing up the stairs unafraid. The voice, soft and filled with concern, was compelling. It lured him to the top of the staircase. For what felt like a solid minute, there was dead silence again. Evan stood there, breathing heavily. The door of Bright's room was halfway cracked open, which was unusual since they always left the door wide open. After he mustered up enough courage to approach the adjacent guest bedroom, Evan took a quick peep.

Nothing.

He sighed with relief. But his heart began to thump louder. Evan came to the realization that the voice was most certainly coming from the nursery.

Evan…come…here.

The voice was louder this time.

Evan… Evan… Evan.

He took a few steps towards the nursery, beginning to feel slightly numb. With the little courage that was left, he pushed the door slightly, enough that the crib was visible. Now, the voice had become silent. As he pushed a little further, he saw a figure standing in the corner. His blood ran cold. *Who was that?*

The figure looked up from underneath a sheaf of long hair.

"Samantha?" Evan said, his voice shaking.

She was still. Her hair draped limply down both sides of her face, and pain filled her beautiful eyes. Tears ran down her pale cheeks.

"Help me… *please*."

A knot formed in the middle of his throat. The hair on the back of his neck stood erect once again.

"What?" he managed to say.

Her wrenching sobs rang in his ears. Evan moved closer.

"Please help me," she whispered.

"Help you with what…?"

Before he could take another step towards her, in the bat of an eye, she was gone, leaving him standing alone in the nursery, confused. *What had happened to Samantha? Wasn't the SEA protecting her from Derek? What did this mean for his family now? Was she trying to tell him something?* He stood in Bright's room feeling hopeless and increasingly insane. He, too, began to sob. Evan buried his face in the palm of his hands. He was terrified of what else was lurking in the darkness. His life felt as though it had become a living nightmare.

Evan knew deep down that as long as the SEA existed, their lives were never going to be at peace. For a second, death felt like it might be the only freedom.

He wiped his tears with the back of his hand and looked around the room, trying to not let another tear escape.

What was going to come next?

***

Shadow tossed and turned in the hospital bed. The pain medication was slowly wearing off. Dull pain in her wrist was beginning to make its way to the surface. Her nose felt swollen and sore. The accident replayed in her dreams, resulting in her body going into defensive mode. In her mind's eye, she saw herself in the car, looking out of the driver's side, still trying to grasp what it was that she was avoiding on the road, which had caused her to swerve the car. A blurry vision of a woman quickly appeared and faded. The sound of a vehicle raging towards her played loudly in her ears. Now, the focus shifted to the black SUV speeding towards her. Her hand reached for the gear shift to move out of the way and avoid a deadly accident, but before she could turn the gear into reverse, her world turned black.

Laying on her side, her eyes slowly flickered open,

everything a blur. For a moment, Shadow was confused about her whereabouts, but within a couple of seconds, she knew where she was. She recalled the stitches she had received the day before. Everything was coming back to her, piece by piece. She slowly rolled herself onto her back. When the room came back into focus, a silhouette in the corner immediately caught her attention. Her eyes bulged and froze in position. All she could hear was the pounding of her heartbeat ringing in her ears.

It wasn't Evan. She recalled the argument they had gotten into about Evan staying the night because of her safety. He'd gone home, from what she remembered.

And then there was movement.

Shadow frantically looked for the nurse call button, but she was unable to think clearly and couldn't find it.

"Shadow..."

The voice was eerie yet familiar. Shadow desperately wanted her hunch to be wrong.

Marvin appeared out of the darkness.

For a moment, Shadow stopped looking for the nurse button to stare at him, just to make sure she was seeing correctly. *Marvin... how long had he been there? How did they let him in?* When her mind fully registered who it was, she screamed as loudly as she could, her eyes remaining fixed on his face.

"Help! Somebody help! Someone, please help me!" She looked at the door, waiting for a nurse to come rushing in.

"No one's coming, Shadow. No one's coming to save you," he chuckled.

Panting, Shadow looked from left to right.

"No, no, no," she whimpered.

When she felt the alarm cord underneath her back, she pulled it out as quickly as she could. She looked at the remote, spotting the nurse button on top. She pressed it once and then again.

Marvin chuckled and reached over for the remote. "Shadow, you need to learn when to exhaust your efforts and when it's pointless." He put the remote back in the console.

Shadow tried to roll on to her side so she could make an escape, but instead groaned in agony.

"Where do you think you are going?" he asked, calmly. He proceeded to sit down at the foot of her bed. "You need to rest and heal."

Shadow began to sob. "Please... just leave me alone. I don't want you here. I don't want you, Marvin. I just want you to go away... please... just leave me alone. I'm *begging* you, please. *Please go.*"

Marvin gazed steadily at her for a moment. "I can't. I can't let you go, Shadow."

"But you have to," she cried. "You're ruining my life. You took my baby from me."

"We belong together. You know that. Now, the three of us can be a family together. I love you, Shadow. I know that deep down, past all the hate you have for me, you still love me, too. I understand we will have to work to repair our relationship, and I am willing to do that. Come home."

Shadow pulled up the sheet over her face. "I don't want you. You need to leave and bring me back my baby—"

"I don't want to leave. I belong right here, with you. When you come back home, you can see him. Unfortunately, I can't give him to you before then."

"*Noooo!*"

The room fell into silence.

When she no longer heard his voice, Shadow slowly pulled the sheet away from her face. The hospital room was empty. She looked in every corner and he was nowhere to be found. Her heartbeat slowly began to normalize. Perhaps it had just been part of a dream? Sure enough, the alarm console sat in its holster at the side of the bed; outside, she could hear the distant murmur of voices. Despite this, Shadow wasn't entirely sure. It seemed so real. The fear remained.

Dream or not, Marvin was never going to leave her alone. Her heart sank knowing she couldn't do anything about the reality of her life. Not only did she feel lost, but she knew she'd been defeated. He was always going to have a hold over her life. Whatever he wanted, he would receive.

What was the point of living if she was going to be enslaved?

CHAPTER 29

The following morning, after Shadow was released from the hospital, Evan drove her straight home. He peered over at the splint that she was required to wear for her broken wrist. Shadow was instructed to wear the orthopedic device for a few days before a cast would be placed. Her nose was still rather swollen, and bruises appeared below her hairline and underneath her eyes. From what the nurse had informed them, it was going to take at least a week before the bruises began to fade away.

"What are you thinking about?" Evan asked, noticing the awful silence.

"Marvin." Shadow shifted her gaze to the window and watched passing cars.

The unexpected response caught Evan off guard. "Oh..."

"He showed up last night."

"At the hospital?" He gripped the steering wheel tighter in frustration. "This is—"

"No, not at the hospital, Evan."

"Then where?"

"In my dream. But it was so vivid. It seemed so real..."

"Oh..."

"He kept telling me to come home and that it was the only way I would get to see Bright. And..."

Evan reached over and softly rubbed her thigh with his eyes focused on the road. "Take your time, babe."

Shadow closed her eyes and drew in a deep breath. As she let out her breath, she focused on the sound of her exhale. The mention of Marvin's name alone was a trigger for her anxiety. Her voice cracking, she continued. "He wanted us to be a family. It felt so real. The dream felt so real."

"You're a hundred percent sure that he wasn't in the room with you?"

"Yeah... I think so. He was there one second and gone the next. None of the alarms were working, and I know they were hooked up. I just can't get away from him and it scares me. I feel like the dream means something."

"Well... dreams, in a way, *communicate* with you. Whatever is in your subconscious, they replicate that. All your fears come to the forefront. The timing of it, the accident, Bright being kidnapped. It all makes sense. But..."

Shadow faced Evan, with her eyebrows furrowed. "But what?"

Evan pulled apart his theories in his brain. "But what if it was a *hallucination*?" he asked, turning his head towards her.

Shadow looked confused. "But it *wasn't.* I was asleep, dreaming."

"Okay. I'm just saying—"

"Evan," Shadow snapped. "It wasn't a hallucination. Why would you say that?"

There was a brief moment of silence.

"It's because when I was talking to the detective, he said a witness to the accident saw you swerve the car, almost like you were trying to avoid hitting something. But there was nothing and no one on the road."

Shadow's lips parted, but nothing came out. She remembered only bits and pieces of the accident. In her mind, she replayed everything she could remember in order and realized there *had* been someone there on the street.

Her pounding headache made it difficult to focus and think clearly. She rested her head back on the headrest with her eyes closed, in the hope it would fade away.

"When I was driving, I *did* swerve. I thought I was going to hit someone. I didn't know who it was, but it all happened so fast..."

"Or it was a figment of your imagination..."

Shadow slowly shifted her head in Evan's direction. Her chest began to feel as though it had been set on fire.

"I don't know, Evan."

He peered at her, seeing the confusion and hurt circulating in her eyes. The conversation he had with Roy began to play like a broken record. A part of him wanted to keep the conversation to himself: Roy was far from being clear about why they needed Bright and how it was going to help not only Evan but Shadow and Bruce as well. On the other hand, maybe, just maybe, this would help Shadow recall something important that she may have had blocked out or simply forgotten.

Evan bit his lower lip out of hesitation.

"So..." Evan began, feeling quite nervous about Shadow's reaction. "I went to my father's house yesterday. That's where I was and—"

Suddenly, Shadow's pounding headache dulled to a mere nagging pain.

"What in the world compelled you to go to your dad's house?" Shadow asked, her face flushing with anger.

"I don't know. I just wanted to find a lead."

"It's bad enough that we have the SEA following us, and now you're just voluntarily walking into their trap? Are you crazy? Do you have some sort of death wish that I don't know about?"

Evan thought about it for a moment.

"I hadn't thought of it that way. I shouldn't have done that. I'm sorry."

Shadow closed her eyes once more, feeling her head pound harder again. "Well, did you find anything?"

"Um, no, but your dad showed up there."

Shadow's eyes fluttered open. "My dad was there?"

"Yeah," Evan responded, taking a quick glance at Shadow before turning his attention back to the road. "He said that your hallucinations were going to come back, and that he knew about mine. Apparently, they're going to get worse. He also said you were going to lose yourself, and that giving up Bright was for the greater good. Giving up Bright is supposed to not only benefit the both of us but my father as well."

"What the f—"

"Yeah, I know. He was vague about everything. Nothing made sense."

Shadow's mouth remained agape. With her right hand, she held her head, unable to comprehend the information Evan had just shared.

She looked at him and asked, "I don't ever remember having *hallucinations*."

"That's why I was asking if *maybe* you had a hallucination, because when the detective said you swerved your car to avoid hitting something, what your dad said to me kept coming back to me. If he says you've had them in the past, then maybe... maybe they're coming back, but slowly."

Shadow ran her fingers through her hair, flustered. "But why? Am I eventually gonna to start remembering my past life too, then, huh? I mean, I know we were a part of each other's lives, in another lifetime, but my recollection is blurry. It's nothing like yours, vivid and so damn haunting."

"The only reason why I'm even entertaining the idea is because of what your dad and the detective said. That's it. Otherwise, I wouldn't even have thought about hallucinations in the first place."

"I don't know what I'm supposed to do with this

information."

"I think we need to start preparing for them, *if* they do become regular and vivid."

"Great, I thought I was going to be the normal one out of the two of us." She smiled wanly.

Evan chuckled at Shadow's ability to crack a joke even under their current circumstances. "I love you and we're gonna get through this together."

"I love you too." She took a moment to reflect on the possibility of living a life filled with hallucinations and taunting memories of her past life. "What I don't get is how Bright fits into all of this. He's just a baby."

"I know what you mean. Maybe we'll find out once we get Bright back? I don't know. Sky or my dad should get some sort of idea, you'd think."

"I hope so. I just wanna hold my sweet baby and have him home again."

"Me too."

It was difficult for Shadow to fathom that her own father was behind all of this. That he was the one who ran the agency and had set a plan in motion to kidnap her baby. Her entire life was in question. The man she thought she knew never really existed. The man she grew up to love and adore, who had tucked her into bed most nights, who'd told her that he loved her more than anything in the world, was capable of doing something beyond her own comprehension. It terrified her.

***

When they pulled into the driveway, they noticed an unfamiliar car sitting in front of their house. At the front door, waiting patiently, was Detective Lucas.

"Who's that?" Shadow asked, immediately on the alert.

"That's the detective who was on the scene after your accident."

They unbuckled their seatbelts and stepped out of the car. When they approached the front door, Evan greeted the detective.

"Detective Lucas. It's nice to see you."

"Hello, Evan. I was just about to leave."

Evan shook his hand and replied, "We came just in time, then. This is my wife, Shadow."

Detective Lucas extended his hand and held her gaze for a moment. "It's nice to meet you, Shadow," he finally said. "I'm so sorry for what happened."

Shadow stared at him a moment before forcing a smile and nodding. "Yeah."

Once they were inside, Evan made Detective Lucas a cup of coffee and then returned to the living room. He placed a coaster under the cup in front of the detective.

"Thank you," Detective Lucas said, eyeing the steam rising from the cup as it quickly vanished into thin air. "I'm just going to get straight to the point here."

"Okay," Evan responded and took a quick glance at Shadow, who seemed to have become lost in her own thoughts. He slipped his hand into hers, feeling her fingers softly move against his.

"There's no easy way to say this. From the security

footage we were able to obtain for review, there wasn't a license plate we could track down for either of the SUVs. We used facial recognition for the two men who stepped out from one of the vehicles, but there was no match in our system."

Evan nodded. He knew realistically there was no hope of the police department tracking down whoever it was that kidnapped Bright. However, he realized he'd been holding onto hope regardless, and so felt his heart sink after hearing Detective Lucas deliver the disappointing news.

"So… you're saying there's nothing you can do."

The detective pursed his lips before responding. "I'm going to keep trying and exhaust every effort to help find your son. I can't make any promises. I need to be honest with you: things aren't looking so good. I don't want to give you or your wife any false hope. I can't sit here and tell you that we've got leads when we have none. Tracking down who did this… it's almost like trying to find a needle in a haystack. But at the end of the day, you just never know."

Evan nodded.

"Whoever did this... they were smart, and they weren't newbies in this game."

"How about the witnesses? Weren't they able to provide you with information? Or anything that would help?"

"I questioned everyone there at the time of the accident. There wasn't a single person who could give me any concrete details about the accident, or who they saw or what they looked like. From the security footage, these men were in and out in less than a minute. Plus, majority of the time, witnesses aren't able to recall exact details. They go back and forth with their stories. Things become a blur. Facts begin to lose their credibility, and then we all end up back at square one."

Evan looked at Shadow, who had been listening to the entire conversation without making a sound. "What do we do now? Just wait to hear back from you?"

"While we do more digging, and find pieces to the puzzle, the best thing for the both of you would be *not* to go out looking for answers yourselves. People tend to do that when they feel hopeless. It's never a good idea, and it can put you in danger, compromise the police investigation. And we don't want that. Go about your regular day, as much as you can, or take some time off work, if you need to. Everyone's different. Some need to distract their minds and some people don't. Do what works for you. I don't want to give you false hope, like I said, but we're working our hardest to find your son so we can bring him back home to you."

"Thank you. We appreciate it."

"Of course," Detective Lucas replied.

When Detective Lucas rose from the couch, Evan and Shadow followed suit.

"Thank you. I'll be in touch."

"We look forward to hearing from you."

Evan opened the door for Detective Lucas and watched as he began to make his way to the driveway. Halfway to his car, he stopped and turned to face Shadow, who had been watching him. "Take care of yourself, Shadow."

Once he was out of their sight, Evan closed the door behind them. He looked at his wife and proceeded to wrap his arms around her.

"What are you thinkin' about?"

For a moment, they held each other in silence. Then, Shadow's voice broke the stillness. She pulled away slowly, her face filled with concern.

Her voice quivered. "I need to sit down."

Evan desperately wished the detective had brought better news. Shadow appeared to be reeling with shock.

"Yeah, of course."

They headed back to the living room and took a seat on the couch. He slipped his hand into hers, feeling a sense of calmness travel through his body. With everything that was going on in their lives, despite what Shadow had said about their relationship, he knew in his heart they belonged together. They were stronger together and brought the best out in each other.

Shadow looked at him and smiled. "I love you, okay? I don't know what the hell is gonna happen tomorrow or the day after, but I'm going to be right here with you."

Evan, teary eyed, nodded and softly responded. "I know, babe. I know. What's going on, Shadow?"

Shadow smiled, trying to figure out how to say everything on her mind without overwhelming them both. She knew once everything was out in the open, it was only going to make matters worse.

A tear droplet landed on her cheek. "Evan… I don't

think that was a real detective."

He gripped her hand a little tighter. He, too, took a moment to find the proper way to deliver what he wanted to say, taking her feelings into account. "I know, right now, everything and everyone is under question. You've been through an ordeal. It's normal you'd feel suspicious about anyone unfamiliar…"

"Evan... I know what you're thinking. But I'm *not* being paranoid. That guy… I've seen him before. Before you say anything about 'maybe I'm mistaking him for someone else' or 'maybe I saw him at the grocery store…' or that 'I'm confused because I was in a car accident'—no. *He's not who he says he is.*"

"But… he was at the scene… and the police officer knew him. I saw his ID—"

Shadow leaned forward, her eyes now filled with terror. "Babe, listen to me. He's *not* a detective. I sat here as he talked and watched him. He felt so familiar, and I couldn't figure out where I knew him from. It took me a minute but I figured it out. Listen, when I was a kid… he used to drop by the house to see my dad, late at night. *Regularly.* That voice, the eyes. That's the same guy. I always thought they were really good friends. I never was under the impression that they worked together and my dad never mentioned anything about them working together. And now he's here? It's too much of a coincidence that he *just happens* to be a police officer who *just happens* to show up at the scene of my accident, all these years later. He works for the flippin' agency! He has to. Maybe that's why he would drop by at night to talk about the agency and whatever they work on over there." Her eyes widened. "Look! He didn't even touch his coffee. Probably because he didn't want to get his fingerprints on the mug—"

Evan sighed. "Do you think, maybe—"

"Evan! I'm not crazy. Trust me. Just because I was in a car accident, doesn't mean I've lost my marbles. That guy... 'Detective Lucas'— he isn't a detective. He either works with my dad or for him. Or maybe he does work for the police department as a detective and works for the agency at the same time. I don't know. If he's on the inside, it makes things easier for my dad and anyone else to cover their tracks and dismiss any type of evidence that will potentially hurt the agency and their own agenda. Do you see what I'm saying?"

Evan pondered over Shadow's theory. The more he thought about what she said, the more it began to make sense.

"You're convinced that you've seen him at your parents' house?"

She nodded. "I have no doubt. And he gave me this *look*... like, he wanted me to know he was toying with us."

Evan let out a deep sigh. He was beginning to feel a little overwhelmed. It hadn't crossed his mind for one second that the agency would go as far as having law enforcement and special agents under their control. He felt stupid for not being more cautious. They couldn't trust *anyone*.

"How come you..." he began, holding his tongue when he realized what he was about to say might seem like an attack on Shadow, "...didn't tell me this before we let him inside our home?"

"I wasn't a hundred percent sure about it myself. I wanted to make sure his voice sounded familiar and that he was the same man I'd seen before," she said pausing. "He works with my dad. I know in my gut that Detective Lucas is part of my dad's team or whatever you wanna call it." She sighed heavily. "I don't... I don't know what to think, Evan. It's really all too much. What's real and what isn't... I have no clue. What world are we living in?"

"The one where our lives are controlled by a secret agency," he answered. "It's almost like our lives have become chess pieces. One wrong move, and we're out of the game. We have no control over anything at this point."

She leaned back, resting her head on the back of the couch. After a moment, she slowly turned her head to face Evan.

"I'm *so* scared," she whimpered.

Shadow wiped away a tear, trying to refrain from crying, but it was the only thing that made her feel the slightest bit better. Knowing there was nothing he could say right now that would help, Evan offered Shadow the one thing that any human being needed in a moment of grief, uncertainty, and terror. He moved closer and wrapped her in his arms, needing the comfort just as much as she did.

CHAPTER 30

Venice gazed at her mug as her hands continued to tremble. She brought the tissue to her face and dabbed the corners of her eyes. Willow emerged from the kitchen with two energy bars and sat beside her on the sofa.

"Venice, my dear, you need to eat something."

"I can't... I don't have the appetite, honey. But thank you."

Willow set the energy bars on the coffee table and slipped his arm around Venice. He gently rubbed her shoulder and, leaning forward, kissed her forehead.

"Is there anything you need or I can do that will help you feel better?"

Venice wiped her nose and shook her head. "No. There isn't," she said. "I hate this."

"Do you mind sharing what your vision was about?"

Venice mused over his question for a while. The vision replayed in her mind, over and over. She was heartbroken and torn about what she needed to do. In her mind, she ventured down the two paths before her: on one, life would remain the same if she chose not to run interference, and on the other, Bright would come home, but at the expense of another loss.

"I know where Bright is."

Willow's eyebrows rose. "You know where he is? That's good news, isn't it?"

"Yeah," she sniffled. "Can you get my cell from my purse? I don't have the energy to get up."

"Yeah, of course. You don't want to take just a little bite?"

"Maybe in a bit."

Willow retreated to the kitchen table where he'd seen her purse and brought back the rather large gadget.

As he handed Venice the phone, he asked, "If you know where Bright is, then why the tears?"

Venice glanced at Willow before reaching for her cellphone. She looked at it, knowing this phone call was going to change everyone's lives.

"Because," she started, "there's always a consequence when you interfere with your higher power, when you tell the people involved about the visions. I'm not God, but when I decide to play interference because *I* want things to go the way I want them to, there's always going to be some sort of suffering involved—a price to pay. That's the cost of saving someone."

"What if you let them find Bright on their own? Bruce, Sky, Evan, the police? Then there wouldn't be any consequences, right?"

Her eyes flickered towards Willow.

"They're never going to find him if I don't tell them where he is. I really wish there was another way..."

"You sure?"

"Yeah."

Willow sighed. "I feel so helpless right now. I want to say the right thing, but I—"

"I know, honey. Just be here with me. That's all."

He kissed her on the forehead and slipped his arm around her. "Okay." He watched as she pressed the buttons on the phone. "Are you sure there isn't anything I can do?"

Venice pursed her lips and grazed his cheek with her forefinger. "I'm absolutely sure."

As the phone rang, her heart sank.

"Hi," Venice said softly.

"Hey, Mom," Bruce replied on the other end.

Before she could question herself any further, Venice spoke again. "I know where they're keeping him."

CHAPTER 31

That evening, Bruce called for a meeting over dinner at Evan's residence. Amid the chaos, sadness, terror, and ambiguity, Bruce knew that food was and always had been the temporary cure for heartache, and so he had brought over an indulgent dinner consisting of spring rolls, chow mein, eggplant parmesan, pasta marinara, cheese pizza, paneer tikka masala with naan and rice. For dessert, there was Evan's favorite, chocolate fudge cake with hazelnut whipped frosting from Bernie's, and a classic New York cheesecake.

Bruce looked around the table at Evan, Shadow, Denise, Ryan, Venice, and Mr. Brar. The absence of Nate and Bright was glaring. A smile would appear across his face whenever he heard Evan or Denise chuckle, and then suddenly, the reminder of what was to come brought him back to reality. This was a moment that wasn't going to last forever, and he had to cherish it—every bit of it.

Once the table was cleared away and everyone was

halfway finished with dessert, Bruce cleared his throat. "This isn't something I want to end the night on, but… I want everyone to be on the same page about what's going to happen in the next few days," he began. The mood quickly shifted from mellow to tense. The others listened attentively, each having their questions ready.

"Taking down the agency is the least of our worries, for now. It's a major player in what's happened, but what's more important right now is that we bring Bright home and find the person who administered the drug to Nate. Furious can't begin to describe what I'm feeling right now, but putting emotions aside is the only way we're going to be successful in the mission. Sky has been digging into Nate's case," he said, peering over at Denise and Ryan. "She will find who did this, and then we can discuss what you guys want to do from there. This person is linked to the SEA and knows enough to understand how to administer drugs."

"In a perfect world, I'd want this person dead, if I'm being honest. But right now, we just want our life the way it was and Nate to wake up and have him home. That's all," Ryan said.

"I understand," Bruce said. "As soon as I hear back from Sky about any potential, strong leads, you guys will be the first to know."

"Thank you," Denise responded.

"As for Bright, we know where he's located. We definitely wouldn't have found the place if it weren't for you," Bruce stated slowly, shifting his gaze onto Venice. "I've got some of my agents keeping an eye on the property, logging all activity taking place there. I'll be finalizing the plan tonight and Sky will review it before we brief the agents tomorrow afternoon. The following day, we're going to drive out to the location and set the plan in motion. It's going to be myself, Sky, and our other mission agents; the field agents will already be in the area before we get there, keeping the property under surveillance."

"Sorry to interrupt, Bruce, but it seems as though you've forgotten that I'm a part of this mission. We discussed this," Mr. Brar said.

A blank expression filled Bruce's face. He looked down at the table before meeting Mr. Brar's eyes. "You've done *a lot* for this family. This operation is a huge risk, and with—"

"What are the risks?" Evan jumped in.

Bruce glanced over at him, sensing he couldn't brush over his question.

"It's a safe house, where Bright is. Meaning those protecting it will be armed, with orders to defend the location at all costs. If something goes wrong… we're looking at a lot of damage. When they find out agents on the inside have been colluding with outside operatives to scupper the SEA's plans, there'll be hell to pay for all the agents involved. I'm not going to focus on the negative, but that's why we've allocated tomorrow for Sky to review the game plan so we know what we would need to do if things were to go haywire."

The room fell silent as the magnitude of the situation

settled in. Everyone retreated to their own thoughts.

"What kind of damage are you talking about?" Shadow asked. Worry filled her voice.

All eyes were focused on Bruce.

Bruce let her question sit for a moment before giving a response. "Given the fact that we know how they operate, that we know they're going to be ordered to defend that safe house, no matter what, we could lose some of our team, if not all. That's the worse-case scenario, I would say. Anything besides that, we can recover from. But we can't get someone back."

Venice's mind jumped to the vision she'd gotten earlier in the day. Hearing the words come out of Bruce's mouth reminded her that there was no preventing what was going to happen once they went to retrieve Bright. Her heart plunged down to her stomach. She held back the tears that wanted to escape so desperately.

"I'm going. I'm on the team," Mr. Brar inserted. "Bright's my family too."

Bruce opened his mouth, but before he could say anything, Mr. Brar interjected once again.

"There's nothing you can say that's going to stop me."

"I don't feel comfortable with you being on the mission," Bruce said sternly. "We've got some of the best agents on the team. You need to sit this one out. There's *way* too much risk involved. You shouldn't have even been on our first mission to begin with. Life's fragile and so are you."

Mr. Brar raised an eyebrow. "You don't need to remind *me* how fragile life is," he said, hinting at the truth Bruce still withheld from his family. "You're forgetting the type of agent I once was, Bruce," he stated. "I've got this."

His eyes cold, Bruce stared at Mr. Brar. "Fine."

Mr. Brar muttered as he rose from his chair. "He's just as much of my family as he is yours. This guy..."

Mr. Brar withdrew to the backyard, where warmth filled the air and the sky had turned violet. Venice quietly joined him.

"What was that all about?" she asked, tucking a loose strand of hair behind her ear.

Mr. Brar looked over at Venice and then back at the pathway in front of him. He choked back tears.

"I've lived a very fulfilling life, and I don't want to waste whatever time I have left thinking and stressing about what's going on out there. I told Bruce that I was in from the get-go. I don't understand what's holding him back now. I'm healthy. Great shape. There's nothing keeping me from being there with them. I'm just a little frustrated, that's all."

"I understand your perspective, but it also doesn't make sense to put anyone else at risk if they don't need to be. Even you would agree."

Mr. Brar pursed his lips. He knew Venice had a point there. "Okay. Fine. I'll give you that, but I made a vow to myself long before any of this happened," he said, pausing for a moment, recalling the conversation he'd had with himself one night. "You guys are the only family I have left. When it comes to family, it doesn't matter what it is, you do whatever is necessary. I have to do this, Venice.

If something happens out there while I'm here, sitting around on my ass, I won't ever forgive myself. You know what I'm talking about."

For a moment, neither of them said anything. They gazed up at the stars, letting his words hang in the air between them.

"You need to let go of having control over every situation that comes up. I tell this to my clients all the time. I know it's hard because I find it difficult to let go of control. But we can't always be the hero. You've helped this family beyond measure. You've done so much for us. It's our turn to take care of you and be there for you. It's been long overdue if you ask me," Venice said, softly.

Mr. Brar snorted. "You're being ridiculous. You don't owe me anything."

Venice tried again. "It's our turn, Mr. Brar."

"That's nonsense. You guys have always been here for me." He wrapped his arm around Venice. "You're my family and I love you beyond this world. But this isn't going to change the fact that I'm still going."

"Did you listen to a word I said?"

"I did. But I need to do this... for my family. You fight for what and who you love. It's something I've always lived by, and I wouldn't be staying true to my word if I sat back and let Bruce go on his own."

"He's not going to be on his own."

"You know what I mean."

"I just..." Venice started to sob.

Mr. Brar hugged her tighter. "Nothing's going to

happen. We're all going to come back safe and sound. You have nothing to worry about. Alright?"

For a second, his words comforted her, but her vision came rushing back.

"You don't know that."

"Yeah, I know, but we can't indulge in our negativity either." Mr. Brar sighed.

Venice remained quiet.

"Willow is a lucky guy, Venice."

Venice tilted her head upwards and got a glimpse of the smile that played on Mr. Brar's lips before meeting his eyes. "When did Bruce tell you?"

Mr. Brar chuckled. "Soon after Willow told him about his plan of proposing to you."

Venice wiped a tear from the corner of her eye. "That boy can't keep anything to himself."

Mr. Brar chuckled and gave Venice a tight squeeze. "Some things he cannot."

CHAPTER 32

In the dark room, the light crept through the curtain gaps. Even though Sky had been here only a few times, the mandatory requirement for all SEA agents to learn how to memorize unfamiliar floor plans well enough to walk them blind folded, she was able to move easily through the space.

She walked around, looking at some of the photos that hung above the mantel. Others were placed on the side tables next to the couch. From the pictures alone, they appeared to be the happy family you'd see on TV or in the pictures that came along with the photo frame. She knew her brother *appeared* happy, but a hint of skepticism lingered in the back of her mind.

People were good at covering up their true emotions. She believed his wife was out of his league, and the only way their marriage had worked to date was because money played a colossal role. Oftentimes, she wondered when she'd get a call from him, spilling the truth about his relationship and what a mistake he'd made. If that happened, Sky knew she would let him vent; she would console him, and she would try very hard not to pointedly remind him that she'd warned him repeatedly about his choice for a wife— and that he'd chosen not to listen.

The bottom line was that she didn't like her sister-in-law. To say that she was fake was an understatement, and it was a personality trait that made Sky's skin crawl. She had a list as long as her arm about all the things she didn't like about the woman, but in the end, like every good sister, she had to put her personal feelings aside and get on board with her brother's life decisions.

She padded into the kitchen, noticing, even in the gloom, that a lot had changed since the last time she was here. It was no surprise to her that everything in this home had to be up to date. Having the latest and best version of everything seemed to be an ongoing requirement, if the conversations she'd had with her brother and the interactions she'd had with her sister-in-law were anything to go by.

She peered at her watch with its light-up screen and made her way over to the nook. Carefully, she pulled out a chair and made herself comfortable. Any moment now, her brother would come downstairs for a light snack. According to her field agents, it was around two fifteen when he would regularly make his way to the kitchen.

Now, all she had to do was wait.

As time passed, she found herself drumming her fingers on the table, shifting in her seat every few minutes, beginning to doubt if her brother would appear. There was also a fifty percent chance that the person coming down in the middle of the night could be her sister-in-law. That was an eventuality she wasn't prepared for, but she didn't care. She'd think of something if it came to it. Just as her mind grew clouded with negativity, she heard the footsteps she'd been longing for. This was the moment of truth.

The kitchen lights flipped on, and her brother appeared out of the darkness. At first, he didn't notice another body occupying a seat at the table. She watched as his eyes slowly adjusted to the light. He rubbed his face as he moseyed his way over to the refrigerator.

"Hey, Zack."

He froze midway when he heard the familiar voice fill the room. He turned around cautiously, his face gripped with fear and uncertainty.

"Fuckin' shit, Sky..." he gasped.

"It's been a while."

"What in God's name are you doing here? It's the middle of the fuckin' night. This is trespassing."

"You know what, just calm down a bit. Have a seat," she offered. "Let's have a little chat."

Zack furrowed his eyebrows. "It's..." he looked at the clock that hung on the wall and then met her eyes, "... two twenty in the morning. This couldn't wait until later? And how the hell did you get in here?"

"For someone who's half asleep, you sure ask a lot of questions," Sky said, "I'm just going to get straight to the point. You were the one who administered the drug which put Nate in a coma, correct?"

Zack's mouth was agape.

"It was you, wasn't it?" Sky repeated.

The shock on his face said it all.

"Can you at least nod for me? Nod if you were the one who administered the drug. It's not that hard, Zack."

When Zack finally got the courage to speak, his voice trembled. "Oh my god...You're one *of...them*! You work for that secret agency!"

"Hey, I'm not here to talk about my life decisions. Did you or did you *not* administer the drug to Nate? Your son's best friend? Should I drag your whole family in here? Will that get you to talk?"

"No," he replied, his voice raspy. "I didn't have a choice. I agreed to do it before I knew who it was," he said, defending himself. "I–I... I wouldn't have done it if I knew it was going to be Nate. I swear."

Sky was taken aback. Not because he'd finally confessed, but by how weak her little brother was. As a doctor, she assumed he would have a backbone and stand up for anything that went against his moral code and ethics; she was mortified by how easily he'd been able to jettison any sense of empathy and compassion he had in his heart.

"That's pathetic, Zack. You always have a choice!"

"Shhh! Don't raise your voice. You're gonna wake up Greece."

"You think I give a shit? You took their son away. Did you even *think* for one second how you'd feel if it was

Skylar? Huh? Did you even think about that?"

"They said if I didn't do it, then they were going to come after Skylar. So yeah, I *did* think about what it would be like if it was Skylar. What else was I supposed to do? Let my kid die?"

"No, but you could have called me and told me. I could have helped you."

"We don't talk for months, and you expect me to come to you and ask for help? Are you fuckin' kidding me?"

"When you're told to *murder a child*, you ask whoever the hell you can to help you. You made your bed with the wrong people."

"I panicked, Sky. I didn't know what else to do…"

"Well, brace yourself, because for the rest of your life, you're going to be living in fear."

"Huh? Sky…. wh-wh-what are you talking about?" Zack asked, his voice desperate.

She could see the horror in his face. "Did you really think that they were just going to ask you to do this one task and then leave you alone?"

Zack appeared dumbfounded.

"You're on their payroll, Zack! You're done. You're their little bitch now. You and *your* family."

He shifted his weight in his seat. "There has to be a way out of this. There has to be, right?" he asked, his fear kicking in high gear. "Right, Sky?"

"No, Zack, there's no way out. This is it," she said. "This is your life now. You're done."

His eyes widened and glazed over with terror. He ran

his hands through his messy orange bed hair, sprang out of his chair, and began to pace back and forth.

"You have to help me," he blurted mid stride.

"That's not how it works, Zack! This isn't just a one-time deal or a contract you can get out of once it ends. Your life is theirs now. Every time they need you to do something, they're going to expect you to deliver. And if you don't... I'm sure you probably already know what's going to happen."

"So... what do I do?" he asked frantically.

"I don't know."

"Sky," he hissed. "Tell me what to do. Please, I'm begging you."

"You know how they say it's never too late? Well, in this case... it is. The agency doesn't operate on kindness or compassion. It's all about their clients and their needs. You're just a means to an end. And you should start preparing yourself for when Denise and Ryan find out you were the one who kidnapped their son and nearly killed him."

"Please, don't tell them. *Please.* I'm already regretting this and feeling guilty—"

"Oh, boo hoo. Cry me a river. You should've thought about this before—"

"If you were in my shoes, what would you do? Huh? What would you have done?"

"Off the top of my head... I wouldn't have folded so quickly. I would have challenged them. I would've asked for help. I would've looked for an alternative route. I would've done everything I could to make it difficult for them to get to me. And if I've learned anything at the agency, the number one reason why people are so quick to do whatever the SEA asks is because of the lump sum of money they offer or ...they have something on you. You've done something that you can't get yourself out of."

She waited for him to confess what she already knew.

"I'm in over my head," he blurted. "We own things we no longer can afford. I've spent so much money. Greece... she wants this lifestyle that needs upkeeping. And—"

"Then don't buy shit you don't need. She doesn't work. Did you ever think about telling her she needed to get a job? And do her part around here instead of looking like a human barbie? Maybe if you learned how to put your foot down and spoke up occasionally, you wouldn't be in this financial mess. You wouldn't have had to take out that loan, right?"

Zack appeared perplexed. "What... how did you know about that?"

"How'd you think?" Sky asked. "You're a doctor, aren't you? You're smart. You should already know the answers to your own questions," she said, pausing for a moment. "I did my research and put two and two together. It's not rocket science."

"There was an incident... with a patient, who died under my care," he confessed. "I made a mistake during the surgery. I'd been up for forty-eight hours. I wasn't thinking straight, but it was on me. The family filed a lawsuit. It wasn't looking good for me. They were talking about jail time. I wasn't gonna be able to practice anymore, or for at least a while... and then Marvin showed up said he could help—"

Sky scoffed at the name. "*Help?* He didn't help you. All he did was manipulate the situation and make things worse for you. Did it ever occur to you that maybe he had been keeping his eye on you? You didn't find it odd that he showed up precisely around the time you were down on your luck? C'mon, Zack. You should have known something was off."

The room fell back into silence. Sky pondered over what was going to become of her brother's life. It scared her, the thought of losing her only brother, but at the same time, she knew he'd brought this upon himself. Her entire life, she had cleaned up after his messes because she was his older sister and she felt obligated. But there came a time in everyone's life when they had to take a step back and let their loved ones figure things out on their own. No matter what, she was going to love him, but he had to figure this out himself. And quite frankly, there wasn't anything she could do, even if she wanted to.

"So, that's it? You're not gonna help? You're my sister, Sky. I need you."

Sky rose from her chair. "You should start getting your affairs in order. Be prepared for the worst. Make sure you have a will in place in case Skylar loses you both. And it probably would be a good idea to let Greece in on your actual financial situation and what you did. She'll probably leave you... I don't know. But seriously, prepare yourself for the worst. It's going to get ugly. And Denise and Ryan.... I don't know what they're gonna do once they find out you were behind this, but you're gonna want to mentally prepare for that conversation, as well. The SEA will protect you as long as you work for them, so at least you don't have to worry about walking out of your home in handcuffs."

"Sky," he whispered. Tears of regret streamed down his cheeks. "I'm sorry."

"I'm not the one you should be apologizing to," she said, making her way out of the kitchen. She peered over her shoulder and choked on her words as they slipped out. "I love you, Zack."

CHAPTER 33

Bruce gaped at himself in the mirror. He still had one last thing to do, and as much as he wanted to drag it out, he knew once they brought Bright back home, he would have to say something. As much as he wanted to avoid the uncomfortable and heart wrenching conversation, he knew Mr. Brar was going to nag him until he finally told his family about his declining health.

Everyone had said their goodbyes the night before after dessert. As expected, the night had ended on a somber note. Bruce and Sky weren't letting themselves think about the chance they wouldn't make it back home and that as a result, Bright would remain in Roy's clutches.

In the early morning, the team gathered at the warehouse Sky had secured from Enrique for one last briefing of the mission to rescue Bright. Stacy stood at the back of the room, her arms crossed over her chest, as she listened to Sky review the location where Bright was taken. When Sky had informed her of the sudden change of plans and the new mission they were going to embark on, Stacy didn't hesitate to join the team, when she was asked.

Sky held a tablet in her hand, which projected a three-dimensional blueprint of the building into the air. Every so often, she would use her fingers to rotate the blueprint, or pinch the thin air to zoom in and get a closer look at the interior of the home.

"It's going to take us three hours to reach our destination, point B. It's just another mansion in the countryside used as a safe house. It's a fairly new property. Only five years old. I'll go over the tech we'll be using in a bit, but I just want to go over the drive to point B. We've got four sedans ready to go. Bruce and Mr. Brar will be in one, Stacy and I will be in the second one, Andrew and Prem will be in the third and then Aabish and Santokh will be in the last vehicle. We're all taking the same route. Keeping it simple. As you guys know, these sedans have the invisibility option."

"Oh, sick!" Andrew exclaimed. "I've only been on one mission where we used those."

"We won't be going into invisible mode until we're a hundred yards away from the driveway, when Mike gives us the go-ahead to enter the premises. Don't activate the invisibility until *after* we reach our checkpoint, which is the street sign after the stop sign, right *before* the driveway to our location—Endings Way. We'll check in with everyone once we get there and remind you, but I know you guys are all capable of understanding simple instructions."

"Mike's already gonna be on the premises? How come Bruce's not taking the lead on this one?" Santokh asked, taking a quick glance at Bruce, who had been laser focused through Sky's briefing.

"Mike's team is surveying the property right now. They've been in the area as of yesterday morning. I'm passing your second question, Santokh. It's not important to our mission. Any other questions?"

"Just to clarify, we're the only agents going into the house?" Prem chimed in next.

"Yeah. Mike's team of four will remain on the ground, physically active on site, while we go inside and retrieve the baby. Any other questions before I move on with the gear that you guys will be wearing? You guys should be very familiar with the plan by now, but please don't be afraid to speak up if there's something that was unclear to you in the packet."

The packet that Sky had given to the team included the details of the agents on the task force, their objectives, technology that was going to be used during the mission, game plan, the floor plan of the home and everything else important associated with the mission. It was understood that all agents on the mission were to know every detail by the time the briefing took place, which always happened the day of the execution.

Stacy watched as the agents shook their heads, signaling to Sky to move ahead with the next run down.

"Alright." Sky moved on and pulled up the gear that all the agents were required to wear on her tablet. Sky looked at the three-dimensional images of the equipment for a moment. "The gear we'll be wearing is invisible, like I said, but not many of you have had the opportunity to use it. The gear is not tricky to operate. You wear it like you would wear your regular clothes. There are zippers all around the outfit, so you're able to unzip if you need to treat a wound. There's a button underneath both the left- and right-hand sleeve, which you will push to activate the invisibility mode. By not clicking that button, you'll defeat the purpose of wearing the gear. It's happened before. So, make sure you don't forget to press the button."

Stacy paid close attention to Sky as she demonstrated the gear. Wearing the full-length equipment, with the simple press of a button, everything but Sky's head had become invisible. The room filled with *oohs* and *ahhs* as they gawked at Sky's invisible body and her floating head.

"That's wicked!" Andrew shouted. "There's no way we're goin' in with just a-a head, though. How does that go invisible?"

"Good question. There's a button inside your right chest. You'll feel it and all you do is tap the button and... let me show you."

When Sky tapped at a button on her chest, multiple thin clear shields appeared from the neckline of the suit, forming a wall around her head. As each piece of shield came together, forming a dome around Sky's head, her face began to disappear. Within three seconds, Sky had become completely invisible, leaving the team in awe once again.

After a moment, she was visible to the team once more.

"Now, to deactivate the suit and headgear, you reverse the process. You can connect your devices to these suits. So, if you're wearing a smartwatch or are using a Slinc—which I know all of you have used at some point in your missions, and which we're using today—you'll be able to see everything in this shield that you would see on the screens of those gadgets. Except for the glasses. Those you will have to wear, while the other gadgets you can keep on you. There weren't enough Slincs for everyone, so we had to check out the glasses instead."

"How do we link the Slinc to the suits?" Aabish asked.

"In the settings, you click on Bluetooth, and it will pick up the name 'Sea 901' followed by a unique three-digit code specifically for each suit. When you each get your suits, you'll find a code inside, by the tag. You'll match that code to the one on your screen when you connect. *Don't* connect with just any suit. That will be a mess. This suit is also voice activated, so if you say, for example, 'show me blueprint' the blueprint of the house will appear."

"So, we can command the suit to show us whatever we'd see on our Slincs?" Andrew asked.

"Exactly. Whatever information the Slinc provides you with, you can use the voice command to pull that up so it's right in front of you. That way, you're not reaching for your Slinc or holding it in your hand throughout the entire mission. Any other questions about the suit before we move forward?"

Aabish raised a hand.

"Go ahead."

"We'll be using the Slinc and glasses to communicate with the team, correct?"

"Yes."

"Okay. How would that work with the suit?"

"It's the same, but handsfree. The suits are programmed with everyone's agent numbers and names. You can take calls from individuals and have a group conference, which is what we will be doing, obviously. The cool thing about these suits is that they are soundproof. You can scream bloody murder with the suit on—once activated of course—and no one around you will be able to hear you. Even though we won't need earpieces with the suits, we'll still be using them. If the suit malfunctions in the middle of the mission for some reason, at least you will still be able to keep contact with the rest of the team. Any more questions?"

"If there's some sort of malfunction with the communication, how will we know where we are in relation to each other if invisibility mode is still activated?" Stacy asked.

"Good question. We have six Sparks that we can use, one for each room."

Sky quickly pulled up the gadget on her virtual screen. A round silver-plated ball appeared, rotating slowly in the air in front of the assembled agents.

"This is what a Spark looks like. It's one of the gadgets that are used the least in missions. What this does is help with uncovering anything that might be in invisible mode. These are best used in small spaces. So, let's say we walk into a room that looks empty. How do we know it's *really* empty, if we don't have clear audio communication channels? We *don't*— unless we activate the Spark. What this little bad boy will do is reveal everything in that room for about a minute before it shuts off to be recharged. It's not great at tracking moving objects, but should indicate the locations of any agents waiting in position or moving slowly. We only have six of these babies, though. We have to use these only if and when we really have to. Now, let's say you're not using a Spark, or can't for whatever reason... the best way to get in touch with your team is to use your Slinc and send a message that way. Your glasses can do the same, if you guys remember. All you have to say is 'send message' and then voice-to-text will be activated and we'll get your message even if your suit is no longer operating the way it should be."

Sky reviewed her team before going over the next item on her list. "Mike will be using the fly to get a look inside while we're en route to the location."

"Isn't there a chance that whoever is protecting the property will also be wearing invisible gear?" Prem asked cautiously.

"As far as the agency is concerned, invisibility tech is still in the early stages of development—they're not even at the suit prototype stage," Sky explained. "We had some of our agents duplicate the program that allowed us to use these suits that can operate at the level we need them to. For once, we're ahead of the SEA. They won't know what hit them."

"Got it," Prem answered. "How many of their agents will be on the property?"

"As of right now, there are four visible agents positioned in the backyard. Given that they're not expecting any visitors, because it's a safe house and there's no way we would have found the place if it wasn't for the help of an—*informant*, I would say there will be a few agents working inside. I'd be lying if I said we have a solid count."

"It's always fun to be on our toes," Prem responded softly.

"That's why we've compensated you guys... very generously for this."

All the agents present knew this would be their last mission if they were captured. If the worst happened, they'd be subjected to interrogation and torture. Their retirement benefits would be revoked as punishment and for the remainder of their life they would be under surveillance.

"What about the no-kill rule?" Andrew asked.

Sky and Bruce exchanged glances with one another.

The no-kill rule was implemented by the SEA to ensure every agent was safe. In some cases, agents had found themselves seeking vengeance or at the very least had been a part of brutal fights due to a botched mission. The no-kill rule applied to all agents within the agency, and stated that no matter what happened, agents were under no circumstances to kill another member of the agency.

"Our mission is to retrieve the baby safely from the home. At this point, if we have to kill an agent to get to the baby, we will. The no-kill rule doesn't apply today," Sky answered, feeling the tiny hairs on the back of her neck rise. "I know it's not how any of us have operated in the past, but they *will* try to kill us when we come. They're going to keep this baby at all costs."

Stacy's eyes flashed to Aabish, whose hand darted straight into the air for another question.

"Shoot," Sky stated.

"In the packet it said that we're going to have smoke bombs, the baby carrier, masks, goggles... all things we've used before—but a Snake Knife? I'm not familiar with a Snake Knife. I've never even heard of it."

"Oh," Sky responded, taken aback. "No worries." Quickly, Sky pulled up an image of the Snake Knife which agents were going to have access to during their mission. "The Snake Knife has a rigid edge which releases poison when it comes into contact with a body. The poison won't kill a person, but it will incapacitate them. It's said to feel as if your body is melting, like it's on fire. Persons wounded with the Snake Knife continuously sweat and hallucinate to the point they are unable to function. Tests suggest the Snake Knife can cause victims to want to kill themselves. The psychological effects are severe. There's nothing they can do to counter these effects: it's a matter of letting it pass."

"Oh god. I wouldn't wanna be on that end of the stick," Aabish replied.

Stacy had only raised her hand halfway when Sky immediately called on her. "Yeah?"

"Has Mike's team located where the baby is within the safehouse?"

"As of right now, he's predicted to be on the second floor, where all the bedrooms are located. We'll know once Mike gets that fly inside the house. Any other questions before I move forward? Any questions about your positions?"

Everyone shook their heads confidently.

"Okay. We're almost done. When we're inside the house, we'll have less than ten minutes to complete the mission. Our goal is to get the baby out of there and every single member of our team out alive. In the event we have an agent who is shot or killed, you are expected to continue with the mission. I have appointed Santokh to be our eyes and ears from the outside should anything happen to Mike or his team. I want whoever retrieves the baby to be the first one out of the house and off the property. Everyone else goes second. We take any fallen agent with us. That will be our last priority. I hope it won't come to that." Sky's face was solemn.

After Sky had answered lingering questions, and reviewed other items on her list, the team began to dress in their gear. They packed their backpacks with gadgets and other necessities such as first aid kits. As each agent double checked to make sure they had everything they needed and their gear was operating correctly, they stood aside and waited for the rest of the team to finish packing and getting ready.

Once all the agents were equipped and ready to

depart, they headed out of the building. They split up into their designated teams into the sedans and started their journey to the safe house. Even though the drive was three hours long, it was far from dull. A huge portion of the route wound through grassy green fields, occasionally broken up by swathes of cherry trees, against a backdrop of mountains. Most of the agents stared out at the view, lost in their own thoughts. And some fantasized about what they were going to do with the paycheck they would receive once the mission was completed.

Twenty minutes away from their destination, they entered the town of Pond View. The homes dotted on either side of the road were large and expensive. They sat on at least a half an acre of land, each with a dirt pathway leading from the main road to the house.

As they drove past the houses, Mike dialed into the team's Slincs. Bruce used the voice activation option to call the team in.

"Everyone on?"

One by one, each agent chimed in, confirming they were all on the same channel.

As they drove down the path towards Endings Way, the road began to incline slightly. Their three-hour drive was nearing an end. As instructed, all the vehicles turned their invisibility mode on as they approached the sign.

Every agent except for Bruce and Mr. Brar was ready to get into position.

"I'm nervous," Mr. Brar confessed.

"Yeah, me too. I just want this to be a quick, in and out

mission, but we're dealing with the SEA here. Those ten minutes are going to feel like an hour."

Mr. Brar sighed, wishing the same.

"I love you, Bruce."

Bruce chuckled, feeling his fear kick into high gear. He glanced at Mr. Brar, who was looking directly at him. "I really wished you listened to me. You shouldn't be here."

"I'm doing this for my family. You know that."

"Alright. You guys invisible?" Mike asked over the Slincs, from his position behind a row of rose bushes on the left side of the house.

Bruce peered in his rear-view mirror to confirm before giving an answer. "Yeah. We're good to go."

"Alright. We've done a sweep around the property. Four agents are positioned behind the property. We're all positioned around the property for backup, but you guys are up now. There are two agents inside, but I don't think that's it—I just think there must be more. It's been fairly quiet inside. The doors are kept closed, so we haven't been able to get inside each room. Although we did hear a baby's cry from the right side of the upstairs hallway. There are three rooms it could have come from. You guys know the drill."

"Okay. We're going to pull into the driveway. Need clearance."

"Yup. All clear."

After each vehicle passed the street sign, the first driveway on their left was their destination. Tall Cupressus Sempervirens trees stood on both sides of the property, keeping the view of the house private from the street. As they entered the driveway, they were met with a brick paved road, unlike the other homes they had come across, which had dirt paths. On either side of the driveway were more Cupressus Sempervirens. As they neared the house, they emerged from the corridor of trees, and the safehouse itself was finally visible. It was a large, Mediterranean style house painted the color of chantilly lace, with a seed brown trim and window frames. The double front-door was flocked by pillars. Large windows filled the first floor; those on the second floor were smaller. A four-car garage with Spanish style doors nestled to the right of the house. In front, there was a large fountain, featuring two white marble fishes that appeared to have jumped out of the water and frozen in place above it. The fountain, and the colorful flower bed at its base, formed the center of a turning circle out front.

Sky's team parked their vehicles off to the right side of the property, parallel to the rose bushes. They studied the property, each reviewing the game plan in their minds.

Mike's voice escaped from the Slinc. "I'll let you guys know when it's clear to get out of the vehicles. Once you're in, no more than ten minutes in the place. Get the baby and get out. Fast."

"Copy," Bruce responded.

As they sat in their vehicles, patiently waiting for the go ahead, the front door of the home opened.

"Hold," Mike emphasized, knowing at this very moment, Bruce's team was ready to deploy.

An agent stepped out from behind the door, with his hand slipped behind his back. He stood in the doorway and studied the view. After a few moments, the agent, apparently satisfied that all was well, returned back into the house, closing the door behind him.

Bruce muted his Slinc, keeping the conversation between him and Mr. Brar.

"I've never been this agitated on a mission before."

"Of course you haven't. This is your *grandson* we're rescuing. The stakes are high and the sooner we're out of here, the quicker we can get Bright home."

"All clear," Mike's voice echoed again.

Bruce and Mr. Brar turned to one another one last time before activating their gear into invisible mode.

"I'll see you soon."

Mr. Brar nodded. "Love you, son."

"I love you too."

Bruce and Mr. Brar quietly slipped out of their vehicle and carefully began to creep towards the fountain, using it as a safeguard. Sky and Stacy joined them on the other side of the fountain. The next half of their journey would lead them to the front door.

On Mike's cue, Andrew and Prem sprinted their way to the garage and took cover. Aabish and Santokh were the last to depart. As they began to make their way to the left side of the house, near the flower bushes, they were forced to halt in position as the front door opened once again.

"For fuck's sake," Andrew hissed.

This time, the agent didn't stay idle in the doorway. He

walked out of the house, closing the door behind him, and began to near the fountain.

"Don't move," Mike instructed Bruce's team.

Bruce and Mr. Brar watched as the agent neared the fountain, sending a wave of anxiety through their bodies. With one knee planted on the ground, and the other close to their chests, they remained frozen in position. Though their muscles ached in this unnatural crouch, neither Bruce nor Mr. Brar dared to move even an inch. When the agent came to a halt, each member of Bruce's team focused on him, unsure what had brought him out for the second time.

"What the fuck is he doing?" Sky asked, frustrated. "We're wasting time. We should've been at the front door by now."

"I know you guys are eager to move up," Mike answered. "But there's no way they know anyone's here, remember? I don't know what he's doing outside, but just sit tight. He has to go back in at some point."

They watched as the agent pulled a gun—a Glock, by the looks of it, Bruce thought—out of his back pocket and admired it before reinserting the weapon back into his pocket. After taking another moment and assessing the property for anything out of the ordinary, the agent returned again to the house, and closed the door behind him.

"What the hell was that?" Stacy shouted.

"Just another loonie from the agency. Obsessed with weapons for no good reason," Andrew replied.

Mike's voice came over their headsets. "The entrance is clear. He's heading upstairs. On my say-so, everyone finish their course."

Once Mike gave the agents clearance, Andrew and Prem sprinted towards the backyard, Bruce and Mr. Brar following their lead. Sky and Stacy navigated their way to the front door, while Aabish and Santokh continued forward, taking cover by the flower bushes.

Stacy and Sky pressed their backs against the wall next to the door.

"You're up, Stacy," Sky stated.

With her heart pounding and adrenaline flowing through her body, Stacy pulled out a tool from her back pocket, using it to unlock the door. As she maneuvered the tool inside the doorknob, her hand trembled. In her ears, the team's words of encouragement flowed, but it didn't make her task easier. She had to get the door unlocked quickly, making as little noise as possible. Bruce and Mr. Brar took cover behind a tree in the backyard, where the four patrolling SEA agents were visible, while Andrew and Prem waited patiently by the side of the house. Once Stacy unlocked the front door, the next phase in the mission would be underway.

Turning the tool to her left, Stacy heard a slight noise from the door mechanism, indicating it was now unlocked.

"Unlocked the front door," Stacy announced.

Mike again. "Get yourselves through that door. Bruce, Mr. Brar, Andrew and Prem, you guys wait for them to be in the clear before entering through the back door."

"Gotcha," Bruce responded.

Slipping the tool back into her pocket, Stacy wrapped her hand around the doorknob, gripping it hard and slowly turning it as quietly as she could. Before Stacy could turn the knob fully, bullets came piercing through the front door, one striking Stacy in her upper thigh.

"Shit!" she screamed, jumping to the side of the door. "Fuckin'..."

"Stacy—you hit?" Sky said in a panic.

"I'll be fine," Stacy grimaced, pressing down on her leg with one palm. "It's just a flesh wound. I'm gonna need to rinse it with alcohol." Stacy quickly pulled out a small bottle of alcohol and unzipped the side of her suit, pouring the liquid over her wound. She gasped as the alcohol hit the bullet wound.

"I forgot how much this hurts," she said, her face scrunching in agony. "More importantly—how the hell did they know we were coming?" she hissed. "Is there a malfunction with the invisibility feature?"

Mike's voice came over their headsets once more. "All suits are at optimal functioning," he said, his voice tinged with something like panic. "They shouldn't be able to locate us—"

"Where are their agents?" Bruce interrupted.

"Looks like the second floor, but we're having problems detecting them all," Mike answered. "Somehow, they know we're here..." his voice became garbled, and shots rang out from inside the house once more.

"Mike?" Bruce said. "Mike, come in." There was only

static and the muffled sound of gunfire now over the Slincs. Bruce and Mr. Brar watched the agents each pull out their weapons.

"Mike, I can't hear you," Bruce said again, checking the connection to Mike's Slinc as he pulled out his gun. "I'm not getting a response from Mike. Can anyone else hear him?"

"No, sir," Andrew answered.

"Same here," Sky acknowledged.

Still, Bruce waited for Mike's order, knowing their original plan was no longer viable. Seconds which felt like minutes passed and Mike remained silent. A sense of uneasiness ran through Bruce's body. Something wasn't right.

"Mike," Bruce repeated. "You there? You're leaving me no choice but to move forward without you and your team." He waited for a response, but heard only the ragged sound of his own breathing inside his suit.

Inside, the firing came to a halt. A familiar voice suddenly echoed through their earpieces. "What a nice surprise, Bruce."

"Who's that?" Prem asked.

The tiny hairs on the back of Bruce's neck stood erect.

Mr. Brar hissed, "It's that son of a bitch, isn't it?"

"Remember me?"

"Marvin..." Bruce declared.

CHAPTER 34

Marvin chuckled as he stood over Mike's dead body. "Now, how many of you are out there? I just want to make sure we get a head count for the body bags."

"I'm gonna come after you once we're done here," Bruce said sternly. Without saying anything further, he cut his connection with Mike's set.

"Everyone's gonna need to cut their sets off from Mike's."

One by one, all the agents disconnected their sets from Mike's and confirmed with Bruce that they had done so.

"Aabish and Santokh, get in contact with the other field agents."

"On it," they both answered.

"All this fucking planning... gone to shit," Bruce said, aggravated. "How did this happen?"

"You're forgetting who you're dealing with," Mr. Brar responded. "We may be two steps ahead of everyone else, but the agency is *always* ahead."

"Sir..." Aabish muttered. "About Mike's team..."

"What's the status?"

"They've all been compromised. They're not answering."

"Fuck," Bruce whispered. This was one of their worst-case scenarios, and it had already played out sooner than he'd ever expected. He had to think fast.

"Santokh, you're taking over for Mike."

Santokh, who hadn't moved since the shots had been fired earlier, took a glance at the SUV, and responded. "Crystal clear, sir."

"So, plan B?" Stacy asked.

"Yup," Bruce responded.

It was evident what that meant. They were under the instruction to do whatever was deemed necessary to accomplish the mission.

Santokh quickly dashed to the SUV and ducked down behind it. "I'm back in position," he announced. "Alright you guys. Stacy, you're up next. Sky will follow her lead. Bruce and Mr. Brar, you guys need to wipe the agents out in the backyard. Andrew, Prem, and Aabish— enter the house from the back door. I'll need a check in once everyone is inside."

"Good luck to everyone," Stacy muttered under her breath.

***

Inside, on the landing above the staircase, a SEA agent stood silently in position, waiting for them to enter. Outside, Stacy pulled out a hand grenade and took a few deep breaths before setting everything in motion. She kicked the door open and tossed the little ball of fury to the left of the house. The thud and clink of the grenade hitting the floor drew the SEA agents' bullets away from Stacy and Sky, allowing them to make their move further inside the home.

Behind the house, Bruce and Mr. Brar pulled out their weapons, preparing to kill. The SEA agents were now scattered around the premises, one standing just a few feet away from the back door.

Mr. Brar pointed his gun at the agent by the back door. "Good night," he whispered. A single shot to the head brought the agent to his knees. Immediately, the remaining SEA agents swung around and fired in Mr. Brar's direction, missing their target. "One down and three more to go," Mr. Brar muttered.

"I'm at the back door," Andrew's voice echoed over the headsets. "Santokh, I need clearance."

"I'm not picking up any movement on the Slinc. Just keep your guard up."

"Going in."

With no one in sight, Andrew slowly made his way over to the house and slid open the back door.

"I'm in," Andrew stated.

"Prem?"

Santokh waited for Prem to check in.

"Prem, I need your check in."

Santokh allowed a minute to pass by, hoping against hope to hear Prem's voice over his headset. But there was no response.

"Agent fallen," Santokh said flatly. One by one, the team disconnected themselves from Prem. Bruce, who had trained Prem and had hired her for all his top missions, aimed his gun at the SEA agent now advancing to the back door with tears in his eyes. His finger resting on the trigger, eyes focused on the agent, Bruce took a deep breath, keeping his emotions under control, and squeezed the trigger. There was a loud pop. In an instant, the agent was on the floor. Very quickly, a pool of blood became noticeable in the grass.

He heard Mr. Brar's raspy voice trickling through his earpiece. "You need to be quicker, Bruce."

Ignoring Mr. Brar, Bruce adjusted his position and pointed his gun at the second SEA agent now advancing towards the house. Without hesitation, Bruce pulled the trigger, sending the agent tumbling over to his death. "How do they know to move to the house?" he mumbled through gritted teeth.

For a moment, there was something approaching silence.

"She was a single mother, Prem—" Bruce said. "—kids just five and eight." In that moment, Bruce was reminded of his past and how Evan and Denise grew up with no parents, just like these two young girls would.

"Bruce," Mr. Brar sighed. "We'll make sure the girls are taken care of one way or another. You need to focus right now."

"Yeah," Bruce responded, pushing his emotions down deep into the pit of his stomach.

The last SEA agent outside began to fire in their direction once he saw his colleague hit the ground.

"Bruce, Aabish and Mr. Brar. Head for the house," Santokh urged.

"Going now," Bruce communicated, running towards the home, dodging bullets as he went.

"Roger that," Aabish said. As he promptly made it around the corner, a SEA agent became visible. Aabish pulled out his weapon and fired in the agent's direction. Missing the agent by less than an inch, he pulled the trigger once again.

"Mr. Brar. Need your check-in. Aabish?" Santokh's voice was filled with urgency.

"Gotta bring down the last agent out here," Aabish answered.

Laying on his stomach, on the sharp green grass, Mr. Brar kept his focus on the agent who was still firing in his direction.

"Mr. Brar! I need your check in *now*!"

The air continued to fill with gunfire, as the grass peppered with bullets.

The terror in Santokh's voice amplified. "Last call, Mr. Brar!"

With the gun pointed at the agent's forehead, Mr. Brar shut one eye and pulled the trigger.

"Got 'em," Mr. Brar exclaimed.

"Damn," Aabish whispered. "You got a good eye, sir."

"For fuck's sake, Mr. Brar! Respond when I'm calling!" Santokh was angry now. "Why aren't you guys inside the house yet?"

With a chuckle, Mr. Brar replied, slowly getting up from the ground. "How is it that I've been off the force for more than a decade, yet I'm the only one who has his shit together?"

Bruce let out a chuckle as he peered through the window inside the home, near the back door. "Santokh—they seem to be shooting straight at us. It's almost as if they know our locations. Something's not right. We can't afford to lose anyone else," he said, rolling his eyes to himself. "Am I the only one who is weighing the odds of any of us leaving this place alive?"

"That ship has sailed, son," Mr. Brar responded. "I'm moving towards the house now."

"Same," Aabish added.

"Heading in," Bruce replied. "Where's Andrew?"

"He's inside the house," Santokh responded. "Remember: be as quick as you can inside."

***

In the front hall, smoke from the grenade explosion hung in the air. The SEA agent positioned at the top of the stairs seemed to have disappeared. Sky and Stacy crept forwards.

"Inside," Stacy said.

Sky replied, "Ditto."

Suddenly, the agent at the top of the staircase leapt up from where he'd been crouching out of the way of the explosion and aimed his gun towards Stacy. Instincts taking over, Sky pulled out her weapon and aimed for his forehead.

Pow! Pow!

The agent dropped to his knees and hung over the staircase.

"Thanks," Stacy whispered.

"C'mon, we gotta—"

A loud chuckle echoed over the intercom, surprising both women.

"Wait a minute. Wait. Just. A. Minute. You ladies really believe you will make it all the way up the staircase when I can *see* you? Haven't you all worked it out yet? Your precious invisibility gear *doesn't work*. Not for *your* team, anyway. Not with the new technology we have here. We just wanted to have a little fun before we struck. Saw the cars parked out front."

Sky's heart dropped to the pit of her stomach.

There had to be new technology the agency was secretly developing which hadn't been brought to the board's attention. Not to her knowledge anyways. It was capable of detecting the invisible gear. That was how the SEA agents were able to locate them. *They'd been vulnerable the whole time.* It was apparent why it had been kept a secret and away from the board's eyes and ears: there was no doubt in Sky's mind now that Roy and Marvin had collaborated to enhance the capabilities of the current technology available to the agency.

Stacy looked around her, trying to figure out where the

voice was coming from. Exactly where was Marvin located?

"You guys," Bruce's voice filled their ears. "You in?"

"He can *see* us," Stacy responded through gritted teeth.

"And he can hear you," Marvin sang.

If Marvin could see them, there was no point in hiding. Both Sky and Stacy disabled their invisibility suits. They glared at each other, feeling defeated.

"Oh shit!" Santokh exclaimed. "Oh shit! Oh shit! Oh shit!"

"What?" Bruce asked. How could things possibly get even worse?

"*Fuuuuuuck*!"

"What the hell is going on?"

"There's a pool of blood on the kitchen floor. Andrew's not responding. Someone's gotta check for the body. I think they got him."

"Fuck," Bruce said under his breath.

"If he's dead, then we have to assume they have his Slinc. Which means—"

"They'll know our game plan," Sky concluded. "If they don't already."

Santokh's voice again. "Nope. Not happening. Not on my watch. I'm gonna kill Andrew's set from the rest of ours."

"Just do it," Bruce blurted.

"We need to get back on track," Mr. Brar inserted. "We're out two agents already."

"Disconnected it, Sir. Bruce, Mr. Brar... one of you guys needs to check the kitchen for his body. Sky and

Stacy are still in the entryway. You guys are closer."

"That'll be me," Mr. Brar replied.

In the entryway, Sky pulled out her phone and texted Stacy a series of instructions. She couldn't risk telling Stacy the plan aloud when Marvin could hear them. When Stacy's eyes met hers, they both nodded in agreement.

They both looked around for any visible cameras. Each step they took was a risk, not knowing what they might trigger, given that it appeared all kinds of advanced technology was clearly being utilized that they hadn't been aware of until now.

"We're coming in."

The sound of Bruce's voice brought a sense of peace to Sky. She held onto the feeling, knowing it wasn't going to last long.

They were approaching the most difficult part of the mission, and she felt her hope for successfully accomplishing their aims slowly disappear. In hindsight, they had gone unprepared. Everything they had considered, prepared for, their alternative plans—they were all no use. Marvin and the agency had blocked them from all angles possible. They had access to technology that Sky's team weren't even aware of. She'd thought the invisibility feature would give them the advantage. What she and her team were in now was a death trap. Without the protection afforded by invisibility, they were sitting ducks for Marvin and his goons.

"You have to be *extra* careful," Sky responded.

Bruce could sense the terror in her voice. He forced

himself to sound more confident than he felt. "Don't worry. Don't panic, Sky. You know we got this. He's messing with our heads."

Stacy whispered, "I've never been more terrified in my entire life. How do I know I'm not gonna trigger some sort of explosion, or that the next step I take isn't going to be the one that gets my head blown off?"

Sky wanted to reassure Stacy that wouldn't happen, but she had no idea what Marvin might do. Her mouth remained in a grim line. They heard the back door open and then close.

In the kitchen, Bruce, Mr. Brar and Aabish also disabled their invisibility mode. They stood beside the breakfast nook for a moment, before Mr. Brar moved into the bright white kitchen, scanning the periphery as he did so. Bruce examined the room, trying to figure out where the cameras were hidden. Aabish checked his surroundings like a hawk on high alert.

Mr. Brar cautiously approached the kitchen island and walked around it to find the pool of blood that Santokh had spotted on his Slinc. Mr. Brar crouched down, and carefully ran his hand over where he suspected the body would be. He felt nothing.

"There's no body," he said, feeling his heart sink.

"You got to be fuckin' kidding me," Santokh raged.

"No body," he repeated.

Mr. Brar analyzed the white tile flooring, but it was clear of any traces of blood which indicated the body had been transferred. "There's no sign of his body. This was just a way of getting us all in here, of slowing us down... we're not prepared for whatever they're equipped with. It's not looking good for us."

Mr. Brar rose and examined the rest of the kitchen out of curiosity. It was evident that this house was a home for someone. Water droplets rested on the stainless steel of the sink, and dish towels hung from the oven door. Making his way to the refrigerator, Mr. Brar opened the doors and found it to be stocked with food. Who was living here? Did this home belong to Roy?

"Andrew's dead..." Santokh thought out loud.

Santokh and Andrew had been recruited to the agency on the same day. Although they didn't spend too much time on missions together, they had found solace in one another when being an agent had taken a toll on their mental health. Over the years, their bond as brothers had strengthened and they knew they could count on each other whenever either one of them needed support. "His family's never gonna get his body," he whimpered. "They're gonna have to have a funeral with—"

"Santokh," Mr. Brar shushed. "We need you to focus."

Santokh's somber voice filled their ears. "Yeah."

In the front hall, Marvin's voice rang out again.

"Stacy, it's nice to see that they've seen potential in you," Marvin snickered. "What do you ladies plan on doing, *if* you make it out alive, now that you will be terminated from the agency? Any thoughts?"

Stacy peered around, still unsure of where the hidden intercom was. It was apparent that the house had been designed to allow a relatively small force to defend itself through using this advanced technology, which seemingly could take down a whole army remotely.

Back in the kitchen, Bruce looked around him and above. "Why don't you face us like a real man instead of hiding behind a screen?" he hollered.

Bruce checked each corner for cameras but found nothing. Whatever devices the SEA was using to watch them, they were highly sophisticated.

Marvin chuckled. "I want to watch you struggle for your life, Bruce. However, before there's more bloodshed, I am willing to let you all walk out, unharmed. This is your chance. If you continue with your rescue mission, I guarantee you that none of you will make it out alive. He's ours now. Don't waste your time and your precious lives trying to bring him back home. He *is* home."

"Fuck you!" Bruce yelled.

Marvin let out a manic laugh. "Well, it's settled then. Continue as you were. But don't say I didn't warn you."

"Sir," Aabish said as he approached Bruce. "You guys gotta get upstairs. We're running out of time."

Bruce peered down at his watch, agreeing. "We'll meet you out front. You got this." He gave him a pat on the back as reassurance.

Aabish nodded and responded, "See you on the other side, sir."

Aabish would remain on the first floor, on guard, while the rest of the team headed upstairs. Granted, it was a lot of square footage that he was expected to cover, but with two agents gone, now the duty fell solely into his hands.

Bruce turned to Mr. Brar and nodded. They moved along the hallway towards the front hall, staying vigilant. If Marvin's agents had access to invisibility tech even more advanced than their own, that meant that in any given moment, there was a chance they could be ambushed, shot, held in a chokehold or have their throats slit. It was all Bruce and Mr. Brar could think of as they made their way to Sky and Stacy. The unexpected kept them on edge.

"Ladies.... this is it," Bruce said. "Have your weapons ready. Be alert. You'll be able to sense the movement around you."

"For someone who hasn't worked in the field for over a decade, you are still pretty sharp," Marvin replied.

"Shut. The. Fuck. Up. You asshole!" Bruce hollered. "I'm coming after you next. I will *kill* you. Don't fuckin' underestimate me, Marvin."

"Don't entertain the idiot," Mr. Brar said calmly.

The house roared with Marvin's eerie laugh. "Oh! You are *too funny*!"

As Bruce and Mr. Brar appeared out of the hallway, they stood right underneath the ceiling of the upstairs landing, using it as a shield. They could see Sky and Stacy in opposite corners, also avoiding becoming a target in a fire storm.

Bruce halted. He linked eyes with Sky, and then with Stacy. They both nodded, knowing their next move.

Bruce pulled out a smoke grenade and tossed it in the center of the entryway, allowing them to make a run for it. Bruce and Mr. Brar sprinted towards the staircase. As Bruce took a few steps, a punch to the face took the wind out of him. He tripped over the step and tumbled, right before getting a grasp on the railing.

"Fuck."

Marvin's chuckle filled the air.

"Oh boy, that was rough to watch," Marvin bellowed.

Bruce looked up, trying to get a sense of where the unseen SEA agent was. His ears were still ringing, so he was unable to hear the agent's movement—or anyone else's—at that point.

Bruce took another step forward, receiving another punch to the jaw. Excruciating pain filled the lower half of his face. With no time to spare, knowing roughly where the blows were coming from, Bruce kicked into space as hard as he could, feeling his foot connect with the solid mass of a body. When the ringing in his ears subsided, he heard a thud, realizing the agent had fallen.

Mr. Brar stopped in his tracks. He reached into his suit, pulled out one of the Sparks, and tossed it towards where the thud had sounded. The shape of an agent lying crumpled on the floor flickered into view through the smoke. The agent reached for his gun and pointed it up at Bruce.

Things seemed to move in slow motion. Bruce's hand leapt for his gun, but before he could pull the trigger, a shot rang out and the agent on the floor slumped down, dead. His motionless body was visible for another few seconds before the Spark lost charge and he became invisible once more. Bruce slowly craned his neck back and peered at Mr. Brar, who stood, gun raised, his eyes fixed on the fallen agent. His mind couldn't fathom what had just happened. Although they were now unable to see the agent, blood was seeping into a dark pool beneath the body which still lay there.

"Bullseye," Mr. Brar whispered.

Bruce took a step forward and leaned over the pool of blood, groping the air until he found the shield around the dead SEA agent's face. He found the button at the collar and pressed it, disabling the invisibility suit and lowering the face shield. The first glance at the agent's face caused Bruce to jump back and almost lose his footing. He grabbed the stair rail to steady himself. His heart was pounding, and his ears filled with nothing but his own heartbeat.

"What the fuck…"

Evan.

"Are you seeing what I'm seeing?" he asked Mr. Brar.

Mr. Brar had begun to creep up the staircase and didn't have a visual of what Bruce was looking at.

"Hold on." He turned and looked down over the banister to where Bruce crouched next to the fallen man. When Mr. Brar saw the agent, he felt his stomach twist and his head droop down to his chest. He could feel his legs becoming numb.

"Why does he…. that *can't* be Evan. It's… it's not possible." Struggling to get words out of his mouth, Mr.

Brar felt a rush of panic in his stomach, rising with each passing second. He turned around and faced away from the staircase. Feeling pressure behind his eyes, and in his throat, he opened his mouth. Like a waterfall, his breakfast came rushing out.

"Mr. Brar!" Sky screamed from across the hall. She raced up the stairs, her eyes wide with concern. Stacy followed behind her.

"That can't be him," he moaned. He wiped his mouth with the back of his hand. "No. No way."

"What's going on?" Sky asked frantically. When she saw Mr. Brar's face, she came to a halt.

Mr. Brar bent over and retched again.

Bruce's eyes filled with tears as he lowered himself to the step.

"That's not him," Sky said, panting. "That's *not* him. We know he's back home with Shadow—"

"You sure about that, Sky?" Marvin interrupted.

Sky folded her hand into a fist and closed her eyes. Marvin's voice alone made her temper rise. Right now, she needed to remain calm and collected for the sake of their team.

"Bruce," she said softly, "that's *not* Evan. Trust me. It's not him. Marvin's trying to get in your head."

When she met Bruce's eyes, she had never witnessed so much sadness. She couldn't imagine the pain he was currently experiencing, believing that his only son lay dead in front of him. However, it wasn't Evan lying on the floor. That agent was a clone.

"But… he looks just like him, Sky," Bruce whimpered.

Sky pressed her palms together and brought them up to her face.

"Bruce, he just *looks* like Evan. But it's not him."

Bruce peered back at the dead agent, still feeling uneasy. He had forgotten what a lifeless face looked like. With a bullet in the middle of his forehead, the agent's pupils were fully dilated.

"Promise me."

"I promise you," she said, hurriedly.

He heard a raspy voice behind him. "We gotta keep going, Bruce."

Bruce wiped the beads of sweat above his upper lip with the back of his hand as he turned and met Mr. Brar's eyes. "Yeah."

Bruce leaned over and shut the dead agent's eyes. A part of him wanted to grieve the agent's death because somewhere out there, someone had lost either their brother, father, son, or partner. He'd never felt remorse for anyone in the field unless he had built a deep connection with them. However, given that he was looking at a doppelganger of Evan, he felt sadness in the pit of his stomach.

"Aww…he has feelings," Marvin mocked over the intercom. "Only a DNA test will prove whether or not that's your son."

"Don't listen to him, Bruce," Mr. Brar reminded.

Bruce traveled up the stairs, keeping his guard up and tuning out Marvin's voice, even though it was getting under his skin. Mr. Brar followed, staying on high alert, with Sky and Stacy right behind them, their weapons raised.

Once they reached the top of the stairs, Bruce looked left and then right.

"Split up," he announced.

Separated into their teams once again, Bruce and Mr. Brar took the right side of the house as Sky and Stacy took the left. Bruce traveled down the long hallway with Mr. Brar right behind him. As they approached the first door, a hissing sound filled their ears.

"Where is that sound coming from?" Mr. Brar asked.

Bruce peered around and spotted a small white nozzle sticking out from the wall at ankle height. As his eyes traveled down the wall, he realized there were hundreds of them. Suddenly, there was another loud hissing noise and the hallway filled with a thick, choking gas. Bruce and Mr. Brar began to cough almost immediately. Bruce assumed the gas would either kill them or at the bare minimum leave them unconscious.

"Mr. Brar, put on your mask! I don't know what this shit is but I'm guessing we don't have long before it hits our system."

"Two minutes," Marvin chimed in gleefully.

Mr. Brar covered his mouth with his elbow and searched for his mask.

"I can't find it," he said, his voice muffled. "It's okay. I'll be fine. We have to keep moving."

Bruce slipped on his mask and added eye goggles for maximum protection. He shook his head out of frustration.

"It's in your back pocket."

As gas filled the hallway, Bruce turned around to quickly help Mr. Brar find his mask.

"I checked both pockets—it's not—"

Aggravated, Bruce responded harshly. "For fuck's sake. Turn around and I'll check your backpack. It has to be in there." He moved towards him, gesturing for Mr. Brar to turn around so he could access the backpack.

Mr. Brar met Bruce's eyes. If he couldn't sense the frustration through Bruce's voice, he could certainly see it in his eyes. "Okay, but look, this—" suddenly, he froze.

Mr. Brar's mouth remained agape, but no words came out. His eyes widened with terror. Someone dragged Mr. Brar backwards. He tugged desperately at the invisible arm threaded around his throat.

"Bruce...," he said, choking.

"One sec."

Bruce pulled out his gun and aimed past Mr. Brar. Shots began to fire back in Bruce's direction, a bullet entering his shoulder.

"Ah... *fuck*," Bruce groaned.

Ignoring the pain, Bruce fired more shots, again missing the invisible SEA agent using Mr. Brar as a shield.

The hair on the back of Bruce's neck stood tall. He watched in horror as Mr. Brar slowly slid to the floor, blood oozing from what looked like a knife wound on his back. With perfect timing, Marvin deactivated his camouflage, revealing himself as the agent who had stabbed Mr. Brar.

"Give up, Bruce," Marvin said. "It's over, don't you see?"

He released the knife from his hand. The sound of it clattering onto the hardwood floor pierced Bruce's ears. He glanced at the Snake Knife that lay on the floor, blood dripping from the blade.

His eyes focused on Mr. Brar, who was groaning in pain. *Everything's gonna be okay. We just need to get him to the hospital,* Bruce repeated to himself, trying to remain calm. His hands began to tremble, making it difficult to hold his gun with the stability he needed for his aim. It was the first time Bruce had felt helpless. Bruce fixed his gaze on Marvin. He wanted to pull the trigger and end Marvin's life on the spot, but he couldn't. His hand felt paralyzed. The emotional wall that he had put up had slowly begun to come down.

"Aabish," Santokh's voice entered through their earpieces. "Bruce needs backup."

"Heading up."

"Drop your gun, Bruce," Marvin purred.

"Put on your mask and goggles!" Bruce yelled to Aabish. "Finish me off, Marvin. What are you waiting for?"

"Drop your fucking gun, Bruce."

"Not happening." Bruce's chest filled with agony and pain flowed through his body, knowing right in front of him, Mr. Brar was slowly dying. "Need a car ready for Mr. Brar," he said, trying hard not to choke on his words.

Marvin chuckled. "You really think the old man's going to live? The Snake Knife poison might wear off but the multiple fatal stab wounds sure won't, you know."

Bruce's ears homed in on the sound of footsteps traveling up the staircase, disregarding the gun pointed directly at his face. Right now, his focus had shifted to getting Mr. Brar out of the house and to the nearest hospital.

As Aabish neared towards the top of the staircase, Marvin pulled his trigger, piercing Bruce in the chest with a bullet. Then another.

Bruce groaned in agony. Marvin glanced in the opposite direction as Aabish appeared in his peripheral vision. That one second was all it took. Bruce quickly pulled the trigger of his gun as he tried to maintain his balance. With one clean shot in the head, Marvin plummeted to the floor beside Mr. Brar. Bruce leaned against the wall and watched as Aabish sprinted in his direction.

"Sir—"

"I'm fine. The bulletproof suit took most of the impact. You need to get Mr. Brar outta here and… to the nearest hospital. Snake Knife. Stabbed in… in the back. Go!"

As Aabish turned over Mr. Brar's body, his eyes flickered over to Bruce, who was managing to stand.

"Sir, we still haven't found the—"

"Hospital. Now!" Bruce roared.

Aabish carefully lifted Mr. Brar's limp body off the ground. "Got it."

With tears in his eyes, and out of breath, Bruce watched as Aabish carried Mr. Brar out of the hallway. In his mind's eye, all Bruce could see was the look on Mr. Brar's face right before he plunged to the floor. He stood still for a moment and stared down the hallway. *He's going to be fine*, he told himself. Santokh's voice rang in Bruce's ear. "Sir, do you need me inside?"

Through gritted teeth, Bruce responded, "No… stay there. We should be out in less than five."

With the time ticking, and in increasing amounts of pain, Bruce accelerated as fast as he could to the first door closest to him. Using one hand, with his gun in the other, he opened the door with caution. The room was perfectly set up for someone who had planned on staying for a while. The white bedding matched the wallpapered walls. In the corner, next to the dresser, was an armchair. A chest stood at the end of the bed. No sign, however, of baby Bright.

At the other end of the corridor, Sky and Stacy opened a second door, taking the necessary precautions. Stacy stood back, ready to fire if needed.

As Bruce advanced to the next door at his end of the hallway, a shrill scream pierced the air. Before Bruce could muster up the strength to call out to Sky and Stacy, he heard gunshots.

"Bruce…" Stacy's voice sounded in his ear.

"What? What?"

"The SEA agent is down... but Sky was attacked with a Houlkin."

Sky cried out in pain. "It hurts!"

The Houlkin was a circular tool with metal teeth which penetrated the skin. To increase the pain and risk of complications, the Houlkin released battery acid into the victim's skin, causing a second or third-degree burn.

"Sky, listen to me," Bruce said in a soft soothing voice. "We're almost done here. You're going to be fine. I promise. Just hang in there, sweetheart."

On the other end, all Bruce could hear was Sky hollering at the top of her lungs as the pain and the burning of her skin continued. Trying to tune out Sky's cries for help, Bruce finally opened the second door to find another bedroom neatly arranged.

Stacy's voice chimed in.

"Sir, I just checked the third room on this side of the house. He's not here."

"I have one more bedroom to check."

"I'm heading your way," Stacy replied.

"Keep guard for now. I'll call for backup if I need to," Bruce responded as he moved along the hallway.

"Got it."

"Santokh, there's no one else you can see on your Slinc that's up here?"

"No sir, but..."

Stacy marched her way down to the opposite side of the house, stationing herself in the hallway.

"What is it?" Bruce asked, beginning to become aggravated. They were running out of time. It wouldn't be long until more SEA agents descended upon the safehouse. He began to turn the handle of the last door.

"Someone just pulled up in front of the house."

"For fuck's sake," Bruce said, holding his hand in position.

For a brief moment, there was dead silence between the

two of them.

"It's Roy, sir," he stated. "He's got three agents with him. And they're all armed."

"Take out the two agents. Leave Roy," Bruce answered.

"Consider it handled," Santokh responded.

"Stacy, when Roy gets inside, just a shot in the leg. Maybe two. We're not killing him."

"Wait? Why?"

"We're gonna need him alive."

Echoes of gunshots drifted upstairs.

"One guy down," Santokh announced. "I don't have eyes on Roy."

"If we kill Roy right here, right now, the agency is done," Stacy concluded. "We need to get rid of him, now."

"Not until we find out why they took Bright," Bruce replied.

Stacy sighed. "Alright." She lowered herself to the floor, keeping her gun pointed at the door while she patiently waited for Roy to enter. From her position, she would be able to get a good visual of Roy in his entirety.

"Just a heads up, we only have two SUVs left," Santokh told them. "The tires of the other two were compromised in the initial shooting. I heard the air leak out."

"Where is the other SEA agent?" Stacy asked.

"Give me a second. I don't have eyes on him."

"Hurry up!" Sky interjected. She had propped herself up against the wall, riding the pain as much as she could, wanting the sweet release of death or at least unconsciousness to arrive. "I can't do this," she cried.

"Hang in there," Bruce urged.

He carefully pushed open the door to the final room.

"Bingo."

Bruce stood in a nursery. The walls were painted in Chandelier Sparkle, a pale yellow shade, and the room, to his surprise, was carefully decorated with a jungle theme. Monkeys hung from tree branches. Parrots flew across the room while a few Toucans sat on the branches. Tigers roamed below, looking for their next prey. A changing table sat against the wall to his right and next to it was the cot. In the corner opposite the window, was a rocking chair. The hardwood floor was hidden underneath a beige shag rug. It was evident Roy's plans of kidnapping Bright had been put in place the minute he had heard the news Shadow was pregnant. This was not a rush-job by any means. "I've got eyes on him."

Through the rails of the crib, Bruce could see Bright staring at the baby mobile. He let out a tiny yawn as he moved his arms up to his face. Bruce breathed a sigh of relief to see the baby unharmed and healthy. To his surprise, Bright remained calm and unfazed by the gunfire that traveled throughout the home.

Stacy continued to watch the front door carefully, waiting for the doorknob to begin turning. When the gunfire finally settled outside, there was a moment of peace.

"Santokh?"

Stacy waited for a response. The other end remained mute. Given their luck so far with this mission, Stacy was inclined to add another death to her imaginary tally board. Out of all the assignments Stacy had completed, none had compared to the one she was currently on. Everyone had always gone home to their families, minus perhaps a few days in the hospital after a major injury. She sighed deeply.

"Sir, we're another agent down."

Bruce let out a deep sigh. "Too many—"

"Wait, hold on a minute. I'm still alive," Santokh responded, panting. "Don't count me out just yet."

"What the hell man?!" Stacy sputtered.

"Sorry. Thought I was a goner there for a minute. I pissed my pants. It took me by surprise."

"I needed that," Sky giggled weakly. "Ow...ow... it hurts to laugh."

Suddenly, the front door opened, and Roy stepped through it into the entryway. Stacy didn't hesitate to fire. She released the trigger, firing three rapid shots, hitting Roy in the lower leg and ankle. He let out a loud groan and hit the floor.

In the nursery, Bruce heard the gunshots from downstairs and knew there wasn't much time. He had to get Bright out of the house as quickly and safely as possible.

Bruce rushed over to the crib, taking his backpack off and setting it on the floor.

"Hey there, little buddy," he said, feeling the tone of his voice change from panic and stress to soft and calm. "You're gonna go back home to your mommy and daddy. They're waiting for you."

An unexpected yet beautiful smile crept up across

Bright's tiny face.

"Yes, they are!" he exclaimed, as he pulled out a buckle carrier and unzipped the top half of his suit. Once he had the carrier fastened, Bruce reached into the crib and lifted Bright out, safely placing him into the carrier.

"We should be on our way back already," Santokh pointed out over the headsets as he kept a lookout for any signs of newcomers. "There could be backup on the way for all we know. When are we going back for our fallen?"

"Roy's on the floor trying to recuperate. We don't have much time, sir."

"I'm on my way out," Bruce responded. "We won't be able to do that, Santokh. By the time we come back for their bodies, the SEA will have already picked them up."

Bruce navigated his way out of the nursery and back into the hallway where Marvin's body lay lifeless. Moving swiftly and with caution, Bruce headed along the hallway, where he could see Stacy in position, with her gun still pointed at Roy.

"I'll put a bullet in your brain," Stacy warned as Roy reached for his gun.

Roy hesitated for a moment before deciding his life was far too important to jeopardize and dropped the gun to the floor.

"Now slide it away." Stacy's eyes remained fixed on Roy.

Groaning with effort, Roy did as she asked, then held his hands weakly over his face in a gesture of surrender. Keeping their eyes fixed on Roy, Bruce crept down the stairs towards the front door.

"I'm gonna go get Sky, sir."

Sky's voice beamed through their earpieces. "I'm coming," she said breathlessly. Sky trudged her way down the stairs, shocking both Stacy and Bruce.

Bruce could see the blood seeping from where the Houlkin had dug into her skin. The weapon was clearly no longer embedded in her flesh.

Stacy looked over her shoulder and asked, "How did you take it out?"

"*I* didn't," she said, sounding almost as shocked as Bruce and Stacy felt.

Her response raised serious and important questions. It was evident someone else had removed the gadget, but who? And why? Sky's lips curved upward slightly as she gazed at Bright and then at Bruce. "I think it's time we got the hell outta here."

CHAPTER 35

Bruce sat at the kitchen table, his eyes slightly swollen and pink as he blankly stared at the urn. It had been a week since Bruce received Mr. Brar's ashes. It had come as a surprise to Bruce that the agency hadn't withheld them, given he and his team—except for Santokh, who'd not been caught on surveillance during the Bright rescue mission—were all now blacklisted, their names on watch lists for the rest of their lives. Bruce's heart hadn't accepted that Mr. Brar was gone. This was a loss that Bruce knew he was going to grieve the rest of his life. Mr. Brar's last moments replayed in his mind's eye, as they had replayed every single day since it'd happened. He had dreamt of it. And when he was alone in his thoughts, all he could see was Mr. Brar lying in front of him, slowly taking his last breaths.

It felt surreal.

Bruce had imagined Mr. Brar living until *he* was turning old and frail. Even though he had his fears about having

Mr. Brar on their team for the Bright rescue mission, he hadn't seriously entertained the thought of losing him. Becoming injured? Yes, perhaps. But death? No.

His heart was in shock, to say the least.

The sound of Sky's voice pulled him out of his thoughts.

"He was one helluva guy, huh?"

Bruce cleared his throat and responded, "Yeah."

Bruce's eyes followed Sky as she neared the table; for a moment, his focus shifted to the scar on her neck, which would surely fade over time. However, the marking of the Houlkin would remain, even if only faintly.

She walked over with a black folder and pulled up a chair at the table. Sky rubbed at the scar left by the Houlkin absentmindedly as she looked over the folder. Bruce watched her and thought about how lucky she was to have survived.

"Does it bother you?" he asked, gesturing to the scar.

"No," Sky replied. "It's a badge of honor." She grinned. "Plus, this is how you'll know it's me, if you ever come across another one of the agency's clones—remember that SEA agent who looked just like Evan? They're clearly further along with the clone research than I knew." Bruce swallowed, thinking back to that awful moment when he thought it was Evan lying dead on the floor of the safehouse.

"So clones don't have scars?" he asked.

"Nope," Sky replied. "They're replicas of our DNA, so any injuries or changes to the body—ear piercings, say, or tattoos—are not cloned, as they're additions."

Bruce contemplated this for a moment. "So... you're saying it's possible that Marvin could have been a clone. Which would mean..."

Sky looked up from the folder, her eyes widening slightly as she grasped the gravity of what Bruce was implying. "He's most likely not dead," she said, slowly. "But I think he's the least of our concerns right now."

"This is beyond my comprehension," Bruce replied, frustrated. "Why would someone, who works for Roy, remove the Houlkin for you? I've been trying to figure it out..."

"It's been on my mind, too. It makes no sense. The agent could have easily killed me. Instead, my life was spared. I'm grateful to whoever had the heart to let me live. Maybe it's not important who it was?"

Bruce offered an undecided shrug. "Or it could be the key to the answers we're looking for?"

"That could be very possible," she said, placing both hands on the folder in front of her. "We're gonna have to revisit this conversation a little later. There are some things we need to discuss first." As Sky opened the folder, Bruce began to shake his head in disapproval.

"Sky... I don't wanna do this right now."

"I know, I know," she said sympathetically. "But as we're still reeling from our loss, *they're* working and plotting."

"He was..." he said, choking on his words. Bruce covered his mouth as he tried his best to maintain his composure. "I've never met someone as selfless as him. He was there for my entire family when I wasn't.

Twenty-seven years, Sky. Who would do that? And now... he's gone. Just like that."

Sky leaned forward and took his hand, intertwining her fingers with his. She held his hand tightly, knowing he needed her. But, at the same time, they couldn't put what was right in front of them on the back burner.

"You guys were really lucky to have him in your life. Extremely lucky. His aura was very gentle and kind. I miss him too, Bruce."

"I think you just described who he was perfectly," he said with a sniffle.

Sky smiled and gently gave his hand a squeeze. "We have to do this."

Bruce sighed, knowing he wasn't going to be able to escape from having this conversation.

"Alright," he said. "Let me go put this away."

Sky's hand slipped from his. "Okay."

Bruce picked up the urn and stepped out of the kitchen. He walked into the living room and looked for a temporary resting spot. After a few minutes of deliberating with himself about where to put Mr. Brar's ashes, he finally decided on the coffee table.

Sky pursed her lips and opened the folder, getting straight to business.

"Wait," Bruce began as he walked back into the kitchen. "Before you begin... I gotta tell you something."

She looked up, gazing into his eyes. "What is it?"

"I decided I'm not going to tell my family about my diagnosis."

She raised an eyebrow. "Bruce!"

"I know what you're going to say."

"That's a jerk move, you know that right?"

"Really? Because the way I see it… they're going to have to face another loss. And how is that period of time going to look like for them, knowing their dad is dying? I want them to enjoy every single day of their life. If last week has shown us anything, it's that life's short. I don't want to rob them of time and the happiness that they can enjoy."

Sky pondered his reasoning.

"I understand where you're coming from, and it makes sense, but—"

"There it is."

"You can't run away from the truth or hide from it. You did that once and look how it turned out for you. Once you're… gone, all they're going to have left is questions. And is that what you want for them? To leave them with more questions? It's not fair. You have to tell them. I'm not saying right now, but in the next few weeks or something. Sooner rather than later."

Bruce leaned back in his chair and admired the woman who sat before him. His heart hurt thinking about leaving her, too. His eyes glistened with tears, but he forced down his sadness.

"Okay. Fine."

"Thank you. Now, back to what we need to discuss."

"Shoot."

"First things first— Zack Moore is the one who administered the drug to Nate."

"*Zack Moore?*" he said, bewildered. He asked again, not sure if he had heard her correctly the first time. "Zack Moore... Skylar's dad?"

Sky broke eye contact and nodded. "Yup."

"Your *brother?* How do you feel? Are you—"

Sky shrugged. "He's an adult. He knew what he was doing. He could have done anything besides almost killing an innocent young kid. A kid that was his own son's best friend, *your* grandson."

"True. It's just... that he's your brother. Your only sibling."

Sky forced a smile and looked back down at her folder. "You don't have any siblings either," she reminded him. "And the way I see it, neither do I, any longer. I can't dwell on that decision anymore, Bruce. He did what he did, and now he's going to pay for it. That's how it works."

Bruce wanted to press further but held back. Like him, under duress, Sky tended to focus on the practical, omitting whatever emotion she might feel, the feelings surfacing later, once everything was settled. He was going to allow her to come to him when she was ready to talk about how she was really feeling about Zack.

She looked up at him and rested her elbow on the table. "I don't know if you want to tell Denise and Ryan who was responsible for what happened to Nate, but I think I would want to know if I was his parent. Keeping people in the dark about the truth is never a good idea."

Bruce mulled it over for a moment. He ran his hands through his hair then brought them forward to the table, clasping them in front of him.

"I agree they should know, but—"

"There are no buts, Bruce," she blurted, wide-eyed. "See. This is your problem. You say one thing and then back track. You lost twenty-seven years of your life with your kids. Do you want your daughter to wonder for thirty years about who did this to her child? It's always going to be in the back of their minds."

Taken aback by Sky's sudden outburst, Bruce let out a soft exhale.

"Maybe we should talk about what's *really* going on, Sky, and this all can wait."

"No. All of this is important. Everything else can wait."

Bruce pursed his lips and let out a deep sigh.

"Look, I get why they should know. I would want to know as well, but this person is from their inner circle. This could lead to them both living in a constant state of paranoia. That's no way to live," he sighed. "Their lives are never going to be the same, regardless. I don't know... if we share this information with them, it might make it worse for Ryan and Denise. At the same time, it's a natural human tendency to want to know, even if you're really not going to gain anything out of it."

Sky nodded. "That's something you're gonna have to figure out then. Just keep in mind, what the agency did to Nate was their way of sending you guys a warning. Zack was the perfect person for them to use to administer the drug because he was familiar to Nate and because he was facing a legal battle that Marvin could exploit. Denise and Ryan have their son back but that doesn't mean—"

"Yeah, I know. They'll never be done making threats until they have what they want."

"Glad we're on the same page."

Bruce studied her. He sensed she was beginning to put up a wall and, if he knew her at all, it was only a matter of time before she snapped.

Sky turned her attention back to the file. "Next thing on the list. Mr. Brar made me the executor of his will."

Bruce's eyebrows furrowed. He was perplexed. "He left it with you? I thought he would have appointed me. I've known him *way* longer than you have."

Without looking up, Sky responded, "He was going to ask you, but he knew it was going to be extremely hard for you, so he gave it to me."

Bruce pushed back his chair and went to the refrigerator. "What does it say?"

"It's pretty straightforward. You guys are allowed to take whatever you want. He wants Evan to keep his wife's books. He wants any of the religious text or paintings that can't be dropped off at the temple, to be burned. Everything else, he wants us to donate to charity. The memorial service is set for Wednesday."

He turned from the refrigerator and pulled out a can of Coke. "You already—"

"Yeah. We gotta keep the train moving."

He stood in the middle of the kitchen and pulled back the tab, letting the snap and the sizzle of the soda fill the air for a moment.

"Why Wednesday? Why not Friday? What's the rush in doing his memorial Wednesday? It's not like he's going anywhere."

Sky offered a sympathetic look as she peered into his eyes. "Bruce, I know this is really hard for you. I know that. But the longer we hold onto his ashes, the longer it's going to take for you to actually begin grieving."

Bruce reflected for a moment.

"Yeah, I know," he admitted, sighing heavily. He sat back down and placed the can on the table. "So, what's next on the agenda?"

"One of the other things Mr. Brar left behind for all of you was his retirement fund."

Bruce raised an eyebrow. "What?"

"He wanted to keep you guys safe, even if he wasn't here, so the money he left for you guys could cover private security."

"Wow... I can't believe he didn't tell me any of this."

"He probably didn't think he needed to have the conversation with you just yet." She smiled sadly.

"That day... I don't think I even gave Mr. Brar a hug. And I snapped at him when he couldn't find his mask. I really wish I hadn't done that."

Sky nodded, unable to muster up any words in response. She found herself thinking about the day she would have to say goodbye to Bruce. All her emotions began to rush back to the surface.

"I don't think we have a recent picture with him as a family." Bruce leaned back in his chair, a faraway look in his eyes. "You know, he loved kheer? It's an Indian dish that's made with rice, milk, and sugar. I don't know why I didn't bring that to the dinner we had..."

As Bruce reminisced, Sky's mind continued to be filled with thoughts of the day Bruce would be gone, too, and her eyes welled up. Not wanting Bruce to see her in such a state, Sky quietly excused herself from the kitchen and walked into the bedroom with her hand over her mouth. She sat at the edge of the bed and silently sobbed. How was she supposed to say goodbye to Bruce? She couldn't wrap her mind around it. It was unfair.

She wasn't alone for long before Bruce noticed she had quietly slipped away.

"Babe." Bruce's voice neared as he walked down the hallway. When he approached the bedroom and saw Sky wiping away her tears, he immediately made his way to her side. "Hey, hey, hey...what's wrong, Sky? Talk to me." He wrapped his arm around her and pulled her close to his chest. He felt her body tremble and her sobs become muffled as she buried her face in his chest. "Talk to me."

"One of these days...you're gonna leave me, too."

As her words hung in the air, he hugged her tighter. He didn't have the right words. Were there right words for something like this?

She pulled away and peered into his eyes. "How am I supposed to live without you, huh? My heart..." she choked. Her lips quivered as she spoke, her voice now softer than it was before. "I'm... I'm trying to keep myself together, but I can't. How am I supposed to do this?" she asked, tears streaming down her face. The pain that she had been hiding so well had finally surfaced. "*How*? I don't want to do life without you. I really don't," she said, shaking her head. "There has to be something we can do..."

Bruce clenched his jaw. His vision became blurry as he gazed at Sky. They had fallen in love some time ago, when they believed they were going to grow old and travel the world together. It broke his heart that he was not going to be around to watch Sky grow old, or to watch his own children and grandchildren evolve. It tore him apart knowing that some of the promises he had made to her had become mere empty words.

There was nothing he could say that was going to make her feel better.

"You gave me a home in your heart, and I'll always be there, no matter what." He hugged her tighter and kissed her forehead. "I love you, Sky. I would go to the ends of the Earth for you, over and over again. You've been my sunshine, ever since the day I met you."

She buried her face in his chest, feeling broken and calm all at the same time.

She'd been used to losing people; that was something that came with the territory of her job. But it seemed easier when there was no sign of death just around the corner.

"I love you, too," she cried.

CHAPTER 36

Shadow rested at the bench after finishing her two-mile walk. With her headphones plugged in, she couldn't hear the sound of the children playing tag or the dog playing fetch with its owner, barking between throws, or the picnic that was taking place fifty yards away from her. It hadn't been a year since she'd moved to Lake View, but so far, Cherry Park was by far her favorite spot to relax and sit with her worries. It was calm and peaceful, regardless of whether there were swarms of people or if she was all alone. It was also the place where she had first felt the depth of Evan's love for her. This place was always going to hold a special significance for Shadow.

Feeling ready to get back on her feet, Shadow bent down to pick up her water bottle. As she sat back up, she got a glimpse of the man sitting at the end of the bench, who hadn't been there the moment before.

"Hello, Shadow."

She recognized her father's voice. When she met his

eyes, her heart plunged to the pit of her stomach.

He was dressed as she always remembered him, in all black from head to toe, except for the crisp white collared shirt. And now it made sense to her: he was the leader of a sinister organization, and the outfit was fitting for the line of work.

She had no reason to be scared of her own father, but if she had learned anything in the past few weeks, it was that he wasn't who she thought he was. And that terrified her, even though she didn't want to feel that way.

"What are you doing here?" She felt her heartbeat begin to race. This was the man behind everything she was trying to escape from. He had created hell on Earth for her family.

Roy peered towards the pond with his hands clasped in his lap. "I haven't seen you in almost a year, and that's all you have to say?"

He craned his neck sideways, an unpleasant look on his face.

"Let's not play games here, Dad. You're the last person I want to look at. You ruined my life and then took my baby from me. How do you… *what's wrong with you*?" she hissed.

"It's not about how I could do this or that, alright? There are bigger things in play here."

"So, you're telling me that your daughter's and your grandson's lives are meaningless and have no value?"

"In life, you have to make decisions, and some of those decisions require you to look at the greater good."

Shadow scoffed. "I'm just appalled. Not even angry.

I don't have time to be angry. Just *appalled* that I don't mean shit to you." Her eyes glistened with tears, but she refused to let her father see how he'd torn her apart.

"There are things that I can't tell you, Shadow."

"That doesn't excuse anything you've done. My entire life was built on a *lie*... does Mom know?"

He nodded.

"She knows?!" She felt her heart sink.

"Look, you can be mad at me all you want, but this is all for a good purpose."

"I'll never understand how you can walk around and act like you did nothing wrong. You run a secret organization that has probably taken thousands and thousands of lives. And you were ready to sacrifice me for something you claim is 'for the greater good'. You expect me to believe this bullshit you're feeding me?"

Roy stood up and met her eyes. "You're alive, aren't you?" His eyes flickered towards the arm that was now wrapped in a cast.

Shadow's mouth was agape. This wasn't the man who'd raised her. She'd never known her father to be so insensitive, snarky, and cruel.

"I'm hanging on by a thread," she hissed.

"You may not remember this, but when you were younger, you remembered who you were in some other life. And then you began to suffer from flashbacks as a kid, hallucinations. Your grandfather suffered from them and so did his father. I've seen what happens, Shadow. As you age, hallucinations lead to delusions. You start to believe and live your life like you're this other person that doesn't really exist. Eventually, you go off the deep end. You're not *you* anymore and that will cause you to lose your life, your family, your job. You'll lose everything you ever cared for. *I* saved you from that. Is that what you want for Evan? He suffers from that, too, doesn't he?"

Shadow felt the hair on her neck stand up. The moment of her accident came flashing back. The memories *were* coming back...

Flustered, she asked, "What else are you hiding?"

"You want to know the truth?"

"That's all I've been asking."

"Okay."

She lowered her voice. "Why him? Out of all the men out there, why Marvin?"

"He's ambitious. He would have made a wonderful husband and father, Shadow. He would have always protected you. He was one of the finest agents I had. Good looking. Only child. A good build. I made him a promise that if the two of you got married, he would become the head of the agency once I stepped down. The agency belongs to the Hex clan and we're going to keep it that way. Picking who I wanted to take over gave me some sort of relief. He would have made a fine leader."

Shadow cocked her head backwards in disbelief. "I can't believe this. I really can't. He was the devil."

"The devil was once an angel too."

Ignoring her father's pedantic response, she followed with her next question. "And Detective Lucas... he used to come to the house when I was younger, didn't he?"

The lack of response from Roy told Shadow all that she needed to know.

"I hope there's a special place in hell for people like you," she screeched. "You've inflicted *so* much pain in such a short amount of time. How do you live with yourself? If I—if I saw you dying in front of me, I wouldn't save you. I wouldn't!"

Roy shrugged, ignoring the brief flash of pain her words caused. "Fair enough. There are a lot of things I can't tell you, Shadow. You have to understand that. If you love your family, you'll make the sacrifice and give us Bright. We need him."

He watched the expression on her face switch from anger, to disgust, to sadness, to confusion and then back to anger. He had protected her for as long as he could until she became an independent adult. He couldn't share everything he knew for her safety, and it killed him to not be able to defend himself fully. Of course, he loved his daughter, despite what Shadow thought. In her defense, she wasn't in the wrong to be angry with him.

In his eyes, she was always going to be his little girl whom he'd loved so deeply. But he had to let her go and love her from arm's length, even though it was far from what Shadow thought love and protection should look like. Everything he had done, he had done in Shadow's best interest. And he hoped one day she would come to find that he wasn't as evil as she currently believed him to be. Until then, this was going to be the nature of their relationship.

"That's it? You feel no guilt for what you did? The pain you caused my family. Nate? Any of it?"

He didn't answer, saying only, "Try calling your mother once in a while. She misses you," instead, his voice somber. With that, Roy stood up, turned his back towards Shadow, and began to limp away. In mid stride, he stopped in his tracks and turned towards Shadow. "The safehouse... where we had Bright... how did Bruce find it?"

"It looks like you're not the only one who has secrets."

A tight grin appeared across Roy's face. "Don't worry. We'll figure it out soon. And one more thing."

"What?"

"I still love you. I always will."

Shadow watched with unease as her father walked off into the distance. It took every fiber in her body to keep herself from falling apart. There was a part of her that felt that she needed to save him from whatever it was that had transformed him into this unrecognizable person. He had assured her that he'd always loved her. Surely deep down inside he was still the caring, loving father she'd grown up with? But she knew it wasn't her job to fix him, either. Perhaps he couldn't even be fixed. Tears streamed down her face. It dawned on Shadow that her father was never again going to be a part of her life; there was never going to be a chance for them to rekindle and repair their relationship. Not after this. Even though Shadow didn't want to believe what her heart and mind were telling her, she knew that this was the end of their relationship. What her father had done was unforgivable.

Taking in the last view of her father as he became a blur in the distance, she turned around and retraced her route back home.

CHAPTER 37

During Shadow's walk on her way back home from Cherry Park, the conversation with Roy continued to play in her mind like a broken record. She'd been left with more questions than answers. Her father knew about her memories, which she had thought started only a year ago, but he was claiming she'd had them as a child. Why couldn't she remember? Whatever the SEA was working on now, Bright was their golden egg. But why Bright? He was just a baby. What purpose was he supposed to serve? Roy had provided no answers.

When she reached the house, she recognized Denise's black Lexus parked in the driveway. The grey Audi that Willow drove was parked right beside it. By the sidewalk was Bruce's black Range Rover. But before she reached the front door, her attention veered towards Mr. Brar's house. Every day she would look at the porch, hoping he would be sitting there. Even though they'd known each other only a short while, it felt as though she'd known him her entire life. His smile was bright and contagious. Filled with love, it was something she was going to miss dearly. It wasn't until now that she realized how one soul could have such a great impact on not only just her life but on everyone else around her.

As she stood there, absorbing the reality of Mr. Brar no longer being in their lives, conversations between the two of them came rushing back. She recalled the moment she and Mr. Brar had been left alone together in the backyard one evening when Evan slipped away into the kitchen to check on the pizza baking in the oven.

"When things get tough, and they always do, don't run away from each other," he'd said. "Any problem you face can be resolved by working together. If he runs or you run when life throws curve balls, it will take a toll on your marriage. If you want your partnership to last, don't run. Don't doubt whether you two belong with one another. I've never seen him this happy. He looks at you like you're magic. That certainly isn't an exaggeration."

Shadow knew she'd remember his words forever. At the time, she'd agreed with Mr. Brar—of course she would stand by Evan, and he her—but when she'd been put to the test, hadn't she just wanted to run?

Shadow headed for the front door, pulling out the house key from the pocket in her leggings. When she stepped inside, she heard laughter, which was quite shocking after what felt like weeks of tension and sadness, and which made her immediately wonder what had put everyone in such a good mood. She went to the kitchen and found Evan, Bruce, Venice, Denise, Ryan and—*Nate?* sitting around the table, plates of cheesecake before them.

"Aunty!" Nate shrieked. "You're here!" He jolted from his chair and ran over to Shadow, who was standing by the door, baffled, unable to comprehend what felt like a miracle. Nate was back? And healthy? Her nephew flung his arms around her waist and gave her a big squeeze.

Shadow wrapped her arms around Nate, blinking back tears, and looked up at everyone.

Her voice trembled as she spoke. "He's awake... he's awake." She could see tears welling in Bruce's eyes, too. Denise and Ryan were nodding their heads, smiles beaming.

"*Yeah*! He woke up yesterday morning!" Evan exclaimed.

"Yesterday morning?"

"Yeah," Denise chimed in. "The doctors wanted to run some tests and keep him overnight to monitor him, just in case. That's the short version, anyway..." Denise smiled and signaled to Shadow that they would spare the details for another time.

Shadow understood and nodded. She looked down at Nate, who hadn't let go of her.

"You have no idea how happy I am to see you!" She kissed his forehead, feeling a sense of relief overcome her. She had blamed herself for what had happened to Nate, even though Evan had reassured her that she couldn't have prevented it. But now that he was awake, and breathing, the part of her that felt responsible was finally diminishing. Her heart felt just a little lighter, and for that she was grateful.

"How's your baby cousin doing?"

Nate looked up at her with a grin, pure innocence radiating through his eyes. "I got to look at him. He's sleeping. Can I hold him when he wakes up?"

"It's almost time for his next feeding, Nate," Evan asserted. "He'll be up pretty soon. You can hold him afterwards, bud."

"Yeah, it's almost that time," Shadow added.

"Okay," he answered. Nate quietly slipped away to join the rest of the family at the table and continued to play on Ryan's phone.

"Sweetie, come sit down and have some cheesecake," Venice said.

"I'm going to skip the cake," Shadow chuckled. "Let me just rinse this and I'll be right there," she said, waving her water bottle.

"How was your run?" Bruce asked, following her to the sink.

Shadow paused. The conversation at Cherry Park with her father resumed in the back of her mind. Bruce had been an agent for so many years. Yes, he'd been a part of a plan to take down the SEA, but how much did she really know him? If her own father was able to lead a double life all these years, what was preventing Bruce from doing the same? Before she allowed her mind to run away with theories and suspicions, she took a breath and reminded herself that not everyone was like her father. She studied him for a moment and then replied, "It was good. How come Sky isn't with you?"

"She's working on some things. She wanted to be here though. She'll be there tomorrow for the service."

"How are you doing? Are you still in any pain?"

"No, not as much as before. How are you doing with everything?"

"I don't know. I'm glad that Nate and Bright are home. But we lost someone so special. It's just a lot to take in, if I'm being honest."

Bruce sighed. "Yeah, it is. But we're all here for you guys, you know that right? Whatever you need, we're here."

She met his eyes, feeling a pang of sadness. Her mind harked back to the moments her father had been there when she needed him the most. It was as though Bruce was now filling in his shoes.

"Thank you," she said.

Bruce nodded. "No worries. How long is that cast staying on for?"

"Uhm...a few weeks."

"Let me know if there's anything I can do or if there's anything you need. Whatever it is. I'll be here."

Shadow pursed her lips and replied. "Thank you. I appreciate it."

Bruce hugged her tight before retreating to the rest of the group.

When Shadow finished rinsing her bottle, she let it dry on the dish rack. She walked towards the bassinet in the living room and peered into it at her little bundle of joy.

Even doing absolutely nothing, Bright was able to restore her heart and dissolve all her stresses. She grinned and softly touched the tip of his nose.

Evan slipped his arm around her waist and kissed her neck.

She met Evan's eyes and felt grateful for the man who didn't give up on her. She thought back to their wedding, when they'd exchanged the vows they'd written themselves.

Through the storms of life and the glorious days that feel heavenly, I'll be right there beside you, because baby, I ain't goin' anywhere.

Despite their ups and downs, which any healthy marriage endured, there hadn't been a day that Evan didn't put in all his effort to make sure she felt loved and was safe.

She softly grazed his cheek. "I love you," she whispered.

Evan smiled and tugged her closer. He felt his heart explode a little with happiness. "I love you more."

Someone cleared their throat from across the room. Evan and Shadow both turned their heads, to find Denise beaming with joy.

"So, we wanted to share some exciting news with you guys," Denise began.

Evan and Shadow turned around.

"What is it?" Evan asked.

Denise reached for Ryan's hand, barely able to contain her excitement.

Ryan chuckled. “She’s been dying to share this with you guys.”

“Oh, spill the beans, Denise!” Venice shouted with joy.

“We’re pregnant!”

“No way!” Evan bellowed. “That’s amazing!”

“Wow! That’s wonderful news,” Bruce chimed in.

A round of congratulations came from everyone in the room as they all exchanged hugs and congratulated Denise and Ryan on their pregnancy.

“I know it's early to share but we’ve got a little bun in the oven.”

“That’s so exciting, Denise!” Shadow added. “I’m so happy for you guys!”

Evan made his way over to his sister and congratulated her with a big hug.

Venice leaned forward and grasped Ryan’s hand. “Congratulations, you two!”

The room was filled with joy, and it felt like a normal day: for a moment, they had forgotten about their loss. They had forgotten all about their worries and fears and what was to come next. They hadn’t had too many days like this one in the past year.

It felt like a breath of fresh air.

It brought hope.

***

Later that evening, after dinner was served and the house had become quiet again, Evan sat in bed propped up against a pillow while he checked his emails on his laptop. He scrolled through a few, dreading having to go back to work in a month's time. Not because he didn't enjoy teaching, but because it was going to be time away from Bright, and he was soon going to learn that babies did grow up fast. Too fast. Not only was Evan slowly absorbing the idea that they were going to transition back into their somewhat regular life with a newborn on their hands, but the loss of Mr. Brar was still settling in.

When Bruce had broken the news to Evan, his emotional wall of denial had gone up in seconds. His mind couldn't immediately understand what had happened. Even days later, it still felt as though it was the first time he was hearing about Mr. Brar's death. Evan's job as a psychology teacher, and all the knowledge of the human psyche that came with it, was of little use when it came to his own grief. Like everyone else, he simply couldn't wrap his mind around the idea of Mr. Brar no longer being here. The reminders came in waves: he would no longer be able to have conversations with Mr. Brar on the porch like they used to; Mr. Brar was no longer going to be there for advice that Evan might need. He was never going to see Bright grow up.

He looked over at Bright, who was laying on his back next to him.

A smile danced on his lips as he leaned close to give him a peck on his soft cheek. It amazed him how much love he had to give to a little human who did nothing but eat, poop, and sleep. He couldn't imagine his life without him. It was a concern that they had no plan in place about how they were going to navigate the future. There was no doubt in their minds that the SEA was going to attempt to abduct Bright once again. But right now, all they wanted to do was absorb every single moment they had with their son.

"Hey there little guy," Evan said, softly rubbing Bright's stomach.

Bright was in a grey onesie that Shadow had eventually managed to wrestle him into. Denise assured them this was a struggle for all new parents. Along with dressing a newborn, Shadow had found breastfeeding to be extremely painful, which was also normal for some mothers from what she had read and had resorted to bottle feeding. It wasn't how she had envisioned her experience as a first-time mother, but she was grateful that Bright was happy, healthy and back home nonetheless.

Bright's tiny hands moved closer to his face that had scrunched up for a moment as his beautiful blue eyes looked up at his father.

"You make the same face Mommy makes when she's tired, but yours is cuter."

Shadow chuckled as she stepped out of the bathroom. "I heard that." She rubbed her neck with the cream she had squeezed onto her hands and smiled, waiting for a snarky response.

"That's why I said it... out loud," he winked.

Shadow shook her head and giggled as she made her way to the bed.

"I can't believe Venice is engaged. I'm so happy for

her," she grinned.

"She deserves the world and Willow is finally getting married to his high school crush."

"They're so cute together," Shadow gushed.

Shadow crawled into bed and leaned against the bed frame. She gazed at Bright in awe.

"I wonder what he's thinking about." She leaned in and kissed the tip of his tiny nose. "You're soo cute, my love," she said in a baby voice. "Yes, you are. Yes, you are, my sweet pea."

"You've got me. He's probably wondering what we look like. Babies can't see very clearly."

"I remember reading that in one of the books we bought."

They gawked at their baby and soaked in every second they could.

Evan reached over and softly grabbed her cheek and pinched it. "Tell me."

"Tell you what?" she asked, meeting his eyes.

Evan lowered the screen of his laptop and shifted it onto the bed.

"Your face said it all after you came back from your run. Something was bothering you. What happened?"

She studied his eyes. As much as she wanted to lie and keep the conversation with her father to herself, just so Evan wouldn't worry, she knew at one point, the truth was going to come out. Then, it would be a completely different conversation and she knew it wasn't worth losing his trust over.

She sighed and broke eye contact. "I… uhm…

saw my father."

"Oh…?"

She met his eyes again. "Yeah. He showed up at the park. When I was taking a break, he came and sat right down on the bench I was sitting on."

Evan felt his stomach turn and tried as hard as he could to keep himself calm. He already knew this conversation was not going to go anywhere positive.

"What did he say?"

Shadow looked down at Bright and caressed his soft, brown hair. "It's not what he said, but what he implied. He said he saved me from these hallucinations, the ones you have. It seems like they run in my family, though I have no memory of that. He was vague about everything, and I have more questions about my whole life now. I feel like I'm never really going to get the answers to them, you know? I'm hurt and confused. And I'm angry because he's my dad. Parents are supposed to protect their kids, right?"

"Yeah. That's supposed to be their primary goal. Loving and protecting them."

"He says that's what he was doing, but look at what's happened since I moved here. And my dad's been behind all of it. How is *that* protecting me?" she asked, frustrated. "He wants me to feel like I'm responsible for everything and moving forward, I'll be responsible for whatever happens next because I'm choosing to keep my son." Shadow wiped the corner of her eye. "I'm so mad. Pissed. Sad. Heartbroken. But… I feel numb at the same time. I don't know how I'm supposed to deal with this. It's just too much, Evan."

"I know, honey."

"And then a part of me wonders about the future, not just for Bright, but for you, too. He said these delusions lead to losing your life. It just got me thinking... what if we both lose ourselves? How do we know how long it will take? What's going to happen to Bright? And then I started to wonder like, what if giving up Bright to the SEA is actually a good thing in the long run?" Her lips began to quiver. "I feel like I'm gonna go crazy with all these thoughts because no one can answer them for us. And my dad's not gonna give us the answers."

"It's hard to know what the truth is at this point. They've been watching us, and they're master manipulators. There's no denying that."

"Yeah."

"So, he could be telling the truth and trying to do a good thing—and I know we'll never see it that way—or it's just another lie to get what they want. But it's hard to believe he's telling the truth with everything that's happened. Since he's not allowed to share what's going on behind closed doors... we have to do what's right for us, whatever that may be. We have to take it one day at a time, though."

Shadow pursed her lips. "This is never gonna end, is it? This is our life now, huh?"

Evan looked away for a second before meeting her eyes again. "Yeah, until they take down the SEA, I think we're going to have to stay on our toes. I hate that it's what our life has come to, but we can't also keep thinking about what decisions we *could* have made, either," he said as he held her gaze for a moment.

Shadow looked down at her hands and studied her fingernails.

"I know," she said, her voice breaking. "I think... there's a part of me that's just so sad that I don't have my family. I mean, I do, but my parents aren't in the picture and finding out the truth about my dad and who he is... it just makes me..." She paused to take a deep breath and peered into his eyes through a blur of tears. "I never thought in a million years that this was what my life was going to look like, you know? I should've been able to experience every milestone in my life with happiness in my heart, but instead, there was fear. I just... miss being able to breathe and not have to worry about whether or not I'm being followed or... worry that someone might be hiding in our house... you know?"

"I know, hun." Evan reached for her hand and kissed the top of it. He held it close to his chest as he gazed into her eyes. "You've been through a lot, more than I have, but now, and tomorrow, and the day after, I want you to remember that you don't have to do this alone. We're in this together. I've told you this before. You have to stop thinking that everything is for you to handle on your own. This is *not* your burden to carry. We'll take it one day at a time. And the good thing is that we've got security now, so even when I'm not home, you won't be alone. That should help with the stress a little bit."

Shadow remained silent, letting his words register. Somewhere deep down in her gut she knew this was just the beginning. The war was just getting started.

CHAPTER 38

Sky yawned quietly as she watched the entrance of the Lake View Hospital from the backseat of the AMG GT 63. She glanced at her watch and saw it was two thirty in the morning. Early morning field work had never been her cup of tea, but now that she was no longer a part of the agency, Sky and Stacy would have to do all the grunt work, sending the information back to the few agents left on the inside of the SEA Sky knew they could trust.

She had been waiting for an hour in the parking lot, which, despite the time, was partially full and illuminated to ensure the safety of the staff and the patients as they left the building. Sky was beginning to become agitated. She had been out of the field for a long time, and this moment only reminded her how much she didn't miss it. She killed the time by scrolling through her social media feed and keeping an eye out. Eventually, she spotted her target walking out of the automatic hospital doors; white coat still on, briefcase in one hand and red hair bright under the parking lights.

"Piece of shit," Sky muttered under her breath.

The doors unlocked and Zack opened the car door. He tossed his briefcase over to the passenger's side and lowered himself into the driver's seat. Once he slammed the car door shut, Sky pulled out her knife. Like a snake, she wrapped her arms around his neck, the blade almost piercing his pale skin.

"I'm surprised," she began. "That with the type of work you do for them, they don't have a security detail for you," she hissed.

Zack's pupils dilated with fear. "Please don't kill me," he whimpered.

"I'll spare you your life if you tell me what's going on in there."

Scared of having his throat slashed, Zack sat frozen in terror. He thought about his words carefully. Sky couldn't wait.

"What the *fuck* is going on in there, Zack?!"

"Can we calm down a little bit... *please*?" Beads of sweat quickly began to form at his hairline.

Sky pressed the blade against his skin harder this time. "Do you want to bleed to death? It's a long and painful death."

Zack shuddered and wheezed out a ragged breath.

"I really don't know anything—"

"Cut the bullshit! Nate didn't just 'wake up' miraculously. I saw the reports. *Tell me*."

"How do you know it wasn't a miracle, huh? You should try going to church—"

Sky pressed the blade a little bit more, just breaking the surface of his skin. He winced in pain. "This is not the time to be a smart ass. I'll slit your throat and figure this out on my own. *Or* you can stop being a little *bitch* and tell me the truth. How did you do it and why?"

Zack remained quiet.

"*Tell me how!*" Sky pressed the knife further as blood began to slowly ooze out of his skin.

"It's..." he said, taking deep breaths.

"It's what?!"

Zack's chest rose up and down rapidly out of panic. "It's a trial medication, and there was a chance it wasn't going to work. And..."

"And what?"

"And I didn't want you to kill me. You're all I have. That's why I did it," he finally admitted. Zack closed his eyes, feeling a little relief trickle over him.

"So, you reversed his condition?"

He nodded aggressively.

"I want to hear you say it."

"Yes," he mumbled.

"How did you do it?" she asked, pressing the blade harder against his skin once again.

"Can you ease up on—"

"How?!"

"I just told you!" he squealed. "I injected him with the drug, the antidote."

"So, you knew it was going to work."

"Yeah, the reversal works but..."

"But what?"

"There are some side effects we're still working on fixing."

"What are the side effects?"

"Well... seizures are one, though that's more immediate. So, it looks like he's clear from that. The other ones we know of are memory loss, and possible paralysis."

"Fuck, Zack! When do the side effects kick in?"

"I don't know, Sky! I don't have all the answers for you. Like I said, it's a *trial medication*."

"There's more," she said, murmuring under her breath.

"Can you put your knife away? It's really hurting me."

"What else do they have you inventing in there?" she asked, pulling the knife away from his skin.

"This is the only thing I'm working on."

"Are there others?"

"Doctors?"

"Yeah. Are there other doctors?"

"I'm not sure."

"Do you know anything about Project X? Or a medication called Xanderlate? Has anyone said anything about it?"

"No, no."

"Are you lying to me?" she cried out, pressing the knife against his throat once again.

"No! I swear! I swear I'm not lying to you. I swear on Skylar's life."

Sky debated for a moment if she should let Zack go, or

send a message to the SEA in retaliation for what they had done to Nate. When she had first arrived at the hospital, Sky had made up her mind that she was going to kill Zack, but now she realized that as much as she despised him for what he'd done, he was useful to her.

"You're working for me now. You understand?"

"What?" he asked, sounding frantic. "You want me to be a double agent? I have a family and a son! I can't—"

"Maybe next time use your brain, or did you lose that while you were in med school? Anyways, I'll let you know what I need and when I need it." She pulled the knife away and took a close look at the blade. She pulled out a handkerchief from her back pocket and wiped away the blood from her knife. "Like I said, you got into bed with the wrong people."

"They're gonna kill me if they find out I'm working for you."

"That sounds like a *you* problem. I gotta go. I'll keep in touch."

Zack's lips began to quiver, and his eyes glinted with tears. "Please, Sky..."

"We're done here."

Sky stepped out of the vehicle and strolled towards the sidewalk, making her way down the street. She felt invigorated. She had begun her career with the SEA decades ago, but it wasn't until now that she truly felt she was serving her life's purpose. Things were beginning to click in her mind, but still had many unanswered questions.

She couldn't help but think: if the SEA had created the

injection that had been given to Nate, what else were they working on?

CHAPTER 39

1936

It had been three years since Samantha started a revolution. WIP.

Leading a movement that was more powerful than anything she'd ever experienced before had been a rewarding journey. She was helping pave the road for women. She had become an advocate for those who had been silenced for far too long and had taken various issues, whether it was taxation on feminine products, or funding education for the poor, to the board. So far, she had come back from her meetings with the agency victorious. Samantha's partnership with the SEA gave her the support and funding she needed for the work she was passionate about.

She had been praised in newspapers for her efforts and the change she was bringing to low-income communities, minorities, and women. She had conducted interviews covering the protests and rallies held all over Pool View and Lake View for women who were the victims of domestic abuse. The world was slowly becoming familiar with the name Samantha Hall and what she stood for. Her own story, however, hadn't leaked to the press—her relationship with Derek and the extramarital affair that had led to a baby boy, the fact she still had no knowledge of his whereabouts. The SEA had made her a promise to keep her personal life from slipping through the cracks. She had been a huge asset for the agency because of the amount of money she'd brought in from her supporters.

Knowing that she could accomplish whatever she set her mind to, Adrian had helped Samantha enroll into college to pursue a career as a lawyer. She was driven to fight for human rights and against injustice. Although it was a long road ahead of her, and law school was going to be far from simple, she was determined to excel in her studies.

Even though she had her hands full with being the leader of WIP, there wasn't a day that she didn't think of her baby boy. It wasn't until now that she and Adrian were able to refer to their son by the name they had picked out: Colton.

***

It was a cool Saturday afternoon. The sky was clear, and the temperature was in the low seventies, which was perfect in Samantha's book. She sat outside Café De La Vue Sur La Piscine, at a small table decorated with a mosaic design of a snail. She picked up her cappuccino and took a short sip before setting it down on its saucer. The restaurants around her were filled with customers, and the crosswalks were filled with rowdy people. She had been feeling anxious about this day for the past week. Samantha had changed her outfit three times, finally settling on a half-sleeved, floral-patterned yellow and white day dress paired with a white fedora hat. Her lips were painted a deep red, reminiscent of a vibrant rose.

Samantha took account of her surroundings and, in particular, looked for a woman with short blonde hair and a short stature. The most important of the details she had provided Samantha was that she was nine months pregnant. Therefore, she would be hard to miss in a crowd.

As Samantha picked up her cup to take another sip, it dawned on her that her intake of caffeine wasn't helping with her anxiousness about this meeting. She set down her cup, deciding not to finish the rest. When she looked up again, Samantha saw the woman she was expecting walking in her direction, wearing thick black sunglasses and a polka dot sundress that skimmed gracefully over her porcelain skin. Her lips were colored a soft pink that matched her blushing cheeks. Samantha's eyes narrowed in on the baby bump. She thought of the nine months she had carried her own child and felt her heart drop into the pit of her stomach.

The woman extended her arm with a beaming smile as she introduced herself. "You must be Samantha." She removed her sunglasses, revealing bright, sea-blue eyes fringed with lashes darkened by a generous coat of mascara.

Samantha shook her hand and smiled. "Yes, that is me."

"I'm Gia. Gia Hart," the woman said, as she pulled the chair out and made herself comfortable.

"It's a pleasure to be acquainted with you, Gia."

"Likewise. How are you doing?"

"I'm… okay. You must be excited to become a mother."

"It feels surreal. She was hard to conceive, but everything happens for a reason, don't you think?"

"I suppose. Have you picked out names for your baby girl?"

Gia gleamed with excitement. "Yes! We settled on Venice. It's such a unique name."

"That is indeed a beautiful name," Samantha said with a wistful smile.

"Thank you. Now, enough about me. Let's talk about the future."

Samantha pondered over the reason why she had scheduled the meeting with Gia in the first place.

"I just want to find my son."

"How old is your son?"

"He will be turning three this year."

"What's your son's name?"

Samantha considered the question for a minute. "We never got a chance to name him. He was taken away from me. We wanted to name him Colton, but… I don't know the name he has been given."

Gia offered a frown and replied. "I'm so sorry to hear that."

Samantha pursed her lips and acknowledged Gia's sympathy.

"Here. Give me your hands," Gia said.

"We're going to do this right here?"

"Yes, darlin'. Now, give me your hands."

Samantha brought both of her hands in front of her and placed them in Gia's palms.

"Thank you. Now, I'm going to channel your energy, and hopefully it will lead me to a vision to help me determine where your son is."

"Okay."

"You have no idea where he could be?"

"No, not at all." A little skeptical, Samantha asked, "Out of curiosity, how long have you been doing this?"

"About five years now. I have a ninety percent success rate."

Samantha had come across Gia's ad in the newspaper and figured while the SEA was still searching for her son, she needed to take the initiative, as well.

"I'm going to close my eyes now," Gia said.

"Do I need to as well?"

"Not if you don't want to," she chuckled.

Gia proceeded to close her eyes while Samantha scrutinized her facial expressions hopefully. The next few minutes passed in silence. From time to time, Gia would murmur something under her breath and her eyebrows would furrow, as if encountering something behind her closed eyelids. Slowly, time passed, and Samantha watched with intent. Gia tightened her grip around Samantha's hands. Then, her head slowly lowered to her chest.

After a short moment, she looked up and met Samantha's eyes.

Samantha was taken aback by how tired Gia's eyes appeared. She had been channeling her energy for less than ten minutes, but it appeared as if Gia had been hit with a storm. Her eyes were strained, and her vibrant skin now appeared dull.

"What did you see?"

Gia remained silent for a moment.

"What did you see?" Samantha asked, desperately.

"Dark energy," she said in a hushed voice. "Your son is surrounded by dark energy. He's closer to you than you think."

Samantha felt her heart plunge into her stomach once again. "Where is he? Who has him?"

Gia's eyes glistened with tears. "He's right here in Pool View, but the people he's with… they will end your life if you go after them."

Samantha's eyes widened with sadness. "But he's my son, and I want him back. He belongs with *me*."

"I'm sorry, darlin'," Gia said, choking on her words. "I don't know what else to tell you."

"You have to tell me where he is."

"I don't have the exact location, but there is a wooded area that he has been to with his adoptive father and their other son. There's nothing there as such, but I see them in that place. It's an important location, from what I feel."

"Is that all that you can tell me?"

"I'm afraid so. Samantha… they're dangerous people. They will hurt anyone who gets in the way of their family. I would be *very* careful."

"My son was taken from me. I didn't choose to give him up. He's *my* family."

Gia pursed her lips and nodded.

"I understand, darlin', but these are folks who can't be reasoned with. In the end, I can't control your decision. However, whatever you choose to do, please be careful and make your safety a priority. They are *very* dangerous people."

Samantha nodded. "Thank you for your honesty." She reached for her purse and pulled out an envelope, which contained the payment for Gia's services. "Here you go," she said as she handed the envelope to Gia.

Gia took the envelope and slipped it into her purse. "Your baby should have never been taken from you. I will never understand your pain and I sincerely mean that. But… here I have someone in front of me, filled with so much love to give… it would pain me to know something happened to you as you were trying to bring your son back home. That's all."

"I appreciate it," Samantha said with a faint smile.

"I hope you find peace. I really do."

Samantha nodded as she rose from the table. "Thank you."

Walking away from the cafe in the opposite direction, all Samantha could think of was how she was going to find her baby boy. Although she had no clear leads, she did have the SEA at her disposal. They had been working on finding the baby, but all leads so far had only brought them to dead ends. She hoped the information Gia was able to provide her with would help lead the SEA to where her son was.

It was a step in the right direction, she thought.

***

Derek had been in the Lincoln-Zephyr for the past forty-five minutes, handcuffed and surrounded by two agents, one on each side.

"The least you can do is tell me where we are going."

Neil looked into his rear-view mirror and chuckled.

"When we get there."

"The handcuffs are unnecessary."

"You are entitled to your opinion, Derek."

"Almost three years being on the board and trust has not been established?"

"Trust? We are far from that."

Derek scoffed. "Put a bullet in my brain then."

"That's not an option, unfortunately."

Derek smirked. "I am sure Stephan will not be happy to hear about my experience today."

Neil gazed into his rear-view mirror, not offering a response.

The truth was, after Stephan had seen Derek's performance as a member on the board, and how he had delivered on his promises, Stephan wanted to expand their relationship. Derek had been a godsend. Neil, however, wasn't entirely convinced Derek belonged with the agency, even though he had shown loyalty and displayed signs of trust. As always, Neil kept his guard up and took it upon himself to put in place necessary precautions—hence the handcuffs.

The next half hour passed in silence. Derek rested his head back on the seat, feeling agitated and uncomfortable. He took the time to contemplate the last three years of his life, which he usually refrained from doing because deep down there were regrets he wasn't ready to acknowledge.

He still missed Samantha. One night, heavily drunk and weeping to himself on the kitchen floor, it hit him that he had lost someone who had truly loved him, even after all the abuse and heartbreak he'd put her through. As time went on, though he was going through women like paper in a notebook, Derek finally admitted to himself that he was still in love with his wife and was always going to be. He needed her back in his life.

If he was able to change the past, Derek would change every instance that had allowed Samantha to fall in love with Adrian. He would have become the man she deserved. It tore him apart that he had been so vile towards her. If only he could have had a moment of clarity, of seeing what his behavior had truly become! Then he would have changed. Instead, it had taken him losing Samantha, his soul, and his dignity, to make him realize who he truly was and what mattered in life.

Since then, he had changed as a person. He had made the effort to take roads that strayed away from evil.

People who'd never received respect from him were now beginning to. These changes that had taken effect within him over the past two years had slowly made his life a little brighter. He was far from perfect, but he had no urge to retreat to malice or threats. He was slowly shifting from illegal activities to more legitimate businesses. However, the greed for money still existed.

"It's time," Neil suddenly announced.

It took Derek a few seconds to understand that it was an instruction for the agents to cover his face with a duffel bag. It went from day to night in a short moment.

"This is utterly ridiculous. I'm already handcuffed."

"We do what we're comfortable with."

"I'm not going to get far, if I decided to escape."

"There is always that chance, which we're not willing to take."

Roughly twenty minutes later, he felt the vehicle slow down. From what Derek could ascertain, they had pulled onto some sort of rutted track that was leading to a fairly secluded place: there was no traffic noise, no people, nothing other than the crunch of gravel and stones under the car's wheels as it lurched over the uneven ground. He felt the car slow down even more.

Ten minutes later, the car came to a full stop and the duffel bag was removed from Derek's face. He looked out of the car window to find the sun slowly setting. Around them, they were surrounded by redwood trees with nothing else in sight.

"Pull him out," Neil ordered, stepping out of the car.

Moments later, Derek found himself pulled roughly out of the car, his hands still in cuffs.

"Easy," Derek snapped. "For fuck's sake!"

Neil gave each of the agents a quick glance, acknowledging that roughhousing wasn't needed just yet.

As Neil began to traipse forward through the trees, Derek was hustled along after him by one agent, while the other followed close behind.

After a few minutes, Neil turned around and said, "We're almost there."

While they walked, Derek absorbed the beauty of the forest. Underneath his feet he could hear the crunching of the leaves and the snap of branches. His ears slowly began to disregard the noise from down below and focused instead on the birds chirping above him. The further they walked, the darker it became as the sun fell beneath the horizon.

It was the first time Derek feared what was waiting for him once they reached their destination. He had concluded there was no way to escape from the forest; in either direction he looked, all he could see was trees. If they had come to kill him, this was going to be the perfect place.

They walked out of the trees into a clearing the size of a football field. Derek hadn't ever seen anything like it: though they were still surrounded by forest in all directions, in front of them, about a hundred feet from where they stood, was a metal post with buttons and a speaker. An intercom.

"Welcome to the agency," Neil proclaimed.

Derek raised an eyebrow and craned his neck towards Neil.

"Where is it?"

"Right in front of you."

Derek chuckled nervously. As far as he could see, there was nothing in front of him. "I don't see anything."

"You're correct. It's not visible to the naked eye, but it is there. The agency is protected by a layer of invisible paint."

"There is such a thing as *invisible paint*?"

Neil nodded. "Today, we are going to file your paperwork. We thought it was time for you to see the agency as well."

"We signed the paperwork three years ago..."

"Each board member receives a bonus and security after their first three years serving on the board. Stephan chose not to include that in your initial deal. He's had a sudden change of heart. You will sign the documents in order to receive your bonus and security."

Derek had learned to trust his gut early on. Neil wasn't telling him the truth. At least, it wasn't the entire truth. "You are forgetting that I practice law," he said. "I have worked long enough to know when someone is covering up the truth. What are you not telling me?" he asked, staring into Neil's eyes.

Neil made his way towards the intercom. "We can discuss that when the time comes," he replied over his shoulder.

The agent took hold of Derek's arm once again and

proceeded to follow Neil.

Derek watched as Neil pressed the red button. A few seconds later, a man's voice was heard over the speaker.

"Name and agent number please," said the man.

"Neil Harper. Agent number is four two six... five, seven zero, zero... six, one, eight, eight, eight."

"One second please."

A moment later, the man confirmed Neil's clearance. Then, the other two agents gave their information and, like Neil, they, too, were cleared.

"I'm bringing in Derek Will for paperwork."

"He will need to sign in with the receptionist once you enter."

"Yes, sir."

What Derek witnessed next was unlike anything he'd ever seen in his entire life. He knew if he shared this encounter with his friends, he would be nothing but a laughingstock. First, the sound of ringing filled his ears. Then, out of thin air, an opening appeared to an escalator. The sight left him speechless.

Neil took a glance at the shock painted across Derek's face and grinned.

For the second time, Derek felt fear prick his chest. There was no doubt in his mind that the SEA was hiding something, but what? Surely, they wouldn't handcuff and blindfold him if they really were only showing him around the agency? Only time would reveal what the SEA had planned for Derek.

Neil moved out of the way. "After you," he said

graciously.

In Neil's eyes, he still saw Derek as the man he used to be.

And for once in his life, Derek was terrified of what would become of him. He had worked hard on bettering himself, seeing how his old life had cost him Samantha. He'd slowly changed his ways and wanted to become a better man, knowing there was more to life than corruption and power. But something in his gut told him that the SEA had other plans for him. Plans that would rip his humanity apart—the humanity which had taken long to rebuild.

He feared returning to his old self again.

CHAPTER 40

It was half past ten. Sky sat across Bruce at the kitchen table with a black folder in front of her. When he'd seen the folder, Bruce knew there was more information that needed his attention.

"So, listen to this. I've been wracking my brain, trying to work out why on earth the agency wanted Bright in the first place. And I remembered something. A few years ago, I had a meeting with Roy."

"Uh huh..."

"When I was in his office, there was a document on his desk. It was labeled *Project X.* Underneath it, in a small font, it said *Medicine Xanderlate.* And it was something that none of the board members knew about, because it was never brought to our attention or discussed in our meetings. I didn't think anything of it at the time, thinking that maybe later down the line, whatever it was, we would be informed about it. But it never happened—the board was never briefed on Project X."

Bruce nodded to show Sky he was following so far.

Sky continued.

"When I was doing a routine check at Lake View Hospital, on the tenth floor, I decided to go into the lab. It wasn't a part of the checklist for that visit, but the scientists were on their break, and I was just curious to see what they were cooking up in there. Anyways, I go in and I'm scanning the place and there's a sheet of paper hanging off the table. Me being me, I went to go look at it. And the heading read *Xanderlate.* The same word I'd seen on that document in Roy's office. I looked it up on Google and found *nothing*—absolutely no mention of it at all, anywhere. So *that* was a red flag. What's not Google-able, these days? Then, when Nate made a full recovery from his mysterious injury, the alarm went off in my head. Something wasn't making sense to me. So, I paid a little visit to Zack. It turns out that the SEA has the antidote to the drug that was first given to Nate. He didn't just wake up on his own. Zack gave him the drug which brought Nate out of his coma."

Bruce leaned back in his chair, overwhelmed by the new information Sky had shared with him. "Wait—is that what Xanderlate is? The drug used to put Nate into a coma? Or the antidote? Either way, if they're working on biological weapons like that—that's something they address with the board, don't they?"

"Add that to the list of questions," she responded. "I asked Zack if he knew about Project X or Xanderlate... he said he didn't, and... I believe him. But it seems a bit too coincidental that the SEA has been working on some mysterious drug and then Nate falls into a coma because of a … *mysterious drug*, doesn't it? I don't know what Xanderlate is for or what it does, so my theories could be off. I looked through the agency's database when I first came across Project X, and the only thing that came up was this organization called WIP. It was one, single-page document that stated Project X was moving forward with its next phase, and the agency was going to begin cutting ties with WIP."

"Hold up. What's WIP? And how is that connected to Project X?"

"I did a lot of research about what WIP is—*was*—actually, and I found this article. There wasn't much about Project X that I could find." Sky pulled out a clipping of an article and pushed it towards Bruce. "WIP was a women's movement starting around 1934, led by this woman named Samantha Hall. Essentially, she was a trailblazer in her time. Fighting for women's rights on a whole new level during her time, a voice for the abused. She was advocating for eliminating tax on feminine goods. It's all in there, the things she was trying to achieve, but that was the only article that I could find on her and the whole organization. Putting two and two together… I believe WIP no longer fit the agency's agenda, whatever it was at the time, and they got rid of it. Somehow WIP and Project X are connected. I just don't know exactly how yet."

Bruce held up the clipping. His focus shifted to the picture on the right of a woman standing outside, protesting with signs displaying words he couldn't quite make out.

"That woman kinda looks like Shadow, doesn't she?"

"Which one?"

Bruce laid the article on the table and pointed towards Samantha.

Sky leaned forward and bobbed her head. "Oh yeah, she kinda does."

He reached for her hand and asked, "So, what do you wanna do?"

"I want to know *why* they're working on Project X. *What* does it do? How was WIP linked to Project X? I didn't think Project X was important until I saw Nate's test results and talked to Zack... imagine what else they're keeping a secret."

"Tell me if I'm following correctly. You want to—no, you're *going to* dig into this, which means the SEA will have to continue to exist in order for you to do that."

"Bruce, whatever it is, it's bigger than us, and, yes, I don't think we're in a position to destroy the agency. Not right now at least. The SEA has a bigger agenda, clearly, and *maybe* that's where Bright comes in. Perhaps he plays a huge role in some way. I just don't know yet. We have our chance to find out."

Bruce ran his fingers through his hair and let out a deep sigh. "Well... this is another long conversation we're *both* going to have with everyone. At least they will have security as long as the SEA is still around. How are you gonna do all of this now that you and Stacy aren't part of the agency?"

"I have other agents who I trust with my life and are still with the agency. I'll get in touch with them once I map out my thought process and give them some starting points. We'll come up with a game plan and get to the bottom of whatever the agency is working on."

Bruce revisited the conversation they'd had earlier. He was looking forward to spending more time with Sky now that they were both off the force. Traveling the world with Sky seemed like the perfect temporary escape and felt they both very much needed the getaway. However, he saw the passion behind Sky's eyes for this new mission she was putting together. As much as he wanted to tell her to let go of what the SEA was working on, he couldn't.

"I'm here if you need consulting or a second pair of eyes. Whatever you need."

"I know," she said with a smile. "I appreciate that. Once we figure out what they've been hiding, we can resume our original mission and be done with the SEA for good. Then, we can travel."

"Sounds like a plan, my love."

"Okay. That's it for today."

Bruce chuckled as he slowly rose from his seat. "How about we go into the bedroom and watch a movie. We've got a big day ahead of us tomorrow."

He held out his hand as he neared Sky.

"Yeah," she said with a grin. She closed the folder in front of her and followed Bruce into the bedroom.

CHAPTER 41

Evan sat with his journal in front of him. The journal entries hadn't been consistent since Shadow walked into his life. For a while, he hadn't seen the importance of continuing journaling since he believed the memories were leading to Shadow and nothing more. However, now that they were giving him insights of a world outside of Samantha, Adrian, and Derek, it had become a cause for concern. He was taken aback by the fact that Samantha had met his great-grandmother, Gia. This was the first time he'd seen what she looked like since he had no pictures of her—the exact reason why Venice urged both Evan and Denise to take as many pictures as they could.

With everything in mind—conversations and events that had happened in the past month—Evan was beginning to believe his memories were pointing him in the direction of the SEA.

But the question that irked him was, *why*?

The knock at the door caught Evan off guard. "Yeah…?"

Shadow opened the door and pursed her lips. "Everything okay?"

He turned his head around and met her eyes. "Uh, yeah."

Evan faced his desk and closed his journal. He slid it back in his desk drawer and rose from his chair.

"You've been in here for an hour."

"Has it been that long?" He looked at his watch. "Damn, time is slipping away, isn't it?"

Shadow wrapped her arms around his waist and locked her eyes in his. "Is everything okay?"

"Yeah. I was just thinking about how my memories have expanded."

"Do you think they're leading you in a different direction?"

"I'm not too sure."

Wrapped in each other's arms, they let the silence of the room take over for a moment.

Evan slowly rocked from side to side and pressed his forehead against hers. "I miss him, Shadow."

It didn't take her long to piece together who Evan was talking about.

"I know you do. He was a *huge* part of your life. Accepting that he's gone is not going to happen overnight or even in a year. He was your family. You gotta grieve at your own pace, and I know you know that, but I just want you to know that it's *okay* if you're having a hard time with it."

Evan's eyes began to brim with tears. "Sometimes, when I go out to put the trash can or when I'm going for a run… I have hope that he's gonna come out of that house and life's gonna be the same again. I know he's gone, but then I think to myself, what if he really isn't? I used to get that feeling about my dad, where I felt like he really wasn't gone… and it turned out he really *wasn't* gone."

"I get what you mean," Shadow said. "But… your dad was there when Mr. Brar was killed. He saw him, remember?"

"Yeah, I know. It's just that…a part of me is hoping that all of this is a lie, just like my dad's death was. I know it sounds crazy."

Shadow unwrapped her arms from his waist and brought her hands to his face. She held his face in the palm of her hands.

"No. It doesn't sound crazy. It sounds like you're missing your childhood friend. Someone who had always been there whenever you needed them and now they're gone. And it probably doesn't help that you're not registering all of this like you thought you would. Maybe after we say our last goodbye, it'll start to sink in. I mean, the last time you lost someone was when you were four. In a way, this is going to feel all new to you."

"Yeah. You're probably right."

Shadow ran her fingers through his hair and grinned. "You *are* a psychology teacher, right? This is the type of stuff you study and teach for a living."

Evan mocked her. "Very funny. On a serious note, thank you for listening and being there."

"You and me 'til the end baby," she responded. Shadow pulled away and met his eyes once again. "Speaking of baby, Bright's going to be up for his feeding any minute now."

"You want me to feed him?"

"I got this one. Can you get his bag ready though? We need to head out pretty soon. The memorial is in a couple of hours, and I was in the middle of packing before I came down here."

Evan nodded. "Yeah, I got it."

Not too long after Evan had packed Bright's bag, they were off and on the road to Highland View, to celebrate the life of Mr. Brar.

***

Paradise Way was the location Mr. Brar had requested for his ashes to be scattered. It was an hour away from Lake View, and it was also the first time Evan had heard about it. The name sounded unreal, but after a quick Google search, they learned it was, indeed, a spot on the outskirts of town.

Bruce and Sky traveled together in the car for the first time. At this point, there was no need to go anywhere separately, now that the SEA had discharged Sky from her position with the board. Had the circumstances been different, there would have been excitement and joy about the fact they no longer had to hide their relationship. It had put a strain on their partnership when even the simplest things had to be planned out strategically for the sake of their careers with the agency.

Denise and Ryan, along with Nate, who had been busy

playing an educational game in the back seat, drove down the hillside listening to The Chainsmokers.

"How are you feeling?"

Denise looked to her side through her sunglasses. "Feeling better than before. I just wish peanut butter didn't make me nauseous." She subconsciously placed her hand on her stomach.

"Say goodbye to peanut butter and jelly sandwiches," Ryan chuckled. "It's been a really weird time, hasn't it? With everything going on..."

"Yeah. It worries me about tomorrow, you know? We're living in the unknown. I mean, realistically speaking, we always are, but knowing that there are people out there who are out to get you and you're just a pawn in the grand scheme of things... that in itself is terrifying. They don't care about what happens to the rest of the world."

"That's what I was thinking about this morning." Ryan peered into his rear-view mirror to make sure Nate's headphones were still plugged in. "What if we moved?"

Denise pondered over his suggestion.

"It's not that I haven't thought about it," she finally said. "But... at the end of the day, we can't really run even if we wanted to. If they want to find us, they'll find us. One way or another, they'll get to us."

Ryan pressed his elbow against the window and rested his head against his knuckle. He let out a deep breath and responded, "Yeah, I know. I was hoping you would give a different answer. I was hoping there *was* a different answer."

Denise reached over and rubbed his shoulder. "I wish I had a different answer for you, hun. It's gonna be a huge adjustment, living this way, but we have a lot to be grateful for, after everything that's happened to us, too. Things could've been worse."

Ryan shifted his position and took her hand and slipped it into his. "That's absolutely true. We've got to take extra precautions, though, and install high-end security cameras for the house."

"I agree. I'll take a look once we get back home. We have a lot to do, now that I'm thinking about it. Gotta get the nursery ready. We gotta buy new clothes and literally everything else. I have to start distributing my projects… jeez, it's gonna be so hectic."

"Oh, yeah. It's gonna be a crazy nine months. Remember your lists? I don't miss those *at all*."

Denise chuckled, remembering the phase she went through in which every day consisted of a list of things she needed to complete. At first, it enabled Denise to be productive, but after they found out they were having their firstborn, her lists had become extravagant. Instead, she had become overwhelmed with the amount of work that needed to be completed. She underestimated how weary she was going to become not only with the pregnancy, but also running Storm Inc., which was also her baby at the time. At the end of each day, Ryan would get an earful, because Denise couldn't manage her time properly, even with the lists she had created.

"I remember how annoyed I made the both of us. You

remember the fight we had because I lost my list and I accused you of throwing it away?"

Ryan snorted as he watched the scene replay in his mind's eye as if it had just happened yesterday.

"I almost shit my pants. Your hormones were already all over the place, and I remember thinking, 'she's gonna kill me.' That was the first time I was genuinely scared of you."

Denise covered her mouth as she laughed. "I know! I saw it in your eyes, and I remember feeling really bad afterwards because I found it underneath all the clothes I was trying on before I left for work that morning."

"*So* excited for those hormones again," he said sarcastically.

Denise giggled and gave his hand a squeeze. "No lists this time. I promise."

She glanced over at the GPS and noticed they were ten minutes shy of their destination.

"Nate, honey," she said, rotating her neck slightly. She could see him in the corner of her eye, his eyes glued to the screen. She reached back and massaged his knee, getting his attention.

"Yeah?" he asked, pulling one of his earbuds out.

"It's time to put the iPad away."

"Okay," he replied, with his eyes still fixed on the screen.

"*Away*, away. We're almost here."

"Okay... *fine*," he replied solemnly.

Nate pulled out the remaining ear bud and turned off the device.

"How long are we gonna be here?" he asked as he put the ear buds back into their case.

"For an hour maybe," Denise replied.

For a short moment, the car fell silent.

"Dad…"

Ryan looked into his rear-view mirror and answered, "What's up buddy?"

"Can we get ice cream afterwards?"

"Yeah, why not? Ice cream sounds good."

"Yay! And…"

Denise peered over her shoulder and responded, "What is it hun?"

"I'm ready to be quizzed."

"For what buddy?" Ryan asked, peering in his rear-view mirror.

"You said I could get a puppy if I learned how to take care of it."

Denise and Ryan exchanged quick glances with one another. It had completely slipped their minds that they'd promised Nate a puppy. That conversation felt like it had taken place years ago.

"If you get all the questions right, then yes, we can get a puppy," Ryan answered.

"Yay! I want a labradoodle!"

Denise raised an eyebrow. "I had no idea he even knew what that was," she chuckled to Ryan.

"I get the feeling he's gonna ace the test."

"I'm gonna name him Pickle," Nate exclaimed.

"Oh jeez," Denise sighed as she rubbed her belly. "I don't

know how I'm going to make it through this pregnancy without puking every time I hear the name 'Pickle'."

Ryan let out a soft chortle as he reached over and softly rubbed Denise's arm.

Evan looked at his GPS and began slowing down, realizing the destination was close by. They had pulled over to the shoulder, seeing they were close, but there was no sign of an entrance. Shadow glanced over at the screen and then looked out the window. On both sides of the road there was a beautiful apple orchard, which had started a mile back, and it continued for what looked like another mile. They were surrounded by green hills, with nothing else in sight.

"Is this right?" Evan asked, confused. He put the car in park and peered out in front of him.

Shadow frowned, not knowing herself. "We put in the correct address, right?"

Shadow pulled out her phone and input the address in her app to double check. "Yeah, we're here, but..." She looked out her window once again and noticed a car pulling up behind them. "Wait, I think that's Sky and your dad behind us."

Noticing Evan wasn't moving forward, Bruce pulled up beside him. Without skipping a beat, Sky rolled down her window, resulting in Evan doing the same.

"Hey, you guys."

"Hi, Sky. Hey, Dad."

Shadow politely waved at Bruce and Sky.

"Our GPS says that we're here, but I don't see any sort

of entrance."

"Just follow us," he motioned to the road ahead. "Your grandma and Willow are already there," Bruce hollered.

"Okay." Evan put the car in drive and peered into his rear-view mirror for oncoming traffic before pulling back onto the road.

Soon they were following behind Bruce, only to find out that the entrance to Paradise Way was just a hundred feet away.

"Oh, wow," Evan chuckled, as he pulled onto the dirt road that split the apple orchard. "It was so close."

Shadow smirked. Over her shoulder, she glanced at Bright, who was quietly sleeping.

As they pulled in, the road became more of an uneven dirt path. The view was captivating. On both sides of the road were big, beautiful apple trees with dark green leaves that looked as though they would be soft to touch. Red delicious apples hung from the tree branches, ready for harvest. As they continued along the path, every now and then, the sunlight would hit their windshield through the gaps between the trees. The dust rising from under the tires shimmered in the air when the sun rays struck.

"I wonder why Mr. Brar picked this spot," Shadow pondered.

"If I knew him at all, there's definitely a reason why he brought all of us here. But we probably won't learn why, though."

"Well, that sucks. It's such a beautiful place and almost completely secluded from the rest of the world. Looking at all these apples makes me want to bake an apple pie," she said, giggling. "These lands are usually privately owned by a farmer, right?"

"Yeah. We wouldn't be able to pass through if..."

It didn't take long for them to connect the dots. They glanced at one another in utter confusion.

"No way," Shadow said in a shock.

"This can't be all his. There's no way. He would've mentioned it to me at some point."

"You think your dad knows about this?"

"I would think so..."

When they reached the end of the road, ahead of them lay a large flat open area of grassy green and a cliff that felt almost out of place. The steep cliff overlooked a beautiful, empty sandy beach. The sound of the waves hitting the rocks could be heard from up top. Unlike other beaches, this particular beach was free from squawking seagulls. The only visible entrance down to the beach was a small man-made stairway, on the left-hand side of the open lawn area.

Evan and Shadow spotted Venice and Willow, who had been enjoying the ocean breeze by the cliff.

As Bruce parked his car, Evan did the same. Denise and Ryan arrived shortly after and parked next to Evan.

It was a bittersweet moment; a moment everyone had been dreading for the past week. The sun was shining bright, bouncing off their sunglasses. The place inspired a calm feeling that none of them had experienced anywhere else in recent times. To Evan, it almost felt as if Mr. Brar was walking amongst them. And for the first time since Mr. Brar's death, Evan felt at peace. He was unsure how long the feeling was going to last, but he wanted it to last forever.

From a distance, Evan spotted Venice and Willow making their way down to greet the rest of the family. They all huddled together, dressed in black, exchanging hugs and kisses.

Denise and Ryan fawned over Bright, who had awoken but was ready to fall back asleep at any given moment.

"Look at those big blue beautiful eyes," Denise said with admiration. "He's already a heartbreaker."

Shadow chuckled. "How have your mornings been?"

"Well, I can't have peanut butter anymore."

Shadow frowned.

"She had one bite from her sandwich, and she was already running towards the trash can," Ryan said. "I had to finish it for her like a champ," Ryan teased as he patted her back.

Denise raised an eyebrow and tried her best to refrain from laughing.

Ryan nudged her, continuing to tease her. "You couldn't even watch me eat it."

Denise covered her mouth and laughed silently.

"Shadow had some pretty weird cravings," Evan chimed in as he peered at his son. He kissed the top of his head and nuzzled his cheek with the tip of his nose. "I caught her eating a bowl of ice cream and barbeque chips in the middle of the night once," he said, looking up at Shadow.

Shadow smirked as she responded. "You really want to go down this road, mister?"

Venice chuckled as she neared Shadow. "As a kid, he would pair the oddest foods together."

"Oh my god, he did!" Denise chimed in. "What was it that he used to love eating? And he would *beg* you for it when we went grocery shopping..."

With Sky by his side, Bruce smiled through his heartbreak. He had missed their entire lives and could only learn about them through stories.

"How can I ever forget?" Venice replied with a grin. "I don't know what came over you, but it didn't sound appetizing."

"What was it?" Sky asked curiously.

"Oh, I remember," Ryan recalled. "Denise told me. You had quite a few."

Evan shook his head in disbelief. "Nope."

Ryan snickered as the spotlight continued to shine on Evan. "It was hamburgers with peanut butter."

"Gross," Denise added, making a face. "Oh my god, that is disgusting. Just thinking about it makes me want to throw up." She held her hand up to her mouth in disgust.

"Jeez, the aftermath probably was just as bad," Sky responded with a chuckle.

"And the other one that I remember was—"

"Avocado toast with jam," Denise inserted with a sour face. "*So gross.*"

Shadow covered her mouth, her eyebrows furrowed, suddenly beginning to feel queasy. "How was that *tasty*?"

An embarrassed Evan shrugged his shoulders and pretended to ignore the conversation.

"Tasty? It hardly looked appetizing. But that wasn't the worst one," Venice responded with a giggle. "He would sometimes treat himself to ice cream with... pickles!"

"Pickles and ice cream?" Bruce asked in amusement. "My goodness...that's quite a pair."

"I was just a kid!" Evan protested. "I was being creative."

Shadow rubbed his arm, with a grin across her face she couldn't quite wipe off.

"That's actually not a bad combo," Willow declared.

Venice raised her eyebrows.

"It looks like you and Willow have some things in common," Ryan inserted.

Ryan's comment invited a round of laughter. Even during a time they expected to be filled with pain and sadness, they found solace in each other's company.

***

From a distance, Mr. Brar and Mrs. Brar walked through the orchards, hand in hand. They watched as their family shared laughs and smiles with one another after all that they had been through.

"Bhuhadur," she said softly.

"Yes, my dear?"

"Watching them laugh and smile breaks my heart a little."

He stopped in his tracks and gazed at his wife in wonderment. "Why is that, sweetums?"

Mrs. Brar, who was a couple of steps ahead now, turned

around and tilted her head, eyes glazed. "What are they going to do without you? They need you now more than ever. They can't escape from their lives to come here every time things become difficult or when the SEA—"

"Ekam," he said with a soft smile, "they'll figure it out. We're all called back home when we've fulfilled our life's purpose. I have a feeling they're going to be back here more often than they think."

Mr. and Mrs. Brar followed the family that now existed in their memory as they made their way through the orchard.

Bruce turned midway and gazed at the sign, feeling it was time to set Mr. Brar's remains free.

"Shall we?" Bruce asked, scanning the group.

Everyone slowly and solemnly hiked towards the sign that read 'Paradise Way'. Bruce carried the urn close to his chest, feeling at peace, which he wasn't expecting. Prior to arriving at Paradise Way, he thought this was going to be one of the hardest days in his life, but what he was feeling was far from what he'd predicted.

Whether it was that they had begun to accept Mr. Brar's passing, or simply the environment they were in, there wasn't much sadness amongst them anymore. Instead, they felt a power and strength here, which had been lacking back home. In their hearts, they felt the love rise in their bones.

"This place feels like what home should feel like," Shadow said quietly to Evan.

"That's exactly what I was thinking."

Venice turned midway and chimed in with a smile across her face. "It makes you feel safe, calm, and at peace, doesn't it?"

Shadow patted Bright in his black baby wrap softly, as his eyes became heavy. "It does. I wish everyday felt like this."

Once they reached the sign, they all stood side by side, facing the ocean. The sound of the waves hitting the rocks filled their ears, and they could taste the salt in the air on their lips.

"I think we should all say something," Bruce said, the reality of what they had come to do finally setting in.

"Why don't you start?" Venice suggested, as she peered down the line.

Bruce nodded. His eyes left the urn and focused on the horizon. He took a moment to gather his thoughts as best as he could before beginning.

"Mr. Brar… where do I begin? The universe pulled you out of the game when we were just getting started. Ah…I struggle with the fact that I didn't say thank you as often as I should have or tell you how much I loved you. I just thought I had more time. This sucks," he said, choking on his words. "You kept my family together and safe. I don't know anyone who would have devoted so much time and love to their neighbors, caring for them as their own family. The world lost an angel. We were beyond lucky to have you in our lives, for as long as we did. I thought we would have had more time to sit and talk… about life, the things we experienced being agents, just anything really. You were there for me when I was at my lowest and... I thought I had time to repay you for all that you did, but... you were taken too soon. I really don't know what to do or say because it's not going to bring you back. There's a hole in my heart, Mr. Brar. You were the light in my life for such a long time... I didn't deserve you. I really didn't." Bruce's lips trembled as he tried to keep his composure. His eyes brimmed with tears. "I love you and I'm going to miss you terribly."

Sky gently rubbed Bruce's arm, feeling her throat become dry, now that it was her turn to say goodbye to Mr. Brar. "I wasn't fortunate enough to know you as long as Bruce did," Sky began. She peered at the calming ocean with a heavy chest. She wiped her tears with the back of her hand, suddenly feeling a sense of loss all over again. "But for the time I did get to spend with you...I came to realize how pure your soul was. Your laugh... oh, man. It made me so happy to hear you laugh. I'm going to remember it when I'm having a bad day or just missing you. You treated me not just as an agent but as your daughter. There was nothing but love in your heart for me, and I can say with confidence that anyone who has ever had the chance to meet you, would feel the same way. I wish I had said this, and maybe at the time I didn't realize it, but thank you for loving me. I love you, too."

Mr. and Mrs. Brar watched the family speak, hearing every heartfelt message each of them shared, even from where they stood across the grass.

Evan folded his hands in front of him and took a moment

to reflect on his time with Mr. Brar. "I don't have the right words for everything that I'm feeling or what you meant to me, but...uhmm..." Evan covered his mouth as he cried quietly. The sound of the waves splashing against the rocks filled the silence. Everyone around him wiped away the tears from their faces, feeling broken and a little lost. Once Evan regained his composure, he continued. "I'm thankful for every moment we got to spend together. There's a part of me that still believes I'll see you later, sitting on the porch, waving over at me. We'd talk about anything and everything. I don't think I'm ready to accept life without you just yet. There were a lot of conversations we were supposed to have. I'm going to miss sitting on that porch with you. I'm going to miss the way you hugged me when I needed it the most. I'm going to miss you talking about life and everything you learned along the way. I'm going to miss your energy and positivity. I'm going to miss your voice. Your smile. Your laugh. You have always been a role model for me. I'm the man that I am today because of *you*, and I hope that I can be half the man you were for my family. You'll always be in my heart."

"Sky kind of stole my words," Shadow sniffled with a slight chuckle. "When someone loves you unconditionally and talks to you like they've known you for their whole life... greets you after a long day at work, as if they've been just waiting their entire day to see you..." Shadow's eyes filled with tears, and what she wanted to say now seemed difficult. This was her last goodbye, and every fiber in her body was refusing to accept the truth. "I'm going to miss that. You went to save our son and lost your life in the process. Who would do that?" she cried. "I promise you that you will never *ever* leave our hearts, and Bright will grow up to know you as the hero that you are. Thank you for everything, Mr. Brar." Shadow wiped her tears with her hands and gave Venice the floor, not knowing she had set off a chain reaction of tears.

Venice cleared her throat and dabbed her eyes with a tissue that she had tucked away in her pant pocket. In the short moment, the vision that she had prior to the mission replayed in her mind. Venice was reminded, again, that Mr. Brar's death had been the result of her interfering with the universe. The decision she had made pained her deeply, but Bright was merely a baby with his entire life ahead of him. The choice had been a heavy one, but she knew it was exactly what Mr. Brar would have advised her to do.

"There's a lot to say about a man who took a piece of our hearts with him. I miss you more than my heart can handle. I found comfort in our friendship. You were always there for me, for everyone and… I'm never going to stop missing you. You helped me raise Evan and Denise. I'll never forget those times. You were the support that I needed even when I thought I could handle everything on my own. You kept this family together. I hope you know that. It's because of you, we're all here together. Thank you for everything you've done for us and showering us with *so* much love and kindness. We all love you so much."

Willow cleared his throat, trying to find the right words for someone who left an everlasting impact on everyone's life. "Thank you for showering this family with endless amounts of love," Willow expressed. His hand slipped into Venice's and tightly gripped it. "I wish I had met you sooner in life. I really wish we had more time. Please rest in peace, Bhuhadur. Your presence is going to be deeply missed here."

Denise followed Willow's speech, holding back tears. "Mr. Brar, ever since I was a little girl, you… always made me feel like I was your number one priority. You treated me like a princess and your arms knew how to mend a broken heart. You were *always* there. No matter what. I remember when I first started Storm Inc., you pushed me to keep going when all I wanted to do was give up on my dream. Your love for Mrs. Brar gave me hope that one day I would find my person when I struggled to find my partner in life. I honestly don't know what my life would look like if you hadn't been a big part of it. You gave us all strength when we felt like quitting. Heartbroken doesn't even begin to describe the pain I'm feeling," she said, wiping the corner of her eye. "It's gonna be hard visiting Evan and knowing you won't be there on the front porch. Your smile. Your voice. Your eyes. Your warmth. I'm going to miss all of it so deeply."

Ryan, knowing it was his turn, and that he was the last person to say his piece, took a moment as he overlooked the ocean. "You know what I still find insane?"

Denise's wet eyes landed on Ryan, confused where he

was going with this speech. Everyone peered down the line, briefly stunned.

"You fooled an entire secret organization into thinking that you were handicapped, *for years*. You even had us fooled up until now. So... how do we know that you're *actually* gone? What if you're really out there living your best life? And you're just waiting for the perfect time to come back and visit us? What if—"

Denise nudged Ryan in disbelief. "Ryan!" she hissed. "What's wrong with you?"

A faint smile appeared across Ryan's face. "I don't know if you're here with us, but everyone's giving me the glare over here. What they don't know is that you once told me when the time came, I had to make sure to stop the weeping. And I did. Everyone stopped for a quick second," he said, managing a small laugh. "But I had no idea how hard it was going to be because all I wanna do is cry with them." Ryan's eyes brimmed with tears. He let out a deep sigh and closed his eyes. "I followed through with my promise. Now I get to say what I wanna say." Ryan took a moment to find the right words to express how he'd felt. "How are you gone? It's not fair, man. My heart's in pieces. You were the dude that you could have any conversation with, no judgment. You were like a second father to me. I'll always remember the advice you gave me and the unconditional love I received from you. I know I always talked about quitting drinking because it just isn't good for you but I never got around to doing it. I had pictured the day in my mind, when I gave up drinking. We were gonna celebrate with some chai. I guess that wasn't in the cards for us, huh? So, I'm making you a promise that I quit today in your honor. Cheers to the man who didn't need alcohol to weave through life. Rest in peace, my friend."

They stood in silence for a moment before it was time to release Mr. Brar's ashes.

Mr. and Mrs. Brar reached the top of the cliff and stood beside Bruce.

"You have no idea how long I've been waiting for this moment," Mrs. Brar said, resting her head against his shoulder.

"Me too, Ekam. We're finally together again," Mr. Brar said with a smile. He softly kissed the top of her forehead.

Bruce opened the lid and took a quick glance inside of the urn. Although Mr. Brar's memories would continue to live on, the last of his earthly remains were all in this one vase. Bruce took a step forward and tested the winds with a wet finger to know which direction he needed to disperse the ashes. He looked back at his family, his eyes slightly pink, his lips pursed. Then, he turned back to the ocean, feeling it was time to do what they all had come here for.

Mr. Brar put his hand on Bruce's shoulder, wishing Bruce could feel his touch. "I know you can't hear me, but I'm always going to be here with you in spirit."

Tears streamed down Bruce's cheeks, feeling the unbearable pain of acknowledging that Mr. Brar was no longer with them. "Goodbye, Mr. Brar," he whispered as he scattered the ashes.

They watched in silence as the specks of dust slowly became one with the wind until they were no longer visible to the naked eye.

It was official. Life as they knew it was never going to be the same again.

Bruce turned around and put the lid back on the urn. "Shall we go?"

"We were gonna take Nate to go get some ice cream. You guys are all welcome to join if you want," Ryan ventured.

"Yeah, that sounds nice," Venice answered as she dabbed the corner of her eyes with a tissue.

"There's Zack's Ice Cream Parlor," Evan advised. "We'll hit it on the way back, if you guys wanna check that out."

Denise and Ryan looked at each other for approval. "Yeah, that works for us," Denise decided. "Dad, will you guys be coming?"

Bruce nodded. "Yeah, of course."

As they made their way back to their cars, Sky stopped, suddenly remembering an important duty Mr. Brar had left her with.

"Evan! Denise!" Sky called out.

Everyone came to a halt and turned around.

She pulled out a small red envelope from her back pocket and held it out. "This is for you both. I almost forgot about it."

Bruce's eyes bounced from Sky to Evan, to Denise, and then back to Sky.

"What is it?" Denise asked, reaching for the envelope.

Sky smiled and said, "Open it and take a look."

Evan neared Denise while the rest stood nearby, confused.

Denise and Evan both read the short note. Their eyes followed each line until the end of the note where Mr. Brar had signed his name.

They looked up at Sky and then Bruce, mouth agape. Then they faced each other, not knowing how to digest the last message Mr. Brar had left with them.

Denise handed the note to Evan and put her hand over her mouth, flabbergasted. "Oh my god," she muttered.

Evan's eyes flickered from Sky to Bruce. "He left us with… all of this," he said to Bruce, looking back at the apple orchard.

"This was all *his*?" Bruce asked in disbelief.

"Yeah," Sky responded. "He and his wife had bought this land fifteen years ago as an investment and, five years later, decided to grow an orchard. He had told me about it very briefly, but I had no idea that he was leaving it for you guys. What blew me away was that they only kept enough money to keep this place running. The rest of the profit went to organizations that helped widows, supported people of color, provided education for families who couldn't afford to send their kids to college without a loan… stuff like that."

"It almost sounds like he wanted to do what he could do to prevent anyone from having to join the agency, or go to them for help," Bruce suggested.

"That's one way to look at it."

"He left all the paperwork with me. The one thing he

asked was for you guys to continue their work and to keep the farm running in the family. Everything's laid out, so it won't become a burden. It was the last thing he wanted for the two of you."

"Wow," Ryan exclaimed. He stood with his hands on his hips, unsure of what to make of this news. "What else is he hiding?"

Evan chuckled. "He really did in fact leave us with a little piece of him and Mrs. Brar."

"He honestly did," Denise said, finally realizing there was now a place her family could come to escape life's miseries, even if it was just for an hour or so.

As the others talked about the orchard, Evan's mind began to make connections that hadn't been so clear to him earlier on. The charities Mr. Brar had quietly supported with this place were the very same groups Samantha advocated for. Was it just a strange coincidence? Or did Mr. Brar know about WIP? If so, how much did he know? If Mr. Brar had, indeed, played a role within the organization founded by Samantha, had he met her at some point? And, if so: why hadn't Mr. Brar mentioned the similarities Shadow shared with Samantha?

What was his true motive for leaving the orchard behind for him and Denise?

Evan had the feeling, yet again, that there was something far bigger going on than what he could have imagined. And it had every bit to do with the SEA. He wondered if Mr. Brar had known what Project X was, or whether he had even heard of it. His eyes flickered to Venice, who was watching a game of thumb war between Nate and Willow, standing with her arms crossed at her chest, lost in thought. She was notorious for keeping secrets. Why hadn't she mentioned that their grandfather, Dean, had been raised by an adoptive family? Although he had never met his grandfather, who had passed away before he was born, he'd seen pictures and heard amazing stories about the man. Evan was intrigued by the information that had been kept a secret. However, there was always the possibility that his grandfather had never shared that part of his life with Venice.

Were there other secrets that she had hidden from the family? Did his great-grandmother, Gia, ever share her encounter with Samantha with Venice?

There was only one way to find out.

Evan looked over to where Shadow stood nearby, admiring Bright and surveying the land that was now also hers. Bruce had turned to face the ocean one last time. Evan believed each of them held information that would help complete the puzzle that he'd been working on in his mind for the past year. He couldn't help but think Paradise Way was going to lead them to new revelations about the SEA and what Shadow's ancestors had been working on for generations. Evan felt he was closer than ever to finding out the truth about Project X and quite possibly the agency's motives for kidnapping Bright. His memories were finally starting to make sense.

***

"Ekam," Mr. Brar said softly.

"Yes, my darling?"

"What's home like?"

Mrs. Brar slipped her arm around his waist and hugged him tight.

"Home is what everyone's searching for here on Earth. Peace. Bliss. Tranquility. There's no pain there, Bhuhadur. You're finally free, my love."

Mr. Brar ran his hand through his beard and sighed with relief. "I'm ready to go home," he said with a grin.

He turned back one last time and watched his family quietly mingle with one another. A faint smile appeared across his face before he turned his face towards the ocean. Their hands intertwined, and together they began their walk into everlasting peace.

***

"Should we get going?" Ryan asked.

"Yeah, I'm ready," Denise answered.

"Bright's first family trip!" Shadow exclaimed softly as she gazed at Bright, who was still sound asleep.

"Well... technically it's his second," Evan pointed out, "but we won't count the first one as one. It's not a trip that we need to remember, if I'm being honest."

"Bruce..." Sky called out.

Bruce slowly turned around and met her eyes. "Coming."

He caught a glimpse of Evan as he headed back and smiled.

It was evident to Bruce now why Mr. Brar had left Sky

with the responsibilities of his estate instead of him. It was time for Bruce to take the back seat and focus on the things that mattered, like restoring his relationship with his family and being present. It was all in front of him. Life was too short. And in his case, it was extremely short.

Sky held out her hand, waiting for Bruce to take it.

"What were you thinking about? You kinda zoned out there."

"You can plan as much as you want, but life has a funny way of showing you that it has its own plans. It really is unpredictable."

She held his hand tight. "That's why we need to enjoy it as much as we can, with whatever time we have left."

***

From afar, in the depths of the apple orchard, Dean Storm watched as everyone made their way to their vehicles. He watched as Willow opened the car door for Venice. It reminded him of the times he had done the same for Venice. Ryan slid behind the wheel, with Denise and Nate already seated and buckled in. Evan helped Shadow carefully take Bright out of the baby wrap to put him in his baby seat. Bruce and Sky's hands slipped apart as they made their way to their seats. From where he stood, Dean could see the scar of the Houlkin. He could still hear Sky's loud cries from that day as he carefully removed the gadget from her skin.

In his pocket, the vibration of his ringing phone caught his attention. He pulled out his phone and saw the caller

ID: Roy. He allowed the call to go to voicemail.

"Oh, Venice," Dean said ever so softly. "Why did you have to meddle?"

He observed the cars leave the orchard, one by one. How relieved they must all feel, he thought, now that things seemed back to some semblance of normality. And how wrong they all were, he thought, about that.

Every ending, after all, was also a new beginning.

CPSIA information can be obtained
at www.ICGtesting.com
Printed in the USA
LVHW112113220422
716981LV00004B/221

9 781732 234420